the Rosetta Cylinder

Neil Pollack

iUniverse, Inc.
Bloomington

The Rosetta Cylinder

iUniverse books may be ordered through booksellers or by contacting:

iUniverse
1663 Liberty Drive
Bloomington, IN 47403
www.iuniverse.com
1-800-Authors (1-800-288-4677)

ISBN: 978-1-4759-5913-0 (sc)
ISBN: 978-1-4759-5915-4 (e)
ISBN: 978-1-4759-5914-7 (dj)

Library of Congress Control Number: 2012920808

Printed in the United States of America

iUniverse rev. date: 11/19/2012

For Karen

The Cosmos is all that is or ever was or ever will be. Our feeblest contemplations of the Cosmos stir us—there is a tingling in the spine, a catch in the voice, a faint sensation, as if a distant memory, of falling from a height. We know we are approaching the greatest of mysteries.

In all the galaxies, there are perhaps as many planets as stars, ten billion trillion. In the face of such overpowering numbers, what is the likelihood that only one ordinary star, the Sun, is accompanied by an inhabited planet?

Carl Sagan, *Cosmos*

PROLOGUE

"DAD'S DYING. COME HOME."

Steven Carter hadn't realized how seriously ill his father had been. The lung cancer was extremely virulent, and his father had taken a terrible turn for the worse in just three weeks. Although Steven hadn't spoken very much to his father, Don, for the past two years, he immediately hopped a plane from Denver to his parents' apartment in New York City. Now he stood by his parents' bed with his mother, Diane, and a nurse from hospice care who was attending to his father's needs. Although Don Carter was only in his early sixties, his cancer-ridden, emaciated body made him appear far older to Steven.

"I'm glad you're here," Diane said as she stared at her husband, whose breathing was becoming increasingly labored. The morphine drip used to ease his pain was also hastening his demise. It would only be a matter of hours, a day at most.

"Can he hear us?" Steven asked.

"Sometimes yes, sometimes no." She wiped a tear from her eye and then moved closer to her husband, bent over, and said, "Don, Steven is here."

It seemed a struggle for Don to open his eyes and turn toward his son. He nodded slightly in recognition and then said to Diane weakly, "Show him."

Steven stepped closer to his father's side and asked, "Show me what?"

Don's eyes closed as he appeared to fall back to sleep.

Diane turned to Steven and said, "Follow me." She walked out of the bedroom and into the living room, trailed by Steven. "The nurse doesn't have to hear this," she said.

Puzzled, Steven asked, "Hear what?"

Diane pointed at the couch. "Sit down. I need to show you something." She left the room and returned one minute later, carrying a box. She sat next to Steven.

Steven stared at the box. "What's that?"

"I know you and your father have had your quarrels over the years, especially that last one, almost two years ago."

"You don't have to bring this up."

"No. I have to. In many ways, you were right. He wasn't that great a father."

Steven shook his head. "I don't know how you could've lived so long with a man who was always tilting at windmills, just like that other Don. There were times I thought he was crazy. Why the hell would an archeologist have to spend practically all of his spare time searching for UFOs?"

"I know he should've spent more time with you when you were growing up." Diane paused, groping for the correct way to begin. "Many years ago, before you were born, your father worked for a time in Peru."

Steven appeared surprised as he said, "You never told me that."

"He was there for just over a month. I was there too, but only for a few days. A couple of days after our return to Manhattan, two well-dressed men—federal agents, probably CIA—knocked on our door. They used not-so-veiled threats to tell us that if we didn't want to see the inside of a mental institution or prison for the rest of our lives, we needed to forget everything that had happened in Peru. They didn't say it, but we knew that something like a well-planned car accident wasn't out of the question."

Steven's jaw dropped. "Our own government wanted to silence you? About what? They sound like Mafia hit men."

Diane smiled wryly. "Small potatoes next to these guys."

"Again, why would they want to keep you quiet?" He shifted uneasily in his seat.

"They didn't want other governments searching for what your father had found. Also, the United States didn't want to jeopardize its relationship with the new Communist leader, Mikhail Gorbachev."

"Slow down," Steven said as he shook his head in disbelief. "How could my father have affected anything in the former Soviet Union? And what did he find that's so important?"

Diane placed her hand tenderly on top of his. "In the time since you left, he's finally put onto paper what's been gnawing at his soul for so many years. And remember, I was in Peru with him. It just affected him more than me. Two years ago, when your father learned that he had terminal cancer, he finally figured, what could they do to him that his cigarettes haven't already done?" She lightly tapped the box. "In this box is the manuscript he's been working on for almost two years. It tells the story the government never wanted made public. He wants you to have it."

"What should I do with it?"

"It doesn't matter anymore. What matters most is that at least *you* believe it." She held out the box for Steven to take, which he did.

"Read it, and you'll finally know what I've known all these years: that there are reasons for his seemingly insane obsession. Your father is not and never has been crazy. His story—*our* story—begins before you were born, in Peru."

CHAPTER 1

The Mountains of Peru: 1985

THE ELDERLY PRIEST AND the twelve-year-old boy sat next to each other in the front pew of the weathered wooden church, the largest structure in their tiny, rural mountain village. They were alone, save for the mahogany, life-sized statue of Christ on the cross that gaped sadly down at them in the dimly lit, postconquistador house of God. The scent of paraffin permeating the air served as a reminder that here, in this poverty-ridden, spiritually rich region of Inca descendants, death was as much an accepted part of life as was birth.

The normally self-confident Indian boy fidgeted, ill at ease, as he anxiously wondered what he'd done to deserve a private audience with the most revered man in the village.

The priest, sensing the boy's discomfort, didn't delay his task. His speech had the ability to admonish while educating, the result of decades of accumulated worldly wisdom. "Your mother has asked me to speak with you, Paco, regarding your wandering alone, far from the village."

"I know it's dangerous," replied the bronze-skinned Paco Rivera with his usual self-assurance, "but I know these mountains as well as anyone. Nothing will happen."

Ah, invincibility, the priest thought. *A proper but often deadly characteristic of the young.* "You must understand that your mother worries about you. Why do you insist on exploring the highest of our slopes?"

Paco momentarily contemplated lying but chose otherwise, knowing better than to lie to a priest, especially here, under the gaze of those sad, mahogany eyes.

But Paco's hesitation was telltale to the wise old priest, and he spoke with a kind yet firm voice. "Come now, Paco, tell me your answer. And remember, I expect the truth and nothing less."

Paco looked into the priest's gray eyes, eyes that Paco knew could tell if he were lying, and instead attempted withholding the truth. "I've done nothing wrong, really. I like to go find things, that's all."

"What things?"

"You know, stuff. I'm curious. I like to explore." Paco nervously tapped his foot, hoping he'd successfully avoided having to divulge his ambition.

The priest shrugged his shoulders. He wasn't yet satisfied with Paco's answers and continued to probe. "And exactly what 'stuff' are you looking for? Certainly not rocks."

Paco's head tilted downward as he diverted his eyes away from the priest's and noticed the golden crucifix that hung by a long gold chain from around the priest's neck. Staring at the crucifix as though it were both a warning and a suggestive cue to be truthful, he answered softly, "Gold. I ... I look for gold."

The priest smiled knowingly and tried not to sound condescending as he replied, "Gold? In Ochoa? I didn't know we've discovered gold here."

Embarrassed, Paco answered, "We haven't. At least not yet."

"And you are going to be the one who finds it, I suppose?"

"Yes!" Paco replied with conviction.

"And what will you do with it if you do find it?"

The question surprised Paco. *Everyone knows what you do with gold,* he thought. He answered the priest with youthful exuberance. "It will make us rich! We can buy anything we want. I would surprise my family with presents. Dozens of them."

The priest brought the palms of his bony hands together as though chanting a prayer. "Paco, Paco. Gold is not as important as you believe it is."

More confused than impressed by the priest's words, Paco asked, "Don't you want to be rich?"

"I *am* rich, only in other ways."

"I don't understand," Paco said, shaking his head.

The priest placed his hand over his heart. "I am rich here, in spirit. I need no gold. My son, one day you'll discover that all the gold in the world cannot change your soul's ultimate destiny."

Paco sat silently, as the priest's statement was beyond his capacity to fully comprehend. He knew there could be no winning a battle of wits with the priest, for the priest's answers to any and all questions had been thoroughly practiced for some two thousand years by countless priests before him.

Paco also knew the priest to be very wise. But if he was right, why did so many people hunger for the precious metal? He had to ask. "Father, doesn't gold mean money, and doesn't money mean buying things? Doesn't that make people happy?"

The priest recognized that he was once again grappling with the age-old dilemma of delicately balancing the nourishment requirements of the spirit and the flesh, and knew he must choose his words carefully. "I agree that the average person would say yes to your questions, but I tell you here and now, the thirst for gold can never be quenched. It is like being an alcoholic; the more you have, the more you thirst. Man's search for gold has brought him far more anguish and pain than contentment."

The priest saw confusion in Paco's eyes. *Time,* he thought. *It will take the seasoning of time for young Paco to grasp the full meaning of this conversation.* "Paco, your mother worries about you, and now I am worried. But my worry is twofold, as I worry for both your body and your soul. Promise me you'll forget about wandering off in search of gold."

Paco paused. *A priest,* he thought. *Why did I have to be asked this by a priest?* "I ... I'll try, Father." Paco sincerely believed he had thus far avoided lying.

The priest had hoped for a more definitive response, but he readily accepted what was offered. "I hope so, Paco. You'll be far better off. Now go home. Your mother is expecting you."

Paco crossed himself, genuflected in the direction of the son of God, and hurried out of the church with a sigh of relief. He vowed to honor his promise to the priest and would try his best to avoid the golden lure, although something told him that he might be unsuccessful in his effort.

Paco Rivera was always adventuresome, although for a boy of twelve this wasn't unusual. A thin, athletic-looking boy with dark, Indian features, he had lived his entire life in the small village of Ochoa, sixty miles outside of Lima, Peru, and loved to roam the beautiful, mountainous area surrounding his village. His mother, Rosa, a squat, rotund woman, knew that Paco was the most likely of her seven children to be missing at mealtime when she took her usual head count. More than likely her first-born would be off again exploring the area where the ancient legends had told of the Mochica, ancestors of the Incas from whom the people of Ochoa believed they were descended. The Mochica had flourished for several hundred years, from approximately 200 AD to 600 AD, and Paco, having visited museums in Lima on class trips with his school, had seen for himself the artistry of the Mochica in pottery adorned with beautiful hand-painted figures, in textiles woven by careful and patient hands using every stitch that is known today, and in metal objects of beautifully sculpted bronze. More than anything else Paco ever had experienced, the golden figures he'd seen at the museum ignited his imagination.

The legends told of old gold mines in the mountains not far from his home, and the existence of these golden museum pieces was proof enough that his ancestors had indeed mined for gold in his mountains. Exploring the countryside was great fun for Paco, but the thought of discovering gold added a pleasant touch of excitement and mystery.

In school, Paco had learned that it was the lust for gold that motivated the Spanish conquistadors in their conquest of Peru. Led by Francisco Pizarro, they captured the Inca ruler Atahualpa and mercilessly slaughtered thousands of the Incas even though the Spanish troops numbered only 180. Superior armor, guns, cannons, and especially those frightening horses, which didn't exist anywhere in the New World, tilted the scales of war in the conquistadors' favor. A ransom was paid for the life of Atahualpa amounting to some twenty million dollars in gold and eight million dollars in silver, but the Spaniards, fearing the power of Atahualpa, brought him to trial on prefabricated charges and condemned him to death by burning at the stake.

Atahualpa was obsessed with the desire that his body be preserved like the mummified bodies of his ancestors and therefore pleaded that he not be burned alive. Atahualpa had seen terrible forms of torture and death, such as skinning alive, pulling out eyes, or breaking heads with stones, but nothing was as repulsive to him as was burning at the stake. His spiritual self had to be forever preserved. If he didn't disappear physically from this world, he would still reign on, even in death.

Pizarro therefore offered to proclaim death by strangulation for Atahualpa if Atahualpa would agree to become baptized as a Christian. Agreeing to this antithesis of values, Atahualpa was then baptized Jean de Atahualpa and was immediately pushed down onto a crude wooden chair. A Spaniard then threw a leather thong garrote around his neck. Into the loop he placed a stick, which he twisted tighter and tighter until the last of the Inca rulers was strangled to death. This ignoble event of 1533 marked the beginning of the end of the Inca empire, the People of the Sun.

The gold that the conquistadors so ruthlessly sought brought little happiness to them. Many were killed, including the chaplain, Valverde, who had baptized Atahualpa. Valverde was caught by the Incas, who killed him by pouring molten gold into his eyes. Pizarro had one of his Spanish rivals, Almagro, beheaded, but in 1541, vengeful supporters of Almagro assassinated Pizarro by stabbing him, and it was rumored that much of the gold was still stashed in the surrounding hillsides of Lima. Legend said that when news came of the murder of Atahualpa, gold that was being shipped by llama was hidden by the Incas, and although many were tortured by the Spaniards, the gold was never recovered. Young Paco Rivera often dreamt of finding that lost treasure.

The following day began like most other mornings, with Paco attending the local school near the center of the village with four of his brothers and sisters. The village, like most of earthquake-prone Peru, rests on huge faults in the earth's crust. Occasionally, a fault slips, enormous areas of land vibrate, and an earthquake is born, lives but for seconds, and dies slowly, fading into aftershocks. During one of the lessons, while Paco was writing a small composition, he noticed his normally neat handwriting becoming sloppy. He looked up at the startled teacher, who had ceased speaking in midsentence. She instantly sensed that an earthquake was about to strike, a relatively common occurrence in this part of South America, and ordered the children out of the school and into the safety of an open area. As with most other earthquakes, the epicenter of this one was either far enough away or would have too little energy to do more than shake and rattle the school and village. This earthquake was a bit more powerful than most, registering 5.0 on the Richter scale, but would it do no more damage than creating small cracks in building and roads and causing rockslides in the higher elevations of the surrounding mountainsides.

Once home, the children were warned by Rosa not to wander far from the village too soon after the earthquake. Aftershocks could cause a loose rock to come crashing down a hillside. The village, lying in a valley between the mountains, would be safe. But the adventurous Paco would obey his mother only until the following day.

The next afternoon, ignoring the prior warnings of his mother and the priest, Paco decided to explore his ancestral mountains. After a walk of about one mile on the dirt road leading out of the village, Paco turned off the road and headed for higher ground, passing tons of newly fallen rock debris. He climbed higher and higher while thoughts of golden treasure pirouetted through his mind. The gilded sun was slowly sinking behind him when a burst of reflected light caught the corner of his eye, thirty feet overhead. Paco believed that this was merely the reflection of a shiny piece of rock, but his imagination got the better of him. He pushed still higher to find some hidden treasure, perhaps even the golden treasure of Pizarro!

As he climbed higher, the mountain became steeper and the footing became increasingly treacherous, even for someone as surefooted as Paco. He could no longer see the shiny spot because a ledge of rock was jutting out directly below it. Finally, after deftly scaling the almost-vertical wall, Paco carefully pulled himself up to a point above the ledge from which he was able to see the place where the light had reflected.

To Paco's amazement, this was no rock at all! What he saw embedded in the rock was a cylindrical metal object that was golden in color. His heart began beating faster. This must be some golden piece left by Pizarro's conquistadors. He would make his family rich! His father, Herme, would be so proud of him. This would more than make up for the time he had borrowed and lost his father's only watch.

The excitement in him swelled as he began to try to remove the metallic object. First he attempted to wobble it loose by placing his hands on the sides of the cylinder and tugging with all his strength, but it wouldn't budge. He realized that it was solidly embedded in the rock, so he picked up a piece of granite the size of a grapefruit and with both hands brought it smashing down onto the encasing rock, trying not to hit the cylinder. After several attempts at loosening the rock, his arms became tired, and some of the blows glanced off the cylinder. *Don't hit the cylinder,* he exhorted himself. He knew that damaging it might lessen its value.

Paco soon tired. His arms ached from the weight of his makeshift hammer of granite, and he felt uncomfortably warm, unusually warm. He was sweating profusely and couldn't remember being as hot as this. He felt on fire, far more than when he had his worst fever, and began to feel light-headed. *I'd better get down from here*, he thought, feeling faint. He tried to move his feet but couldn't. It was as though they were planted in cement. He was burning up and losing consciousness. The pain from the heat was so great that his numbed mind grappled with only two choices: hold on and incinerate, or let go and fall.

The intense heat engulfed him to such an excruciating extent that there remained no choice. Paco let go. As he fell backward, he thought how interesting it was that the cylinder appeared to glow.

The ghostly glow was the last thing on earth that the glinting eyes of Paco Rivera would ever see. Lost among the jagged rocks far below, his shattered body wouldn't be found for two days.

CHAPTER 2

THE CORONER'S OFFICE IN Lima served many outlying towns and villages, including the village of Ochoa. An unusual case had been brought to the attention of the chief coroner, Dr. Alberto Lopez, by an assistant, Carlos Garcia. A young boy had been found by the municipal police after a two-day search, and it seemed to assistant Garcia that it would be an open-and-shut case of an accidental fall upon the rocks by an overly adventuresome boy. His skull had been split open by a jagged rock from a fall of perhaps thirty feet or so, and the body bore multiple contusions, several broken bones, and much internal hemorrhaging. But something else about this case puzzled Garcia, and he felt compelled to bring it to the attention of Dr. Lopez, even though he knew Lopez didn't like being bothered by his assistants.

Lopez was sitting at his desk in his office, poring over what seemed to be a mountain of paperwork, when he heard a knock at his office door.

"Come in." He looked up and saw a reticent Garcia enter.

Garcia walked over to the desk. "Dr. Lopez. I'd like to discuss case 3190 with you, if you have a few moments."

Lopez glanced down at the papers on his desk and, with a sigh of resignation, responded, "Sit down, Carlos. What seems to be the problem?"

Garcia sat down in a chair facing Lopez's desk. "I'm not quite certain. A young boy, Paco Rivera, was brought to us by the municipal police. At first, no foul play was suspected—"

"And now you suspect something?" Lopez interrupted.

"Well," Garcia replied, "I'm not sure. The head was severely lacerated, and I'm sure that the immediate cause of death was from a blow to the head caused by a fall. But the body was found face down among the rocks about forty-eight hours after the fall, and yet certain burn marks appear on the ventral part of the body, especially on the face, neck, and upper chest."

"Perhaps," Lopez speculated, "the boy didn't die immediately and lay for a few hours on his back?"

"Possibly, but the boy was fully clothed when they found him. Also, and this is very strange, the palms of his hands, especially the fingers, received the worst burns of all." He held out his hands to emphasize the point.

Lopez thought for a moment. "Perhaps, and I'm just groping now, a hot spring or hot rock exposed by the earthquake could have burned him, and he then fell to his death?"

"That might make some sense, except for the clothes. They were perfect and untouched." He hoped Lopez would deem this information important enough to warrant disturbing him.

Lopez paused again in thought. He was almost happy for this little mystery to break up the tediousness of the day. But now he seemed more concerned than ever. His eyebrows turned downward as he spoke in a softer voice than before. "Could we be dealing with some type of sex-crazed torture-murderer or something who may have burned the boy and then placed his clothes back on him?"

"Possibly," Garcia replied, "but the burns are so uniform … the same all over." Garcia needed help, but he dared not ask for it.

Lopez sat silently for several seconds, realizing that without actually verbalizing it, Garcia was asking him to examine the body. He therefore said, "I think it's time I viewed the body." As he stood up, he thought, *this had better be warranted.*

The two men walked down the corridor to the morgue, where the lifeless, bluish form of Paco lay in cold silence on a slab.

It had been several years since Lopez had performed an autopsy himself. Paperwork and making sure his staff kept to their timetables was now his job. He viewed the cold and rigor-mortis-stiff body of Paco Rivera lying unclothed, except for a small white cloth covering his groin, a practice which always puzzled Lopez. Surely the young boy was well beyond feeling embarrassment.

The only other thing attached to the body was an identification tag that hung limply by wire from the big toe of the right foot. As a young medical student, Lopez had thought how odd it was that the first time the big toe became truly useful for anyone was when lying dead in a morgue.

The strange burn marks on Paco's body that Garcia spoke of had been why the police referred case number 3190 to the coroner's office. Otherwise, Paco's death would have immediately been ruled accidental and the body would have been turned over to the parents for burial.

Lopez began to examine the body. The thick, pungent smell of formaldehyde permeated the room but of course went unnoticed by Lopez and Garcia, as did the sight of Paco's internal organs lying grotesquely lifeless next to the body on the examining table. To medical examiners, this was merely a job to be done, day in, day out. Little of their time or energy was ever spent on becoming emotionally involved in the cases that unceasingly passed through their offices. Besides determining the cause of death, their job was also to add to the body of knowledge of the medical profession through pathological determinations of the causes of death as a possible aid to others in finding solutions for preventing or curing certain illnesses. But such sophisticated analyses were seldom the case here, especially in cases involving the peasant population. The tediousness and monotony of the work often led medical examiners to joking in bizarre ways, such as, when removing a scalp in order to cut a skull open to reveal the brain for examination, remarking, "That's a hair-raising experience." Medical examiners would practically roll on the floor over jokes like these, especially ones with sexual overtones, of which there were too many to count. Sometimes fingers probed orifices from the outside in and sometimes, freakishly, from the inside out. This was not a job for the squeamish. Respecting the dead wasn't easy in a place where the dead were cut up and categorized like so much meat.

After examining the thin, broken body of Paco, Lopez began to speak. "I see what you mean. Very puzzling. Appears almost like a severe sunburn rather than burns inflicted by fire or another hot substance. Have the police opened up an investigation yet?"

"No. They're waiting for our recommendation first. What do we tell them?" He hoped Lopez would be able to arrive at some plausible explanation.

Lopez thought of the paperwork that already faced him. Besides, the police in the area were generally inept, especially in cases involving children of impoverished families. He began thinking aloud. "Could the burns have been made before he fell? Could he have then put his shirt on and fallen afterward?" Lopez paused for a moment and then began to speak, sounding as though he actually believed what he was saying. "Here's what I believe occurred. The boy fell asleep among the rocks, on his back, with his shirt off and palms up. He awoke, put his shirt back on, and, perhaps because of his hurting hands, lost his grip and fell to his death."

"Yes," Garcia answered, "that does sound possible." *But not very probable,* he thought. Still, if Lopez ascertained the cause of death and certified it, Garcia would be relieved of his responsibility for this case.

"It's the only explanation as I see it," Lopez concluded. "I'll notify the police that we've determined the death to be accidental. Release the body to the family as soon as possible. And thank you, Carlos, for bringing this case to my attention."

Carlos Garcia was happy that the case was closed and that Lopez was pleased.

As Garcia turned and walked out of the room, Lopez stood thinking, *What a brilliant administrator I am. Everyone will be happy with this decision.* Yet case number 3190 still puzzled him. Something about the burns seemed peculiar. But his holiday was soon approaching, and he had to get rid of the paperwork piled high on his desk. And anyway, the boy's death certainly appeared accidental, and nothing he could do would bring the boy back to life. *Let the family bury him,* he thought. *They've suffered enough as it is.*

CHAPTER 3

I<small>F ANYONE IN HIS</small> college days had told Don Carter that he would one day wind up in Lima, Peru, and like it, he would have said they were crazy. But here he was and loving it. Lima was the one truly modern city of Peru, with its ornate cathedrals, plazas, the Torre Tagle palace, and the magnificent suburbs of San Isidro and Miraflores with their graceful homes and gardens of roses. Lima was a city of fine hotels, elegant restaurants, theaters, parks, and wide commercial and cultural exchanges with the rest of the world. Yet the contrast between Lima and the rest of mostly poverty-stricken Peru is astonishing. To many people, Lima is Peru.

Unfortunately for Don, his recent separation from his wife, Diane, was placing a damper on his trip. But being thousands of miles from memories of Diane and being able to expand his knowledge by working with things he enjoyed gave Don a new lease on life. Working at the University of Lima as an archeologist was wonderful. He was an assistant to Dr. Romero, a well-known figure in anthropological circles, renowned for his work on Incan culture. Don's job was to help date and categorize pieces recently found in the surrounding areas of Lima. Don spoke fluent Spanish, having taken the subject for four years in both high school and college, and had spent a semester abroad in Puerto Rico during his sophomore year.

One of the nondegree assistants in the department was a young man named Diego Gonzales. The department utilized several persons as assistants to aid in physical chores such as digging, carrying supplies, driving vehicles, and so forth. They were persons who were deemed bright enough to be helpful but who could never afford to continue their education at a university. They earned a decent wage compared with the general population of mostly uneducated Peruvians, especially those from the so-called Sierra, a term used to describe anyone from the high elevations. Big-city dwellers tended to look down on persons from these areas and, in general, had little knowledge of the peoples of the Sierra.

Diego Gonzales grew up in a small village in the Sierra and always did well in school, at least by comparison with the other children. But as almost all children of the Sierra, Diego had to drop out of school at an early age to help with the farming and livestock that were the mainstay of his people. As with most people of the Sierra, Diego spoke almost no English.

Diego worked closely with Don, and they got along well from the start. Don had just turned twenty-eight and had told Diego of becoming recently separated, and so the two men often dropped in at the local bars in the city during evening hours. Diego was a nice-looking young man of twenty-four, and he seemed to know what places the best-looking young women of Lima frequented. Diego attempted to fix Don up with an old girlfriend of his, but although separated, Don had no desire to go out with anyone, at least not yet.

While sitting in a bar with Diego one evening, as both men smoked cigarettes, Don thought about the good times he and Diane had shared. His face wore a melancholy smile as he recalled the day he decided to surprise Diane with an engagement ring. He'd hidden the half-carat ring under her pillow in the apartment they had shared for the past two years. He waited with anticipation for her to come home from work, and rather than simply handing it to her, he decided to play a game of hot and cold in order for her to find it. The game would later seem silly, almost childish, whenever he overheard Diane excitedly relate the story to her friends, but he remembered it now as one of the happiest times of his life as she groped her way around the apartment, humoring him in his game, unsuspecting of what the result would be.

Diego noticed his dreamy-eyed expression and asked, "It's her again, yes?"

"It is," he answered softly. Time had made the unpleasant memories almost vanish, and he longed to see Diane again. He hoped that once he got back to the States they would somehow work things out.

Diego was proud of the fact that he had landed a job with the university. He knew he was bright and was an astute learner, and this fact had impressed the officials who hired him. In the five years Diego had worked at the university, he had learned much about the history of his people and Peru, picked up a tremendous wealth of information about both anthropology and archeology, and become well respected for his abilities as a competent aide.

Diego had been introduced in Lima to things he'd never known existed while growing up in his small village of Pataz. He was amazed at how many rich people there were in the big city of Lima. Since coming to Lima, Diego had met some wealthy Limoneros who had interests in Incan art. These aristocratic, erudite Peruvians had palatial residences and were revered patriarchs who would have an often attractive and privileged wife and many servants. They collected original paintings of Goya, Picasso, or Matisse. They would visit France or Spain regularly and could also speak English, French, or Italian. They would casually mention their lunch date the previous week with some famous bullfighter or painter. These were the epitome of the cosmopolitan man. And they were also persons to respect, for they often donated money to further the study of archeology.

Diego hoped that one day he would somehow become rich, and possibly famous, and adorn his own hacienda with the artwork of famous painters. Perhaps he would discover some amazing ancient ruin and write about his adventures in finding it. Maybe they would make a documentary about him, or even a movie about his life, or …

A knock at the laboratory door brought Diego back to reality. Don was calling for him, as he usually was at this time of day, asking Diego if he was ready for lunch. The two men generally ate in the cafeteria, where they would talk shop or discuss local events. Invariably, Diego would lead the discussion to some girl whom he'd recently met. But on this day Diego appeared solemn, and Don questioned him about his mood.

"Something bothering you?" he asked while sitting at a table across from Diego in the noisy cafeteria.

"I just received word from my cousin who lives in Ochoa that his oldest child died from an accidental fall. The funeral will be held tomorrow in Ochoa, and I guess I should attend." He bit into a ham sandwich.

"I'm sorry. Were you close with him?" Don was genuinely affected by the sad news.

"Not really," he said as he swallowed. "I haven't been to as many family functions in the past few years as I used to. Poor kid. He had a lot of heart. I guess he had too much heart for his own good."

"Want some company?" Don asked.

"What?" replied a surprised Diego.

"Tomorrow's Saturday, and I don't have any plans."

"You don't really have to …"

"I'd like to go. You seem depressed. Hey, what are friends for?" Don also thought it might be interesting.

"Why not? But there's going to be plenty of sobbing and wailing tomorrow." Diego was clearly appreciative of Don's offer. "I'll pick you up with my car tomorrow at seven thirty."

The next morning, the two friends set out for Ochoa, which was over an hour's ride to the east of Lima. They arrived at about nine and quickly found the Rivera house, a windowless, hut-like home. Don knew that the homes of Ochoa were typical of many of the country's small, isolated villages, containing perhaps two hundred people living with no radio or television, no phones, and no electricity. He saw that the village was composed of thatched houses made of adobe (mud brick) and knew they were similar to those built by the Incas in which the inhabitants slept on blankets on the floor. The men worked the fields with primitive hand tools while the wives were almost constantly engaged in making thread on a hand spindle or weaving cloth on a handloom.

The funeral and burial was a totally solemn religious affair, as befits a Catholic death. Pizarro's conversion and execution of Atahualpa was both an end and a beginning, as the Roman Catholic Church soon became the one cohesive force influencing colonial Peru. At its inception the conversions were not all voluntary: some of the Indians were beaten or had their ears cut off as a means of persuasion. But the church had evolved to become the focal point of not only spiritual but also cultural and artistic endeavors. Being Catholic was now a way of life, from baptism to marriage to burial.

The elderly priest who had conducted the funeral service and had briefly eulogized the young boy appeared stooped and even older than his years. He inwardly accepted responsibility for Paco's death, and it weighed heavily on his shoulders. He believed that he had failed Paco and the Rivera family in not being able to prevent the boy from scaling the treacherous slopes. He told himself that if he had done a better job, if he had been a better priest, Paco would still be alive. But was death the proper punishment for not following his advice? The priest wasn't surprised that he was unable to make sense of God's checks and balances. He could never fully understand. But understanding God was not his domain. Serving him was. And he had served again in the burial of a boy, once so full of life, who searched restlessly for an unworthy dream and who was now at rest and with God. *Yes,* he told himself, *the boy is at eternal peace. God's will is wise.*

On his way back to the church, the priest was stopped by Don and Diego.

Diego asked, "Why was Paco climbing, if it was so dangerous?"

The priest diverted his eyes downward. "He was looking for gold."

"In Ochoa?" Diego shook his head.

"I tried telling him the thirst for gold is unworthy, but he did not heed my advice."

"If I had thought there was gold up there," Diego mused, "I might have gone too."

The priest placed his hand on Diego's shoulder. "Then I will give you the same advice. The search for wealth for wealth's sake will not bring you contentment. Do something worthwhile … maybe help those less fortunate. If money comes with it, so be it. You can always donate to the church or other charity."

Don thought about his conversations with Diane and wished she were here, listening to this wise old priest.

Diego pointed at the priest's golden crucifix and said, "Just give me the gold."

The priest frowned and walked away. His duties complete, he returned alone to the church. As a tear streaked down his cheek, he lit two candles for Paco Rivera: one for his body and one for his soul.

Don, born a Protestant but with little religious upbringing, was unaccustomed to the open display of grief that he encountered during the funeral. But to Diego, only one thing seemed out of place, which he felt important enough to mention to Don: the simple wooden casket had been sealed throughout the funeral. As four men with leather straps lowered the child-sized casket into the grave, Diego quietly asked Don if he had noticed that fact.

"What of it?" Don replied softly, standing next to Diego.

"They always let us view the body one last time, but not this time. Just seems strange," he remarked as he watched them commit Paco's body to its eternal resting place.

After the burial, the two men met with the father of Paco, Herme Rivera, who greeted Diego with an unexpected remark. "Diego," a mournful Herme said, "you noticed, of course, that the coffin was never opened."

"Yes, I did, and I wondered about it. I would have liked to have seen him for one last time," Diego said with sincerity.

"Paco was a handsome boy, but the way he looked, I couldn't allow people to see him," Herme said, shaking his head slowly and sadly.

"What way?" Diego asked. Then, sympathetically, "Did the fall damage his face very badly?"

"His face was very badly sunburned," Herme replied, touching his own face for emphasis.

"Sunburned?" Diego asked. He sounded quite surprised, and Don glanced at him quizzically, wondering what the concern with sunburn was all about.

"Yes, at least that was what the police told me the coroner had said." The doubt within him was expressed in his voice as he continued, "But I've seen sunburns many times, and this looked different, much worse. His body, his arms, and especially his hands were badly burned, too. Besides, Paco was very dark. He never got sunburned, at least nothing like this."

Don's interest was now stirring. "What do you think caused the burns?"

"I don't know," Herme answered. "Paco was wearing his shirt when they found him. The shirt wasn't burned, and Paco never liked to take off his shirt."

"Puzzling," Diego said. "What do you think, Don?"

"I don't know. If the coroner examined him—"

"The coroner," Diego interrupted, "has been known to spend his time on big-city murder cases of prominent persons or government officials. He doesn't have time for *peasants*." His disdain was obvious.

Don asked, "Where was Paco found?" He could feel the detective in himself becoming aroused.

"A mile outside of town," Herme replied.

"Can you take us there?" Don asked.

"Yes, but we've looked around and found nothing. But if you like, you can look around the area also. Maybe you can find something we have missed, or maybe something the police didn't seem to have time for."

The three men got into Diego's beat-up 1972 Chevy and drove the dusty mile to as close as they could get to the spot where Paco was killed. The dirt road, dating back to pre-Inca times, lay in a small, natural valley between two imposing mountains that loomed like giant watchtowers on either side of the road. Most of both mountains appeared dark green from the vegetation covering them, although an occasional granitic, deep-gray outcrop could be seen as a reminder of the hard, rocky crust that lay beneath the thin topsoil.

Part of the mountain to their right, the one at whose base Paco's body was found, was now an exception. The earthquake had split open the face of a good portion of the mountain, about a hundred feet wide and three hundred feet high, as though it were merely rock candy. Much of the mountainside now lay at the bottom as sharp-edged, variously sized rocks, from pebbles to boulders, of mostly granite, containing assorted amounts of the minerals quartz, feldspar, and mica. The rock had sheared off in a manner that left a gouge in the mountainside, rendering that section of the mountain as a steep, almost vertical cliff.

They began walking up the sloping mountainside, over and around the rock debris and toward the place that Paco was found. This, Don thought, was rugged but also beautiful country. A wonderful place to die of old age. Paco was far too young.

"Here it is," Herme directed. "You can still see the blood-stained rock."

Don and Diego glanced briefly at the thick, dark-brown, coagulated blood stain that covered part of a two-foot-wide boulder. Clearly it was the fall that had ultimately ended Paco's life. Don swallowed hard at the sight of so much blood and then turned away and looked at Herme, who began to sob but was quickly able to control himself. Wiping tears from his eyes, he said, "I must be getting back. Rosa will be needing me."

"I'll drive you back," Diego offered.

"No, I'm fine. It's a fifteen-minute walk, and I think I could use a few minutes to be by myself."

"You're sure?"

"Keep looking. I'll see you back at the village."

Diego placed his arm around Herme's shoulder and said, "We'll stop by the house when we're finished here."

A forlorn-looking Herme turned and began walking back toward his village. Paco, his first-born and favorite son, was no more. He was in the hands of God now.

The two men began searching among the rocks, not knowing what they were looking for. They traversed the rocks for about fifteen minutes, to no avail.

"Listen," Don said, "there's nothing here. Paco could've climbed much higher than we did, and even if he had, what could have burned him?"

"I have no idea," answered a disappointed Diego, "but I wanted to satisfy myself. Maybe the coroner was correct. Stranger things have happened in this world. We might as well go back." Diego lit a cigarette with a match, inhaled deeply, and shook the match to extinguish the flame.

"Okay," Don agreed. It was late, and he was getting hungry.

Don and Diego returned to the car. By this time of day, the sun had begun to approach the distant mountain in its daily journey toward the west. The bright sunlight that now bathed the mountainside would soon slip behind the mountain as the car began moving down the road with Diego at the wheel. Don turned and looked back at the mountain as the car started toward the village.

"Man, a lot of rock came off that mountain," Don said.

"From the last earthquake," Diego replied with a yawn.

A flash of light from over the spot that Paco had been found caught Don's eye.

"Stop the car," Don shouted.

"What?"

"Just stop the car."

Diego brought the car to a halt. "What is it?"

"I saw something. Turn the car around and head slowly toward the spot," he said, pointing back from where they had come.

"Okay, if you say so," Diego responded as he turned the car around. The car headed slowly back, and again the sun's light briefly reflected off something that lay above the spot where Paco was found.

"Did you see that?" Don asked, a bit excited, expecting a similar reaction from Diego.

Instead, he answered casually, "Probably some shiny rock or something. The mineral mica can reflect sunlight like that."

"But," Don insisted, "there's also a chance that it's why he fell, trying to reach it."

The car stopped, and the two men got out and walked to the location where Paco's body was found.

"Do you see it anymore?" Diego asked, looking up the steep incline.

"Not from this spot. We have to climb up those rocks if we're going to see if anything is there."

"My cousin apparently thought it would be worth it."

"Unfortunately for him and his family, it wasn't," Don remarked.

"It's almost dark. We should be getting back."

"But something up there attracted his attention enough to make him take the risk," Don said, pointing toward midmountain.

"My cousin had a wild imagination. He probably saw the same spot you saw as the sun was setting and went up to have a look. Probably thought it was gold." Diego stooped and picked up a rock.

Don turned and faced Diego. "Couldn't it be?"

"Not very likely, at least not right around here. No one has ever found gold in Ochoa." Diego threw the rock and watched it rebound off the mountainside and arc to the ground in a parabolic curve.

"Well, there's still a chance of it, isn't there?" Don asked, appearing more wishful than inquisitive.

"You sound exactly like my cousin. You got the gold bug?" Diego kidded.

Embarrassed, Don replied, "No. Well, maybe a little. I mean, gold was found all throughout Peru at one time or another. Maybe the earthquake uncovered a place that no one could have discovered before."

"Maybe," Diego answered. "But it doesn't matter because it's almost dark and we'd better get back."

But the mystery of the burns still nagged at Don as he asked, "Why did Paco's body have those strange burn marks that Herme described?"

"Good question, and I have absolutely no idea. Maybe we can return to this place in the daylight. But I'm telling you, it's nothing. A piece of mica or quartz glistening in the sun, that's all."

"I still would like to go up there, just for the hell of it," Don said, straining to no avail to see what had glistened in the sunlight.

Observing the interest that Don was displaying, Diego said, "If you're really determined to have a look, we can come back tomorrow. To tell you the truth, I'm curious myself, especially about those burns."

They turned and walked back to the car, and then they returned to the Rivera home and said their sad farewells without mentioning anything about the shiny spot.

Once in the car again, Don asked, "Why didn't you tell them about the shiny spot?"

"I don't know. It didn't seem very important news. Why didn't you?"

"I don't know either. I guess I was waiting for you to mention it. They're your cousins."

But they both did know. The possibility, no matter how remote, that the shiny spot might be something of archeological value, or better still, something golden, was enough of a lure for any man. That possibility's seductive powers were instinctively held in secret.

CHAPTER 4

Downtown Lima springs to life at night like nowhere else in Peru. That evening, after returning to Lima from Ochoa, Don and Diego visited the Café Enrico, a popular night spot for young, mostly single, white-collar workers, and the two men sat at the bar sipping their beers and smoking cigarettes, adding more toxins to the already smoke-filled room.

In college, Don had learned that as with all cosmopolitan cities, Lima's bars and restaurants serve as a nocturnal breeding ground, satisfying the primordial urges of nourishment and reproduction in order to ensure the survival of the species, yet Don and Diego were understandably oblivious to such lofty thoughts. Diego constantly glanced around the room at the various tables in search of some good-looking females, and Don listlessly paid attention to his drink.

"Look at the women in this place. You see the three girls over there?" Diego enthusiastically pointed them out.

Don gave a perfunctory turn. "Yeah, I have eyes."

"What do you think of the honey in the middle?" He practically drooled his eagerness.

"She's okay, I guess."

"Just okay? I thought you said you had eyes. What you didn't tell me was that you're blind. She's gorgeous."

Don turned again to glance at the young woman only as a courtesy to Diego. "Yeah, she's nice."

"And I suppose if Bo Derek sat on the stool next to you in the nude, you'd say 'she's nice'?"

Don hadn't been listening, lost in thought, and replied, "What did you say?"

"What the hell is the matter with you? First you're blind, now you're deaf. Next you'll be speaking to me with grunting noises."

"Sorry. I was thinking, that's all."

"About what?" Diego playfully poked him in the ribs. "About going back to the shiny rock, eh?"

"Reminiscing," Don said, staring straight ahead, focusing on nothing in particular.

"Ay, it's your wife again, no? You have to get over her, or you'll have to either join the priesthood or do a lot of making love to your television set."

"What can I say? I'm thousands of miles from her and enjoying my work here, but I can't seem to get her out of my mind."

"Out of your heart is more like it, my man. Face it, you still love her."

"Always have."

"So she dumped you?"

"It was sort of mutual."

"So then she doesn't love you?"

"To be honest, I believe she still does. There was a time I thought we had a cosmic relationship."

Diego wore a puzzled smile. "Cosmic?"

Don took a paper napkin off the bar, ripped it in half, and demonstrated how the two ragged edges joined perfectly together. "In the entire cosmos, only one piece of paper will fit the other. I thought that was me and Diane."

"Then why did you separate?" He was clearly confused. Was the institution of marriage so different in America?

"It's a long story, but let's just say that her expectations of my earning power were set way too high."

"Ah, money. Must be a billion marriages a year that end over money."

Don turned and looked at Diego. "You think only that few?"

They laughed a good laugh, especially Don, and he felt some of the depression lift.

"You're right, Diego. I have to lighten up. But I don't think I'm ready to start seeing other women. And I *am* still married." Don extinguished his cigarette in an ashtray on the bar.

"What if she's seeing other men?" Diego instantly regretted asking that question, as he didn't intend to return Don to his depressed state.

"It's a thought I've tried putting out of my mind."

"Or you'll go out of your mind?" he asked, empathizing with his lovesick friend.

"Maybe so. We were married six years. But I don't think she'd begin seeing other men, at least not yet."

"She must be some good-looking woman."

"She is, and more." He stared at the condensation rolling down his beer glass.

Diego, sensing Don becoming melancholy once more, attempted to sound cheerful. "Got any photos of her?"

Don had a wallet full but hadn't looked at any of the photos since his arrival in Peru. He reached into his back pocket, pulled out his wallet, extracted several photos, and handed them to Diego.

Diego viewed each photograph, one by one, for several seconds each, intermittently nodding his head in approval. "She's dynamite. You left this to come here?"

"It isn't that simple." Don was uncomfortable. He wasn't one to easily bare his soul.

Sensing Don's annoyance, Diego said, "I didn't mean to pry. I meant she seems worth going back to."

"You ever been married?"

"Not yet."

"Before I got married, I pictured marriage as a way to have a permanent partner who you can not only have great sex with but who you love and share things with—goals, common interests, your life."

"You don't have to be married to know that it doesn't always work out that way."

"Sometimes, problems you never even knew could exist pop up, and you slowly drift apart. We're both stubborn people. We never seemed to be able to find a happy middle ground on some important issues."

"Maybe once you're back home in the States, things will be different. I hate to sound like a preacher, but maybe the two of you need to grow up a little. If you want to know what poor is, just go back to Ochoa. I know because I grew up in a village just like that."

Don paused for a moment in thought. "You're probably right. We certainly weren't starving, and other people have far worse monetary problems than we did, but they don't all get divorced over it." Don's spirits were now markedly lifted.

"Why don't you phone her and tell her how you feel?" Diego cocked his head in the direction of the pay phone.

"I don't think I'm quite ready for that. The last thing I need is to call her and get into another argument. Maybe in a few days."

"Think about it. After all, we have plenty of time on our hands. No girls, but plenty of time."

They laughed again. It felt good to Don, and he changed the subject. "Hey, what about tomorrow? Back to Ochoa?"

"Sure, why not? But I'll bet you a beer it's only a rock."

"Come on. You have to give me odds on that one."

"When llamas speak Spanish. Even money."

"You drive a hard bargain. For a beer." Don thrust his hand out for Diego to grasp, and they shook heartily, not only to seal the bet but also out of friendship.

CHAPTER 5

LATER THAT EVENING, ALONE in his apartment, Don sat at his kitchen table, drinking coffee and smoking. He thought about the events that led to his being in Peru. If he hadn't recently been separated from Diane, he would never have left New York.

He had met Diane at a college social when they were sophomores, and they had an instantaneous attraction for each other. He was somewhat shy and she somewhat outgoing, but each liked the opposite trait in the other.

He was of medium height and build with light brown hair, and most people considered him handsome. His personality had a certain seriousness that, for Diane, conjured images of the stability provided by her father, who had died suddenly when she was only fifteen. And Diane loved the gentle demeanor Don demonstrated in his dealings with people, especially with her.

Diane was a petite girl with dark eyes and dark hair whom Don found extremely sexy and exciting. He was further attracted by her poise and intelligent sense of humor. She had an uncanny ability to assess situations and take control of them, sometimes armed with an insightful wit. Their friendship led to an engagement followed by marriage one month after graduation. Don and Diane. It seemed perfect.

She had studied business while he majored in premed. He'd always been a good student, and everyone thought he'd become a fine doctor one day. But his grades slipped in his final two years after moving into an apartment in New York City with Diane. She was a distraction he wasn't willing to give up. His applications to medical schools were rejected. Instead, he found a job working for a museum as an aide to one of the professors, Dr. Anton Steinert, with whom he'd taken a couple of archeology courses. He had thoroughly enjoyed the courses and had managed to do well in them. Don had a genuine interest in archeology, finding the study of the ruins of ancient man fascinating. He didn't feel as though he was settling for second best, for, in actuality, his desire to become a doctor had burned within his parents but only smoldered within him personally. To his parents, having a son who was "The Doctor" was the epitome of the successful parent, a medal to be worn and carried around wherever they went as testimonial to the brilliant upbringing that their child had received. But it hadn't been Don's dream, except by default, and he had never really known what future career he wanted for himself. Now one thing had become clear to Don; he found archeology challenging and interesting and knew he enjoyed it, enough to perhaps pursue a lifetime career.

Don recalled sitting in the front row of a lecture hall at New York University. What he had seen and heard from Dr. Anton Steinert had been pure enchantment; the old man's words had mesmerized the former premed student. The genesis of Man, the dawning of what would eventually become the human race, as told to the graduate class by the elderly professor of archeology, stirred Don's emotions as though he were approaching the greatest of human mysteries. He was thrilled by the idea of determining the roots and origins of his own ancestry as well as the beginnings of all humankind. It was a major curiosity; he felt the need to know what it was that made human beings what they are. The German-accented old man, who had much to conceal concerning his own personal history, taught archeology, the study of the ruins of ancient Man. He combined knowledge, experience, and the love of his subject with such skill and passion that his words flowed with the rhythm of a finely tuned instrument. His words indeed became music to the ears of Don, for whom school had at one time lost much of its significance. Academically, Don had floundered, but he'd rediscovered his academic direction in the embodiment of the old professor's words. In spite of what others had said, especially his fiancée, Diane, about his change of heart concerning medicine, archeology became his profession.

Dr. Anton Steinert was an expert on South American ruins and had taught his college classes much about Peru. Don had learned about places and things that fascinated him as no other college subject had ever done before. Steinert made it come alive for him, and Don looked forward with excitement to attending his lectures and discussing the past of Man. He listened intently as he heard the professor describe strange and mysterious places high in the mountains of the Peruvian Andes, where the windswept slopes stand majestically, silently, as they have for eons past. The professor vividly depicted how lush greenery now hides many of the secrets of ancient Peru, where, some fifteen thousand years ago, humans in America trekked their way from the Asian continent across the frozen Bering Strait into Alaska and the rest of North America and then down through Central and South America, spawning civilizations older and more powerful than the Spanish-conquered Incas of the sixteenth century.

Often referred to as "the old man" by students, Steinert was only sixty-five years old but appeared ten years older due to his old-fashioned mode of dress and from his tormented history—one that left him with a permanent limp. Yet here, in his familiar element in front of the blackboard, he moved with the grace of an athlete and expressed his thoughts in a manner befitting the greatest of thespians. The educator was an impressive sight for an impressionable young man.

The professor further taught that the ghosts of ancient Peru loom especially mysterious to modern man since they devised no written language and are known only by their artifacts of pottery, cloth, and jewelry; their tools and weapons of bronze; and the stone ruins of their once-magnificent cities. He stated that these ruins of places with exotic names, such as the famed "lost city" of Machu Picchu, demonstrate that the ancient peoples were master builders, skilled in mathematics, and able to build aqueducts for irrigation. They also devised superior calendars and were knowledgeable about much of the heavens.

Don had pictured himself making wonderful and remarkable discoveries deep in the steamy jungles of South America as he read that in 1911, the explorer Hiram Bingham, scaling a precipitous two-thousand-foot slope led by a little boy acting as his guide, discovered, partly concealed beneath centuries' worth of moss and trees, "the work of a master artist … Surprise followed surprise in bewildering succession. We came to a great stairway …

The sight held me spellbound ... the principal temple ... Would anyone believe what I had found?"

Bingham had discovered Machu Picchu, the most spectacular sanctuary of the Inca Empire that had still remained undefiled by conquerors. Today, Steinert lectured, only the echo of the distant enchantment of the Incas' timeless land remains, and their pyramids and walled cities are still to be marveled at by modern man, thousands of whom are drawn each year to these ruins due to some inherent fascination with their past. Don longed to visit such places.

Steinert had visited many such ruins and related how he was always uncontrollably gripped by a strange sense of loss in not being able to know more of these people—how they lived, loved, died. Who were they, and what happened to them? Were they anything like modern man? What would it feel like to have lived in their time? "Conjecture is all that remains," he said, "but if one closes one's eyes among these ruins and listens with the perception of the sightless, he can almost hear the melodic sounds of the ancient woodwinds playing their melancholy songs." Steinert knew much of the riddle that is the Inca, but he lamented that the enigmas surrounding these people would probably never be fully revealed.

Approximately four thousand years ago, these people invented a very significant technology: large-scale cultivation of maize. The farming that followed agricultural invention made the growth of cities possible, and great cities were thus built that included large temples rising high toward the heavens. Don had asked, "How did these ancient people manage to become so advanced?"

Steinert answered that some present-day theories of reasons for this increased technology include the possibility of contact with ancient Egyptians who drifted their way by raft across the Atlantic and thereby influenced these ancient peoples. The possibility of this voyage was demonstrated by the Norwegian Thor Heyerdahl, who sailed the currents in 1970 aboard his papyrus raft, the Ra II. Another theory, he said, even went so far as to suggest that ancient alien astronauts had landed in Peru thousands of years ago and influenced these people. "But to this day," he continued, "the reasons for the technological advances of these ancient Peruvians remain largely uncertain, and in spite of its earlier glory, the Inca Empire was destined to crumble and decay."

Don had felt a surge of excitement pulse through him. No foreign lands or buried treasure did he find, yet determining the true course for his life gave him the exhilaration of a Marco Polo discovering new worlds. Don was now an explorer finding his direction in life, and Steinert was the compass.

The needle had pointed away from medicine and toward archeology. Don became an apprentice archeologist and was thrilled that it was under the tutelage of Dr. Steinert, an exemplary role model.

Don finished his coffee and cigarette and then climbed into bed, but his mind was still running on all cylinders as he continued to think about both Steinert and Diane.

Dr. Steinert worked as a part-time curator for the Metropolitan Museum and as an expert consultant on ancient South American ruins. His job was to authenticate the artifacts the museum bought for its collection in terms of age and origin. Although Don had a very limited archeology background, Steinert was willing to hire him for several reasons: Don was quick to learn, was eager to learn more about archeology and take graduate courses, and spoke fluent Spanish. Since Steinert specialized in South American ruins, knowledge of the language would be advantageous.

Don loved the work although the salary was low. But with Diane working for a Madison Avenue advertising agency, they more than made ends meet. Don attended graduate school at night and earned his master's degree in archeology.

Working with Dr. Steinert was a joy. His knowledge of archeology was enormous. He had lived, studied, and worked at several South American universities for some twenty years before coming to the United States. Don learned that Steinert had emigrated to Argentina from Austria soon after the Second World War, but Steinert was generally closemouthed in matters about his past, mysteriously avoiding any conversations concerning it.

Each day at the museum brought some new challenge to Don. He felt as though he were a kind of Sherlock Holmes trying to unravel the mysteries of civilizations that had flourished hundreds and even thousands of years ago. The only drawback to the job, a large one indeed, was Diane's attitude toward it. She had expected him to become a prosperous doctor who would earn lots of money, enough for her to eventually retire from the advertising business, raise a family, and never worry about finances. She wanted to work freelance and then get back into the business once the children were off to school. Don's present career, she believed, would get them nowhere. In fact, in their six years of marriage, she had more than doubled his salary and was beginning to feel boxed in. She wanted to begin having children but couldn't see how it would be possible to give up her job. She didn't think it was feasible to continue working full time in a demanding industry and raise a family at the same time.

Diane's worrying over money arose from the fact that her father had died of a heart attack when Diane was only fifteen. Her father had been a linotype operator for a large newspaper and made enough money to provide for Diane and her four older siblings, but upon his passing, life became much harder for her and her family. Diane had to learn to do without many of the things her more affluent friends took for granted.

Diane's feelings on the matter of Don's profession began to take its toll on their marriage. At first, Don would attempt to brush her protestations aside with jokes. He enjoyed telling their friends that when he died he wanted his ashes spread around Bloomingdale's so that he could be sure that Diane would come visit him at least once a week. But eventually the matter became more serious. Their discussions became all-out arguments, and the fighting became so severe that they began to drift apart. Inwardly, they still loved each other, but the arguing became a game of stubborn wills. They began to make marital threats with the hope that the other would back down, knowing how serious the threat was.

Don hadn't expected the day he moved out to be as traumatic as it was. The emptiness he felt was only relieved by throwing himself into his work, so when the opportunity arose for him to take a short-term position for one semester at the University of Lima, he jumped at the offer. Steinert was willing to give him a leave of absence, knowing how beneficial the experience would be.

Don turned over in his bed. Tomorrow's trip back to Ochoa would take his mind off Diane.

CHAPTER 6

THE NEXT DAY, DON and Diego set out for Ochoa, and the two men's curiosities brought them back to the place where Paco had begun to climb. The side of the mountain had sloughed thousands of cubic yards of rock, most of which lay as unsorted rubble at their feet. The part of the mountain where the shiny spot was thought to be was almost a sheer vertical cliff, only slightly less than perpendicular. But the shattering of rock during the earthquake left innumerable jagged-edged stepping stones, which it seemed would allow them to scale their way up to the ledge that blocked the shiny spot from view.

After climbing several feet, they could see nothing out of the ordinary. They climbed still higher, with Diego cautiously leading the way.

"Do you see anything?" Don asked.

"The ledge of rock is blocking my view. This is getting to be dangerous." Diego nervously looked down at his feet. "I can't believe I'm doing this to see a rock."

The men climbed higher, finding it increasingly difficult, much as Paco had. Neither man was adept at this sort of thing, but they made no mention of that fact to each other. If the surefooted Paco could fall to his death, why couldn't they? But each man pushed still higher, grasping rocks with his hands and feeling for solid footing with his feet. Their fear of injury or death was overcome by the slimmest of chances that something up there, above the ledge, was worth the risk.

About fifteen minutes had passed, although it had seemed to them far longer, when the ledge was reached, with Diego still leading the way. He peered over the ledge and, to his amazement, saw a bright metallic object that he recognized as being man-made. Diego called out, "I see it! Take a look!"

Don stuck his head over the ledge and saw the metal object embedded in the rock. The object was cylindrical in shape, had a bright, shiny golden color, and measured approximately twelve inches in length and six inches in diameter. About two-thirds of it was protruding sideways out of the solid rock, which had been cracked open by the earthquake.

"This is it," Don exclaimed. "Paco was probably standing right where you are."

Diego reached out with his index finger and touched the cylinder. "Close enough to touch this and try to ...wait a second. Could this be what burned him?"

The two men glanced at each other with knowing looks, and in unison they ducked under the ledge. Their excitement was almost too much to control as a myriad of questions and possibilities crossed both their minds.

"This is unbelievable," Don remarked. "Was it hot when you touched it?"

"Not at all."

"Then maybe it was made with radioactive material mixed into the metal they were using."

"Sounds crazy," Diego replied. "How would they have carried it? Look what happened to Paco."

"Also, how did they get it up here? It wasn't placed with rock pushed against it, but rather the rock was melted around it and solidified. Maybe it was caught in a lava flow that hardened around it. You got a pretty good look at it. Does it appear to be of Incan origin?"

"I saw no markings. Only a fairly smooth, rounded surface."

They paused, still in their crouched positions below the ledge, pondering the mysterious object.

"Don, whatever it is, it may be an important find. Can you imagine if it's mostly gold? We might even be able to write a paper on it together." He was only half joking. Diego had always believed he was bright, but he knew that he lacked the educational credentials to be published.

Ignoring Diego's statement, Don said, "We've got to get it out of the rock first, and we have to keep this a secret until we do. We'll have to get some equipment: a Geiger counter, a lead box, some tools, and most of all, a radiation suit, just in case my guess about it being radioactive is correct."

"I agree. We can probably get everything from the department. The suit may be a bit difficult to explain." Diego looked down to check his footing.

"We'll say we're on a dig that may bring us near some uranium ore."

"Sounds phony."

"But old Manolo won't care. All he cares about is having all his precious equipment returned to the storeroom."

They quickly placed some rock debris in front of the golden object in order to hide it from possible further discovery and drove back through the village, stopping briefly to pay their respects to the Rivera family but saying nothing regarding their find. Don and Diego sang songs during the drive back to Lima and dreamed of how great the find might be.

For Don, the excitement lay in the intrinsic value of the find itself. Very few archeologists could ever claim that they had found anything truly unique during their digs. Yet here he was, in Peru for only one month, and he had found something, whatever it was, on which he could write an article and have it published in one or more national scientific journals. The object would be donated to the Peruvian government as a national treasure. Who knew? This could be the first step in being promoted at the museum back in New York, and it might even be the foundation for the dissertation he would write for his hoped-for PhD.

But mostly, he hoped that his accomplishments here would impress Diane enough for her to reconsider her attitude toward his chosen profession, which could then lead to a reconciliation of their marriage.

But Diego viewed the object in purely monetary terms. Radioactive or not, if it were indeed gold, it had to be worth a small fortune, even if they had to melt it down and sell it piecemeal. He saw this as an opportunity for him to rise above the aide's position that he knew would otherwise be the highest-paying job he could ever aspire to, lacking the degrees that were essential for promotion but that he could never afford to attain. Perhaps he would use the profits to get an education, or maybe to purchase some hot automobile that the chicks would love to be seen in. Even better, he'd be able to start a business that might eventually make him a millionaire.

Both men thought to themselves, *Yes, the golden object could be the answer to my dreams.* But with their thoughts unspoken, they couldn't have realized that their visions were in direct contradiction to each other.

CHAPTER 7

THE COASTAL CITY OF Lima faces the ocean to the west and thus takes longer to receive the sun's radiant energy than many cities of the same longitude, as the mountains to the east effectively block the fireball's warmth until the middle-aged, yellow star rises above the great crests of the Andes. The hazy morning fog hadn't yet burned off as the two sleepy-eyed men met at the university, having slept restlessly in anticipation of the day's future events.

After obtaining the needed equipment, the two men drove the sixty miles back to Ochoa, making sure to take a different route through the village to avoid being seen by the Riveras. They drove off the road as close as they could to the site and exited the car.

"What if we're seen?" Diego asked. "Especially once one of us puts the suit on."

"First of all, I hate to pull rank on you, but since I'm the big enchilada and you're a lowly assistant ..." Don bantered.

"Okay, okay. No problem, your majesty. I'll stay at the bottom and watch for any cars or pedestrians. If I see anything in the distance, I'll shout. You can duck down and squeeze behind a rock near the ledge."

The radiation suit consisted of alternating layers of aluminized Mylar, nylon, and rubber, similar to the fabric used by astronauts. The helmet fit loosely over the head and had flaps that hung on all four sides down to shoulder level. A rectangular, tinted glass window allowed the user to see straight ahead well enough but restricted peripheral vision. In tropical climates, the suit had the tendency to become uncomfortably warm. They knew Don would have to work quickly.

Don got into the suit with the aid of Diego and carried a lead box large enough to place the cylinder into. They hooked the other equipment to rings attached to the waist of the suit, including a Geiger counter, a hammer and chisel, and a camera. While Diego stood lookout, Don climbed carefully, slowly, up toward the ledge. The first thing he knew he must do would be to test the hypothesis of radioactivity. Then he would determine if the suit and lead box would be enough of a shield against the radiation.

After about twenty minutes of arduous climbing, made more difficult by the cumbersome suit and lead box, he arrived at the ledge directly below the cylinder. He readied the Geiger counter and carefully held the tube of the counter over the ledge with one hand. The counter had been clicking steadily due to the usual background radiation, and Don held the tube as close as he could to the cylinder, in fact even coming to touch it, but the level of radiation only increased slightly. Curiously, the cylinder's radioactivity wasn't powerful enough to have caused the damage it had done to the boy.

Don placed the Geiger counter on the ledge and left it on. Next, following correct archeological procedure, he photographed the cylinder and the surrounding rock and measured the exact position of the object relative to that surrounding rock. He then began to chisel at the rock that encased the cylinder. The rock was extremely hard. *No wonder,* Don thought, *that poor Paco had trouble, working with only his hands and perhaps another rock as a hammer.*

Don hammered with the care of a sculptor. This type of work wasn't new to him after his many field expeditions with Dr. Steinert. He knew that he must be careful not to damage the cylinder, but standing precariously on rocks, and overlooking a ledge, made the job difficult. The suit was bulky, and the harder he worked at the rock the more his perspiration began to run into his eyes. The helmet prevented him from rubbing his eyes, and his vision became blurry. He was also becoming hot and tired, and he accidentally brought the hammer crashing into the cylinder.

"Damn it." He didn't want to damage the cylinder, but as soon as he struck it, the Geiger counter began to click wildly. The reading on the meter showed extremely high levels of radiation, and Don ducked under the ledge for protection. Even with the suit on, those levels would be dangerously high. Don waited for a minute and then realized that the Geiger counter had almost ceased clicking. This was incredibly strange. He stood up and, this time quite by design, struck another blow with the hammer against the cylinder. Once more the radiation level increased enormously, and he again ducked under the ledge. *This is fantastic*, Don thought. *Paco must have struck it at least several times until he was severely burned and then fell to his death.* He waited for the clicking to subside and then began to chisel around the cylinder once again. The rock began to break apart, and Don was able to place his gloved hands around the ends of the cylinder until he began to slowly wobble it loose, being careful not to jar it. Finally, the cylinder was freed from the mountain's grip; it was heavier than Don had thought it would be.

Just then, Diego spotted a car approaching and shouted toward Don. "Don, get down!"

Don was extremely tired, and in his rush to hide behind a rock by the ledge, he almost slipped and fell. He tried to grab hold of a rock with one hand, but the weight of the cylinder and his confusion made him drop the cylinder. Don watched, horrified, as the cylinder went crashing down onto the jagged rocks below. His Geiger counter clicked furiously for the next two minutes, and Don hid behind one of the larger rocks.

The approaching car slowed to a halt as the driver spotted Diego and his car. "Need some help?" the man called out through his window, leaning toward Diego.

"No, no." Diego answered nervously. "Just doing some rock collecting, but thank you for asking."

The man in the car waved and drove off.

Diego turned and ran toward the rocks. "Are you all right?" he called up to Don.

Don pulled the helmet off his head. He was perspiring profusely. "Yeah, I'm okay, but I dropped the damned cylinder. Shit!" He began to descend.

"Where is it? Is it ruined?"

"Wait. I'm coming down. Don't touch the cylinder even if you see it." Don then climbed down to where Diego stood. "It fell over there, by those rocks."

They walked closer to the rocks with Don carrying the Geiger counter.

Diego asked, "Is it radioactive?"

"Sometimes."

Diego's eyebrows raised. "What do you mean by 'sometimes'?"

"This may sound crazy, but it's radioactive only when you hit it," Don said as they scanned the area ahead for the cylinder.

"You don't look like you're in a joking mood, so I'll assume you're either mistaken or your Geiger counter has gone crazy."

"Let's find the thing and you'll see."

They walked over some debris and then spotted the cylinder lying in a pool of melted rock.

"My God," Diego exclaimed in disbelief. "It melted the rock! How could that happen? What is this thing?"

"I haven't the slightest idea." Don was equally amazed at the sight of the hot liquid rock. "All I can tell you is that it's very heavy, and it only gives off radiation when struck. That fall must have made it give off mega doses of rads. Enough to melt rock. But look at the Geiger counter. It's as if it's hardly radioactive at all."

"And that's what burned Paco," Diego said, pointing at the cylinder.

"I'm sure of it. And we should still put it into the lead box just in case." Don placed the box onto a rock next to the cylinder.

"Be careful," Diego cautioned. "Do you think the fall may have damaged it?"

The men moved closer to the cylinder. Don used his gloved hands to gently roll the cylinder away from the rock, which was now cooling and hardening. The cylinder didn't have a mark on it, except for some small raised dots on its surface, which appeared to have been placed there by design.

Given that it had no scratches or dents from the thirty-foot fall, Diego and Don instinctively knew that the cylinder couldn't be made from the soft yellow metal Paco had searched for, but Diego still clung to the hope that maybe it was worth something to someone. It had to be. His future might depend on it.

"Don, I'm not the expert on these matters, and I know that governments keep these things very top secret, but do you suppose we've come across some sort of nuclear bomb, perhaps lost by some plane or something, and that it could have melted its way into the rock on impact?" He believed a nuclear device could be worth untold sums of money to the right bidder.

"I wish I had something clever to say to you, because that's the craziest thing I have ever heard anybody say in my entire life, and yet I don't have any better answer. Let's put it into the box and get out of here. We can speculate further once we get it back to the lab and examine it more closely."

After placing the cylinder into the box, they packed up everything and began the drive back toward Lima, with Diego at the wheel. Both men lit cigarettes and inhaled greedily.

"Don, whatever it is, I doubt it's Incan or made of gold." He glanced at the lead box, which was placed between them on the front seat.

"I agree, but then what is it?" Don held his hand on top of the box to keep it steady. The Geiger counter was at his feet, monitoring radiation levels with its steady clicking.

Diego turned toward Don. "Maybe we *do* have some miniature CIA atomic bomb that can be exploded from a satellite."

"In Ochoa?" They both laughed at the ridiculous thought.

"Okay. So maybe it's not a nuclear weapon. You have any better ideas?"

Don thought for a moment. "The United States has an enormous communications network around the world, much of which is related to national defense. I wonder if this cylinder sends out signals in order to help guide planes … bombers, maybe, or satellites, or even missiles?"

"Why place it in rock, and how did they get it in there?" Diego asked, still tending to his driving.

"I don't know how it got into the rock, but maybe it's so important it had to be placed there to avoid detection. Maybe it's some new, top-secret, high-tech device that they wouldn't want to get into enemy hands." Don patted the lead box.

"Maybe we'll know soon enough."

They arrived at the university and, this being Sunday, were able to enter the laboratory alone. The laboratory was a cluttered conglomeration of shelves filled with books, magazines, and journals; walls papered haphazardly with maps, posters, and charts; counters filled with a variety of instruments; and tables filled with samples of rock specimen and artifacts uncovered in recent digs, all used alternately either as tools of teaching or for what college professors truly enjoyed, their own research projects.

Once inside the lab they gathered up the necessary equipment and prepared to perform various tests. One test involved connecting a radio to an amplifier and tape recorder to record any signal that might be given off by the cylinder. Don played around with wires for a while, linking the radio to the amplifier and tape recorder, while Diego busied himself with collecting materials they would need to determine the type of metal the cylinder was made of. Within twenty minutes they were ready to test the hypothesis that the cylinder was some type of guidance or communications device.

Don called to Diego, "All set."

"Great." Diego walked over to Don. "What do we do first?"

"We check the Geiger counter constantly as we lift the cylinder out of the box. I don't want to take any chances." Don lifted the cylinder out of the box and gently placed it on a table. "I think if we slowly change the frequency on the radio, we will eventually hit the correct frequency, if in fact there is one, and record some sort of signal, possibly some kind of coded message. Whoever placed it in the rock obviously went through an awful lot of trouble getting it melted into the rock. Maybe the signal tells them where the cylinder itself is located."

"Sounds like a spy movie, Double O Seven," Diego quipped.

Don kidded back, "You know, Odd Job, you could be right." He then added, "Maybe it does involve some sort of spy network."

"But just who is spying on whom?"

Don pointed at the cylinder. "Maybe we'll find out."

Don began to slowly turn the dial, picking up various local stations but nothing that sounded loud enough to be transmitted from a source next to them. They expected the signal, if there indeed was one from the cylinder, to be quite a bit stronger, and therefore louder and clearer, not only due to the proximity of the cylinder but also because the walls of the building would have a blocking effect on the signals from the local radio and TV stations.

Don continued turning the dial, occasionally picking up some song that Diego began to gyrate and spin in place to while humming a tune.

"You call that dancing?" Don chided mildly, glancing at Diego.

"The girls lo-ove when I move like this. You should try it sometime."

"I did. We called it disco, only it died." He held back a smile.

With an air of mock-superiority, Diego said, "Americans don't know how to turn the chicks on. Too stiff when they dance."

"Oh yeah? You ever see *American Bandstand?*"

"American what?"

"American … forget it," Don replied, remembering where he was. He continued turning the dial.

Seconds later, a powerful signal was heard from the radio.

"Wow, listen to that. The cylinder is definitely giving off this signal. I'll bet I'm right," Don said immodestly, proud of his earlier hypothesis. "This thing is probably some kind of aid to guidance or in communications." He suddenly frowned. "Jesus, something just occurred to me. Someone is going to be more than a little angry with us for disturbing it. What if they can trace it here, to the university, by those signals?"

But before Diego could contemplate the seriousness of Don's question, he shouted, "Wait a second!" Diego had had his ear trained on one of the speakers, and he put up his hand, motioning for Don to stop talking. "Do you hear it?" They were both thrilled that the monolithic, inanimate cylinder was internally, electronically, very much alive.

Don strained to concentrate on the strange noises coming through the speaker. With a puzzled yet astonished expression, he looked at Diego and said, "It … it's a person speaking at very high speed … seeming to say the same thing over and over again. Do you understand any of it?"

Diego listened a moment longer and then answered, "No, I really don't. It's going much too fast to understand or make out the individual words. Maybe if you could play it back on your tape recorder at a slower speed, we could hear it better."

Don examined the recorder but saw that it had only one speed. "Nothing. No way to vary the speed on this old thing. And even if we could, we'd probably eventually have to turn the tape over to a specialist in linguistics or decoding. I'm sure that whatever the message is, it wasn't meant to be easily interpreted. My guess is that this thing sends out some sort of coded voice messages to military-related planes, but I'm still baffled at how it could do that while embedded in rock."

"Really strange," Diego said as he shook his head at the perplexing question concerning the entombment of the cylinder.

Don turned off the radio. "We can worry about the tape tomorrow when we get our hands on a better tape recorder.

Diego said, "Let's see if we can open this thing. There has to be something important inside to hide it like that."

Don shook his head. "I don't think we should. Who knows how much radiation could leak out."

Diego smacked himself in the head. "Of course. That would be stupid. But let's look for seams or openings or something."

They slowly rolled the cylinder across the table, cautiously listening for the normal, steady click-click-click of the Geiger counter. Both men leaned over the cylinder, silently galvanized by its potential power and by knowing they held something highly unusual before their eyes, the mystery of which was totally engrossing. They were experiencing the rarest and most exhilarating of moments, when time passes unnoticed.

"Do you see anything?" Don asked while staring at the object.

"Only a bunch of raised dots. I wonder what they're for?"

"No idea. Some secret message or something." Don scratched his head. "I doubt we'll be able to figure out their meaning."

Diego nodded his head. "Forget the dots for now. The metal. What do you think it's made of?"

"Where'd you put the testing equipment?"

Diego walked over to a table on the opposite side of the room, picked up the testing materials that he'd earlier made ready, and placed them on the table next to the cylinder.

"What do we do first?" Diego asked.

"From its color, luster, and strength, we certainly know we're dealing with some sort of metal or metal alloy. If we could crack this thing open, we might be able to tell something about it by its crystal structure. But since we can't do that, we'll have to rely on surface testing alone. There's a chance we might still be able to identify it, or at least narrow it down to a few possibilities."

"You sound like a college professor. What do we do first?" he repeated, impatiently.

"The hardness test. It's fairly easy." Don picked up the hardness kit, which contained ten minerals rated from one to ten, in order of hardness. Number one, talc, was the softest, and number ten, a diamond chip, was the hardest. He would test how hard the metal was by attempting to scratch its surface with one of the minerals in the kit. The lowest number to scratch the metal would be equal to its hardness. This would not, by itself, identify the metal, but it would help narrow down the possibilities with the help of other tests.

Don knew the casing was quite hard and thus began with number seven, quartz, the hardest of common minerals. He took the one-inch-long quartz crystal in his hand and attempted to scratch the cylinder, but he could not. "Okay, we know the metal is harder than seven."

He then tried number eight, topaz, with the same negative result. "Nothing, not a mark."

Then on to number nine, corundum, again with no scratch being made. "Well, here goes number ten." But no matter how hard he pressed the diamond chip against the cylinder, he could make no scratch mark.

Diego remarked, "Must be some new high-tech alloy. Maybe we have no test available here that can identify it."

"Could be. But let's try some acids and bases to see if we can get some kind of reaction. Only certain materials will react to specific kinds of acids and bases."

Don applied drops of various kinds of acids: hydrochloric, sulfuric, and nitric. Seeing no reaction, he then applied sodium hydroxide and calcium hydroxide. None of the chemicals showed any reaction whatsoever with the cylinder.

Don rubbed his eyes. "Well, that's not much help. How about magnetism? Diego, get a magnet from that shelf."

Diego retrieved a large, U-magnet and handed it to Don. Don took some straight pins out of a drawer and magnetized them by rubbing them with the magnet. He then attempted to make the pins stick to the side of the cylinder. They fell harmlessly onto the table. "Not magnetic, either. Getting nowhere, fast."

"You know," Diego said, "a thought just occurred to me. How do we know this thing won't explode in our faces if we fool around with it too much?"

"We don't. But if the fall onto solid rock didn't do anything, I suppose sticking pins onto it won't do very much."

"You're probably right. What about density? Can we test for that?"

"No. We don't know how much space is inside this thing, so we can't determine the actual volume of the metal casing. If we could remove a solid piece of the metal, we could do it. But like this, forget it. But good thought."

"I'm out of ideas as far as the metal is concerned. Neither one of us is a trained lab technician, and it seems that's what it'll take to identify the metal." Diego then pointed at the cylinder. "What about those dots? Any guesses?"

"I don't know, but I have an idea. Get me a bottle of ink and a large piece of paper, about twenty centimeters by forty centimeters."

While Diego went for the ink and paper, Don placed a flat metal pan on the table. He then took the ink from Diego and spread the ink in a thin layer in the pan.

"Okay, Diego, time to play newspaper." Don picked up the cylinder and placed it into the ink-laden pan. He rolled the cylinder across the pan until the entire outside was covered in the black ink.

Diego, sounding nervous, said, "Be careful, very careful, or we might become the best-tanned men in all of South America."

"I'm being as cautious as I can. You keep listening to that Geiger counter." Drops of perspiration were beginning to bead up Don's his eyebrows. He picked up the heavy cylinder and placed it onto the paper. "Now watch this little trick." He rolled the cylinder across the paper, making one full rotation with it. The cylinder left ink marks where the raised dots were. Don lifted the cylinder off the paper, Diego wiped the ink from the cylinder with a rag, and then Don replaced it into the lead box. They were now ready to examine the paper.

The two men saw that the paper contained several hundred, maybe as many as a couple of thousand, pencil-point-sized dots.

"All I see are a bunch of dots," Don remarked. "There might be thousands of them of varying sizes, and they're randomly spaced."

"I don't see any kind of pattern to the dots," Diego said. "Maybe we should take a closer look at the individual dots. Maybe they're really microdots, with each dot having its own message or part of a message."

"Good idea. You look at the raised dots on the cylinder with a magnifying glass, and I'll examine the dots on the paper with a microscope."

Diego retrieved a magnifying glass from one of the counters and then took the lid off the lead box and scrutinized several of the cylinder's raised dots. Don placed the paper with the ink dots under the microscope.

After a few minutes, Diego said, "I see nothing. They all look alike, except for their sizes. Some are a bit larger, and some are smaller than the others."

"That's exactly what I see on the paper. The dots appear to be precisely that, dots. And you're right about the varying sizes. I wonder why?" "Want to switch?" Diego asked. "Maybe I'll see something you didn't and vice versa."

"Can't hurt."

They exchanged places but still came to the same conclusions. They conceded for the moment that the examination of the dots had revealed nothing of significant value to them.

"Now what, Don?"

Don sat down on one of the stools, appearing dejected. The comforting clicking of the Geiger counter was the only sound disturbing the quiet solitude of the empty laboratory. He shook his head as if lost in thought and then began to speak, looking directly at Diego, who continued to stand. "I think we should review what we've got here." He grabbed the pinky finger of his left hand between the index and thumb of his right hand, as if ready to count off a list of items. "We've got a metal cylinder made of material that won't scratch and that we haven't been able to come close to identifying; the cylinder becomes highly radioactive when struck by something, which the two of us are totally baffled about. It obviously gives off some sort of signal that we have yet to interpret, and have no idea as to why it would be placed deeply into solid rock if it were meant as an aid in guidance. We're absolutely dumbfounded as to how it got embedded into the rock, and in Ochoa, of all places; and we've got a bunch of dots on a piece of paper." He scratched his head. "We're going to have to get some help with this thing. This is obviously not an ancient Inca artifact. We'll need someone with access to information that we don't seem to have available here. Maybe our guess about it being some sort of secret weapon, or something related to one, isn't so crazy after all."

"Who do you suggest?"

"The only one I can think of immediately is Dr. Anton Steinert back in the States. He's got connections with government officials who may be able to provide some answers for us."

"But what do we do with the cylinder?" Diego asked. "We can't leave it here."

"We'll have to hide it somewhere, maybe bury it outside this building."

Diego thought for a moment. "Agreed. But how can this Steinert help from the United States? It may be our obligation to get help from someone here at the university, or—" he paused, measuring his words carefully. "We might want to determine its real value before we tell anyone about it."

For the first time in almost two days, each man had a few moments to assess the situation from a selfish point of view. Each believed the find to be of at least some significance, and possibly an important one, although neither could figure out what it was they were dealing with. To Diego, this was a Peruvian find. It was also his doing that they had gone to Ochoa in the first place. He trusted his friend, but if some big-shot professor from America got hold of this, how much credit would an assistant with little formal education get? He might be given credit for the dumb luck of helping to discover it, but those persons figuring out what it was would write the papers that would eventually be published. But at least Diego was a Peruvian, and it might make some difference in his own career here, especially if the cylinder had been placed here without the consent of the Peruvian government. Or, and far more important, it might be worth money, perhaps lots of it.

Don, too, was thinking of his own interests. If the authorities here knew of this, they would claim it for their own. Most of the credit for the discovery and any subsequent findings about it would surely go to the Peruvian government or the university; he was, after all, working for the university. Also, being an American, he doubted that he'd be given rights to the object. He felt that he had to discover more about the cylinder's secrets before relinquishing it to the Peruvians. Don wanted to be the person given credit for determining what this was and desperately wanted to be able to write a paper on it. He knew there was a good possibility that it wasn't American property. Perhaps it was the Soviet Union's! Don began to speak first.

"Let's sleep on this. In the morning, when we're both fresh and have had a chance to mull this over, we'll discuss it again. In the meantime, we've got to keep the secret to ourselves, and we have to hide the cylinder."

Diego nodded in agreement. It had been a long day, and the morning might bring a clearer idea of what the cylinder was.

After some further discussion, they decided to hide the lead box, with the cylinder in it, behind some bushes close to the rear of the building, where they could dig a shallow hole.

Diego carried the lead box and cylinder while Don carried a shovel to dig the hole with. They followed the darkened sidewalk to the rear of the building, where a row of thick, six-foot-high hedges was growing between the sidewalk and the building.

"How about here?" Diego pointed out a spot between the building and the bushes.

"It's as good as any," Don answered, and they pushed between the bushes into a space that was about three feet wide and ran the length of the building, parallel to the bushes. Diego placed the box on the ground, took the shovel from Don, and began to dig. Don went back through the bushes and stood watch from the sidewalk.

The earth was soft, and the hole was quickly dug. Diego whispered, "I think it's deep enough."

Don squeezed through the bushes again and saw the shallow hole. "Bury it, and let's get out of here."

They placed the box into the hole and filled the remainder of it with the loose dirt, patting it down and spreading the excess in order to make it appear normal.

Quickly pushing their way out of the bushes, they nearly knocked over a professor who had just finished teaching a late class. The startled professor caught his balance and said, "Christ, you scared the hell out of me."

Caught off guard, Don and Diego blurted out apologies like two blithering idiots. The professor looked at the two men and noticed Diego holding the shovel. "What in God's name are the two of you doing in the bushes this time of night?"

Don glanced at Diego. Diego glanced at Don. They both looked back at the professor and began speaking in unison.

"I lost my wallet," Diego said at the exact moment that Don said, "We're looking for some potting soil."

The professor stared at them and, thinking they were both drunk, turned without responding and walked off, shaking his head and muttering something unintelligible.

Don and Diego looked at each other. Diego asked, "Do you think he believed us?"

Don began to laugh. "Which one? You or me? You lost your wallet? What a stupid answer."

"And you're looking for potting soil?"

They both laughed at their dumb answers.

"I couldn't think of anything else to say," Don said, laughing so hard that he had to hold his side.

Diego, laughing equally as hard, said, "Do you know what that stuffy professor thinks we were really doing in the bushes together?"

They roared with laughter.

Don could hardly speak now as he said, "Then what ... then what ... are you ... doing with that shovel? Practicing a new form of proctology?"

"No," Diego answered with tears rolling down his cheeks. "Some form of kinky, gay sex."

"Jesus, stop, stop. I can't laugh any more. My side is killing me."

After several more intermittent laughs and giggles, they calmed down, shook hands, said good night, and returned to their apartments, still smiling at the incident with the professor. The tension of the day had been relieved.

Don had kept the tape and the folded dotted paper in his pocket. That night, before retiring, he returned to the laboratory and made a photocopy of the dots and a copy of the tape, which he intended to mail the next day to Anton Steinert, along with a letter detailing the events of the past two days. He took it upon himself to swear Dr. Steinert to secrecy, even though he knew Steinert would be as secretive about this as he was about almost everything, especially his own past.

Later that night, Don had trouble sleeping. So many things were bothering him. Having just written the story on paper seemed to crystallize things for him. How, he asked himself, could the cylinder have gotten embedded into rock like that? Anything hot enough to melt the outside rock would surely melt, or severely damage, the cylinder itself. Then there was the metal. It was quite unlike anything he'd ever seen. Even the color appeared somehow foreign. This was certainly not an ancient relic of any Peruvian society. Diego's idea of some type of atomic weapon was certainly a novel one, but Don felt that this too was incredibly far-fetched. He knew of no modern technology that could explain what was in that lead box.

Don was now tossing and turning in bed more than ever. *Not ancient and not modern,* he thought. Suddenly, he felt both weak and exhilarated at the same time. His mind was boggled by the thoughts that were coming to him. He wanted to believe his own thoughts, but common sense told him not to. Was the cylinder an implant from some alien world? He told himself not to think such insane thoughts, but the idea kept making more and more sense. Did he just want to believe it, or was the evidence compelling him to believe it?

But the signal—why was it so weak, when the cylinder obviously had tremendous power behind it? If an alien meant for some thinking being to find it, why not send out a stronger signal? Suddenly, he felt as though struck by a thunderbolt. Excitedly, he picked up the phone and called Diego. "Come on, Diego, pick up the phone," he said out loud.

After six rings, a groggy voice answered, "Who is it?"

"Diego, it's me," replied an excited Don.

"What's wrong?"

"Nothing. Has the thought occurred to you that this object just might be, and I repeat, might be, something from another world?"

Diego yawned. "You woke me at this hour to tell some bad joke?"

"Have you got a better explanation? The metal, the embedding in the rock, the radioactivity that can melt rock but not harm the cylinder, the signal that it gives off, and the dots, whatever they are, cannot be explained by two men who happen to know more than just a little about archeology."

The statement was met with dead silence at the other end of the phone. "Diego, are you still there?"

"What you say makes no sense. We should have been able to tell at least something about the cylinder by now, but to say it's from space? I don't know. Why would it be here, in Ochoa?"

"That's what puzzled me too. Also, why so weak a signal from so powerful a source? Here's what I think. I believe that someone—or, something—placed this object in the rock. The object contains something, messages perhaps, that it wanted found, but not by just anyone. Certainly not by people who wouldn't know what to do with it and might try to destroy it. That's why it reacts against possible destruction with intense radiation. It was meant as protection for itself."

"But they buried it in rock."

"Yes, but they had a signal coming from it, meant to be heard."

"But you said the signal was very weak."

"It's too weak to be detected by us, now, in the present time. But possibly it's not too weak to be detected by some future generation of far greater abilities than we have. I believe this thing was meant for some human civilization far more advanced than ours."

"Why in Ochoa?"

"We don't know how long the cylinder sat embedded in the rock before an earthquake occurred that even they, these aliens, couldn't foresee. Perhaps they saw promise in the relatively advanced civilizations of ancient Peru."

Diego was silent. Could this be true? If so, it would be the greatest archeological find of all time. He would be incredibly famous ... and rich. Fame would be wonderful, but he'd known poverty all his life. Money, great amounts of it, had to go along with fame. He must see to that.

"Listen. I think you've let your imagination run wild. Why don't you get some rest? Maybe in the morning your head will be clearer."

Don felt the wind go out of his sails. The excitement of the day couldn't be maintained, and by now he was drained. It was two thirty in the morning. Perhaps his mind was being overactive. It was crazy. Aliens? Maybe someone was playing a trick on him, or maybe there was some other explanation that hadn't crossed his mind. "You're right. I'm exhausted. I'll call you in the morning."

Don hung up the phone and began to toss and turn once again while trying to sleep. His adrenaline was still high. He got out of bed and added a postscript to his letter to Anton Steinert, even though he felt silly in suggesting aliens.

But as soon as Diego hung up the phone, he dressed and rushed out of his apartment as swiftly as possible.

CHAPTER 8

JOSE MARIN'S LIFE WAS typical of those who had been brought up as peasants in the streets of Lima's Barrio, where people of the Sierra moved when farming became impossible to live by. Poorly educated, he was the third-born of nine children and had seen two of his brothers die from what was simply called infantile disease. The streets were his training ground, and he had learned to steal at an early age. By the time he was thirty-two, he'd made a reputation for himself as someone to be feared. His body bore the scars of many fights, some that included knives. But Marin was proud of the fact that he generally gave more than he received, and liked to boast about the time he blinded someone by stabbing him in both eyes. No one was quite certain of the truth of this story, but his reputation gave him the opportunity to join the Gente, a local group of small-time organized criminals who dealt primarily in gambling and drugs.

Marin had by now become a man who had little regard for people, but he had the wily capacity to be deceptively accommodating to those who could help his selfish needs. He was never quite able to acquire any truly close friends.

With women it was even worse. He knew what he needed them for. He had girlfriends from time to time, but he always discarded them like yesterday's trash.

As a youth of fifteen, he'd participated with two older friends in the gang-rape and murder of a young woman, strangled to death by Marin, who, ironically, was the only one of the three not wanting to participate, fearful of his ability to carry out the sexual act in front of the others. Because of the intense peer pressure exerted on him, he went along with his friends, but his fear made him unable to achieve penetration of the woman, and, flushed crimson with embarrassment, he strangled the life out of the unfortunate, pleading woman with his bare hands while screaming at her that she deserved it. They buried her body in a bog by the river in a shallow grave. Her body was never found.

He secretly vowed never to allow any woman to embarrass his masculinity, and he took great pleasure in committing several rapes during his lifetime (never again participating in a gang-rape), including that of a mature-looking thirteen-year-old girl. Marin enjoyed having power over both men and women. Violence was a way of life for him.

Marin was sound asleep when loud pounding on his door awakened him. Groggy-eyed, he glanced at the clock, which read three thirty a.m. "Who's there," he growled.

"Diego Gonzales. Open up," Diego urged.

Marin opened the door as Diego rushed by him and turned to face Marin in the center of the room. Although not involved in crime, Diego had recently become a favorite of Marin, having been introduced by a mutual friend. Diego was from the Sierra but was known to be very smart, and Marin respected intelligence in his own kind even though he resented it in the rich.

Diego had heard that Marin had contacts in the government and knew Marin was a tough guy, but he didn't know just how tough Marin could be.

"At three thirty in the morning, this had better be good," Marin said, expressionless.

"It is, Jose, it is." He spoke quickly now. "I have something in my possession that might be worth a fortune to the right people."

"What thing? What people?" The word "fortune" aroused him.

"You know about my work at the university. One of the archeologists and I came across what may actually be something from a foreign world, another planet or … no telling how far away." Diego spread his arms out wide.

"You're drunk." Marin was clearly annoyed.

"No, believe me. This is for real. Whatever it is, it can be radioactive at times and is responsible for killing my cousin, Paco."

Marin could see that Diego was obviously sincere, and he was becoming interested. "I heard about him. But how could he be killed by … by what? You haven't told me what you found."

"It's a metal object. A cylinder about twenty centimeters long and ten centimeters wide." Diego gestured with his hands. "We found it embedded in rock, not covered by rock but actually melted into the rock. It sends out signals of some sort. The metal cannot be identified as anything found on earth—at least, Don Carter, the archeologist, believes this. He believes it's from somewhere in space."

The two men stood in silence in the dim light, staring at each other. Diego waited for a response while Marin attempted to digest something that he would have laughed at if it had come from anyone else. Marin could plainly see the seriousness in Diego's face; Diego, the smartest kid from a little town in the Sierra.

Finally, Marin spoke. "Where's this thing now?"

"Buried in a lead box beside a building at the university, behind some bushes."

"Who knows about this?"

"Only Don Carter and I. I just hung up the phone with him. He was very excited. As soon as he convinced me that this might be some alien thing, I drove right over here."

Marin cocked his head to the side. "What do you want me to do?"

"If this thing is a hoax, no harm done. If it's real, Don may try to turn it over to one of his own countrymen, or possibly to the university. Either way, I'd be given little credit for the find and certainly get very little, if any, money out of something that could be worth—well, who knows? It would be one of a kind in the entire world. Who knows what messages some intelligent being may have sent us?"

"Where do I come into this?" Money always attracted his attention, and Marin wanted to hear more.

"You have connections. You're the only one I would trust with this knowledge. If this thing is genuine, you could figure a way that we could sell it to some government. But we must be able to hide it and remain anonymous for the time being, at least until we have a plan. Maybe we could sell it to the highest bidder. Just imagine, the Russians versus the Americans. Could be worth millions!"

"What about this Carter guy? What will he say about your plans?" He knew Carter could be trouble.

"He would never go along with it. I know Don. He'd settle for his name being written up in some journal and writing articles or a book about this. He'd be made a full professor somewhere. Me, I'd still be some nameless Sierra assistant digging rocks. Can you name one crew member on Columbus's ship, or the guide who climbed Mt. Everest with the Englishman? I could retire in Tahiti or Monte Carlo for the rest of my life with the money that this could bring."

Marin spoke softly, hesitantly. "So what do we do about your friend, Carter?"

Diego didn't want to face this question. He'd avoided allowing himself to think about it until now. "I don't know. Maybe we can deal with Don later. Right now we have to get the box dug up before morning. Maybe Don will think someone else stole it."

"He can't be that stupid," Marin said dryly.

Diego raised his hand. "I know, I know. Look, let's cross that bridge tomorrow. Let's get the thing and stash it somewhere else. Tomorrow you can make contact with one of your people, someone who has influence with someone in the government. Once we've made contact, they would know how to give this information to other countries, and the bidding will be on. We could have representatives from each country examine the merchandise in secret, but we must have security for this. Your people would supply the security."

"If this is really worth anything, which I doubt, you'll have to part with a pretty big cut." The businessman in Marin was beginning to make plans.

"I'm not greedy. Half a fortune is better than no fortune."

Marin nodded his head. "Okay, let's get this thing."

"Just be careful with it. It can give off a lot of energy when it wants to."

After quickly dressing, Marin left with Diego in Diego's car. As soon as the car began moving, Marin asked, "Do you really believe this thing is from space?" Marin lit one of his favorite Cuban cigars with the car's lighter and watched the plume of smoke get sucked out of the slightly open window.

"To tell you the truth, I really don't know. But this thing, this cylinder, is so unusual that no matter where it's from or how it got here, it has to be worth money to someone."

"Like who?"

"Either the people who made it or some others who would like to know more about the technology that went into the thing."

Marin thought about Carter. Eliminating him, or at least neutralizing him, would be no problem under normal circumstances. But he knew the situation involved Diego's relationship with Carter, and it would have to be handled delicately. "Your friend Carter won't be happy with you. You do know that."

Diego exhaled long and hard. "Yeah, I know. But if this is worth lots of money, maybe we can cut him in on it."

"You think he'd accept?"

"I don't know. Maybe not. You know how people are who were never poor. They've got all the morals in the world when they haven't ever starved or wanted for anything. You and me, Jose, we know what it's like to be hungry. I would do anything to become rich."

"Anything?" Marin doubted Diego knew what "anything" really meant.

"Well, almost anything. I've heard you've done some bad things, but I know where you're coming from. In a way, they've forced many of us to do things they would probably do themselves if they were in our shoes. But they sit back and pass judgment on us. They can afford the luxury of preaching honesty and morality even though they do plenty of dishonest things themselves."

Marin was highly impressed with Diego's statement. "You know, that's what I've always felt but was never able to say it the way you did. You're right." Then he added bitterly through clenched teeth, "They deserve what they get."

Tending to his driving, Diego nodded in agreement but didn't truly understand the depths that Marin was willing to sink to.

Arriving at the university, they walked briskly in almost total darkness except for a few lights from the building that shone dimly. It was now past five a.m., and the sun would be rising in one hour.

"Over here," Diego whispered. "Behind these bushes."

The two men pushed through the bushes where earlier that night Don and Diego had buried the cylinder. Diego knelt down and began to dig in the soft dirt with his hands. The cylinder was buried only about six inches below the surface.

Marin watched with an air of anticipation. He'd soon see if Diego's wild story was at least remotely possible.

"It's gone!" Diego exclaimed.

"What? Are you sure?" Marin leaned in closer.

"It's not here. I've dug deep enough to hit hard ground. It's gone." Diego sounded frantic.

Marin slapped Diego in the back of his head with an open hand. "You dragged me out here at five in the morning after telling me some crazy *Star Wars* story, and all you can show me is an empty hole?" He flicked his still-lit cigar at Diego. Sparks flew off Diego's chest as the cigar rebounded off him.

Diego merely brushed his hand across his chest as he said, "Listen to me." His voice reflected both impatience and anger. "It had to be Don. He must've come back here and dug it up."

"But why?" Marin quickly answered his own question. "We're here, no? He obviously had similar thoughts."

"That doesn't sound like Don, but for whatever reasons, the thing isn't here, and we don't have it. We've got to find Don." They turned and ran for Diego's car.

They jumped into the vehicle and sped off for Don's apartment, a few minutes' ride away.

Diego pounded the steering wheel with the palm of his hand. "I can't believe he took it. Why the hell would he take it?"

Marin answered caustically. "He wants the money for himself. The rich get richer, remember?"

"Then why did he call me a couple of hours ago to tell me all this stuff about aliens, practically telling me that it would be worth a fortune, if he intended to steal it? It doesn't make any sense."

"Maybe he got the idea after he spoke with you."

Diego shook his head slowly, and exhaled. "I don't know. I know Don, and he's not like that."

"You can't trust those gringos, Diego. We both know that. How much farther is it to his place?"

"Another minute. Just up ahead."

"If he took it, you know he won't be there, don't you? He'll be half way to the United States by now with that thing tucked safely under his arm."

Diego was deep in thought and said pensively, "You know, maybe he didn't take it."

"You said you two were the only ones who knew."

"There was a professor who saw us coming out of the bushes. I wonder if he went back to have a look?" But he quickly answered his own question. "No, no way. The guy had no idea what we were doing there, and he wasn't about to start digging with that tan suit he was wearing. Besides, I think he thought we were drunk or crazy."

Marin impatiently drummed his fingers on the edge of his seat.

After thinking for a few seconds, Diego said, "Wait a minute. The cylinder sends out signals. I had ignored Don's question when he asked if the signal could be traced to the university by whoever made that thing. Maybe they tracked it down and dug it up." Diego pulled the car over to the side of the road and turned off the engine.

Marin responded to Diego's latest hypothesis. "Why guess? We'll know in a minute, but I know people. I'll give you odds your friend took it."

They got out of the car and walked briskly to Don's apartment door. Diego knocked hard, three times in succession. He waited a few seconds and knocked even harder, five times.

Marin said coldly, "He took it. I told you. He's practically home in America by now, and—"

The door swung open with Don standing in the doorway. Don looked at both men and then spoke directly to Diego. "Diego, I didn't expect you this soon." There was a hint of sarcasm in his voice. He didn't ask them in, and the discussion continued in the doorway.

From Don's attitude, Diego instantly sensed that Don had taken it after all. "Where is it? Why'd you take it?" he said angrily.

Jose Marin had been standing to the side of the door but now moved closer to Diego, where Don could see him better. Don cocked his head toward Marin and said bitterly, "And who's this?"

Diego answered, "A friend."

Marin stood quietly, assessing the situation.

Don felt the man was attempting to look menacing in order to intimidate him. Little did Don know that this was the way Marin always appeared.

With more pronounced sarcasm, Don asked, "You walk the streets of Lima with your friend before dawn every morning?"

"You know why I'm here. What did you do with the cylinder, and why for God's sake did you take it?"

"How much does your *friend* know about this?" Don asked.

"Everything."

Don became angry. "First of all, this was supposed to be our secret. It was stupid of you to tell anyone about this. The reason I took the cylinder was simple. I couldn't sleep last night with a thousand things bouncing around my head. About twenty minutes after I hung up from you, I dialed your number again to discuss something else that I'd thought of. When you didn't answer, I was afraid you might've gone back to get the cylinder, so I went there, just in case."

"I see how much you trusted me after all."

"Trusted you? You obviously tried to do exactly what I had suspected. Not only that, but you went ahead and told this guy. Why'd you tell him, and who is he, anyway?"

"I told you, a friend." Diego was feeling uncomfortable. He knew Don was correct. He wasn't supposed to have told Marin, and he could detect the disappointment on Don's face. But what Don didn't understand was Diego's incredible desire for a lifetime of wealth. The thought that this potential wealth might be slipping though his fingers hardened Diego.

"Listen, that cylinder never would've been found if it wasn't for me. Paco was *my* cousin. I brought you there."

"And we were going to share in its discovery."

"And you'd get all the credit. No one would remember some poor assistant with little formal education. And I probably know more about archeology than you'll ever know."

Diego spoke in a manner that Don thought was uncharacteristic of his friend. "I won't argue your knowledge of archeology. Everyone knows that you're the brightest assistant."

Diego now spoke with a more sympathetic tone. "Don, listen. This thing could be worth a fortune, and—"

"So that's it," Don interrupted. "It comes down to money."

"Of course it comes down to money," Diego snapped. "If you think I would pass up a fortune for a line in some magazine, then you're crazy. Besides, we would share in this fortune. You know I wouldn't shut you out, but I knew how you'd think. You'd rather have your reputation made than have the money."

"It isn't just that. What you're asking me to do would be against everything my profession stands for. And precisely who do you sell this to, the highest bidder?"

"Exactly."

"I can't do it. I'm sorry. If this turns out to be what I think it is, it's worth more than money. It would be priceless. It could be the greatest find in the history of mankind."

"And worth a fortune, Don. We could retire for the rest of our lives."

"I can't do it. I just can't. The cylinder has to be turned over to the proper authorities, who would be able to study it and do justice by it. I work for the university. You know that anything we find becomes the property of the Peruvian government. This cylinder would be considered national treasure."

"But we could sell it to a country that would take proper care of the cylinder. Perhaps even your own country, Don."

"And I would be forever disgraced. I love my job. I don't need a fortune at the price of being an outcast, or worse still, an out*law*."

Diego knew Don wouldn't be persuaded.

But Marin's interest was now piqued. He wanted that cylinder very badly. Thoughts of forcing Carter into telling them where it was crossed his mind, but he knew he had to allow Diego to handle his friend, at least for now.

"Diego, we're both very tired," Don said. "Why don't you go back to sleep. When we're both rested, the two of us will discuss this again." Don emphasized "two of us" while casting a glance at Marin.

Diego was tired. He needed time to think. "We'll talk later. Let's go, Jose."

The two men turned and walked toward Diego's car. The sun was beginning to rise.

They had almost reached Diego's car when Marin grabbed hold of Diego's arm and said, "We tried it your way and got nowhere." He turned back and glared at the apartment. "Now we do it my way."

CHAPTER 9

SHE WAS WITH HIM, and he smiled, safe and comfortable, embraced in her arms, lost in her soft, warm bosom. Then she was gone, only to be seen again on some distant cloud with her arms outstretched. Try as he might, he couldn't reach her. He jumped and then jumped again, higher this time, to no avail. He heard the roll of thunder and feared she might be in imminent danger. Then came more thunder, once, twice, three times, far louder than before. It was coming closer, and she must run away from him to save herself. Yes, run, Diane. Save yourself, save …

He opened his eyes, startled by a sharp noise. Then came another. Rubbing his eyes, he realized that someone was pounding on his door. He glanced at the clock. Eight a.m. Diego, back already? Jesus, he was exhausted and in no mood for more arguments. "One second, one second."

He put on his pants and opened the door. There stood two men whom he'd never seen before: a short man and a large, ugly man.

"Get dressed and come with us," said the shorter man with an icy stare.

"What is this, some kind of joke?" Don answered indignantly.

"If this is a joke, then you're the clown," the man said as he stiff-armed Don in the chest, shoving him away from the door and back into the room. The two men followed and slammed the door behind them.

Don yelled, "What the hell is this? I'm not going anywhere with you."

"Oh no?" replied the big, dumb-looking one. "Maybe this will change your mind." He whipped out a pistol from under his shirt and aimed it at Don's head.

Don was extremely tired and confused, although he realized that this had to be connected with the *friend* that Diego had brought with him, but now he was also very much afraid. He'd never so much as held a real gun in his own hands, and now one was being aimed directly at him. His voice trembled as he said, "All right. Take it easy. You'll get no trouble from me."

While Don dressed, the shorter man, Francisco Alcalde, searched the apartment without care, pushing things aside, turning things over, and dumping out drawers. After several minutes, the apartment was a chaotic mess.

"Hernando, it's not here," Alcalde said to the dumb-looking Hernando.

"Let's go," Alcalde ordered Don.

"Where are we going?"

"None of your damn business. Walk slowly out the door and toward the street."

Don did so and was placed in the backseat of a car, where big, ugly Hernando tied his hands behind his back. Hernando sat next to Don in the rear seat while Alcalde drove. During the ten-minute ride, Don tried asking questions but was told not to speak. He obeyed. He'd never been so scared in his entire life. He asked himself, *Could Diego be involved with men like these?* No, he thought, it had to be the other man whom Diego foolishly told about the cylinder. *But they know I'm Diego's friend, and I don't think they would hurt me. They want the cylinder, but I won't tell them where it's hidden.* He told himself not to be afraid, but he still was. After all, Diego might not know these two. Don decided to try to trick them and somehow escape, although he knew escape might be too risky since they had at least one gun that he knew of. He sat still in the rear seat, but his mind and emotions were working at a furious pace.

Ten minutes later, they arrived at their destination. They rushed him up to a room in a weather-worn apartment building in the Sierra section of Lima, and then, using rope, tied him to a chair with his arms behind him. They also tied his ankles together.

The room was dimly lit and sparsely furnished. The shades were drawn on the one window in the room. There was a closet next to a bed, a small couch, and a bathroom containing a toilet and bathtub.

The smaller man, Alcalde, was of slight build and spoke surprisingly softly, yet his voice carried the sound of authority. Don still didn't know his name, but he knew the ugly, dumb-looking one's name was Hernando, since the smaller man had referred to him by that name.

Alcalde's job was simple. He'd been told by Marin that he must find out where a heavy, lead box was hidden. Alcalde was skilled at his craft. He was confident that it wouldn't take long to get the needed information out of the American. He spoke deliberately, standing directly in front of Don and looking down at him.

"Mr. Carter. We know you hid this box. We don't have time to waste here. I'm told much may be at stake. You don't know me, but you've heard of the Gente. We get what we want, even if it means torture or death. We don't want to harm you, but we will if we have to. Tell us where the box is and you'll be released unharmed."

Don wasn't at all prepared for this, although he realized that people were often killed for far less than the potential worth of the cylinder. He'd been drawn into a situation, quite by accident, that seemed more like a grade-B movie than reality. Making matters worse, he was a foreigner. He knew they could probably kill him and hide his body somewhere so that he would never be found, but then he told himself that his imagination was running wild; Diego would never allow that to happen. Perspiration was permeating every square inch of his clothing, but he calmed himself and began to speak. "The box belongs to Peru. It's not for sale."

Alcalde responded coldly, "I'm not buying, Mr. Carter. I'm taking."

"You know what I mean. You intend to make money from this by stealing it from me … no, your own people." He was scared but also highly indignant.

"I don't have time to waste with you," Alcalde said angrily. "Let me show you what will be done to you if you don't tell us where you hid the box. Hernando. Bring it here."

Hernando walked into the bathroom and returned with a live chicken that he carried on one arm. He stroked the chicken with his big hand, and the chicken sat quietly, looking about the room.

"Mr. Carter," Alcalde said, "watch what fate you'll have if you don't tell us what we need to know."

Hernando gave the chicken to Alcalde, walked back to the bathroom, and then returned with a large pair of pruning shears. Alcalde grabbed the legs of the chicken in one hand and its head in his other hand. The chicken began to squawk and squirm. Hernando then opened the shears and placed them around the neck of the chicken. With one violent thrust, he brought his hands quickly and powerfully together, giving off the sound of metal striking metal. In a flash, the head of the chicken was severed, and both the head and the body were allowed to drop to the floor at Don's feet. Blood squirted out of the neck as the chicken's body quivered for a few moments. Some of the blood had spattered onto Don's shirt, pants, and shoes.

Don was horrified at the grisly sight. Blood was all over the floor. He briefly felt like vomiting, with black bile welling up in his throat, but was able to suppress the urge.

"Mr. Carter," Alcalde asked, "are you ready to tell us now?"

Don was quickly back in control of himself. He knew this was merely a scare tactic and they wouldn't dare kill him. They needed information only he could provide, and he'd be worthless as a corpse. The gory scene only served the purpose of angering him. These were animals with IQs of less than the chicken, he thought. He wouldn't tell them where the box was. He was ready for them. He expected them to resort to beating him, but he felt he could handle it. He could feel the adrenaline building in his body, and he took a deep breath before answering defiantly, "You can both go to hell."

"You leave me no choice, Mr. Carter," Alcalde responded. "Are you married?"

The question was asked matter-of-factly and caught Don off guard. He looked Alcalde right in the eye and thought, *So now they're going to threaten my wife. But she's thousands of miles away, and there's no way they'll ever get to her.*

"Married? I'm separated." Small talk was a relief. Perhaps they meant him no harm after all. Maybe he'd called their bluff and now they realized they had lost. He hoped the small talk would continue. "Why do you want to know?" he probed.

"Because you would be very disappointing to her the next time you tried to make love to her."

Before Don could begin to figure out the meaning of those words, Hernando began to unbuckle Don's belt and quickly pulled down his pants and shorts to his knees, rendering Don naked and exposed from the waist down. A feeling of utter desperation and vulnerability washed over him.

Alcalde held Don's tied ankles forcefully onto the floor and straight out in front of Don. Don struggled to move his feet, but Alcalde only pressed down harder with the weight of his body onto Don's knees. The pain from so much weight on his legs would normally have been far more than required to make Don scream, but the fear he now felt effectively masked any pain he was feeling.

Don shouted at Alcalde. "What are you doing? Get away from me."

Alcalde spoke loudly, looking directly up at Don, while still holding his legs out in front. "Mr. Carter, Hernando is going to cut your cock off as swiftly as he cut off the head of that chicken. He's a crazy man. He has done this before, and he loves it. You must tell me where the box is hidden. Is the box worth seeing your cock cut off and dropped onto the floor? Hernando will pick it up and stuff it into your mouth. Is that what you want?"

Don was shaking and losing control of himself as he watched Hernando approach with the pruning shears wide open. Thoughts of being neutered, turned into a eunuch, flashed through his mind. Terror and revulsion gripped his very soul. A scream from deep within his body came bellowing out. "I'll tell you where it is! Just get him away from me!"

Alcalde glanced at Hernando and nodded with a knowing look. Hernando backed away.

"Where is it?" Alcalde demanded.

Don spoke rapidly and frantically while keeping his eyes on the pruning shears. "It's behind the small tool shed in back of the apartment building I'm living in. It's buried on the corner of the shed and covered by a piece of wood."

Hernando smiled. He knew this would work. No one could resist spilling his guts when faced with this sort of horror.

Don was physically and emotionally drained and felt as though he'd better relieve himself in the toilet very soon.

"Pull his pants up," Alcalde ordered, "and get this place cleaned up."

Don's body sagged with relief. He felt as though he'd been drugged, having had almost no sleep and enduring this latest ordeal. But the realization of what these animals had put him through angered Don to his core even though, tied helplessly to the chair, he could do no more than dream of the day he would take his revenge. Somehow, some way, they would live to regret this day. The hatred simmering within Don strengthened him and helped him to begin making plans for his escape.

CHAPTER 10

ALCALDE LEFT THE ROOM while Hernando kept guard on Don.

Two blocks away, Alcalde met with Diego and Jose Marin.

"He talked, didn't he?" Marin confidently asked.

"No problem, man, no problem for Francisco Alcalde," he answered proudly.

"Did you hurt him?" asked a concerned Diego.

"Never laid a hand on him," Alcalde answered. "But he could be a problem to us later."

Diego knew what Alcalde meant and responded forcefully. "He'll be no problem. We'll hold on to him until this thing is finished."

Marin probed further. "But what will your university do when he doesn't show up in a couple of days? They'll start asking questions and maybe call the police."

"I thought of that, and it might not be so difficult," Diego answered. "He'll write a letter of resignation."

Marin shook his head. "They'll never believe it."

"Look, he'll write something like, he had to leave suddenly for the United States. Family matters, maybe, or he's been working too hard and needs a vacation. I'm sure we can figure out something that sounds reasonable. Beside, it'll be written by Don himself, in his own handwriting."

Alcalde and Marin nodded in agreement. It might at least buy enough time to satisfy Diego. Both Marin and Alcalde knew that they might have to kill this Carter fellow sooner or later anyway. "Okay," Marin said. "Let's go find out if this thing you found is worth the trouble we're going through."

Within twenty minutes, the three men arrived at the tool shed behind Don's apartment building and dug up the box. Diego opened it for a brief moment to peer inside, making certain the cylinder was still there.

Although glancing at something that was possibly from another world, Marin and Alcalde weren't overly impressed. Money would impress them.

They carried the box to their car and drove off to a deserted warehouse, where they concealed the lead box under some floorboards and secured the boards with a hammer and nails.

Marin and Alcalde returned to the room where Hernando was keeping watch over Don while Diego set off for his own apartment, where he intended to figure out what the letter of resignation should say. He was also attempting to avoid his friend, Don. Diego thought that perhaps when this was over, although he knew things could never be the same between him and Don, Don would at least take some of the money and benefit by it. Even if he refused the money, Diego thought, Don would still have a pretty good story to tell, by which time Diego would be long gone to some exotic Pacific island.

Marin informed Don that he would have to write a letter of resignation, but not right now. First, they would eat.

All the while that Don was alone with Hernando, Don had been thinking of ways to escape. Perhaps there would still be time to somehow retrieve the cylinder. The fact that he wouldn't have to immediately write the letter gave Don additional time to concoct a way out of his plight.

Later that day, Marin contacted a politician friend of his, a man always on the take, named Julio Mendez. Mendez was told only that he had to contact a man of high esteem in the field of astronomy and arrange a meeting with Marin.

Diego's plan was to allow this astronomer to examine the cylinder to verify its authenticity as being from another world. If, in fact, it did prove to be as they hoped, the expert would be needed to lend credibility in setting up negotiations with the two superpower bidders. Diego knew that the United States and USSR would eventually want to examine the cylinder for themselves and that this could become both risky and tricky. They would have to be very careful.

It took until the next day for Mendez to contact Miguel Solars, a well-respected Peruvian astronomer. He told Solars only that he had knowledge of something that could turn out to be of significance in the field of astronomy and that he needed some expert opinions about it.

Solars's natural curiosity and Mendez's position in government made him agree without hesitation. He further agreed to meet with a Mr. Rodriguez, who was in fact Jose Marin, at a bar in the heart of Lima. Solars was told that he would be driven by Mr. Rodriguez to a location where he would examine something unusual.

The plan was to take Solars to the deserted warehouse, to which Diego had already brought a Geiger counter, some tools, test kits, and a variety of other testing devices that he thought Solars might need, including tape recording instruments for the signals. If everything worked out, if the cylinder could be authenticated as being from some alien planet and they played their hand well with the superpowers, they would then be able to share in wealth beyond imagination.

Julio Mendez was in a predicament. He wanted a piece of the action and knew that if this turned out to be as important a discovery as everyone hoped, his cut would amount to a small fortune. He knew Marin needed someone like himself, a person who could make contacts and gain entree with important persons in both the American and Soviet governments. But Mendez also knew that the find, whatever it turned out to be, would be considered the property of the Peruvian government, which he represented. He wasn't sure whether the Soviet or American governments would attempt to contact the Peruvian government. If they did, the name of Julio Mendez was certain to be conspicuously mentioned. Therefore, after meeting with Marin and Diego Gonzales, it was decided that Mendez would inform his government that he had received an anonymous tip and been asked to help dispose of a purported alien object to the highest bidder.

Mendez would inform his government that the object was safely hidden, and either he or someone else outside their government would be sent to try and deal with these foreign governments. Mendez thought that the Peruvian government would agree with his point that it would be better for someone within the government to go through with this action, so the government would be kept abreast of events, rather than not knowing what was transpiring at all.

Mendez had little problem receiving the approval he required, but he was reminded by the higher-ups that he must inform any other involved government of the claim that Peru had on anything found within Peruvian borders. Mendez agreed to this, but in reality he had no interest in who received the object as long as he received his payoff.

Meanwhile, Jose Marin, calling himself Mr. Rodriguez, met with the astronomer, Miguel Solars, at the designated bar. After introducing themselves, they left the bar and walked to Marin's car. Solars got into the car in the front seat, next to Marin, and was taken by surprise as Marin handed him a pair of welder's goggles whose lenses had been painted black and requested, "Here, put these on."

Solars looked at him curiously and said, "Mr. Rodriguez, I assure you, there's no need for these."

Marin forced a smile and said, "I'm only following orders. Mr. Mendez told me that you must not know where it is you're being taken. Top secret. Government security. You know, all that stuff."

With a sigh of resignation, Solars said, "I suppose if Mendez felt it important enough to keep this so secretive, it must really be that important. But tell me, what is it I'm being taken to?"

"You'll find out soon enough. The goggles, please. We're on a tight schedule." He was being falsely courteous.

Solars pursed his lips and said, "You win, but I hope it won't be a long ride."

Marin didn't answer and started the engine.

Solars slipped the strap behind his head and placed the goggles over his eyes. They fit snugly and totally obscured any light from entering.

On the way to the warehouse, Solars would occasionally ask how much longer it would be, but Marin would only answer that it would take just a short while. He intentionally took a longer route than necessary in order to trick Solars into thinking the location was farther away than it actually was.

Within a half hour, they arrived at the abandoned warehouse. They were met by Alcalde and Diego, who helped the blindfolded Solars out of the car and guided him into the warehouse. Only then, when they were safely inside, did they allow Solars to remove the goggles.

Several beams of light filtered into the old wooden warehouse through spaces in the slats of wood. Solars rubbed his eyes. Then he stared at the faces of Alcalde and Diego and asked, "Who are these men? And where are we?"

Marin replied, "Friends of Mendez. That's all you need to know."

Solars waved his hand dismissively and sounded annoyed as he responded, "Top secret, I know. Why don't we have a look at what's so important."

"Right over there," Diego pointed out.

Solars walked over to a crude, wooden table that had earlier been nailed together by Diego and Alcalde. On the table were the lead box, a Geiger counter, and a variety of other equipment. Looking toward the table, Solars asked, "I assume that what I'm to examine is in the box?"

"Yes, it is," Diego answered.

"Let's have a look at it and get this charade over with." Solars made no attempt to mask the impatience he was feeling. He felt certain that this affair would turn out to be much ado about nothing and was uncomfortable with the types of men he was now dealing with.

Diego lifted the cover, reached into the box, and slowly, carefully, lifted the cylinder out and placed it on the table. "That's it," he said in a hushed voice.

"What is it?" Solars asked, not expecting much.

"That's what we hope you'll tell us," Marin replied.

"Obviously it's a metal container of some sort. How does it open?"

"It doesn't," Diego answered.

"Well, what does it do?" Solars appeared bemused and then asked sarcastically, "Is it filled with diamonds, or money, or ... wait just a second here!" His expression changed to one of indignation as he exclaimed, "If this thing is filled with some type of illegal drugs, cocaine perhaps, I'm getting out of here."

Solars began to turn around when Alcalde grabbed his arm and blurted out, "We think it's from another planet!"

Solars instantly stopped and turned to face the three men. No one spoke for several seconds as Solars looked into each man's face. They expected an enthusiastic response from Solars, but he merely asked, "Is this man serious? Is that what the three of you believe?"

"It is," Diego answered.

"You can't be serious. You're wasting my time. I'd like to be taken back now, if you don't mind," he said, sounding testy.

Marin stepped toward him and spoke to Solars, knowing that persuasion, not force, would have to be the solution. "Listen to me. Examine the object. Give us an hour of your time. It's the least you can do for us ... for Mendez. If it's phony, what harm has been done?" Marin's eyes then opened noticeably wider as he continued, "But if it's for real ..."

Solars looked at him and then over at the table. He shrugged. "One hour. But I'll tell you right now, you've already destroyed some of its potential value if it is what you say it is."

"What do you mean?" Alcalde asked, verbalizing the thoughts of both Marin and Diego.

Demonstrating impatience again, he replied, "What I mean is, look at that thing, out in the open like that. It's more than likely loaded with contaminants."

Alcalde asked, "You mean we could get sick from that thing?"

"If it were really from another world, that wouldn't be beyond the realm of possibility, but that isn't actually what I was referring to. Aren't you aware of the precautions they took with the moon rocks that the American astronauts brought back with them? They kept their samples in totally isolated and sealed containers so that anything they found on the rocks would be concluded to have originated from the minerals of the rocks themselves, not some piece of garlic that may have rubbed off from some careless worker's hands. We would hate to conclude that the moon is in part made of garlic." Solars laughed at his own joke, but the others only stared at him, trying to digest his meaning. Seeing their reactions, he stopped laughing.

Diego responded first. "But we found it just like that. Out in the open."

"Who is we?" Solars asked.

"Me and—"

Marin stopped Diego in midsentence by grabbing his arm. He appeared angry and impatient now. "It doesn't matter. What matters is that we have what we have. I don't care if there's chili sauce all over the damn thing. Is it from space?"

Solars was seemingly lost in thought for the moment. Then said, "But if it's genuine, an alien object as you suspect, then we shouldn't dismiss the possibility that was mentioned by your friend."

"What are you talking about?" Marin asked, clearly confused.

"The possibility that it might contain some foreign strain of disease that we earthlings have no immunity to, no natural defenses against. NASA thought it prudent to place the first three crews that returned from the moon in quarantine for weeks, just in case."

"In case of what?" Marin asked, not fully comprehending or not really listening at this point.

"Did you ever read *The Andromeda Strain*? The novel about a deadly disease that originates in the Andromeda constellation?"

Marin had now lost all patience and shouted, "No, and I don't give a shit right now! All I want you to do is tell us if this thing is from space or not!" His voice had gradually reached a crescendo.

Solars was taken aback. "All right. Take it easy. This man is a prime candidate for a heart attack at a young age. Let's get this over with." Solars was one hundred percent certain that these were fools he was dealing with. He was sure he'd have a good laugh when he told his colleagues of this day.

With Diego acting as his assistant, Solars began to examine the cylinder. He recognized that this was no ordinary hoodlum standing next to him, as Diego's skilled hands and knowledge betrayed him. Solars looked at Diego and remarked, "You've obviously had experience in the physical sciences. Where did you say you worked?"

Diego responded simply, but to the point. "I didn't."

Solars understood and nodded.

Diego had brought a load of needed equipment for the occasion. Solars tested for metal identification with a variety of acids, scratch tests, and other forms of analysis, but he was plainly baffled. The metal was unlike any that he knew of. While he worked, he listened to Diego's recounting of how they had found the cylinder embedded in solid rock and how it could melt rock and emit a powerful source of radiation. Solars decided to test the cylinder for this radiation that Diego spoke of.

They stood well back, behind a wall, while Diego tossed small pieces of concrete at the cylinder, occasionally hitting it and causing a brief but powerful elevation in the level of radiation as detected on the Geiger counter. Solars was clearly impressed.

Then they listened to the signals the cylinder occasionally emitted of what seemed like a man speaking some foreign tongue, for which there was no plausible explanation.

Solars asked Diego about the peculiar raised dots that appeared on the skin of the cylinder.

"Damn it," Diego replied. "I knew there was something else I wanted to take here."

"What did you forget?" Solars asked.

"Ink."

"Ink?"

"We made a pattern of those dots by rolling the cylinder in ink and then onto a large piece of paper."

"What did you find?"

"Dots of different sizes. That's all."

"Were there any patterns to these dots?"

"None that we were able to determine."

"Let me examine these dots on the cylinder itself. Maybe we won't need the ink."

Solars then gently rolled the cylinder across the table, examining the dots. Several minutes passed with Solars occasionally sketching notes and dots onto a piece of paper. When he felt he'd done all he could, he looked up and began discussing his findings. "These dots are definitely star patterns … constellations."

"For design?" Alcalde asked.

"I doubt that very much. These patterns have a purpose. My problem is that I can't seem to figure out exactly what that purpose is."

"Why not?" Marin asked. "You're the astronomer here."

Solars rubbed his chin. "In order for me to accurately determine what they're trying to convey with these dots, I would require special books which will show me the exact position of the stars in the constellations shown on the cylinder. It depicts at least hundreds of stars."

"What's your best guess?" Alcalde asked.

"What really puzzles me is this. When the Americans sent one of their unmanned Pioneer space probes beyond the orbit of Pluto, and therefore out of our own solar system, they sent along star patterns showing where we—the Earth, that is—reside in relation to these other celestial objects. We're in effect telling some alien intelligent beings, if by some remote chance you should find this space probe in some far distant time, this is where and when we lived."

"So," Diego asked, "is this what the cylinder is trying to tell us about them? When and where they lived?"

"Unfortunately, no. The patterns, as accurately as I can determine without the use of charts, seem to be showing the position of the Earth. These patterns appear to be the patterns that we see from our vantage point here on Earth."

"Why would they do that?" Diego asked.

"As I said, if there are indeed aliens involved in this, there's probably a reason for these aliens to have gone through the trouble of placing the patterns on the skin of the cylinder, but without those charts ..."

The mystery of the dots would have to wait.

Completion of test after test only served to perplex Solars further. He became amazed at what was before him. The conclusion that the cylinder might not be of this Earth became inescapable. He had promised them one hour of his time but had given almost three, yet the time had passed unnoticed. Finally when all available tests were exhausted, Solars took a step back and said, "If your story about the cylinder being embedded in rock, killing a young boy, and being able to melt rock and not be affected itself is true, combined with what I've witnessed here today, then I should like to be the first to congratulate you, gentlemen. I believe you might have discovered something that in the past I have only allowed myself to dream about. I can't be one hundred percent certain, but I believe there's a good chance this might be an object from another world." Then, shaking his head slowly from side to side, he said, "And if so, I stand in awe of you for having it in your possession. And I am ... well, it's difficult to put into words what I'm feeling right now."

Not one of the three men fully grasped the true meaning of Solars's expression of emotion, and Marin crudely asked, "How much is it worth?"

Solars stared at Marin with a puzzled expression and answered contemptuously, "Worth? It would be priceless. No price can be set on such an object."

The three men howled with excitement at Solars's words and hugged each other, watched unemotionally by Solars. He knew these men valued money far more than the possible true value of the cylinder, and for the first time he understood what their intentions were. He also knew he had become a pawn in a giant game of chess, but he further knew he couldn't back out now. He would help Mendez carry out whatever plan he intended; after all, Mendez was working for the government. Perhaps he could help Mendez to somehow secure the cylinder and place it where it belonged, in the hands of the scientific community. What Solars didn't know was that Mendez was working for these men and for himself, not for the benefit of the government.

Later that day, Mendez was informed by Marin that the meeting with Solars went off as planned, with Solars fairly convinced that the cylinder might not be an object of this Earth. Mendez was elated. He would now make plans for both himself and Solars to fly to Washington, DC.

CHAPTER 11

ANTON STEINERT LIKED TO say he was Austrian. He had immigrated to Argentina in 1947 but had actually been born and raised in Germany, not far from the Austrian border, in 1920. Small and frail as a child, he disdained athletics for books, which he loved immensely. Although his parents were of modest means, they always made certain that he and his older brother, Klaus, had books to read.

Steinert became enamored at an early age with anthropology and archeology. His books had told him of the fascinating paleontological findings of fossilized bones of great reptiles and, even more spellbinding, of the remains of prehistoric humans with exotic names such as "Java man" and "Neanderthal man." He'd always planned that these things would become involved in his life's work.

Throughout Steinert's early childhood, he never knew anything other than a defeated, inflation-ridden, impoverished Germany, a result of the Great War, as it was called before there were enough of them to number. When the Nazis took power, male youths were expected to join the Youth Corps, which young Anton dutifully did. He loved the uniform that he wore, which gave him a sense of belonging, strength, and pride. He'd never been on any athletic teams in school and now felt as though he were a member of a special team indeed.

He was especially enthralled by the huge rallies that he attended. He had traveled to the Nuremberg Party Rallies, a two-hour train ride from his home, to be one of tens of thousands in attendance. There he was filled with feelings of a stronger, invulnerable self as he watched thousands of flagmen marching in columns into a large stadium surrounded by banners portraying the Nazi Party swastika. The nighttime rallies rendered a surrealistic illusion to the whole affair as 130 antiaircraft searchlights, blazing their intense light vertically toward the black sky, created the effect of columns, their sharply defined beams visible to 25,000 feet and merging as though forming a great cathedral of ice. The dramatic effect of these rallies had a solemn and beautiful effect upon the impressionable young Steinert, but more importantly, they left him with a feeling of belonging and of unlimited strength. He believed there was nothing he wouldn't do for his Führer.

When the war broke out, he had to leave his beloved books behind to join the German army at age twenty. He was an obedient soldier and was quick to learn. He soon became a driver for the infantry, carrying soldiers to various parts of the country. By mid-1944, the war had taken its toll on Steinert. His father had died in 1941 of a heart attack, his brother had been killed somewhere in Russia in 1942, and his mother had perished in early 1944 from an Allied bombing raid. So when volunteers were asked to participate in a special project for the Führer, Steinert gladly accepted with the hope that the task might help alleviate the pain of the war. He was anxious to throw himself into this new project.

As he now sat back in his chair in his office at New York University, thoughts of that horrible day in German-occupied Poland in 1944 crept into his psyche, just as they had done hundreds of times before. He closed his eyes and remembered.

The sweaty-palmed Corporal Anton Steinert squeezed the steering wheel of the truck as he methodically, almost unconsciously, guided the vehicle around turns, potholes, and an occasional bomb crater, seeing, but not actually noticing, the deserted road ahead. What he saw in his mind's eye, what he preferred to see, was what he could sense through his nostrils as he inhaled deeply to absorb the sweet fragrance of the cool, late-spring morning that swirled past him through the open windows. The odors stirred memories of an earlier Bavarian time, of playing near his mother's flower garden and among the freshly cut grass in his rear yard. The remembrance of catching the aroma of his mother's cooking caused him to salivate slightly, while the memory of her recent death brought an entirely different form of wetness to his eyes.

He attempted to relax but was unable to free himself from the tension that heightened with the continual pounding and screaming that emanated from the rear of the sealed truck. The sergeant sitting to his right, appearing undisturbed by those same sounds, turned to the corporal and said with an emotionless voice, "Five more minutes, Corporal Steinert. No more than five minutes."

Corporal Anton Steinert nodded and tended to his driving as the incessant pounding continued, but with rapidly diminishing force. The screams soon became intermittent coughing and moaning. Then, within minutes, there was telltale silence.

Steinert breathed deeply and yet felt as though he was suffocating as the truck approached the designated unloading area. Here, the sweet smell of spring became the pungent stench of rotting flesh. Steinert knew that for him it wasn't yet over, but somehow, soon, it must be. He believed his sanity was depending on it.

The truck was flagged down by two bedraggled-looking men, perhaps only in their twenties but appearing far older. They knew their tasks well and prepared to carry them out. But this was Steinert's maiden voyage, and he dreaded what he knew must follow. He stepped down from the truck onto the soft earth and turned to meet the two others and the sergeant at the rear of the truck. He glanced down at the exhaust pipe, onto which a two-inch-wide hose had been fastened. The hose ran up the side of the truck to an attachment on the roof, where it belched noxious death to those trapped inside.

The sergeant opened the padlock on the rear doors of the truck, lifted the locking handles, and yanked the doors open. Exhaust fumes billowed out as bright morning sunlight shone directly onto the truck's grotesquely lifeless cargo. Forms of naked human beings were piled onto one another in ways that only minutes before would have made them cry out in pain or become embarrassed at their ungainly, immodest positions.

Steinert stared unblinking at the twisted, tangled mass of arms and legs. The unnatural sight was far worse than he'd imagined, and he fought back the nausea that was welling up in his throat. His emotional defense mechanism began to deny the overwhelming fact that these surrealistic corpses were once living human beings. His thoughts wandered, allowing the sight of several naked young women to arouse his sexual fantasies for a split second, but his mind quickly scolded itself for the perverse emotion. Even so, he believed he would forever feel guilt and shame at the memory of that moment.

The bark of the sergeant's orders jogged the corporal back to reality. He was a soldier with a task to accomplish and would have to help the men unload the truck, which was parked at the side of a ditch recently gouged out by a bulldozer. The bodies were to be unceremoniously thrown in for mass burial. But Steinert hadn't expected what was yet to come.

As the men unloaded the warm corpses, three bodies moaned and gasped, unconscious but clearly alive. The sergeant had been through this routine many times before, and the corporal silently glanced at him, allowing his face to ask the terrible questions he couldn't voice.

The sergeant understood. "We shoot the vermin that remain alive. After all," he said while smiling, anticipating his own private joke, "we're humane to dogs, too."

Steinert's voice trembled. "Who shoots them?"

The sergeant laughed, enjoying the scene that had been played out with others before. "You do."

Although Steinert had anticipated the possibility, the answer still pulsed through his head like an electrical current. "M ... me?" he stammered.

"Yes, you. Who else should do it? I've shot so many. I want you to have the pleasure."

Steinert turned crimson at the insinuation that he would enjoy shooting helpless people. Fate had been cruel enough in that the "secret assignment" he'd volunteered for turned out to be driving a death wagon. Until this instant he'd rationalized that he merely drove a truck. It was others who condemned the prisoners and designed and implemented their extermination, not he. *I'm only a soldier obeying orders*, he thought to himself. While driving the truck he had repressed the knowledge that it was his own foot pressing the accelerator that created the carbon monoxide poison that filled the truck. No! He simply drove a truck. It was his job. His military duty.

But now he was literally face to face with helpless human beings whom he'd been ordered to kill with his own hands. The sergeant had seen others flinch at the request, but none had ever turned beet red or responded with such ferocity as this young corporal.

As the veins in his neck protruded, Steinert spat his words venomously. "You animal! If you want them shot, do it yourself. These are people, not insects. You can have the *pleasure.*" He would have continued had he not remembered that he was addressing his military superior. But his face told it all.

The two other men, having just heaved a body into the ditch, witnessed the brief confrontation.

The sergeant saw them watching and knew he must respond in a face-saving manner. He thought, *If this stupid corporal had pleaded with me, I might have had the decency to shoot them myself.* But this insubordinate corporal had made a personal attack on him and his authority, and he began to speak with deliberate pomposity and a touch of anger in his voice, subconsciously mimicking the newsreel's portrayal of Adolph Hitler addressing the German people.

"Corporal, I'm willing to overlook your rude outburst, as you obviously don't have the stomach or the nerve for this job. Maybe you should have been a chef or a latrine orderly." He made no effort to hide his contempt for the corporal. "But I've ordered you to shoot these three. I could have you shot for disobeying orders, but I'm a compassionate man and believe in second chances. Besides, if you don't shoot them, I'll order them buried alive. It'll be your fault if they suffer even more. Is that what you want?" He smiled at what he thought was his incredibly ingenious logic.

Steinert's knees shook uncontrollably, and his body shivered as if caught in an icy blast of wind. He knew there was no alternative to obeying the sergeant's commands. He looked down at the three pathetic individuals lying on the cold, damp ground that would soon become their graves. A man, a woman, and a young girl were all wheezing and gasping for air in varying degrees while their bodies twitched and their arms and legs moved spasmodically. They were obviously suffering. He could think of no adequate solution for these condemned souls, but he believed he must somehow save the only soul left within his power to save: his own. And whether or not he would carry out the sergeant's commands to shoot these three, he was determined to escape this nightmare that was making him lose faith in the German people and in his own being.

Throughout his schooling, young Anton had been a thoughtful, introspective student. From his studies of history he'd synthesized that the actions of human beings were incredibly ambiguous, capable on the one hand of kindness and generosity but on the other of cruelty and genocide. He had learned that these opposing traits can become juxtaposed within mere seconds of each other. And now, he agonized, was it his turn to experience the terrifying fall from the height of human decency? He removed his pistol from its holster.

As he aimed the barrel of the pistol at the head of the ten-year-old girl and began to squeeze the trigger, his mind flashed back to what now seemed a dream in which he remembered his mother, a meticulously clean hausfrau who would berate her children unmercifully if they tracked dirt into her house with their shoes; a house that was dirty meant a house that would attract insects. And for whatever reasons, unknown even to himself, Anton had always felt strangely guilty at the taking of so seemingly insignificant a life as that of an insect. Thus, whenever possible, when he thought his mother and brother weren't watching, he would allow tiny bugs to crawl onto a piece of paper and delight in setting them free outside the house. But occasionally his brother, Klaus, would witness his mission of mercy and would taunt him, yelling loudly enough for their mother to hear, "You scared little twerp, it's only a bug. Kill it!"

But killing, even of bugs, wasn't part of his nature...

Sweat poured down Corporal Steinert's forehead and into his eyes, mixing with tears of hatred and frustration as his index finger pressed harder on the trigger. Thoughts of shooting the sergeant crossed his mind as the sergeant watched him, laughing sadistically, while Steinert lined up the temple of the pitiful ten-year-old's head with his gun sight. Was it the sergeant he heard, or was it his dead brother, Klaus, berating him from the grave? It hardly mattered at this point, for all that echoed in the chamber of his mind, over and over and over as he squeezed the trigger, was, "It's only a bug. It's only a bug. Kill it!"

A shot rang out with what seemed to Steinert the noise that only a cannon could make, reverberating between his temples, while the temple of the young girl blew apart at his feet, splattering his pants and boots with blood and parts of the girl's skull and brain.

Steinert stood motionless except for the involuntary trembling of his body that seemed to emanate from his gun-clenching hand. While gawking at the terrible yet ghoulishly fascinating sight, his body became filled with a swirl of conflicting and confusing emotions. Then, as if being spoken to as a child playing some silly game, he vaguely overheard the sergeant remark that the next one would be easier.

Steinert's carefully cultivated sense of decency became momentarily disoriented by the irrationality confronting him, and his mind screamed its thoughts in bewildering rage. Perhaps the sergeant was right! Maybe the next one would be easier, and then the next, and the next ...

Then, with a sadness far deeper than he could remember feeling, even upon hearing of his mother's death, he said to himself, *Now they'll think I've become one of them, a madman.*

He silently vowed to live long enough to see at least some of the injustices repaid and to achieve something wonderful for mankind. Helping his fellow man would purge him of his guilt. It had to.

In spite of the external military pressure exerted on him to perform his assigned task, he decided on gambling to remove himself from this nightmare. After one week of this duty, the strain on his psyche became so great that he did something he never could have imagined. While getting ready to clean his gun, he "accidentally" shot himself in his left foot, the foot that was used for the hard clutch of the truck. Suspecting nothing, his superiors reassigned him to office duty at one of the truck depots, where he remained for the duration of the war. His injury never healed properly, but to Steinert it was a price well worth paying.

When the war ended, Germany held nothing for him except terrible memories. He crossed into Austria and lived in Vienna for two years, following the results of the Nuremberg trials with an intensity that he himself didn't fully understand. Was he as guilty as they, the leaders who were on trial for war crimes? Steinert told himself that he had to follow orders as befitted the universal soldier, but he also knew he'd done nothing to stop the inhuman atrocities that he'd played such a brief but prominent role in. What could he have done? It was a persistently haunting question to which he would find no definitive answer for the remainder of his life.

In 1947, after saving some money performing odd jobs, he immigrated to Argentina, where he'd heard a large German population was now living. The memories of Europe could perhaps more easily be erased in a new land. He looked forward to beginning anew.

Steinert never told anyone of his past. His life was now his work and his books. He had girlfriends from time to time, but marriage never seemed to be a possibility. He was sixty-five now, in fair health except for a pronounced limp, and always appeared far older. His hair was gray, cut short, and thin at the top. He still wore the same type of wire-rimmed spectacles that he'd worn since his midtwenties. The years had put a few pounds on him, but he was still considered thin for a man of his age. His favorite mode of dress seemed to always include an old-fashioned, European-style cardigan sweater, no matter the weather outside. And always perched on his desk was his cherished Turkish meerschaum pipe, although he was never seen smoking it in class; he simply clamped his teeth on it on one side of his mouth and spoke through the other side.

This particular day had begun as usual. Steinert awoke, drank his two cups of coffee, shaved, showered, and went off to the university office in New York. At ten that morning, while he was sucking on his unlit pipe, his secretary brought his mail in. One parcel immediately drew his attention. It was from Don in Lima. He quickly opened it, revealing its contents of a letter, a cassette tape, and a piece of paper with dots on it. The letter explained everything about the find in great detail.

Steinert leaned back in his chair and thought, *Has Don gone mad?* He laid his pipe onto his desk and then reread the letter much more slowly, taking notes as he went along. *No,* he thought, *this isn't the work of a madman.* Don was always a level-headed young man, and his writing seemed normal, his thoughts well placed on the paper. But what Don was suggesting was too incredible for Steinert to accept without much more evidence.

Steinert examined the dotted paper. Was this meant to be a code of some sort? He stared at the paper for a few minutes, turning it upside down and sideways. One of the positions seemed to ring a bell, and Steinert peered through his spectacles even closer. "This looks like a star chart," he muttered to himself. Making nothing more of it, he put it aside thinking that he should show it to Dr. Kroner, head of the astronomy department.

He then plugged the tape into his tape recorder. What he heard were sounds that reminded him of a person talking at a very high speed. His recorder couldn't be played at a slower speed, and so he planned to drop the tape off at the engineering department before going over to Dr. Kroner's office.

Steinert hurried to the engineering department and gave the tape to Dr. Fred Arnsworth, who was able to place the tape into a variable-speed player.

The two men listened intently as Arnsworth progressively reduced the speed of the tape. It began to sound like a voice speaking at a normal rate but in a language that was unfamiliar to both men.

"It sounds a bit like Chinese to me," Arnsworth remarked. "What do you think, Anton?"

The German-accented Steinert answered, "Ja, it does sound that way. But for some strange reason, although I speak no Far Eastern language, it sounds to me vaguely familiar, almost as though I have heard something similar to it some place."

"Maybe the Chinese takeout down the block," joked Arnsworth.

Steinert simply smiled and then decided that he ought to get over to Kroner before he left his office. He asked Arnsworth if he'd mind examining the tape further in his spare time. Arnsworth said it would be no problem, and Steinert left, saying he would contact Arnsworth later in the day.

Minutes later, Steinert arrived at Dr. Kroner's office and showed him what Steinert was now referring to as his star chart. Perhaps it was merely some copy of a poor man's horoscope.

After a few minutes in silence, except for several "hums" and "uh huhs," Kroner looked up. "Yes, this is a star chart, the kind we astronomers have fun playing around with."

"What do you mean?"

"You are, of course, familiar with the movement of stars from their seemingly set patterns. Stars always move, although they're so far away that the apparent motion is extremely slow. It might take a thousand years or so for a constellation's pattern to noticeably change. Sometimes we make projections of how a particular pattern will be expected to appear in the future, and sometimes we project backward to what it looked like in the past."

"And I have here what?"

"You most definitely have a projection of the past of quite a number of constellations."

"How far in the past?"

"That'll take a bit of time to calculate. Let me find a book that will help us."

Kroner left briefly and returned with a book. He fumbled through its pages, took some notes, and then measured some of the distances between the dots on the paper. After some further calculations using scrap paper and hand calculator, he turned to Steinert. "About four thousand years ago. Does that help you?"

Steinert blinked for a few seconds, not knowing what to think. "It does, danke."

"Where did you get this map?"

"Oh, uh, from a student of mine," Steinert white-lied.

"I'd say your student did his homework. I took a few measurements randomly from various stars and found the measurements to be quite exact. You should tell your student he or she did a nice job."

"I will."

Steinert hurried out. This was either very exciting news or a well-planned hoax. He hoped for the former.

Back at his office later that day, he phoned Arnsworth at the engineering department. Arnsworth had had some persons examine the tape, but they agreed that whatever it meant, pieces seemed to be missing. They couldn't be of any help as yet.

Were the pieces missing, or were the parts misunderstood? Steinert wasn't sure which. There was a third possibility suggested by Don. Perhaps the message being sent couldn't be interpreted by any known means. What if the message was meant for a race superior to ours?

Steinert's mind was clearly playing games with itself. It was exciting to dream of the possibilities that might be if this thing proved to be real. What an incredible find it would be! But Steinert quickly came back to reality. All he had was a note from Don, a star chart showing ancient constellations, and a tape that no one could interpret. Perhaps it was time to speak with Don himself. Steinert decided to phone Lima. Don had left the number where he could be reached. He dialed and waited a few moments.

"University of Lima. How may I direct your call?"

Having lived in South America for almost twenty years, Steinert responded perfectly in Spanish. "I would like to speak with Mr. Donald Carter in the archeology department."

"One moment, I'll connect you."

Another voice answered, "Archeology. Alvarado speaking."

"May I please speak with Donald Carter?"

"Don? Who's calling?" the man asked.

"Dr. Anton Steinert from New York."

"I'm sorry, but Don left for New York two days ago."

"Two days ago? Left for New York? Are you sure you can hear me well enough? It is Don Carter I would like to speak with," Steinert said loudly and distinctly into the telephone.

"Yes, yes. I hear you quite well."

"Did he leave an address or phone number where he could be reached?"

"No, he didn't."

"Are you certain? Perhaps in the main office ..."

"Don has had several of his usual phone calls, and I've checked to find out how he could be reached. Each time, I've been told simply that he left for New York quite suddenly and left no address or phone number where he could be contacted."

Steinert paused for a moment and then replied, "All right, thank you."

Steinert hung up and began thinking. It was quite unlike Don to leave no forwarding address or phone number. Perhaps he felt he had to take precautions with whatever news he was bringing back with him. *But why didn't he contact me?* Steinert asked himself. *And if he left two days ago, what has taken him so long?*

The only person Steinert could think of who might have heard from Don would be Diane. He needed to find Don's home phone number and began searching among the piles of papers on his desk.

CHAPTER 12

DIANE STOOD NAKED IN front of the full-length mirror that hung from her bedroom closet door. She examined her body as if the image before her was someone else's, working her way down from her neck to her slim waist and down to her model-like legs. *Not bad,* she thought in an objective, almost detached manner.

"Eat your heart out, Don," she said out loud. "You could've had this tonight." But her attitude turned nostalgic as she said, wistfully, "And I could've had you."

Suddenly, there it was again. That weird sensation she felt the other day: a premonition, a foreboding that would involve Peru. Her knees buckled for a split second, and she felt weak. She sat down on a chair and attempted to deny the undefined harbinger that was affecting her.

Only once before had she ever witnessed an image so terrifyingly realistic. It had involved her father, just prior to his death. She'd been at the movie theater with three girlfriends when she began to cry, openly enough to catch the attention of one of her friends.

"Diane, it isn't that sad," she had said.

Diane knew it wasn't, but for some inexplicable reason it was her father she saw in grave danger, not the actor on the screen. "I ... I guess it's my period."

Later that afternoon, she arrived home to find an ambulance and a police car waiting outside with lights flashing. Her father had fallen dead of a heart attack in the middle of the living room.

She never told anyone about her premonition, and over the years she had repressed the memory of it, a memory that made her feel that by thinking it, she may have somehow caused her dear father's death.

Repressed until now. The belief that Peru might hold danger for Don brought back the terrible memory of her father's demise. But, she thought, then she was a girl. Now she was a woman, and no one could foresee the future. Her father's death and her prediction of it must have been purely coincidental. The ominous feeling soon passed, and her mood improved. She finished dressing and went off to work at the advertising agency.

Frank Craine was always one of the first to greet her when she arrived at work each morning. He was one of two senior vice presidents at the company and was grossly unabashed at how much money he made, especially around women he liked. He was very much attracted to Diane. Everyone in the office knew he was heavily into coke, the drug du jour, very often leaving a trace of the telltale white powder on a nostril, but no one would ever point it out to him.

A tall, handsome man of thirty-eight, Frank had been divorced for the past eight years. Making it with women was generally no problem for him, particularly those impressed by money. But the attractive and naturally sexy Diane, who had now worked at the company for six years, never glanced his way. He chalked it up to her being happily married. But after her separation (and Peru, he thought, was as ridiculously separated as one could be), he became an uncaged animal sniffing around Diane as though it were the mating season, except that his intended mate wasn't in heat.

As she entered the office, he was right there, Johnny-on-the-spot to intercept her. To his astonishment, rather than giving him the usual "Hi, Frank," and heading off to her desk, she stopped and faced him.

"Frank, do you believe in precognition?"

"No, I'm Catholic," he answered, smiling.

Slightly annoyed, Diane said, "I'm serious." She was already regretting asking him.

"I'm sorry." *What a jerk I am,* he thought. *She wants to make small talk, and I make some stupid joke.* "You mean," he continued, "where you see the future?"

"Something like that."

"I have enough trouble dealing with the present, but if I had that power, I'd sure as hell be on the phone with my stockbroker." This time he refrained from smiling. "Why do you ask?"

"I had this … feeling that Don might be in some kind of trouble."

He sensed his opening. "Come into my office and tell me all about it."

Diane thought, *Maybe he's not such a jerk, after all.*

They walked into his office, and he closed the door behind her, discreetly locking it. It was a spacious office with a large desk in front of a picture window that overlooked Madison Avenue, thirty floors below. The walls bore framed photos of him skiing, biking, jogging, etc. He offered her a seat on the sofa adjacent to his desk and sat next to her.

As she sat down, she crossed her legs, and he noticed how shapely they were. Her skirt became slightly hiked up above her knee, exposing a bit of her thigh.

As she continued speaking, he placed his arm around her back and gently squeezed her shoulder. Diane now realized that he was no ordinary audience. She stopped in midsentence and asked rhetorically, "What are you doing?"

He was like a child in her presence. "I think you're beautiful. Is that bad?"

She stared at him, understanding fully the unusual predicament. He was one of her bosses, and he wanted her.

Frank mistook her pause as a signal that she wanted him as much as he wanted her and, with his highly practiced technique, began to gently caress her breast.

Shocked, Diane clamped her teeth onto his upper arm, biting as hard as she could through his suit sleeve.

Frank screamed in pain and jumped up. "You bitch," he said, more surprised than angry. "What the fuck? That hurt."

Diane stood up and faced Frank, seething with anger. "Not as much as it's going to hurt if you ever come near me again."

"Come on, your husband—or ex-husband or whatever the hell he is—is off in some jungle."

"Then maybe I'll screw every other guy in the office so they can all tell you how great it was!" She turned, opened the door, rushed past the receptionist's desk, and said, "I'm going home. Not feeling well."

She took the elevator down to the street and hailed a cab. Once inside the cab, she sat back and exhaled hard enough to make a slight whistling sound, as though out of breath.

The cab driver heard her. "Tough day, huh lady?"

She answered with little emotion, "Routine, everyday stuff."

"Then I'd sure hate to have your job," he said as he glanced at her through his rearview mirror.

"This is the Big Apple. You have to be tough." And again came that strange premonition of some indefinable foreboding concerning Don. She thought about him being lost in some jungle and said out loud to herself, not meaning for the cabby to hear her, "I hate you, but I wish to hell you'd call me."

"You talkin' to me, lady?"

She responded glibly, "No, just practicing for a play."

"No kiddin'. Where's it gonna open?"

"In Peru," she answered, sounding convincing.

She smiled. She had no idea why she gave the cabby such a silly answer, but at that moment, something about her answer certainly felt appropriate.

Minutes later, she arrived home and, hearing the phone ringing, quickly answered it. "Hello."

"Mrs. Carter. It is Anton Steinert."

"Dr. Steinert," she answered, sounding surprised. "What can I do for you?"

"Do you know where is Don?" he said, to the point.

"In Peru. But you know that."

"I called there. They said he left suddenly for New York with no forwarding address or phone number."

"Don doesn't do things like that." She bit into a fingernail.

"I agree."

"How long ago did they say he left?"

"A couple of days ago."

Diane felt a knot forming in her stomach. "If anyone knows where he is, his mother would certainly know. I'll call her and call you right back." The pace of her speech had noticeably quickened.

Steinert hung up. A few minutes later, his phone rang. It was Diane.

"I'm sorry, Dr. Steinert. His mother knows nothing. She was extremely concerned, so I told her he must have taken a cruise. I lied and said he'd mentioned something like that but I'd forgotten the dates."

Steinert scratched his head and then said, "If you hear from him, please tell him to call me right away."

"And you likewise. I know we're separated, but ..."

"Ja, of course."

Steinert hung up and thought, *Where is Don? Why hasn't he contacted me?*

Diane was shaken. Her eyes darted around the room as though her brain were searching for something to focus on other than the thoughts that were bombarding her. Perhaps the premonition she'd had was coming true. Perhaps Don was in some kind of peril, and she would come to know more of Peru because she would have to go there to identify his body, or attend his funeral, or have his body exhumed and flown back to New York. Or maybe there were only body parts left, or maybe cannibals had left nothing at all ...

"Stop it!" she screamed. She could deny her terrible thoughts and even her past premonition, but she couldn't deny the facts that she heard from Steinert. Why would Don leave Peru suddenly without telling anyone here about it? And why would he be gone for days? Her premonition regarding her father had come true. Why not this one? No. She wasn't some gypsy mystic. *Don will be all right,* she told herself.

She could do no more than anxiously await word of Don's well-being.

Over at the engineering department, Dr. Arnsworth was perplexed by Steinert's tape. He'd worked with the tape for a while on his own tape recorder. Just as Steinert had suggested, it simply resembled a voice speaking some foreign language, except this language was like none he'd ever heard before. It had reminded Arnsworth of a Far Eastern dialect—Chinese, perhaps.

Arnsworth recorded the sounds on his own tape recorder. Later that day, he took the tape and a cassette player to Dr. Yang, a professor in the chemistry department who hailed from Taiwan. Arnsworth played the tape for Yang. Although Yang concurred that it resembled someone speaking in a Far Eastern tongue, it was nothing he'd ever heard before, and Yang had traveled extensively in the Far East and judged that he could recognize most major languages of the area. Arnsworth could think of nothing more to do with the tape except return it to Steinert.

Having gotten the tape back and remembering what Arnsworth had told him, Steinert played the tape again. Yes, it did sound similar to Chinese or some other Far Eastern dialect, but for some reason the language now seemed even more familiar to him than it had before. Steinert still couldn't place it. He felt certain he'd heard something like it before, but where and when he couldn't remember.

Later that afternoon, alone in his apartment, he replayed the tape several more times. It was now bothering him to the point of annoyance. He knew he'd heard something similar but still couldn't put his finger on it. He picked up his meerschaum pipe, extracted a pinch of cherry tobacco from its pouch, and lit the pipe while sucking heavily on it, watching the flame ignite more intensely with each drag.

He began to tire of the mental acrobatics and instead began to wonder about Don and his whereabouts. Steinert had been in Peru only once before, to attend an important four-day seminar in Lima, but that was many years ago while he still lived in Argentina. Lima was a fairly modern city, he thought, for so undeveloped a country. Part of the seminar included a bit of history about ancient Peru and its civilizations. The presenters showed a film demonstrating how similarly the farmers of the mountains lived compared to the ancient Incas, with their primitive tools and irrigation methods, farming on terraces along the mountainsides. They even spoke a language similar to their ancestors, which they called Quechua.

Steinert leaned back in his chair, resting his eyes, and repeated the word out loud. "Quechua." Suddenly, his eyes flew open wide as he again repeated, excitedly, "Quechua. Es muss sein!" He'd heard several of the farmers speak their ancient tongue in that movie, and the tape certainly sounded similar to that. These Indian descendants of a group of the Mongoloid race had come from Asia carrying their Asian form of speaking with them. It had, of course, changed over the millennia, but it still had that Far Eastern flavor to it. He needed to find someone who could speak Quechua, perhaps someone in the Peruvian embassy in New York.

He phoned the embassy and after several switches was told that no one there could speak the language but that a Mr. Acosta in the embassy in Washington, DC, could help him with the translation.

After making contact with the embassy, Steinert made a copy of the tape and mailed it overnight express to Washington.

Acosta received the tape the next day. It certainly did resemble Quechua, and he was able to interpret some of the words, although this language appeared to be even more ancient than the Quechua he was familiar with. Acosta wrote each word, exactly as it sounded, onto a piece of paper and played with the words for a while.

The tape was apparently repeating the same brief message over and over. After much mental wrangling, Acosta was able to determine a message from the tape, one that he believed was as literal a translation as was possible. He phoned Steinert with the news.

"Dr. Steinert, I believe I've gotten as close to the actual message as possible."

Steinert answered, full of anticipation, "Continue."

"Understand that I have a literal translation of the words only. I can't say what they mean, if anything. I leave that up to you."

"I understand."

"The tape's message says something like, 'People able to enter, receive God'."

"That is all?" He'd expected something more definitive.

"That's it."

"How literal do you think is your translation?"

"Well, you know words can always have more than one meaning. If I were you, I'd play around with the words and try to make them fit whatever it is you're working with."

"I will certainly do that."

Steinert hung up and repeated the phrase, "People able to enter, receive God." He began thinking out loud. "Let me see, if you can enter … enter what? Enter the cylinder? If you get inside the cylinder? If you can open the cylinder? If you can break a code? If you are smart enough to determine the message of the cylinder, then you find God? God," he repeated. "Gott equals what? Infinity, power, knowledge, knowledge of the universe. It could mean any of those things."

Steinert realized that the exact meaning was yet to be determined. Maybe Don would be able to figure it out. Perhaps once they could examine the cylinder, the meaning of the message would become clearer. He hoped he'd be hearing from Don in the next day or so.

CHAPTER 13

COLONEL TOM RAWLINGS WAS at his desk, poring over some routine paperwork at the Pentagon and daydreaming, when he received a phone call that should have been nothing unusual. His office at the Defense Department screened many UFO sightings for authenticity. But ever since Project Blue Book had effectively closed the chapter on UFOs arriving from outer space, concluding from the results of their investigation that in no way do UFOs constitute a threat to national security, the only real concern to anyone was Soviet Union missiles or bombers. Other than that, the sightings were fairly routine and dull by the standards of the military that Rawlings was once accustomed to.

This particular job was given to Rawlings as a kind of plum—with high pay, low pressure, and lots of free time—for his years as a Vietnam War veteran. He had served as a fighter pilot in the Air Force and, more importantly, been held for two years by the Viet Cong as a prisoner of war in South Vietnam. He was forty-five, and the war seemed centuries ago. He'd been shot down near Quang Tri and bailed out, only to be captured within minutes by the VC.

Rawlings was a rugged man, always athletic, and prided himself on his ability to act in only the highest military manner. After his capture, he was certain that the Viet Cong would never be able to break him, no matter what they did. Name, rank, and serial number were all they would get out of him.

But this was no John Wayne movie, and broken he was, as were many POWs. The VC played by whatever rules they devised for that moment. His starvation diet was mostly rice, water, and whatever insects happened to crawl into his bamboo cage, which was only large enough to house a large dog. This became Rawlings's home, toilet, bed, and dining quarters for the two years he was held prisoner. The only times he was allowed out was to be interrogated. An occasional kick, a punch, or a casual cigarette burn on the soles of his feet wasn't unusual. Apparently, the only rule they had was to keep him alive. Diarrhea and skin sores plagued him throughout his captivity.

The days became a blur of unceasing, monotonous routine, but one night in particular stuck out in Rawlings's memory. His VC captors had that day lost six of their comrades to the Americans, and that evening they were either bent on revenge or, perhaps, just seeking a way to vent their anger, frustration, and hatred for the tall invaders from twelve thousand miles away.

They dragged Rawlings from his cage by his hair and threw him on the ground, kicking and beating him mercilessly. One VC, a boy of perhaps thirteen, kept jabbing at his groin with a sharpened bamboo stick. The boy laughed and danced around Rawlings as Rawlings attempted to cover himself with his bleeding hands, rolling on the ground this way and that way, depending on which direction the other VCs were kicking from.

They soon tired of this game, and one man, leering at Rawlings, suggested that they hang the American upside down and drop him, ever so slowly, headfirst, into a pail filled with human excrement, until he was forced to breathe in and swallow their waste just prior to suffocating in it.

The men sardonically approved of this idea and began to lift Rawlings off the ground in preparation for tying his arms and legs and suspending him upside down from a nearby tree. Had they simply threatened to shoot Rawlings, he would've accepted it and would probably be dead today, but the ingloriousness and revulsion of suffocating to death on human waste was Rawlings's breaking point. Out of desperation, he screamed at them that if they would stop he would tell them all he knew of American military strength—which, in reality, was very little and outdated.

Having already vented much of their pent-up anger, the VC now saw a chance to gain at least a partial victory. They could have the satisfaction of knowing that they had made an American pilot talk, and perhaps the information given to them would help them gain their revenge by killing many other American soldiers. Thus, they had spared Rawlings's life but ravaged his dignity.

He told them far more than he had intended to, although by the time he told them what little he knew of American military strength and tactics, it was all obsolete. But Rawlings knew that he'd violated strict military code. He rationalized that no American could ever be fully trained mentally or physically for conditions similar to the ones he had suffered through, and especially for long periods of time. Certainly, it was nothing like those old World War Two movies he'd seen, in which the American POW would endure a few slaps in the face and then be sent back to his fellow prisoners, where he would proudly boast that he told those lousy Krauts nothing, followed by several pats on the back and congratulatory cheers.

Nevertheless, inside himself, Rawlings felt violated and humiliated. He wasn't the same after the war, receiving far less than a World War Two hero's welcome. Some of the spark of life itself was gone. He returned home to his wife, two children, friends, and relatives as a vastly different man.

The dozen or so years that had passed since Vietnam had gradually restored Rawlings's former existence, but only outwardly. His job now was relatively pressure free, and his wife and two teenage daughters were as good to him and for him as he could ever have wished. But he rarely spoke of either the war or his time spent as a POW.

He often found himself daydreaming, which helped pass the time when the job became even duller than usual. His favorite escape from reality was to concoct various ways of killing or maiming his enemies. Some of the ways became rather bizarre, such as inventing an explosive that would be detonated only by the presence of urine. He would smile to himself at the thought of an unsuspecting victim approaching a toilet filled with the explosive and urinating to make the toilet blow to smithereens. He roared with laughter at the thought of the same event occurring had the victim been a person seated on the toilet.

The phone on his desk rang, but this call that brought Rawlings back to reality was different. Major Sloan himself was on the other end rather than one of his secretaries. Sloan explained that the reason he was calling was that someone from the Peruvian government, along with a scientist from Peru, had come in person to describe a different and interesting story about an alien object being held for the highest bidder by persons who had the object in their possession. The bidding was primarily meant to be between the United States and the Soviet Union. Naturally, explained Sloan, everyone's first instinct was that this was a hoax. But in this case, an eminent scientist, Miguel Solars, well respected and knowledgeable in this field, had been allowed to secretly examine this object for authenticity. "Solars believes that this may truly be an alien object from …somewhere else," explained Sloan.

Rawlings had long since learned not to become excited by such talk, but this at least piqued his interest. Rawlings figured that it might be fun exposing this one as just another hoax. "Where and when can I meet with these fellows?"

"Right now, Tom, if you want. They're in my outer office."

"Send them up."

A few minutes later, Mendez and Solars appeared at the office entrance with Major Sloan. After the formal introductions, Rawlings sat down behind his desk. Sloan, Mendez, and Solars sat down in chairs in front of the desk.

Rawlings discreetly pressed a hidden switch that activated a tape recorder. Then he spoke first. "Mr. Mendez. Why don't you start at the beginning."

Solars began speaking instead. "Colonel Rawlings, let me begin by stating that I am a respected man in my field and not given to frivolous behavior."

"I fully understand, Mr. Solars."

Rawlings was quickly corrected by Mendez. "*Doctor* Solars."

"I'm sorry, Dr. Solars. Major Sloan here has informed me of your position in Peru and your eminence in the field."

"Fine. Then you will understand that what I am about to tell you may or may not hold true, but there is at least a chance of it. And if it does turn out to be genuine, I believe your government would do well to obtain the object in question."

"What kind of object is it, sir?"

"It appears as a cylinder about twenty centimeters long and ten centimeters in diameter that gives off strange signals and is radioactive, as if powered by some nuclear generator."

"Forgive me, sir, for interrupting, but what makes you believe that this is an alien object and not just a hoax or something man-made?" Rawlings was familiar with a host of ways to dismiss unfounded reports of UFOs and aliens, and he figured this so-called mystery would take him only a few minutes to unravel.

"First, the story of how it was found," Solars said. "Mr. Mendez can better describe these events to you."

Mendez recounted the story told to him by Diego about the boy, Paco, the strange signals, how the cylinder was embedded in solid rock and became far more radioactive when struck, and how it was able to melt solid rock around it and not be affected itself.

Solars again addressed Rawlings. "It is possible that these signals were left as a message for us to interpret. Who can say what information an apparently superior race may have left in that cylinder? One more thing: the metal that the cylinder is made of. I could not identify it with the means I had at my disposal."

"Perhaps," Rawlings replied, "you didn't have the proper testing devices."

"I performed some simple tests—scratch, acid, and so on—which would normally give me a clue. But this material is one that I could not even scratch with my diamond chip. Also, and this is, I believe, most significant, the amount of radiation it emits is apparently lethal, as it was to the Rivera child. And yet the Geiger counter reading dropped from lethal to almost nothing in only a few minutes. I had this feeling ..." Solars paused as if groping for the correct way to express himself, "that it knew I merely wanted to examine it and meant it no harm."

Silence filled the room for perhaps ten seconds, but it seemed far longer. Rawlings leaned over the desk, closer toward Solars. "You're Peruvian. Why wouldn't you give it to your own country, especially since Mr. Mendez is in the government?" Rawlings now looked toward Mendez for an answer.

Mendez replied, "Our government knows of this cylinder, but, unfortunately, it is in the hands of some unscrupulous persons."

"What do they want?"

"A lot of money."

"How much?"

"That depends on how much your government or some other government is willing to pay."

"Why doesn't your own government pay?"

"Our government knows that such a small object could easily be smuggled out of Peru. The men who have the object believe that a bidding war between

America and the Soviet Union would bring untold times more money than Peru could afford."

"The Russians?" Rawlings said, not overly surprised.

"Yes. They have informed the Russians of this matter, and we have been instructed to meet with them at the Soviet embassy here in Washington later today."

"How can my government verify the authenticity of this object to our satisfaction?" It was said with little enthusiasm.

"I have been led to believe that this can be arranged, perhaps through someone like you."

"Fine. I'll clear this with my superiors. I'll get back in touch with you as soon as possible." The possibility of competition with the Communists was always an added incentive for Tom Rawlings.

Mendez and Solars stood up, shook hands with Rawlings and Sloan, and left the office.

Rawlings turned off the tape recorder, ejected the tape, and placed it in his pocket.

Sloan scratched his head as he asked, "I know UFOs are your thing, but do you believe this shit is possible? Aliens?"

"Anything's possible. We've got a radio telescope a thousand feet in diameter in Arecibo, Puerto Rico. SETI, the Search for Extra Terrestrial Intelligence, analyzes radio signals for signs of intelligence from other solar systems."

"How?"

"They look for signs of sequential or repeating signals as opposed to random ones, thinking that only intelligent beings could produce them."

"They find anything?"

"Not yet, but as you probably know, there've been many reported sightings of UFOs, including by people claiming to have been abducted by short, bald-headed beings with grayish skin, pear-shaped heads, and cat-like eyes."

Sloan grinned wryly. "Yeah, and my dog does calculus."

"Listen, the Roswell, New Mexico, incident just won't go away. A newspaper headline in 1947 said something like, 'Air Force Captures Flying Saucer on Ranch in Roswell.' Rumors started flying about dead alien bodies. The air force says there's nothing to the crash, but too many witnesses have come forward with what they say is first-hand knowledge of a crashed flying saucer, dead aliens, and a military cover-up."

"And you believe this stuff?"

"Of course not. Project Blue Book analyzed all the stories concerning UFOs and concluded that there's no credible evidence that UFOs landed here. The flip side is, they can't prove that they *didn't*, at one time or another."

Rawlings then gave a perfunctory salute to Sloan and said, "Gotta go."

Rawlings took the tape recording of their conversation to higher channels in the Pentagon to get their opinions and advice. He was intrigued by the story even if totally convinced that it would soon be debunked. He looked forward to exposing this sham.

Later that day, Mendez and Solars met with Mr. Sergei Simonov at the Soviet embassy and were received with the same skeptical interest that Colonel Rawlings had demonstrated. And, like Rawlings, Simonov knew that he must at least attempt to follow up on this matter, though he very much doubted the authenticity of it. His first impression was that Mendez was another South American trying to dupe the Russians out of more money. As with Rawlings, Simonov asked to be able to examine this object.

Mendez left the office more disappointed than ever. Neither side had shown enthusiasm for the cylinder. He thought that either they were all very good at hiding their emotions or else he hadn't stated his case convincingly. Maybe he and Solars needed to be able to demonstrate more clearly what the cylinder was. But for now, he would return to his hotel room and await any messages from either the Russians or Americans.

CHAPTER 14

STEINERT FELT HE COULD wait no longer. Don hadn't contacted anyone, and it had been two days since he'd received Don's package. He decided to call Lima to speak with those persons with whom Don worked most closely. Perhaps they'd be able to give him some clue as to Don's whereabouts.

After going through various channels, he was told that Don worked with a person who had also become his closest friend, Diego Gonzales. It took several phone calls over a period of a few hours, but finally Steinert was able to reach Diego Gonzales at work.

"Are you Diego Gonzales?" he asked in Spanish.

"I am."

"I was told you worked very closely with Don Carter and that you might know where he is or how he can be reached."

"Who is this?" Diego asked, startled by the call although he believed some kind of inquiry about Don was imminent.

"Oh, I'm sorry. My name is Anton Steinert from New York. I haven't heard from Don in quite some time and thought you might help me locate him."

Diego remembered hearing of Dr. Steinert from Don. He attempted to sound as casual as possible. "He left suddenly, went back to New York or took a vacation somewhere. That's all I know."

"How do you know this?"

"Our supervisor, Dr. Romero, informed us."

"Thank you for your time, Mr. Gonzales."

The conversation was short, and Diego breathed a sigh of relief.

After hanging up, Steinert immediately called Lima again and asked to speak with Dr. Romero.

"Dr. Romero?"

"This is he."

"It's Anton Steinert."

"Dr. Steinert. I know the name. How are you? What can I do for you?" he said pleasantly.

"Do you know where Don Carter is?"

"Yes, he went back to New York."

"Did he tell you where or how he could be reached?"

"Surprisingly, no. I was quite disappointed in him. He was very good, you know. But he left suddenly without saying good-bye, and with no face-to-face explanation. All I received was a letter."

"A letter?"

"Yes, of resignation."

"What did it say?"

"Only that he was tired of work and needed time off. The letter said he was flying home. We haven't heard from him since."

"Was it typed or handwritten?" Steinert asked.

"Handwritten."

"Is the handwriting definitely Don's?"

"Yes, but why do you ask?" Romero thought he detected more than idle curiosity in Steinert's voice.

"No reason. But would you mind doing a favor for me? Could you read the letter to me?"

"Certainly, if you think it's important. You seem to be quite concerned."

"His mother is a bit ill, and we haven't been able to contact him."

"Oh, sorry to hear that."

"Nothing serious. She would probably appreciate hearing what he wrote in his letter of resignation." Lying was easy for Steinert. He had much practice in denying his past.

"I'll get it out of my files for you." Romero placed the phone down and retrieved the handwritten letter. He picked up the phone and began to read the letter verbatim in Spanish.

Dear Dr. Romero:

I am writing this letter to inform you of my intention to leave the university effective immediately and will travel back to New York. I have thought about this for quite some time and feel that I must now return home. I have been working very hard and need a vacation. Afterward, I will decide what I want to do in the future.

I will have already flown out of Lima by the time you receive this letter, so I will say good-bye to you now. Thank you for all you have done to help me.

Sincerely yours,
Donald Carter

"That's all, Dr. Steinert."

"How was the letter delivered?"

"By mail."

"Was there anything unusual written on the envelope?"

Romero was becoming increasingly curious about the questions he was being asked. Now he was concerned. "Do you believe something may have happened to Don? If you do, I think you should tell me."

Steinert knew he had to tell Romero something of his concern. "I'll tell you why I'm a bit worried. Don't you think it's unusual for a person such as Don to resign in this manner?"

"And very unexpected."

"And why was the letter handwritten and not typed as befits such an official statement? And why hasn't he contacted anyone here in the United States?"

"I can't answer your questions with any certainty, but maybe he was so upset at the time of his resignation that he hurriedly wrote the letter by hand. And the letter did say something about a vacation. Perhaps he needed time to be by himself. You do know that he was recently separated from his wife and is possibly still greatly affected by this."

Steinert would normally have agreed with Romero had he not received the package from Don describing the events with the cylinder. But he wasn't going to reveal anything regarding the cylinder to Romero. "I'm probably being overly concerned. Don most likely will show up in a couple of weeks with a terrific tan."

Romero laughed. "Yes, I bet he will. Let me know when he has contacted you, will you?"

"I certainly will. But humor me for a moment longer. Is there anything unusual about the letter? Anything at all?" Steinert didn't know what he himself might be looking for but felt that if Don was indeed in trouble, he would include some kind of clue indicating that fact. After all, Steinert thought, Don made his living deciphering clues.

Romero examined the letter and carefully reread the words. After about one minute, he said, "I'm sorry, Dr. Steinert. I've examined the letter very carefully, and the only things that seem out of order are a few misspelled words. I'm sorry I can't be of any more help to you."

"Well, thank you for your time," Steinert answered with resignation.

He hung up the phone and sat in silence for a moment. "Baffling," he mumbled to himself. He was no closer to finding Don's whereabouts than he had been before. But something nagged at him. He couldn't seem to put his finger on it, but it was something about the letter. *Bad spelling,* he thought. If Don was scribbling a note to himself, he might misspell some words, especially in Spanish. But this was a letter of resignation to his supervisor. It was handwritten, so the blame couldn't be laid on a typewriter.

Suddenly, a thought flashed through him. He grabbed the phone and redialed Romero. Steinert impatiently tapped a pencil on his desk while waiting for the connection to be made.

"Dr. Romero?"

"Dr. Steinert. You're going to have one very high telephone bill if you keep this up," he said whimsically.

"Yes, I know. But one more favor, please. You said there were words misspelled. Could you tell me what words they were?"

"Easy enough. I still have the letter right in front of me."

Steinert waited a few moments and could hear Romero saying "hmmm" to himself several times.

"You know, Dr. Steinert, the interesting thing about these words, and there are six of them, is that they're misspelled in the same manner."

With excited anticipation, Steinert asked, "How do you mean?"

"Well, in each case one letter was left out of the misspelled word. The letter wasn't written in the neatest of handwriting, possibly due to the speed at which it might have been written. I guess in his haste he left letters out of some words."

"Could you read the first example to me?"

"In the first line he meant to write 'escribo' but wrote 'ecribo' instead."

"So he omitted the letter 's' in that word?"

"Exactly."

"What are the five other letters?"

"Let's see. The next misspelled word is missing an 'i.' The third an 'e.' Then an 'r.' Then another 'r.' Then …let's see …an 'a.' Interesting. It spells—"

"Sierra!" Steinert shouted, cutting Romero off.

"Yes, sierra," repeated a dumbfounded Romero. "But what of it?"

"I'm hoping you'll be able to tell *me*."

"In other words, you believe this to be more than mere coincidence?" Romero responded.

"It might very well be. But other than meaning high country or mountains, what else might it refer to?"

"It can also refer to people who live in the mountains of Peru, or it can be a section of Lima called Sierra."

"What kind of section is that?"

"Not one to be proud of, I'm afraid. It's a relatively small area with one of the worst crime rates in all of Lima. Drugs, prostitution, gambling, and so forth."

So that was it! Steinert thought. Don was still in Lima, in this Sierra section. He was ninety-nine percent sure of it. The only missing piece of proof would be obtained by calling the airport. Because Don was in Peru on a visitor's visa, he would need his passport to get out of Peru and would've had to use his own name when buying an airline ticket. His letter stated that he'd be flying out of Lima, and Steinert knew he could check the airlines for Don's name.

Steinert thanked Romero once again and then called the Jorge Chavez International Airport in Lima. He asked to speak with each international airline that serviced the airport and told each airline that he'd cancelled his flight but hadn't received his refund. In each case he was told that there must be a mistake as there was no record of a Donald Carter booking a flight with them. An hour later, Steinert had his proof. Don Carter hadn't flown out of Lima in these past few days.

Steinert knew what he had to do. He must go to Lima himself and try to find the answers to his questions. Somehow, the cylinder, whatever it was, was surely the focus of all his questions. Steinert didn't know what the cylinder was or if it was important at all, but clearly the most important question at this point was, where was Don?

Steinert made plans to leave for Peru for one week. Before leaving, he telephoned Diane to let her know what was happening. Diane still hadn't heard from Don, and she was extremely worried about his uncharacteristic disappearance. Steinert's explanation to Diane made no reference to the cylinder.

Diane discussed the possibility that some foul play might be involved, such as a kidnapping; so much of it was happening these days, she explained. Or perhaps he was in some sort of accident, maybe an auto accident, or was stranded in some way-out place in the countryside.

Steinert assured her that he didn't think anything like that had happened to Don. Still, she was apprehensive and suggested they contact someone in the US government. But Steinert had already made other plans.

"Diane, allow me three days in Peru. If you do not hear from me by then, I want you to go to a locker at Penn Station and read the letter that I have left there for you."

"What are you talking about? What locker?" She was clearly perplexed by Steinert's strange remarks.

"I have mailed you a key with the locker number on it. The letter will explain some things that will mean something only if you do not hear from me within three days. Take the contents of a package inside the locker to the State Department. It might be of some help to them."

"But why wouldn't you contact me? Do you think something might happen to you?" Now she was more concerned than ever.

"Perhaps I am being overly cautious, but I learned long ago to be that way. Remember, allow three days."

Diane hung up. Steinert was acting too mysteriously, she thought. What was in the locker? What kind of information might be inside? And why did he feel that he had to travel to Peru? Did he already know that something terrible had happened to Don? He said he didn't, but was he lying? Diane was now gravely concerned for Don's safety. Dear God, the premonition was coming true, wasn't it? She started pacing back and forth in front of the living room couch. She knew thoughts of Don would pervade every waking hour. But unless she heard from Don or received word of his condition during the next three days, she would keep her appointed rendezvous with Steinert's mysterious locker, one which she believed could provide no substitute for the solace that only the knowledge of Don's well-being could bring her.

The following morning, as soon as she was certain that her mail had been delivered, she opened her mailbox, reached inside, and extracted a few pieces of mail. Quickly thumbing through them, she was disappointed that the key with a Penn Station locker number hadn't yet arrived.

CHAPTER 15

By NINE THE FOLLOWING morning, the Lima-bound DC 10 had departed JFK. Whenever flying, Anton Steinert never failed to marvel at how such a great metallic pterodactyl could ever get off the ground. He had amused himself this day by counting the number of heavyset persons boarding the plane and pushing themselves through the aisles. When one especially obese woman sat with a whooshing sound on her seat, he thought, *Now this plane will never get up.*

But up the silver bird went, and Steinert remembered Lima as it was the last time he was there, back in 1966. He wondered how much it had changed since that time and whether or not the fabric itself had changed. Certainly the circumstances surrounding his earlier visit bore no resemblance to this one. Then he was a guest lecturer at one of the museums; now he was searching for a missing person as well as for the elusive, long-sought-for evidence that other beings inhabited the cosmos.

He remembered Peru as a land of dramatic extremes: arid desert along the western coast and, to the east, majestic snow-capped peaks and lush, forbidding tropical jungles. Even the people seemed to be divided along distinct lines of demarcation, from the technologically advanced seacoast capital where the very rich and very poor lived juxtaposed to each other, to the very primitive peoples of the Sierra, who today live practically in the same manner as did the Inca, half a millennium ago.

Seated next to Steinert was a woman whom he recognized as being a native of Peru by her glossy, straight black hair, her rose-brown skin, and her chocolate brown eyes with a fold at the corners, which indicated the Indians' Asian ancestry. The woman was seated between Steinert and another gentleman, and she passed some of the time talking with the two men. She told them that she was returning home after visiting her mother, who had undergone two operations in the United States.

Steinert asked, "Your mother is well?"

The woman answered with fervent conviction, "Oh, yes, she is absolutely cured."

She asked Steinert his reasons for traveling to Peru, and he answered that he was an archeologist who studied ruins.

She then asked the other man of his intentions, and the man told her that he was a priest planning to work in Peru with missionaries.

The woman's face changed dramatically. She leaned toward the priest, grasped his hand, and said with anguish, "Oh, Father, my mother has terminal cancer and does not have long to live."

Steinert leaned back in his seat. Yes, she certainly was a Peruvian in the deepest sense of the word. He had seen Peruvians display unlimited trust in priests. The church hadn't been able to earn such unconditional respect in all the time that had passed since the conquest by the conquistadors, but Peruvians gave their confidence to priests without hesitation. Steinert felt he understood. In a land of untold poverty, God was their sanctuary, and priests were his flesh and blood messengers.

In late afternoon, the DC 10 made its final approach into Lima. Steinert could see the wing of the big jet pointing downward toward the distant foothills of the Andes. Misty fog was beginning to blanket the coastal area. *Ah,* thought Steinert, forever the pedagogue, *that must be the result of the Humbolt Current which sweeps up from the Antarctic along the hot desert coastline and produces the fog. Yes, Peru is a country of many strange paradoxes.*

The plane landed, and he was soon standing in the busy concourse of what could have been almost any international airport in the world. At the airport bank, armed police kept onlookers behind rope barriers while tourists exchanged their currency for Peruvian money. Steinert remembered getting thirty soles for one dollar in 1966. Now he received 11,000 soles, the result of rampant Peruvian inflation due to its inherently weak economy.

He threw his bags into the trunk of an old, battered taxi, which rattled its way through rough streets on the outskirts of the city. Steinert could see poverty everywhere, with refugees from the Sierra living in makeshift shelters of bamboo and cardboard. He recalled reading that of the eighteen million people of Peru, fifteen million live below the official poverty lines. With a population of six million, the great city of Lima contained one-third the entire population of Peru and had long since burst its borders.

Steinert saw changes in Lima. Graffiti, which hardly existed in 1966, now covered most available walls, with the name "ALAN" prominent everywhere as grassroots tribute to the newly elected president, Alan Garcia, who had promised sweeping social change. Garcia vowed to build a socialist Peru, with respect for human rights, and with his youthful good looks, fiery speeches, and defiant refusal to pay any more interest on Peru's gigantic foreign debt than he believed the country could afford, he was swept into office by a two-to-one margin.

Steinert had read that the problems facing Garcia were enormous, with guerrillas on the left seeking to overthrow the government in its entirety and the military on the right seeking to hold on to as much power as possible. Under the previous government, the military had attacked the rebels' stronghold of Ayacucho, where some seven thousand people died or disappeared. Many were buried in mass graves, their fingers cut off and their faces mutilated to prevent identification. Steinert knew the world could still be an evil place.

The taxi approached the hotel in the downtown, economic heart of Lima, which was altogether different from its outskirts. Tall skyscrapers of steel and glass dominated the skyline, and Steinert thought that downtown Lima might as well have been any major city in the world.

The weather wasn't quite as warm as he had thought it would be at this time of year, but it was still too warm to suit his Bavarian blood. He intended to check into the hotel, wash up, change clothes, and then, as soon as possible, begin his task of finding Don and his mystery cylinder.

Steinert knew that the best weapon he possessed at present was invisibility. His face wasn't known here by anyone except Don, and as far as he knew, no one here thought that anyone from the United States knew anything at all about the cylinder. Therefore, no one would have cause for suspicion. Steinert also hoped that no one would suspect that anyone was searching for Don just yet. If so, their guard might be let down enough to give him the opening he might need.

His plan was to ask discreet questions, by phone if possible, and to find Diego Gonzales. Gonzales, Steinert believed, had to be the key. The letter he'd received from Don stated that Gonzales knew about the cylinder. He worked closely with Don and was his closest friend in Peru, and yet Gonzales had told Steinert in their phone conversation that he knew nothing of Don's whereabouts and made no mention of the events described in Don's letter to Steinert. Yes, he concurred with himself, Diego Gonzales would be his best bet.

Steinert decided to use a fictitious name wherever possible and had registered at the hotel as Karl Grosz. Later, in his room, he phoned the university and asked for Donald Carter. The person answering told him that Carter had resigned and had gone back to New York. Steinert hung up. Obviously nothing had changed, and he would now begin his search. But first, he would get a good night's sleep.

The following morning, Steinert called a secretary at the university and told her that he was a supplier of tools which Diego Gonzales had requested to be delivered to his home address. But, Steinert explained, he was always misplacing things and apparently had lost Gonzales's address. The secretary gave him the address.

The first place Steinert intended to visit was Don's apartment. Maybe some clue had been left behind. He had Don's address from the package that Don had sent, and he arrived by taxi a short while later at the apartment building, stopping at the superintendent's office only to be told that Don had moved out. In fact, the apartment had already been rented to someone else.

Steinert asked, "Did you see Carter move his own things out?"

"Never saw him. He probably left in the middle of the night."

"Were his personal items gone?"

"Would you expect him to leave without his clothes and stuff?"

"No, of course not."

Steinert left the super's office more confident than ever that Don was in grave danger. He would never have sneaked out in the middle of the night and without informing the superintendent. Whoever had him must have been smart enough to remove his personal items so as not to raise suspicion. The apartment was a dead end other than to reaffirm his own belief of the trouble Don must be in. Gonzales was next.

Steinert decided he must be more mobile. He took a taxi to a car rental agency and rented a late-model, compact Pontiac. The agent requested Steinert's driver's license and, observing that he was a foreigner, required that he fill out a form listing his current hotel. Once completed and guaranteed with a credit card, the car was his, and Steinert drove off.

On the way to Gonzales's apartment, Steinert smiled with the amusing thought that he felt a bit like Lt. Columbo, the TV detective. He was excited by the mysteries that might lie before him, but Gonzales's apartment was only a few minutes farther from the university than Don's former apartment, and as he approached the building, excitement soon gave way to a touch of urgency and nervousness.

Steinert drove around the entire block, taking in the sights and sounds in an effort to determine the best way to find Gonzales and follow him. Steinert's main problem was to find out what Gonzales looked like. He had no way of identifying him other than the fact that Gonzales was a young man.

He parked the car down the block and walked into a restaurant, found a pay phone, and dialed the operator in order to obtain Gonzales's phone number. He dialed the number but received no answer. He walked back to his car and decided to wait and watch the people walking into the building. If someone of Gonzales's approximate age entered the building, Steinert would follow him in.

He knew he would have to remain behind far enough to go undetected and could easily lose his man. As insurance against this, he decided to enter the building and find Gonzales's apartment. It was on the third floor of a four-story walk-up, and the climb was enough to remind Steinert of his sixty-five years. He found apartment 3C.

In the car, he had folded a piece of paper continuously in half until it was about a half inch square and a quarter inch thick. He pushed the wad of paper in between the door and door jamb approximately two inches above the floor and checked to see that it was secure and relatively out of sight. If anyone were to open the door, the paper would fall to the floor.

Steinert hurried down the stairs and back to his car, where he took off his shoe and rubbed his sore left foot. He intended to sit there for as long as he had to, sucking on his unlit pipe, until someone who might be Diego Gonzales entered the building.

For the next two hours, Steinert watched the entrance. A couple of old women entered. Several people left. Some children ran in and out of the building. An old man entered. Still no sign of Diego Gonzales.

Steinert became bored and fidgety. Time seemed to move increasingly slowly. What if Gonzales didn't return until much later, in the evening perhaps, or did not return at all? Another hour passed like watching grass grow. More persons entered and exited the building.

A man of about twenty-five or thirty years of age entered the building. Steinert strained to get a good look at his face and quickly exited the car. He walked briskly to the entrance and could hear the footsteps of someone walking up a higher flight of stairs. He heard a door open and close as he cautiously walked up the stairs, trying not to draw anyone's attention. He reached the third floor and peered around the railing, seeing and hearing nothing more. Slowly and quietly, he walked to the door to apartment 3C and looked for the wad of paper, but the paper was still in its former position. It wasn't Gonzales.

Gott im Himmel, he thought to himself. He would have to return to the car. He turned to go back down but realized that someone else was walking up the stairs. Steinert turned around and swiftly climbed toward the fourth floor, stopping on the stairs when his feet were beyond the sight of apartment 3C. If it was Gonzales, he mustn't be seen. Secrecy and surprise would be his greatest weapons.

The footsteps became louder as they approached. Then there was silence, except for the sound of keys jingling. Steinert crouched over and peered below the floor of the fourth floor and the banister leading up. He could see a man at 3C getting ready to open the door. It must be Diego Gonzales, thought Steinert. As Diego put the key into the door, Steinert studied his face, hairstyle, and physique. He must remember this man well. Diego entered the room and closed the door behind him.

As quickly as his limp would allow, Steinert rushed past 3C and out of the building to his car. He would have to return the next morning at sunrise to ensure he would be at the apartment before Gonzales left. Steinert realized that this could lead to a dead end, but his belief that Gonzales was clearly involved was strong, and it motivated him.

Inside the apartment, Diego sat down on the side of his bed without turning on the light. A gray-white light shone through the curtains of the small window that overlooked the clothesline-filled alleyway, a tapestried network so thick that a person who once fell from the roof, four stories up, lived to tell about it.

He subconsciously wrung his hands together, torn between his basically honest self and his desire for wealth, for he was caught in a dilemma in which a good friend might be hurt because of Diego's lust for money. Don didn't deserve to be the victim of a kidnapping, the enormity and seriousness of which Diego was just now realizing. The brief but concerned telephone conversation with Steinert had brought him back to reality. He wished he'd never involved Marin and his thugs, but in the excitement of believing that the cylinder could represent a fortune, he hadn't thought of the consequences of his selfish acts. But he knew he'd gone too far to turn back. He would see to it that Don was released unharmed, and in spite of Don's feelings, he would insist that Don share in some of the profits. *It will all work out, and everything will be all right,* he told himself as he continued wringing his now-sweaty palms together.

CHAPTER 16

THE FOLLOWING MORNING, DIANE stood watch in the autumn chill. She knew he would approach from Twenty-Third Street. He should have been there already, but he wasn't. The empty mailboxes bore ample testimony to that fact. The key was now her only link to some mysterious solution to Don's whereabouts, and she needed that key like some potent metallic talisman. At the least, it would represent some hard evidence that these past two days weren't a dream.

And there he was, unlike wing-footed Mercury, slowly approaching. Rather than wait, she hustled down the street to greet him.

"Hi, can I have my mail? I'm waiting for something important."

The mailman looked up. Given the number of stops on his route, he didn't often recognize his postal patrons, especially when they were out of the context of their addresses. But her he remembered, as there was something naturally attractive about her. "Sure, Mrs. Carter. Got it right here." He searched his bag and handed her several letters, mostly junk mail and bills.

She immediately sifted through her mail, and her face lit up as she saw that the return address on one of the envelopes was Steinert's.

Seeing her reaction, the mailman remarked, "Got it, didn't you?"

"What?"

"The letter you were looking for."

"Yes, I did. Thank you." She turned, rushed back to her apartment, and ripped open the envelope. Neatly tucked and taped inside a folded piece of paper was a key with locker number B189. The note said only the handwritten words, "Penn Station." The key had arrived just as Steinert had said it would, and she would now have to wait only one more day to fetch the locker's secret contents.

She grasped the key tightly enough to feel her own warmth saturating it, believing that it would be her good-luck charm. It had to be.

That same morning, Steinert once again sat in his car watching and waiting at Gonzales's building. He'd waited for almost two hours while the city awakened when Diego appeared from the doorway, turning up the block in the opposite direction. Steinert started the engine, turned the car around, and tried keeping a safe distance behind. Cars passed by on his left as he hugged close to the cars parked in the street. Diego walked two blocks and got into his own vehicle. Steinert made a mental note of the make, color, and license plate number.

Diego's car pulled out, followed by Steinert. While following for about ten minutes, Steinert twice had to risk a traffic ticket in running a changing stop light.

Diego finally stopped the car in front of a café and then got out while Steinert parked about six cars ahead of his. He followed Diego into the café.

The café was crowded with early morning breakfasters on their way to work. Steinert was confident that Gonzales had taken no notice of him and sat at a table not too far from where Gonzales had seated himself. Another man was already waiting at Gonzales's table. Steinert strained to hear what the men were saying, but the café was noisy, and he could only make out unintelligible sounds.

Steinert ordered a cup of coffee and a roll. He watched as the two men spoke animatedly to each other, apparently over something important enough to be arguing this early in the morning.

Thirty minutes later, the other man got up and left, carrying a large bag of sandwiches and coffee to go, followed by Diego a few minutes later. Steinert followed Diego to the university, where Diego entered the archeology building, watched by Steinert.

Diego had continued working at the school in order to keep from arousing suspicion, and it gave him access to equipment he might need in the future regarding the cylinder. Besides, if the cylinder came to no real gain, this was the only source of income Diego had.

Steinert hung around the grounds outside the building the entire day. This time he'd brought a book to read, and though it was not an especially good one, it helped pass the time as he waited for Diego to emerge and return to his car.

Later in the afternoon, Diego walked out of the building and left for home, followed by Steinert. The rest of Steinert's evening was spent uneventfully, sitting in his car outside Diego's apartment, occasionally munching on a sandwich or piece of fruit that he purchased from a store down the block. At ten that evening, he'd had enough and went back to his hotel room feeling depressed that this day had apparently been wasted. The next day he intended to follow Gonzales again. If nothing of importance occurred, he would have to rethink his ideas on how to handle the situation. Time was of the essence, but for now, sleep seemed more important.

The next morning followed the same script as the day before. Steinert followed Diego into the same café, and Diego sat at a table with the same man. This time, Steinert made certain to sit at a table close enough to catch a word or two of their conversation. Once again, they appeared to argue over some matter, and Steinert thought he overheard Gonzales say the name "Carter," but he wasn't sure whether it was just wishful thinking.

The other man ate a small breakfast, ordered some food to go, and again left with a large bag of sandwiches and coffee.

Steinert wondered, *Whom is he buying sandwiches for, two days in a row?* He decided to change tactics and follow the other man. Steinert watched as the man got into a car across the street from the café. Steinert followed with his car.

The man's car entered the Sierra district of town, and Steinert's spirits lifted. Perhaps this would lead to something, since Don's coded message had been the word "sierra". He watched as the car was parked and the man went into a three-story, run-down apartment building. Steinert parked his car and followed the man inside. If nothing was there, it didn't matter. But if this was important, it would mean trouble, and Steinert knew he'd have to come up with a plan. He had to find out which apartment the man went into and what was inside.

The man used a key to enter apartment 202 as Steinert watched from around a corner, only a few feet away. Steinert decided that he needed time to think about his next move. Feeling vulnerable, he walked quietly back down to his car and sat there, trying to work on some sort of strategy.

Only a few minutes had passed when Steinert saw the man leave the building without the package of food. There would be only one way for an older man to respond if indeed the food was meant for Don; he must outsmart them. He sat for a few more minutes in the parked car and made his plan. He must act swiftly and boldly. He got out of his car and walked back into the building.

Meanwhile, inside the small room that was the entire apartment, Don sat on an old wooden, frame bed with his right wrist handcuffed to the headboard. Big, dumb Hernando sat on a couch next to Don and watched an old Western on a black-and-white TV while eating one of the sandwiches that Jose Marin had delivered.

These past days had been an eternity for Don. He'd been dying for a cigarette, but both Alcalde and Hernando seemed to enjoy watching him suffer as they occasionally smoked themselves. Don rationalized that maybe when this ordeal was over, his forced cold turkey would finally make him kick the habit about which Diane was always nagging him—and rightly so, he thought. The most exciting thing that had ever happened to him, and perhaps to anyone, was the discovery of the cylinder, and yet here he was, in a place where he could do nothing except make small talk with a moron and where the most exciting part of the day was when he could eat a sandwich or was given permission to go to the bathroom to relieve himself. The only other moments that caught his interest were when Marin would occasionally inform Hernando of the progress of the negotiations, as told to Marin by Mendez. It seemed to Marin that these negotiations were taking far longer than expected, and he was getting antsy.

Don's thoughts were constantly on how to escape and find the cylinder. Once in a while he thought of how he could kill or mangle Diego if he ever got his hands on him, although inwardly Don doubted that he could actually do so. As a defense mechanism, he tried to be friendly to Hernando and Alcalde, the two who took turns watching Don round the clock. Marin would appear every so often with food, and sometimes a newspaper, but he rarely stayed for more than a few minutes. He discussed the situation briefly with either Hernando or Alcalde, sometimes in the only other room in the apartment, the bathroom. Don's captors would occasionally unlock the handcuffs to allow him to go to the toilet. The bathroom window was securely boarded up, and they would never allow the door to be completely closed. Each man carried at least one gun and one knife and appeared ready and able to use either one.

The longer his captivity, the more obsessed Don became in planning and scheming ways of escape, an escape that very often included the killing and dismemberment of Jose Marin, and especially Francisco Alcalde and Hernando, for making him grovel and feel more helpless than he had ever thought was possible. He'd never felt nearly so humiliated and had certainly never been held imprisoned before, placed in a totally subservient position. When they were alone, he and Hernando, Don couldn't shake the sickening feeling that the big, ugly dumb-ox stared at him too much, too … too intimately. Don would look away, praying to God that the filthy animal wouldn't make advances on him. If he did, Don vowed to fight to the death, if need be, before he would allow himself to be violated by some perverted slob.

Don lay passively on the bed, finishing a sandwich, when a knock was heard at the door. Hernando immediately rose from the chair and went to the door, asking, "Who's there?"

Anton Steinert, standing on the opposite side of the closed door and sounding as self-assured as he could, answered in Spanish, "My name is Karl Grosz, and I was sent here by Diego Gonzales. I must speak with Don Carter." Steinert felt confident that if Don wasn't there, he would be able to talk his way out of the situation as simply an honest mistake. Or maybe he'd be directed to where Don actually was.

Hernando stood by the door, confused. "Why didn't anyone tell me you were coming?"

"I just left Diego. I'm an expert archeologist and must have some questions answered. If you don't allow me to speak with him right now, the whole project will be jeopardized."

Don's heart began to race. Incredibly, the voice was Steinert's! Don knew he mustn't show that he knew the man on the other side of the door, and so he kept still outwardly while inwardly his body became electric.

Hernando still didn't know what to do. He was aware that he was known as having a small brain in a large body and wasn't usually put in a position of making decisions. He opened the door a crack and peeked out at Steinert, who appeared to be nothing more than a scientific-minded old man with spectacles. Judging that there would be no trouble, Hernando opened the door and faced Steinert. Steinert remained uncertain as to the number of persons inside the room.

"Come in."

Steinert stepped into the room and immediately saw Don with his wrist handcuffed to the bed. The two men tried their best to appear nonchalant even though both were extremely anxious. Steinert played his role first.

"Ah, you must be Mr. Carter."

Don remained silent while trying to look as downtrodden as possible.

Steinert thought quickly and said, "I need some information about the cylinder from you, Mr. Carter, but—" he turned to Hernando. "He'll have to be able to write and make some drawings, so you'll have to open the handcuffs. You don't think he'll try to escape, do you?"

"It's okay. I uncuff him when he has to go to the toilet, but don't worry. I got all the protection I need." Hernando reached behind his back and under his shirt and pulled out a pistol. "So I don't think our little American will try anything funny, will you? Or we might have to do a little pruning!" Hernando roared with laughter at the sound of his own inside joke.

Don replied submissively, "You'll get no trouble from me."

Hernando tossed the key onto the bed. Don picked up the key and, with his free left hand, unlocked his right hand from the cuffs and placed the key back on the bed. It was a routine that had been repeated many times before.

Hernando stood out of reach, near the door, while Don, rubbing his sore right wrist, walked over to a small table where Steinert had moved two folding chairs.

Steinert asked Don to be seated and pulled out a piece of paper on which he would pretend to write answers to his questions. Instead, Steinert quickly scribbled the words in English, "Must escape soon."

Both men knew that the longer they waited the more probable it became that someone would return. Steinert knew the kind of men they were dealing with and believed that both their lives were in imminent danger.

Steinert began to make small talk about the cylinder, asking Don to describe how he found it and casually made notes on the paper. He then turned to Hernando and said, "Excuse me, but I need to use the toilet."

Hernando pointed toward the bathroom door and replied, "Over there."

Steinert surveyed the room as he walked toward the bathroom. He knew he must find some possible way for their escape. Maybe he would spot something that could be used as a weapon. He entered the bathroom and closed the door behind him. He noticed that the window was tightly boarded up, and he could see nothing that could be used as a weapon. Time was running out, and Steinert knew he must make his move now. He flushed the toilet, waited a few seconds, and walked out. Turning to Hernando, he asked, "My friend, do you have anything to drink in this place?"

"Only water or some whiskey."

"Whiskey, thank you."

Hernando took a half-empty liter of whiskey from a cabinet. He handed Steinert a glass, and Steinert poured a small amount into it.

"Leave the bottle, if you don't mind," Steinert said.

Hernando backed away from them while Steinert pretended to talk about some technical points while writing on the paper. At one point he wrote, "Go to toilet and distract him."

Don turned to Hernando and said, "I have to use the toilet."

Hernando nodded and backed away from the bathroom door, watching every move Don made. Hernando's hand was behind his back which represented a subtle warning for Don not to try anything stupid. As usual, the door would only be allowed to close halfway.

Inside the bathroom Don could feel his heart starting to pound. Perspiration began to bead up on his forehead. He thought, *distract Hernando, but how? What kind of distraction? Something to get Hernando to take notice of me in here?* Don looked at the open door and then decided to kick the door closed with his foot.

The slamming door caught Hernando by surprise. He instinctively grabbed for his gun, quickly strode to the door, and opened it. The water in the sink was running, and Don was pretending to wash his hands.

"What are you doing?" Hernando shouted, gun in hand.

Don turned to Hernando and replied, "I needed more room, and the door was in my way."

Hernando had no more time to reply. Steinert had already grabbed the whiskey bottle by its neck and had it raised over his shoulder, standing directly behind Hernando. Hernando began to order Don out of the bathroom. Then a glancing blow from the whiskey bottle stung Hernando on the side of his head. Hernando wheeled around and fell backward onto the toilet bowl, but he was only momentarily stunned, and the gun was still clutched tightly in his hand. He began to raise the gun at Steinert, who was still holding the unbroken bottle in his hand. Don grabbed for the gun and pushed Hernando's arm as a shot rang out, entering the wall above the bathtub. Don struggled for the gun while standing over Hernando, who, although stunned, was still extremely strong. Steinert grabbed the neck of the bottle with both hands and, with all the strength he could summon, swung a blow that landed across Hernando's right cheekbone and nose, shattering the bottle. A mixture of blood, whiskey, and glass covered Hernando's face and chest as his body slumped to the side and half into the bathtub, unconscious.

Don shoved Hernando the rest of the way into the tub. He looked at Steinert, who was still holding the broken neck of the bottle in his hand, and exclaimed in English, "Thank God you're here! How'd you find me?"

"No time for that. We leave or we are dead men." Steinert threw the bottle neck onto the floor, and the two men stepped quickly out of the bathroom. Steinert stopped suddenly just as Don reached the apartment door.

"Wait," he called to Don. He turned, entered the bathroom, and picked up the gun that lay on the floor. Returning to Don, he said, "We might need this."

Don nodded and opened the door. Don ran down the flight of stairs, with Steinert lagging behind. Steinert directed Don to his car, which was parked down the block. They jumped into the car and sped off, with Steinert driving, panting furiously and leaning over to rub his left foot.

Don was also breathing heavily, but being decades younger, he quickly caught his breath.

The adrenalin was still flowing as they drove toward Steinert's hotel room. Don noticed Steinert's hand bleeding as it tightly gripped the steering wheel.

"Your hand. Is it bad?"

Steinert hadn't realized that the bottle he'd shattered across Hernando's face had also cut his own hand. He gave a quick diagnosis. "I will be fine. Let us worry about getting you safely out of this place."

Don replied sharply, his voice full of determination. "Not without that cylinder."

"What happened?"

Don related the story of how they had forced him to talk.

Steinert shook his head. "These are brutal men, willing to do anything for profit. Maybe this cylinder is not worth risking your life. Besides, what can the two of us do against them? Maybe it is time to go to the authorities."

Don understood the risks involved, but Steinert hadn't witnessed the power of the cylinder. He desperately needed to find it, even at the risk of his own life, and he responded with authority. "If we do, we'll never see the cylinder again. They intend to sell it to the highest bidder, and it could even wind up in Russian hands. But if we act now, and I mean right now, before they find Hernando and learn that I'm missing, we still have a chance to get it. Besides, I wouldn't trust the authorities around here."

"But how can we find it?"

"We drive straight to Diego Gonzales. He knows where it is, and we'll force him to tell us."

Steinert felt Don was letting his emotions rule his mind and said, "Bitte. You are going too fast. First, do you know where Gonzales is right now? Second, how do we capture him? Third, how do we make him talk and still have time to get the cylinder? What if it is being guarded?"

Don had thought about many of these questions while in captivity. "Look, I know where Diego usually is at this time of day, which is in the office. You'll go in and give some fake name and tell him that you've been secretly sent by the United States to speak with him about negotiations and that he must leave with you immediately. I'll be waiting for you in the car, with the gun."

"You will not be able to use it. We know it, and your friend probably knows it too. I will keep the gun. I most definitely will be able to kill your friend, if it comes to that."

Steinert's voice had a quality in it that Don had never heard before. He sounded too blasé about being able to kill another person. But Don dismissed this thought, rationalizing that the ordeal must have taken its toll on Steinert.

"Okay, you hold the gun. Diego would probably be more fearful of a stranger."

Steinert unexpectedly stopped the car in front of a hardware store. "Wait here," he said as he opened the door and got out.

Don stuck his head out the window and called out to Steinert, "Where are you going?"

Steinert looked back and responded, "I will be a few minutes." Steinert entered the hardware store and disappeared from sight.

Don was now allowed to be by himself for the first time in seven days, and sitting quietly by himself gave him the opportunity for a reawakening of senses and emotions that would normally have passed unnoticed by him. He breathed in deeply and smelled the crisp, clean freshness of the air. He heard the chirping of birds and people engaged in normal, everyday conversation, and he felt free. Free to do any damn thing he pleased. He stuck his head out of the window and felt the warmth of the sun on his face. And then, for reasons unknown to him, his eyes began to mist, and he began to breathe in and out in very small breaths. He couldn't explain the unfamiliar reflex that occurred, but he knew he was crying. He'd often seen others cry like this. Was it joy? Was it sorrow? Was it the release of the bottled-up pressures of these past days? It didn't matter. His life was his own once again, and Don was determined to make the most of it. There remained so much unfinished business he felt compelled to attend to. He wiped his eyes, slightly embarrassed at having cried, even though no one had seen him.

God, he thought. *I could really use a smoke.* But he knew that Steinert only smoked a pipe. Maybe they'd be able to stop somewhere on the way, but he doubted Steinert would want to stop again merely to assuage his craving for nicotine.

Minutes later, Steinert emerged from the store carrying a shovel, clothesline, knife, and heavy tape. He opened the trunk, threw all the items in, slammed the trunk closed, and got back into the car.

"What do we need those things for?" Don asked.

Steinert started the car and looked at Don. "We might need them to help your friend tell us what we must know."

Don was too tired to pursue the issue.

CHAPTER 17

TEN MINUTES LATER, STEINERT'S car approached the university. They decided that if Diego was there and was willing to go with Steinert, Don should hide in the trunk, as they knew that seeing Don would scare Diego away. Don had described how Steinert would be able to find Diego in one of the buildings across the street. Don got into the trunk, and Steinert pulled up to the building.

Steinert got out and entered the building. Several minutes later, he returned and walked by the trunk, inconspicuously saying, "He is not there. I will drive and release you by some dumpsters."

Several minutes later, Don was inside the car and asked, "What happened?"

"He is over at a dig outside Maleta."

"I know the site."

The drive to Maleta gave them time to discuss recent events. Steinert asked, "Do you realize how much trouble we may get in?"

Don responded casually, "I've already seen some of it."

"But what if your friend refuses to talk? What do we do with him?"

Don sensed that Steinert was attempting to make a point rather than ask a question, and he apprehensively replied, "What do you suggest we do?"

"You understand that your friend will not tell us where the cylinder is hidden simply because we are asking. We might have to act swiftly and decisively, and you will have to trust my judgment in this matter."

Don nodded his head in agreement and said, "I understand."

"I am not sure you do. This is, or at least was, a friend of yours. Some unpleasantries may be involved in this affair."

Don understood what Steinert meant. He'd seen countless movies depicting a myriad of ways to make someone reveal their secrets, and he knew there was no way that he himself would be able to torture Diego into telling where the cylinder was. He looked at the gentle, elderly professor driving the car and thought that maybe they were getting in too deeply. This old man would never be able to make Diego talk. Diego was far too street-wise to be tricked into talking, and if he did, his accomplices would do far worse to him than he and Steinert ever could. Doubts began to settle in. Diego would never talk, and they were driving to Maleta for nothing. Still, Don felt he had to ask if Steinert had some kind of plan, some way to make Diego talk. Even killing Diego would do no good. Dejectedly, he asked Steinert what he intended to do.

Steinert replied with an uncharacteristic icy tone in his voice, "We will do whatever it is we have to do. It will be up to your friend."

Sensing the doubt in Don, Steinert decided to change the subject. "How certain are you of the value of the cylinder? Do you still believe it to be an alien object?"

"You received my package. What did you find out?"

"Nothing conclusive, but some very intriguing things. Those dots represent a star chart with stellar patterns as they would have appeared four thousand years ago."

Don perked up and said, "No kidding? Four thousand years ago? Do you suppose this means that there were aliens here four thousand years ago?"

"If they were actually here, it might mean that."

"What about the tape?"

"The tape revealed signals that repeated the same thing over and over again in an ancient language resembling Quechua, something like, 'People able to enter receive God.'"

Don became visibly excited by this revelation and asked, "Are you certain of this?"

"Fairly sure. But its exact meaning is unclear."

"What's your best guess?"

"If … and it is still a big if … if there were aliens in Peru four thousand years ago, these aliens may have left information for some future generation who would develop the technology to make use of that information. Maybe in the ancient Quechua language, God was synonymous with the universe or some similar word denoting vast information within."

Don mulled over Steinert's words. "Right. The ancient Peruvians didn't even have a true written language."

"And perhaps these aliens could have stayed long enough to have had some impact on the primitive people who inhabited the area. Maybe these aliens were the ones who influenced the building of pyramids, not some Egyptian who happened to float his way to Peru."

Only half joking, Don said, "You mean that maybe all those stories about ancient space travelers might not be phony after all?"

"At this point, who can say? There are, of course, those who believe that Peru was once indeed host to ancient space visitors."

"You mean like the book *Ancient Astronauts?*"

"Yes, Gallagher's book. He cites evidence of ancient Inca drawings purportedly showing rockets and space machines."

"And what about Von Doniken's *Chariots of the Gods?*" Don asked. "It's gotten a lot of play back in the States."

"Although I have not personally visited the Lines of Nazca that he writes about, from photographs I have seen of them it is evident that the giant land drawings they made, including a condor, a monkey, a hummingbird, and a spider, were never meant to be viewed from the ground. Some of these lines that they etched into the dry soil are miles long and can only be appreciated from the air. Von Doniken even says that some of the lines were actually a prehistoric airfield."

"You believe any of that? Most people believe, as I do, that these lines were either religious in nature or related to calendar making."

Steinert laughed. "I know it sounds a bit verruckt—crazy—but now, who knows? We might be able to tell much more if we had that cylinder. This could be the most important find in the history of mankind … although with a very big if."

"I agree, and I've had time to think about a lot of things, including my so-called friend, Diego. He was willing to let them do whatever they wanted with me. You can't imagine the humiliation and terror I felt."

Steinert replied simply, "Yes, I can."

"How could you? They were willing to cut my genitals off if I didn't talk."

"I have seen worse."

The statement piqued Don's interest. "What do you mean?"

Steinert, unaccustomed to letting his guard down regarding his past, waved his hand. "Some other time. It is a long story. Right now we must decide if we are willing to risk our lives and do whatever is necessary to get that cylinder. You are prepared for this?"

The information given to Don about the dots and the tape renewed his desire to find the cylinder. "I hate those sons of bitches. I'm ready. I want that cylinder more than anything in the world right now."

"I feel the same way. I have not been this excited about anything in my entire life."

Don realized that they were practically at the site and instructed Steinert to slow down. "Pull the car off the side of the road. The site is just up ahead around that turn and down into a meadow. You should be able to see several people working. Diego is a thin—"

Steinert interrupted him. "Already I know what he looks like. That is how I found you, by following him. I think you should hide in the trunk again until I return with Gonzales. I will signal for you to come out at the appropriate time."

They got out of the car, and Don opened the trunk and climbed in. Steinert closed the trunk hood without locking it, and Don held it down from the inside so that it gave the appearance of being closed.

Steinert began the short walk toward the site. He walked uphill a short distance and then downhill for a few more yards. Just ahead, working at the site, were several persons, including Diego Gonzales. Steinert felt quite comfortable here among such familiar sights and sounds. He could see men working on a mound that they were excavating for pieces of pottery called shards, which, when pieced together, would reveal much about the society that made the pottery. The men were busy using the tools of the excavator, such as spades and pickaxes for digging, sifting screens for separating the artifacts from the loose soil material, and soft brushes and probes for the delicate work of cleaning away dirt before the removal of artifacts from the ground.

Steinert watched a boy carry a pail filled with dirt to be dumped in an area away from the site, and he knew the work being done here was similar to that of archeologists throughout the world. Expert diggers, like Diego, would search for artifacts, and when unique objects were found, they would be photographed, drawn, and described in a special record book. Artifacts were then sorted, cleaned, and labeled with waterproof ink. Fragile objects were wrapped in soft tissue or cotton wool and then packed in large crates. Objects were then taken to a museum or university, where they would be exposed to further examination by experts such as Anton Steinert. At the end of a digging season, the government of a country might take more than half of what had been found for its museums. Any unique objects would certainly belong to the government, although the archeologist would be allowed to keep his own records, photos, and descriptions.

Steinert approached a table where Diego was sitting and cleaning an artifact of pottery that had been found that afternoon.

"Mr. Gonzales?" he asked in Spanish.

Diego looked up at the elderly gentleman standing in front of his table. "Yes. What can I do for you?"

"May I talk with you a moment? I have a message of, let us say, high priority."

Diego detected a bit of mystery in the old man's voice and replied apprehensively, "Concerning what?"

Steinert leaned in closer to Diego and said in a softer voice, "A certain cylinder that my government, the United States, seems to be highly interested in."

Diego looked around and surveyed the area. Seeing that the old man was alone and that they weren't isolated enough from his coworkers, he said, "We can't talk here."

"That's what I thought. I have a car up the road. I think you'd better make up some excuse to leave. Much is at stake."

Diego, sensing that the true meaning was money, lots of it, immediately rose from his chair and walked over to another worker, said something to him, and then returned to Steinert. "I told him I was needed back at the university and that you were giving me a ride."

They walked up the slope to the road, heading for the car. Steinert had tucked Hernando's gun under his jacket and knew he must avoid using it at all costs, at least until they got far enough away not to be heard. They got into the car, Steinert turned the car around and headed back toward Lima.

Diego was brimming with excitement and began speaking rapid-fire to Steinert. "When did you get here? Where's Marin right now? How much—"

Steinert put his hand up toward Diego and said, "In due time. In due time you'll know everything."

Diego nodded, feeling a little embarrassed with the realization that he should have known that these negotiations would indeed require time and delicate actions. He must be patient, he told himself.

Steinert turned off the main road and onto a dirt road that Diego knew led to no place in particular. Puzzled, he asked, "Where are you going? This road leads to nowhere."

"I know. We're meeting someone important up this road."

Diego nodded. "I understand. We must be very secretive about this."

Steinert drove a few more miles until he pulled off the dirt road and into a clump of trees. He looked at Diego and said, "We get out here."

Diego surveyed the isolated surroundings and replied, somewhat surprised, "Here?"

"This is the place."

The two men opened their doors and got out of the car. Steinert walked to the back of the car and opened the trunk while Diego stood leaning on the front fender of the vehicle, watching Steinert.

Don had been waiting in the trunk nervously and yet also excitedly, as he couldn't wait to see the expression on Diego's face when he got out of the trunk.

Diego was shocked and stood up straight as he saw Don climb out of the trunk.

Don stood up and faced Diego with an expressionless face.

Diego began to stammer, "Don …wha … what's going on?"

"Surprised to see me, eh, Diego? Now it's your turn to talk, and we mean right now."

Sensing the threat in Don's voice, Diego became belligerent. "Or what? What will you do, kill me? You're no killer, and you know it."

Steinert had been casually walking toward the front of the car, behind Diego, who was still facing the rear of the car where Don stood. The gun was now drawn and aimed at Diego's back. Steinert then responded to Diego, saying very coldly, "But I am."

Diego whirled around to face Steinert and immediately saw the gun. "Who are you?"

"It doesn't matter. We've already taken care of your friend, the big, ugly one, and I intend to either get the cylinder back or take revenge on you for my friend's inconveniences. Tell us where the cylinder can be found and live. Refuse, and I will kill you."

Don was surprised at how convincing Steinert appeared. *What a great actor,* he thought. But if Diego called his bluff, then what?

Diego raised his chin defiantly and said, "I don't believe you. You won't kill me. You need my information."

Steinert replied sternly. "But if we don't get it now, we lose the cylinder no matter what. Once your friends find out that Don is missing, they'll hide the cylinder in a different location and be on their guard from that moment on. The time for us to strike is now, and only now. You become useless to us in just a short while."

Diego, still unsure of this old man's intentions, began to work on Don's sympathies. "Don, you're not a killer. I know you won't let him do anything stupid. I was foolish to allow them to trick me into helping them with the cylinder thing. I never meant you any harm. Believe me, not the least bit of harm."

Don hesitated before answering, knowing that he must try his best to continue with Steinert's charade and act as tough as he could. But he felt that any lie he told Diego wouldn't be believed.

Steinert, sensing Don's dilemma, began to speak again with that same convincing tone. "Mr. Gonzales, I'm the one with the gun. Your friend cannot stop me from shooting you here and now, so I think you have no choice but to tell us where it is."

Diego tried reasoning with the old man. "If you shoot me, you'll never know where it is, and you'll both become murderers. Is that what you want? To spend the rest of your lives in jail or executed?"

Steinert had heard enough talk and knew it was time for them to act. Still pointing the gun directly at Diego, he told Don to retrieve the tools and rope from the trunk.

Don did so, realizing that he would now have his answer to the question of what Steinert intended to do with these things. Don approached Steinert carrying the shovel, rope, tape, and knife in his hands.

Steinert ordered, "Now the three of us will take a small walk deeper into those shrubs." He motioned with the gun for Diego to begin moving.

After walking about one hundred feet, Steinert ordered Diego to stop and lie down on the ground, face down, with his hands behind his back.

Diego stared at the gun in Steinert's hand, mumbled something barely audible, and got down on his stomach, moving slowly.

Steinert turned to Don. "Cut a three-foot piece of rope and tie his wrists together with it."

Don complied with the instructions as he heard Steinert continue, "Tie it well with several knots, and then tie his ankles together in a similar manner."

After these things were accomplished, Steinert walked closer to Don and handed him the gun. Don had never held a gun before and deliberately kept his finger away from the trigger and pointed the gun toward the sky.

Steinert then cut another length of rope and, bending Diego's legs at the knees and toward his tied wrists, tied the ankles to the wrists, placing Diego in an uncomfortable position.

Diego shouted, "What are you doing?"

"Sei still!" Steinert demanded in German.

Steinert turned to Don. "Start digging a hole from here to here." With his hand, Steinert pointed out a rectangle about four feet by two feet in size. "Dig it about two feet deep."

Using the shovel, Don began to dig the hole in the soft topsoil, piling the dirt on the side of the hole.

For the first time, Diego began to truly worry about his predicament. Being hog-tied and unable to move made him think about his options.

But Steinert, anticipating that Diego must now have become more concerned with this situation, knelt down next to Diego and said softly, businesslike, "You have three possible responses to my question. One is no response. Two is to lie. Three is to tell us the truth. I leave this entirely in your hands. It's your decision whether you live or die a painfully slow death. This hole will become your grave if you lie to us or do not respond. If you tell the truth, you'll be free once again."

Before Diego could begin to fully understand what the old man meant, Steinert looked up at Don and asked him to help roll Diego into the now-completed hole. They began doing so while Diego spat out several curses, which included damning their mothers. They rolled Diego onto his back and onto his stomach again and into the bottom of the two-foot-deep hole. Diego's mouth had picked up some dirt, and he attempted to spit it out. He then turned his head to the side to keep the dirt out of his mouth and eyes in the shallow would-be grave.

He could barely see the two men, but he began to work on Don's emotions once again. "Don, are you going to let him shoot me? Have you gone crazy? Have you become a murderer?" Diego had lost much of his belligerence. His voice had more of a pleading quality to it, a quality that Diego himself was unfamiliar with in his own voice.

Don remained silent, not knowing what to expect from Steinert.

Steinert again began to speak. "I'll ask you once and only once where the cylinder is. We have no more time left. Don and I must make our escape from your men either with or without the cylinder. In exactly one minute, I'm going to bury you up to your neck and place tape over your mouth so securely that you will have no chance of speaking or shouting again. Even if you could shout, there is no one within miles of here. Anyone passing on the dirt road would never know of your existence. If you tell the truth and we find the cylinder, we'll free you in only a matter of hours, either in person or by notifying someone where to find you. If you lie to us, we won't know it until we go wherever it is you send us, and we might even be killed. Then you'll lie here for the next few days with no food or water. Only the animals and insects will know your presence, and they will surely appreciate it. Your head will become a great meal for them. Your body will have everything that crawls in the dirt feeding on it. I doubt you'll last more than two days. Death will be slow and painful. And it will be certain unless you tell the truth. You'll have no decent burial. You're buried so shallow that even some archeologists of the future won't find enough of you to bring back to the lab. You now have one minute to contemplate your future while we cover you with dirt."

Diego lay motionless while trying to grasp the full import of his predicament.

Don picked up the shovel and began to slowly cover Diego's back with dirt. He was relieved that Steinert wasn't being forced to shoot Diego. Don thought that this idea was absolutely brilliant. Diego's life was truly in his own hands now. If he chose to die, it was his own fault. Don rationalized that Diego's death would be more a form of suicide than murder.

Diego could feel the cold and damp dirt landing on his back, hands, and bent legs. He was extremely uncomfortable and began to rock from side to side. The dirt continued to cover him, and soon the rocking became impossible. Only Diego's head stuck out of the dirt. He couldn't move anything at this point, and a feeling of desperation began to take hold of him.

Again, Steinert was the one to speak, slowly and deliberately. "Once I've placed the tape on your mouth, it won't be removed. We leave immediately for the destination you send us. You have one chance to save yourself. I ask you, Diego Gonzales, where is the cylinder?"

Diego had never known such terror. The fear of animals and insects gnawing at his face was too much for him. Besides, he reasoned, if he lived he'd be able to fight back at some later time and destroy these two Americans. That would be pleasure, indeed! But Diego didn't want to lie here in this hole for even one more minute and hoped to bargain his way out of his predicament immediately. "Look, I'll tell you where it is, but you have to promise to let me out of this hole now!"

Steinert responded firmly. "No deals. Just tell us where it is. You have thirty seconds left."

Steinert reached for the tape that had been lying on the ground and ripped off about two feet of the two-inch-wide tape, making a loud, scratchy sound that Diego plainly recognized.

"Ten seconds left and then we must go," Steinert said callously. He began to bring the tape closer.

Fearing the finality that a taped mouth represented, Diego blurted out, "I'll tell you where it is, but I beg you, once I do, don't leave me here."

"Start talking," Steinert demanded.

"It's buried under the floorboards in a deserted warehouse at 316 Entrada Street."

"How will we know which boards to tear up?"

"There are some new nails holding down the boards. They're located about ten feet from the rear door, about five feet from the side wall. Please, get me out of this hole. I'm begging you."

Don, with mixed emotions, looked at Steinert quizzically, but Steinert simply crouched down and wrapped the tape around Diego's mouth until his pleadings became unintelligible, muffled sounds. Steinert wrapped the tape all around to the back of Diego's head, where the ends of the tape overlapped.

Diego squirmed and continued to attempt to shout through the tape, but only barely audible sounds emerged.

Steinert looked down at Diego and spoke directly at him, businesslike. "Diego Gonzales, if you've told us the truth, you'll be out of here sooner than you think."

Steinert then stepped closer to Don, sympathizing with what he must be feeling, and put his arm on Don's shoulder, guiding him away. "Come along. Don't look back. Just turn and go. If he's told the truth, he'll be all right."

Don wasn't sure of his own emotions. Not quite out of earshot from Diego, Don said, "I don't think I have the stomach for this, Anton, I really don't."

"You're doing just fine," he said as they continued to walk away from Diego.

But Diego had heard the name "Anton" and thought, *So the old man was Anton Steinert from New York.* Diego vowed revenge.

The two men reached the car. Don, still having second thoughts, asked in English, "Can we really leave him here?"

"Would Diego have saved you if they chose to maim or kill you?"

Don thought for a moment, biting a nail. "I don't know. I'd like to believe that he would have."

"Well, not to worry. We are not murderers. Either way, we will contact the police and they will find him—unless, of course, it is a trap and we are both dead."

Don was relieved. But he didn't know that Steinert was lying to him in order to calm his nerves. Steinert knew the kind of men he was dealing with and perceived Diego Gonzales as an enemy, a person to be feared. Gonzales's release might help the authorities or the Gente locate himself and Don. No, Diego Gonzales was a doomed man. He deserved whatever fate befell him, and that fate was sealed, as far as Steinert was concerned.

No one but Steinert could know that the subject of death was on his mind far more than it should have been. Nor could anyone have known how little he feared his own death, a condition brought about by a life whose experiences had differed greatly from the average person's. Steinert understood that the unknown realm of death fascinated the average mortal, who, due to his fear of it, insulated himself against it as much as possible, very often avoiding the topic as being too morbid and depressing to discuss. He knew that many people took comfort in the belief of an afterlife, not unlike the beliefs of the Inca ruler, Atahualpa, but rarely did any of them bear witness, as he had, to the actual instant of death, the exact moment that separates life from death. Most cushioned themselves emotionally against the death of others in preparation for the day they, too, must die.

But Anton Steinert wasn't your average person. The events of the Second World War had greatly anesthetized him against death, especially as it related to those whom he believed deserved to die. For decades he'd lived with his own recurring nightmare, attempting to relegate solely to his dreams the deaths of all the innocent people he had helped exterminate. But as much as he tried, he couldn't escape the memories. During his waking hours he would immerse himself in his work in a futile attempt to blot out those indelible memories of that brief but traumatic time. But always, the memories lingered. Occasionally, a certain sound, scent, or image would arouse the suppressed recollections of those baneful events, followed by a deep sense of guilt at having participated in the supreme injustices that can be dealt to human beings by a member of their own species. Steinert persistently rationalized that he had been compelled to obey military orders when he committed his acts, and yet he was perpetually filled with remorse. He loathed those who could willfully transgress and remain unremorseful. He believed those people had, in effect, sentenced themselves to death. He had no compassion for those who voluntarily chose to perform evil deeds. Steinert believed Gonzales had made his choice and, therefore, deserved a fate similar to the one Gonzales would have allowed Don to suffer. Thus, Steinert felt, Gonzales had condemned himself to a justifiable execution.

The men got into the car and drove off. Steinert asked, "You know your friend. Do you think he told the truth?"

"Yes, I do. It's a good thing he thought you were some kind of secret agent or something. You even had me fooled. How were you able to be so cool about this?"

For a moment, Steinert almost told the story he hadn't told anyone in over forty years, but he changed his mind. "Just a natural actor, I guess," he said with a sad smile as he thrust his unlit pipe into his mouth.

Meanwhile, Jose Marin, sandwiches and coffee in hand, opened the door to apartment 202. He began saying, "Hernando, I have your ..."

Then he noticed the empty pair of handcuffs dangling from the bed and no Hernando or Carter in sight. He dropped the bag, ran into the bathroom, and saw Hernando lying in the tub with dried blood caked all over his face and body and pieces of glass all over the place.

"Hernando!" he shouted. But Hernando was still unconscious. Marin reached for the knob to the shower and turned on the cold water. The spray of water shocked Hernando back to consciousness, and he began to move. Marin helped him out of the tub and into the main room, where Hernando fell onto a chair, still dazed and dripping wet.

"Fucking idiot," Marin barked. "What happened? Where is he?"

Hernando remembered the old man and the bottle. "An old man ... came to the door ... said he was sent by Gonzales."

Marin grabbed him by the collar, seething. "And you let him in? You stupid moron. They should have killed you so I wouldn't have to do it myself. Did you tell them where the cylinder is? Did you tell them?"

Hernando cowered. "No, Jose. I didn't tell them anything. He hit me with the bottle, and that's all I remember." Hernando now seethed. "When I get my hands on them ... they will pray for death. This time I'll use those pruning shears!"

"Later. Right now we have to make sure the cylinder is safe."

"I told you, I didn't tell them a thing."

"But we don't know who this man is, where he's from, or what he knows. We'd better get out of here as soon as possible. Get yourself cleaned up and change your clothes. Then we'll check out the cylinder, maybe move it somewhere else, just in case. I'll call Diego and Francisco and tell them to meet us there. We might need some help moving it."

Hernando felt for his gun behind his back and realized that he'd had it in the bathroom. "Where's my gun?"

"What?"

"My gun. Is it in the bathroom?"

Marin looked inside but saw no gun. He shouted angrily, "Did you think they were as stupid as you and left you with your gun? Get up and get going. We've got work to do now, fucking asshole."

CHAPTER 18

THE THREE DAYS HAD now passed with Diane receiving no call from Anton Steinert. She'd received the key to the locker, exactly as Steinert said she would. Steinert had instructed her to retrieve a package and take it to the State Department.

Time had passed at an incredibly slow pace as each day Diane anticipated contact from Steinert or Don himself. Hearing that Don's whereabouts were a mystery only emphasized how much she missed Don. The good times, the pleasant memories, kept creeping into her head. But as each day passed, she became increasingly worried about her husband. It was out of character for him to simply run off somewhere. She began to think and, under the circumstances, almost hope that his disappearance involved another woman. She mused that perhaps he had fallen in love with some sexy South American woman and run off with her.

The more Diane worried, the more she knew that she still loved Don, maybe enough to live with the fact that he might never be rich. If only she could get in touch with him and tell him how she felt.

Putting thoughts of Don aside, she knew she had to get over to Steinert's locker. She recalled how secretive he'd been about this matter and wondered why. *Maybe that's simply Steinert's way,* she thought.

The key had the number B189 on it with the note telling her to go to Penn Station. She caught a taxi and, upon arrival there, took a while to locate the locker. The huge midtown terminal, situated below Madison Square Garden, connects the New York City subway system with several major train lines and is a miniature city in itself with countless shops and eating establishments. After asking directions, Diane needed about ten minutes to find her way to the correct gang of lockers. Once she found them, she inserted the key, opened the locker, and discovered a sealed manila envelope inside. Written on the front of the envelope was only the name "Diane." She stared at it for a few seconds and then placed it into her handbag, resisting the impulse to open it, feeling that whatever was inside should be examined in the privacy of her apartment.

Immediately upon returning home, she proceeded to tear open the envelope, finding a letter, a cassette tape, and a folded piece of paper labeled "Star Chart." Steinert's letter described the entire story concerning the cylinder. It included the possible translation of the tape and explained that the star chart indicated stellar patterns as they would have appeared four thousand years ago.

Diane scratched her head in bewilderment. Aliens? This was too surreal, but if Don and Steinert both thought this could be true, then who was she to dispute it?

The letter further instructed Diane to travel to the State Department in Washington, DC, and present the material only to a Mr. Charles Block. Steinert said that he would contact Block and tell him to expect Diane Carter's arrival. Block was instructed to then take whatever steps he felt necessary upon reviewing the information.

Diane didn't know what to make of Steinert's story regarding some strange cylinder and potential aliens, but at this point she frankly didn't care. Her only objective was the safe return of her husband, and if going to Washington would help, she would certainly go.

Diane caught the next airplane shuttle for Washington and, using the phone number that had been left by Steinert, contacted a secretary at the State Department and made an appointment to see Charles Block at four o'clock that same afternoon.

Block saw Diane right on schedule, as punctuality was his credo. He was a small man, fifty-two years old, practically bald, and with glasses. As Diane entered his office, Block instantly perked up, noticing how attractive she was. *Very sexy,* he thought.

"Come in," he said while motioning for Diane to sit in a chair facing his desk. "Dr. Steinert had told me to expect someone, but I hadn't realized she'd be so pretty."

Diane was used to this sort of patronizing reaction from men, especially those who knew they had no chance in the world of anything except conversation with her, and she took it in stride.

"Thank you, Mr. Block, but I'm here about my husband, Don Carter."

"And you must tell me all about this. Can I get you a cup of coffee, water, or something else? A cigarette, perhaps?"

"I'm fine, and I don't smoke."

"All right then, what can I do for you? Dr. Steinert was extremely vague about the purpose of your visit. He said he wasn't sure you'd even show up, but that if you did it would be extremely important. So why don't you tell me what you've got."

"First of all, as I said, it concerns my husband, who went to Peru for a five-month stay doing research at the University of Lima."

"And he didn't take you along with him?" Block said it with a wink. He loved playing these dirty-old-man roles.

"I work for an ad agency, and, actually, we were separated before he left."

Block thought to himself that if he had a wife who looked like her, he'd think of something better to do than to run off to Lima, of all places. But he could tell that she was seriously worried, and Block got down to business. He leaned across his desk toward Diane and spoke with a more serious tone. "All right, let's get to the problem. What is it that's wrong?"

"It seems my husband is—well, he might be missing."

"Might be missing? Don't you know?"

"He unexpectedly left a letter of resignation and said he was returning to New York."

"And he didn't?"

"No one, including his mother, knows where he is."

"How long has he been missing?"

"Almost a week."

"Maybe he hasn't arrived yet, or maybe he changed his mind and went somewhere for R and R, or—"

"Excuse me, but I know what you're going to say, that I should wait a while longer. But although I'm concerned and realize that in most cases he'd probably show up soon, this is apparently not your usual case. In fact, the reason I'm here at all is only indirectly related to Don. The real reason is this." She held out the package for Block to take.

"What's this?"

"Steinert meant it for you. Once you've read it, you'll understand why I'm here."

Puzzled, Block opened the package and began sifting through the material inside.

He read everything slowly and carefully, briefly examining the star chart and fingering the tape. After several minutes of total silence, he looked up at Diane.

"Do you believe this stuff? I mean, aliens? Are you sure Steinert hasn't been watching the tube too much?"

"I don't know what to make of it. I only know that my husband's disappearance is totally out of character and that Dr. Steinert is one of the most respected men in his field. If this letter you just read says that this may possibly be the truth, then I think you should act on it. After all, what if it really is the truth? And even if it's all fake or a hoax, you'll get credit for exposing it as such."

"Look. I'd love to help, but UFOs and aliens aren't my domain."

"I figured as much. But Steinert apparently felt that you would know the proper channels to go through. You could give the information to someone who can deal with this while helping me by working through your contacts to try to locate Don."

Block sat back in his chair and pondered her words. "I'll tell you what. I'll make some calls to the American embassy in Lima and see if they can come up with anything concerning your husband. I'll also find out whom to send this package to. They'll be able to determine the validity of this alien story for us once it gets to the proper department. How does that sound?"

"I'm relying on you, Mr. Block. I really don't know what else to do."

"I'll get going on this. But please, the second you hear from your husband—and hopefully it'll be soon—call me."

"I certainly will, and thank you." Diane offered her hand to Block as they both stood up. Diane turned and walked out of the room, watched admiringly by Block. *Pretty lady with a crazy story,* he thought.

Colonel Tom Rawlings had placed the report from Mendez next to a pile of other paperwork. It had been forty-eight hours since he'd seen Mendez, and some of Rawlings's aides were researching the credibility of Mendez and the astronomy professor, Solars. He'd pretty much forgotten about the ridiculous claim regarding alien creatures when another report came in that Rawlings believed was more than coincidence. The report came from a Charles Block at the State Department informing Rawlings that Block had received a strange story from a Diane Carter whose missing husband had found a certain cylindrical object in Lima, Peru.

Rawlings informed Block that this information was now deemed part of a top secret project and that Block was to give no further information to this Carter woman. Rawlings and his department would take over from here as this could be important to the security of the United States. Rawlings impressed upon Block the utmost need for total security and reminded Block that he must keep all dealings between himself and Block confidential.

Block, not really understanding or believing the need for such security, agreed to Rawlings's requests. Block figured that this was the way the cloak-and-dagger boys in the Pentagon worked. What Block didn't know was that Rawlings, putting two and two together, feared that this so-called cylinder might actually be, although improbably, an alien object and that he must beat the Russians to it. Who knew what information it might contain? It would be better to have it in US hands than the Reds'.

Over at the Pentagon, after Block's report was received and Rawlings had discussed it with several directors, it was concluded that contact should be made with Mendez in order to set up a meeting. Mendez had stated that only a few persons from each country would be allowed to view the object, and it was therefore decided that if Colonel Rawlings wanted to head this expedition, it was his project. The other directors didn't express it to Rawlings, but it was generally understood that Rawlings was a perfect choice because his position was one that could be vacated for an extended period of time. Also, no one else of similar authority appeared ready to go on what they believed would probably turn out to be a wild goose chase in, of all places, Peru.

Rawlings, on the other hand, jumped at the opportunity of going to Peru after years of boredom at his desk job. His first step would be to gather a crew of aides and scientific experts, who would have to verify the authenticity of the cylinder before any negotiations could take place.

Rawlings was prepared to face whatever challenges lay before him. No one knew the extent to which the battle-scarred Rawlings needed a victory. He ached for redemption far more than anyone had perceived, and no one could have realized that he was willing to sacrifice his life for it.

CHAPTER 19

On their way to the warehouse, Don and Steinert discussed possible plans, should they retrieve the cylinder, which included contacting the American Embassy and getting Don a new passport. They decided to play it by ear for now and leave their options open, depending upon the events that followed.

Forty-five minutes later, they arrived at the abandoned warehouse and parked the car. Don took the jack handle from the trunk of the car. "We might need this to pry up those boards."

They stepped inside the wooden warehouse through an old, creaky side door. Steinert still had Hernando's gun tucked inside his belt and cautiously placed his hand on the handle, as they couldn't be certain of what to expect inside.

Don said in a hushed voice, "I hope Diego told the truth. This place is giving me the creeps."

Steinert moved slowly toward the rear of the darkened warehouse, which was practically empty except for pieces of wooden crates and some empty cardboard boxes and other debris scattered about.

"Look." Steinert pointed. "There's the rear door."

They moved closer to the door as Don said, "Look for boards with new nails in them."

They slowly walked against the wall that Diego mentioned, looking downward at the floorboards, surveying the area from side to side.

Don pointed at a spot on the floor and yelled, "Over here."

Sure enough, shiny new nails held a few floorboards in place. The heads of the nails were protruding about a half inch from the wood.

"Pry them open," Steinert said.

Don knelt down on one knee and wedged the end of the jack handle between the boards in order to pry up the first one while Steinert looked over his shoulder. The wood made a creaking noise as it slowly lifted upward, dislodging the nails.

"That's one. I think I can pull the other one up by hand." Don placed his hands under the second board and yanked it upward in a rocking motion. The nails released, and the board loosened.

With anticipation, Steinert asked, "Do you see it?"

"I see the lead box." Don reached down and carefully lifted the lead box from below the floor.

"Is it heavy?"

"Heavy enough," Don said as he placed the box on the floor. "Here goes nothing." He lifted the cover and placed it next to the box, revealing the golden-colored cylinder. "So Diego told the truth after all."

Steinert moved in closer and bent over for a better look. The first glimpse of the cylinder made Steinert feel as he'd never felt before. Here, in this darkened, decrepit old warehouse, somewhere in Lima, was an object that he believed might actually be from another world, another civilization. The thought of how incredible the object might be made the hairs on the back of his neck stand up, and he felt a tingling sensation run up and down his spine. He stared at the cylinder with eyes agape, as though by blinking he might miss something of great importance.

Ever so slowly, he reached out with his index finger to touch the shiny metallic object. He felt as though he were dealing with the revelation of coming face to face with God himself. The cylinder felt cold to the touch as he held his finger on it for but a few seconds and then withdrew his hand.

Steinert spoke in a hushed, reverent voice, still staring at the cylinder. "Mein Gott. Imagine if intelligent beings from somewhere out there touched this, made this, and left it for us to find. What incredible wonders might be contained within. What marvelous revelations."

He turned to Don. "In all my years, I never dreamed of finding anything such as this."

Don, still staring at the cylinder, said, "I know what you're feeling. Now you know why I had trouble falling asleep that first night. This could be the most unique item in the entire world, maybe the entire galaxy. The beings that made this would obviously be well advanced in technology. There could be secrets within that could help all of humanity—"

"Or harm all of it. It may also contain secrets of energy or of the universe that could be used for destructive purposes." Steinert watched as Don placed the cover back onto the lead box and then continued, "If so, any government would be willing to pay untold sums, even if for no other reason than to keep it out of the hands of its enemies."

Don stood and picked up the box. "I know, and the bidding has probably already begun. Let's get going," he urged.

Steinert nodded as Don cradled the box in his arms, and the two men strode through the deserted warehouse and out the old wooden door to their car.

Steinert asked, "Where do we put it? What if we hit a bump or something?"

"It's okay. I'll hold it on the seat between us. It only reacts when … threatened."

As soon they had seated themselves in the car, two other vehicles turned the corner, several blocks away, and headed toward them. Each man was momentarily frozen in place. Don nervously said, "Get going, Anton, now."

Steinert started the engine. The two other cars were one hundred yards away as Steinert turned the car around, away from both the warehouse and the approaching cars.

Don gasped, "It's them! Marin and Hernando are in the first car, and I think they recognized us. Step on it!"

The second car contained Francisco Alcalde, who had tried contacting Diego but was told that he hadn't returned from his dig at Maleta. Being farther away, Don couldn't see who was driving the second vehicle.

Steinert made a quick left and then right turn as the car accelerated to fifty miles per hour through the streets. Don turned and looked behind through the back window. "They're still there. Lose them or we're dead men."

Steinert answered while concentrating on the road ahead. "I agree. Once they get this cylinder, our lives will to them mean nothing. The only ace in the hole we have is this gun." He patted the gun.

Don, still watching through the back window, said, "Let's hope we don't have to use it. I wouldn't be very good with it."

Steinert didn't respond. He knew he could use that gun, and use it well.

The three cars flew down the side streets with Steinert repeatedly honking the horn, warning pedestrians and other cars to get out of the way.

Don hollered over the noise of the horn and the racing engine, "If we get stuck behind a truck or something, we're finished, unless we can jump out and head for some building with lots of people around."

Steinert answered, "You know this town. What should I do?" His voice was raised, yet calm.

Don thought for a moment and said, "Make a left at the next corner and head out of the city. We can make for open territory and outrun them."

Steinert made the left and put his foot to the floor, rapidly picking up speed. The car swerved around a truck as it continued to accelerate, but Marin and Hernando were still in close pursuit, a tenth of a mile back. But there were fewer buildings now as they continued heading away from the city, and the driving became less hazardous.

Steinert gripped the wheel tightly with both hands while Don held one hand on the lead box to keep it from being jostled. A dog was running alongside the road and made a quick, sudden turn toward the middle of the road as though intending to cross. Steinert saw the mongrel at the last moment, but too late. The car blasted into the dog at seventy miles per hour, and the dog was instantly killed, being thrown over the side of the road and lying there in a mangled heap. Instinctively, Steinert began to press his foot on the brake, but Don screamed, "Don't slow down! It was just a stupid mutt."

Steinert, clearly saddened for the moment, simply said, "I love dogs."

In another place and another time, Don would have comforted Steinert, but all he had time for was to briefly think of what a gentle, kind man Anton was.

The road gradually became deserted so that within ten minutes they were isolated except for passing an occasional car or truck. Steinert had the car wide open at speeds exceeding one hundred miles per hour on the straightaways. The rented car was far newer and faster than the junk heaps that Marin and Alcalde were driving and was especially better on turns, having a far better acceleration rate, and slowly but steadily they began to leave Marin and

Alcalde behind until they were out of sight. Dusk had begun to fall now, and it was becoming darker by the minute.

Don spoke excitedly. "We're losing them. I can't see them anymore."

"Good," was all Steinert was able to say, intent on concentrating on the road.

"Keep the speed up. We need more distance between us. There are dirt roads up ahead, and we can turn onto one of them. Those jerks won't know which road to follow. We can hide out, off the road, until we think the coast is clear."

"But what if they sit on the main road, waiting for us? Is there another way back to the city?"

"There must be. But look, we'll figure something out later. Let's make sure we escape, first."

Marin's and Alcalde's cars were now about a mile back, representing only some forty seconds of time at the high speeds they were traveling.

Don told Steinert to turn left at the next road. He knew there were some ancient ruins up there but was unfamiliar with the site, having never worked in this area.

Steinert turned left and again brought the car to a high speed. The area was almost deserted except for an occasional dirt road that led to farmhouses high up the slopes where farmers worked the terraces first sculpted long ago by the ancient peoples. The car was hitting potholes and rocks at high speed.

Meanwhile, Marin's and Alcalde's cars went speeding by, unaware that Steinert's car had turned off the main road.

Suddenly, Steinert's car hit a giant pothole at high speed. Two loud popping noises were heard by both men, and the front end began to buck and twist.

"What's that?" Don yelled.

"I cannot steer. I think we blew a tire."

Steinert brought the car to a halt. The two men exited the vehicle and strode to the front of the car. To their chagrin, both front tires were blown out.

Resignedly, Steinert said, "The car is done. It will not help us now."

It was almost totally dark outside. They got out of the car and decided to try to push the car off the road and down an incline into thick brush and trees that might hide the car from sight. Don first removed the lead box and placed it alongside the road. They left the car in neutral gear and pushed it off the road, watching it almost disappear. They could hear the sounds of cracking branches and then one final, dull thud as the car came to a stop, its front end resting on a large, fallen tree trunk. The car was only partially hidden from sight, but the darkness made it less visible.

Don picked up the box, and the two men began walking in the same direction as they'd been driving, away from the main road. They cautioned each other to listen for the sound of any vehicle approaching, at which time they would scamper off the side of the road and hide until the vehicle passed.

Don knew that there were ruins somewhere up the road in which they could take temporary cover. They walked for a half hour, and only one vehicle passed by. They hid among the shrubbery and saw only the blinding headlights, but they knew it wasn't their pursuers, as it was heading toward the main road, not from it.

After walking for another fifteen minutes, Don noticed a sign at the intersection of another dirt road. It had an arrow pointing up the slope and the word, "Huarochiri."

"That's it," Don said. "The ruins are up there. We'll hide up there and try to get some sleep. In the morning we'll think of a way to get out of here."

They walked several hundred yards up the slope, with Steinert lagging far behind, and then noticed some low stone walls that were once the foundations of stone buildings that housed a city of thriving people some fifteen hundred years earlier. Don groped his way slowly, feeling for his footing so as not to slip and drop the lead box. Steinert followed, breathing heavily from the climb.

The night was extremely dark, as the moon was nearing its new moon phase, and the stars shone brightly through the clear, crisp evening air. The sounds of insects and their own breathing could be heard, but nothing else, except for the rustling of leaves from an occasional night breeze.

Don saw a larger wall and decided that it would be as good a place as any to try to use as a resting place for that evening. They sat down, backs to the wall, with the lead box between them. Relaxation brought on the realization of how exhausted the two of them were, and they sat silently, motionless, for a few minutes.

Steinert took his pipe from his pocket, filled it with his cherry tobacco, and lit it with a match.

Don was dying for a cigarette but asked, jokingly, "You wouldn't by any chance have some pot for that bowl, would you?"

Steinert smiled. "You youngsters today seem to have a liking for marijuana. In my day, it was alcohol."

Don suddenly remembered Diego. "My God. What about Diego? How will we get him out of there?"

"I do not know. With no phone or car, whatever we do will have to wait until morning."

Don knew that Steinert was right, nodded his head in agreement, and tried not to think about Diego lying buried in the ground.

As Steinert puffed on his pipe, Don found that he was enjoying the cherry scent of the smoke plume.

Steinert decided to change the subject. The surroundings and the night sky were extremely conducive to introspective conversation. "You know, it was here, at Huarochiri, that, some fifteen hundred years ago, a large population of tens of thousands lived and flourished, utilizing the land in a manner that eventually helped lead to their own demise." The teacher in him was beginning to emerge.

"That's true," Don answered. He was grateful for the opportunity to chat about things he loved, especially with this professor whom he had come to respect and love almost as a father. "But they farmed it out. They didn't replenish the soil of its valuable nutrients."

"But," Steinert continued reflectively, "if there is one lesson I have learned from all my research and books and experiences, it is this: a common thread exists for all human beings, whether past or present, Americans or foreigners. We are all so much alike."

"In what ways?"

"In many ways. But I believe the most important for human beings is the struggle not so much for physical survival, for that is the natural domain of all plants and animals, but for mental, or perhaps what I really mean to say is spiritual, survival. All living things are born and must one day die, but the human race alone is cognizant of its eventual demise and therefore seeks meaning of its own existence."

"But isn't that where religion comes in?"

"Ja, it does, but not necessarily an organized religion. What I am getting at is that humankind is in awe of the unknown, the great powers that lie beyond our ability to know them, and that each and every person must come to grips with the fact that one day he or she will be nothing more than dust, wiped off the face of the earth. To many people this is unreasonable, unacceptable. So they create ideas and rituals that perpetuate and justify the idea that there is a greater, more powerful, being out there and that this being, this God, perhaps, will somehow guarantee that their life is not wasted once they are gone. The Incas believed in a life after death. They thought that the spirits of those who had been good during their lives on Earth would join the sun god. The exception was that all the nobles joined the sun god, whether they had been good or bad. In the kingdom of the sun god, they would enjoy a very pleasant life of feasting and no hard work. Evil people were sent to a gloomy, underground world where it was always cold, and the only things they could eat were stones."

Steinert looked upward. "Men have looked at these same stars for thousands of years and wondered similar thoughts. What is up there, what is up there? Is that where my god is, the one who will watch over me when I am dead?"

Don asked rhetorically, "And do we really have any of the answers to those questions?"

"We do not, of course. With all our modern science we know no more or less about the nature of our existence than the people who inhabited this very spot thousands of years ago."

"Except for one thing."

"What?"

"You and I know that there are other beings, aliens, out there, don't we?" Don patted the lead box lightly and smiled.

A small smile also came across Steinert's face as he said, "Yes, that is right. We may not know about God or our own existence, but we certainly know about this cylinder. I guess we are geniuses." The two men chuckled.

Don, now thinking about the cylinder, said, "I wonder if these aliens know more about the nature of existence than we do? Do you suppose that a superior intelligence might also come to know more of God, if there really is a God?" Steinert had, during his lifetime, gone through similar mental contortions regarding the unanswerable, and he knew that these kinds of questions invariably resulted in a resigned frustration. Therefore, he answered, "Who can say?"

But Don continued to grapple with his own thoughts. "I mean, most major religions address the problem of being from nonbeing, creation arising from a void, which to this day I have always had trouble getting a handle on."

"You are not the only one, believe me," Steinert replied. "The greatest minds in the world cannot answer the immensely frustrating question of creation."

"I understand that. But I wonder, what if we were far more intelligent beings? Could we grasp the question of how the universe began, how something was created from nothing? Or could it *always* have been there, with no beginning? Man, it's enough to make you believe in God!"

Steinert politely listened, as his age had given him the wisdom to allow a youthful mind to run its natural course.

Don's monologue continued. "But then, where did God come from? How did this God begin? It just doesn't seem right that we do not—or worse yet, cannot—know the answers to these mysteries. Can you imagine if these aliens know the answers? Do you think they might actually share them with us?"

Steinert thought for a moment. "I suppose it is possible, what you are asking, but we will not know until we examine this cylinder more closely. Who knows what secrets it may reveal? Ray Bradbury said something like, 'What mankind sees in the exploration of space is his last chance at immortality since he invented religion.'"

After such an incredibly taxing day, it felt wonderful to Don to be relaxed like this, listening to his learned professor and dreaming of the unbelievable. But Don still couldn't help thinking and worrying about Diego. It was turning cooler now, and he prayed that Diego would still be alive and healthy by tomorrow.

"I hope Diego is okay. I realize what he did was wrong, but I still could never allow him to die like that."

Steinert understood that with Don feeling the way he did, it would be difficult to allow his former friend to die in that hole, and therefore he had an unspoken change of heart regarding Diego's ultimate destiny. "I know how you must feel. He was your friend. It is much easier to see someone die whom you have never met before and know absolutely nothing about. You can almost make believe they are not even human. It makes it much easier, you know. To be honest, the only reason I would help save your friend is so that you will not be branded a murderer, although your friend probably deserves to die."

Once again, that surprising, uncharacteristic tone in Steinert's voice caught Don's attention. Here was this man of books, this sensitive gentleman who came to Peru to save his life, speaking with such coldness about another human being.

"Anton, I think I've come to know you pretty well over these past few years, but there are times when I feel I don't know you at all."

"That's because you really do not know me," said an expressionless Steinert.

"What's that supposed to mean?"

The combination of the relaxing night sounds, the cool breeze, the stars above, the remoteness of the place, the exhausting day's events, and perhaps the fact that he had kept his secrets bottled up for far too long brought Anton Steinert to the point of finally being able to discuss his past. He spoke in slow, measured phrases.

"I was in the army ... the German army, during the war. I had been given a job driving a truck that would gas men, women, and children to their deaths."

Don couldn't mask the astonished look that crossed his face, but it didn't matter as Steinert wasn't looking at him. He was staring straight ahead with the sightless expression of someone whose head was filled with his own deep thoughts. He continued his tale.

"Sometimes, while unloading the truck of its horrible cargo, we came across some that were still alive. We had to administer the coup de grace. A bullet in the brain. It was better than burying them alive." He paused, drew a deep breath, and continued. "It was my job ... my military duty. I had no choice. Disobeying orders was a most serious crime ... all those people ... beautiful little children ..." Steinert's voice trailed off into silence.

Don stared at the kindly, professorial man sitting next to him. *Yes,* he thought, *now I know you, old man. Now I truly do know you.* Don didn't know how to respond to Steinert's story, and he sat in silence.

After a brief pause that seemed to last an eternity in the stillness of the night, Steinert emptied the spent tobacco by gently tapping the pipe on a rock and then turned his head toward Don and asked, "Do you believe in evil?"

"Evil?" Don replied, relieved that Steinert had broken the ice. "You mean like evil as in bad people?" He didn't fully grasp what Steinert was leading up to.

"No, not really the word 'bad.' I mean evil. A child can steal a piece of gum from a candy store, and that is bad, but it is not evil. The child knows it is wrong, but not so wrong. Or at least not wrong enough that he thinks he is hurting someone in the worst way possible. What I mean is, do you think people have evil within them? Do all people have the ability, given the right circumstances, to carry out what I only seem to be able to describe right now as evil things?"

"Obviously, you mean like what you did." As best he could, Don attempted to walk a thin line between discussion with, and condemnation of, Anton Steinert.

"Of course. I knew the horrors I was helping to commit and was repulsed by them, and yet I carried them out. I killed people, mostly innocent men, women, and children. I killed them with no dignity to their dying. They died much the same death as a room full of flies after you sprayed the room with insecticide. They did not even get a decent burial. They were shoved into mass graves to rot."

Don tried to be sympathetic to Steinert's private agony. "So you believe it takes an evil person to perform these acts, and you're afraid you might be one of them?"

"Actually, no. I have thought so much about this over the years. I have never considered myself an evil person, and yet the paradox is that the heinous acts I committed could only be committed by an evil person."

"Or maybe a basically good person doing evil things due to circumstances."

"But not everyone did these things. Some revolted against them."

"And many were executed." Don had read a great deal concerning the Holocaust of World War Two and very much wanted to show Steinert that he both understood and empathized with what Steinert had experienced.

Steinert knew that, in truth, a plethora of knowledge could never adequately convey the horrors he participated in. But he politely listened, mostly impassively, as Don continued.

"Maybe they're the real heroes of the war, the men who would not, could not, commit these acts. Maybe what you did is just one of our survival techniques. You feared for your own life and were willing to take part in the killing of many others. And even if you had refused, you'd be dead and they would've replaced you in a second, and all those people would have died anyway. Listen, Anton. You know the old saying, 'There but for fortune …' You were in the wrong place at the wrong time. You know what an evil person would be doing?"

"No, what?" Steinert truly hoped for some wonderful, long-awaited relief from his personal hell.

"He wouldn't be talking about this at all. He wouldn't give a damn. You're no more evil than the next guy."

Steinert sat back, feeling a bit of momentary relief. Perhaps he should have spoken to someone about this years ago, he thought. It felt good to have gotten some of it off his chest. It had weighed heavily on him for far too long. But he felt compelled to say something more to Don, feeling too much guilt to accept a young man's partial absolution of his crimes. Staring into the starry night, he spoke softly and deliberately. "Albert Speer, Hitler's architect, who was going to build colossal cities for Hitler that were to last a millennium and who spent twenty-one years in prison for war crimes, wrote something that I have found important enough to memorize. Speer states, 'For there are things for which one is guilty even if one might offer excuses … simply because the scale of the crimes is so overwhelming that by comparison any human excuse pales to insignificance.'" Steinert turned toward Don, looked him squarely in the eye, and asked, "Do you understand what I am saying to you?"

Don paused briefly, trying to grasp the full meaning of Steinert's words, and answered, "Yes, I do."

But Steinert wasn't really sure if Don actually did or, for that matter, if anyone could ever fully comprehend the true meaning of his statement— except, of course, those who lived through it as he had.

Don placed his hand on Steinert's shoulder as though to lend some sort of comfort. Steinert's eyes were closed now. The confession, bottled up for forty years, had drained him of his last ounce of energy. He was asleep, alone with his own terrible, recurring nightmares.

Don sat motionless in the still of the night, leaned his head back, and looked up at the stars twinkling in the clear night sky. He would never mention Steinert's brief confession again, Don told himself. It would remain ancient history. What an incredible thing the war had done to this man. He had killed and yet was no cold-blooded murderer in Don's eyes.

Don closed those eyes and thought once again of Diego. Tomorrow they must find a phone and get him released as quickly as possible. Diego had kept his part of the bargain.

Miles away, those same twinkling stars shone their dim light upon the motionless Diego Gonzales. Insects crawled up and down his face and explored his ears and nasal passages. He could do nothing but twitch to keep the insects away. The tape over his mouth made breathing difficult, as he could breathe only through his nose. The coolness of the damp soil made his nose run, and he labored for air. He could only pray to God that someone would find him soon. He knew he'd told the old man and Don the truth.

CHAPTER 20

THE OTHER CARS, WITH Marin and Hernando in the lead and Alcalde bringing up the rear, had sped by the dirt roads with the men knowing that Don's car could have turned onto any of them. They had driven for a few miles when Marin decided to pull his car off to the side of the road, followed by Alcalde. They got out of their cars and met between the two cars. It was dark now, and they knew they probably wouldn't be able to find Don and the old man before morning. Marin lit a cigar as Alcalde and Hernando lit their cigarettes. The crimson tips seemed to move in ghostly fashion against the black of night.

Marin and Alcalde discussed their next step, intently listened to by Hernando. First, Marin told Alcalde to go back to the warehouse. It was possible that Don and the old man had just pulled up to the warehouse and hadn't gone inside yet. Or maybe they went inside and couldn't find the hidden cylinder. Alcalde was to go now and return as soon as possible to this spot. Marin figured that Don and the old man wouldn't continue traveling away from Lima but would eventually attempt to turn off and lose them. He decided that they would flag down the first few vehicles that came along and ask if they had seen a white Pontiac going at high speed in the opposite direction.

Alcalde took off for the warehouse, and over the next half hour Marin and Hernando stopped three vehicles, and in each case the driver said he'd seen nothing.

Marin knew they had lost the white car for now, but at least they knew the car was somewhere between themselves and Lima.

While waiting for Alcalde to return, Marin paced back and forth like a caged animal. Hernando could only hope that the cylinder was still safely hidden in the warehouse, as he knew of Marin's temper.

A while later, Alcalde's car returned, and Alcalde got out, saying, "It's gone."

By now, Marin was more angry than he'd been in a very long time. Visions of piles of money slipping through his hands were whipping him into a frenzy. The frustration of knowing that nothing more could be done until morning, and the reality that the cylinder might be lost to them forever, erupted into rage against Hernando.

Marin turned toward Hernando, yelled several curses, and began to attack him with his fists. Hernando was stung by several blows, but he merely backed up and leaned against the car, trying to cover his head and face with his arms.

Several more blows were struck by a screaming Marin before Alcalde grabbed Marin from behind and pulled him away from the cowering Hernando, shouting that this would do no one any good. Hernando slumped to the ground while protesting that it wasn't his fault. He'd been tricked by the two Americans.

Marin, having vented some of his frustration, took several deep breaths and calmed down, but he told Hernando that he'd better ride back with Alcalde to avoid being killed.

They got into their vehicles and rode toward Lima. In the morning they would watch for the white car and the two Americans. They would spread word among their friends to be on the lookout for these two. They would also check out the area where the dirt roads forked from the main road, the area where they'd lost them. Maybe the two Americans would hide there, or possibly someone would remember seeing them. It was a long shot, but it would be worth checking in the morning.

The street-wise Marin had one real trump card. When they had first spotted the white car back at the warehouse, Marin had been able to get close enough to Steinert's car to memorize the license plate. Knowing that the car had to be rented, he would contact all the rental agencies in the morning and see what he could find out about the rented car.

The next morning, Steinert and Don awoke with the first light of day. They decided that carrying the lead box around would be difficult and risky, and if they were caught, they didn't want to lose their best bargaining chip. So they dug a shallow hole with their hands and buried the cylinder next to the stone wall where they had spent the night. Before covering it with dirt, they opened the lid to view the cylinder one more time. Its strange golden color glistened in the light of the aurous sun. After burying it, they stood over the spot with the respect given a recently lost loved one.

"Four-thousand-year-old alien object," Steinert said softly. "Astonishing."

Don urged, "Let's go. We've got to get to a phone and get Diego out of that hole."

Steinert nodded, and the two men walked down the slope toward the road, leaving the ruins behind. They knew they couldn't go back to the main road even though that would be their best bet at hitching a ride; they'd be sitting ducks there.

Thus, they walked along the dirt road in the opposite direction from the main road in the hope that they might find either a ride or a telephone.

They had traveled only about one mile when Steinert suddenly stopped. He was breathing heavily. "I am afraid my years are catching up with me. We have not eaten or drunk anything since yesterday, and I am feeling extremely weak."

"We've got to move on. There are farmhouses all around this area. We'll find one soon."

After a slow walk of less than two miles, they came upon a small, adobe, thatched-roof house. A plump woman was sitting by the door sewing some cloth with needle and thread while two young children, perhaps two and four years old, played in front of the home.

Typical of Quechua women, she wore a brightly colored shawl; a thickly woven, brightly colored, gathered skirt; a sweater; and motor-tire sandals. Her legs were bare. She had a lovely face with dark eyes and high cheekbones; a brilliant smile directed at her children frolicking in front of her; and bad teeth. Her thick, black hair was in two long braids tied together at the bottom.

The woman looked up, startled to see two strangers dressed like city folk approaching her on foot. Strangers seldom came up here, and they generally brought only bad news or some kind of trouble. The plump woman stood up, leaving her darning on the chair.

"Who are you? What do you want?" she said with trepidation.

Steinert answered calmly, "Our car broke down. We're lost and are in desperate need of food and water. We would be happy to pay you for helping us."

The woman thought that the old man appeared kindly enough, and they certainly seemed lost. If they intended her harm, they could have done so already.

"I have some food and water to share. Come in."

They entered the dimly lit, one-room house. The same room was used for eating, sleeping, and everything else. There were no toilet facilities or running water within the house. There were only chairs, a large table, and several blankets for sleeping on the floor by the side of the room. Their water was supplied by a stream that constantly flowed past their house from the higher elevations.

The woman drew a hide over the four-foot-high doorway to keep out the wind and dogs. A rooster lived inside, as did guinea pigs, which have shared Andean man's abode for thousands of years, ending up in his cook pot.

The two men could plainly see that no phone connection was possible in dwellings such as this, which were remote from city life not so much in distance as in culture. This was how many of the people of the Sierra lived. They were poor farmers with none of the conveniences of the modern world, not even electricity, relying upon nature to provide for their meager existence.

She boiled hot gruel by blowing on a dung-and-twig fire with a tube. When it was ready, the two men were served some bread and the hot, cereal-like mixture of grains and water—plenty of it—and they devoured everything ravenously.

The woman told them that her husband and four older children were out working in the fields of their hillside terrace farmland.

Don asked, "Where can we find the nearest telephone?"

"The nearest ones are in a small town about fifteen miles from here."

"How can we get there? Do you own a car or truck?" Don naively asked.

"No, no one around here owns one. All we have is our llama and a wagon. They are being used by my husband. About once a month he travels to the town, but this takes hours by wagon."

"When will your husband return?"

"He returns around noon to eat and then goes back to the fields."

Steinert took out some money to pay for the food and handed it to the woman. Although not much money by city standards, it amounted to about ten times as much as the woman thought the food was worth. She gladly accepted the offer.

Steinert asked, "Do you think your husband could give us a ride to town? We would be willing to pay for his services."

"Yes, I think he would." She knew that her family could use the money they would make for this favor.

"Okay," Don said. "I guess we have no choice but to wait."

About two hours later, the husband and four older children returned, and the husband agreed to take them into town for an agreed-upon price. But first they all shared a soup of ground beans and a thick gruel of corn flour and milk. After lunch, Don and Steinert climbed onto the back of the wagon, with the husband driving.

The trip took more than three hours through dusty, bumpy dirt roads. The trip gave Don and Steinert time to talk and reflect. Steinert asked Don if he thought these people were either more or less happy than the average modern man living in the city. Don's initial reaction was to answer that of course these people must be less happy due to the harshness of their lives, having none of the modern-day conveniences that are taken so much for granted by city folk. But after mulling the question over in his mind, he did an about-face. "You know, I'm not so sure they're any less content or happy than anyone else in this world."

"That would have been my first answer," Steinert said. "They are living their lives in almost the same manner as their ancestors, but they have a pattern of life that knows its goals. There is no confusion here as to the meaning of life. They have a deep-seated faith in God that is not easily shaken. It is true their lives are comparatively shorter and harder than the average American's, but there seems to be little doubt as to the course their lives will take. Peruvians like to devote attention to the eternal questions of the spiritual and transcendental values of life. They are eager to express an ultimate concern for 'Algo más allá,' the 'something beyond.' Modern man seems confused much of the time. Just compare the suicide rates of these people to the average city dweller. I am willing to bet it they are far lower here."

"But I could never change places with these people. No way," Don remarked.

"Nor would I. I guess it is a case of keeping them down on the farm after they've seen Paris."

They laughed at the bit of humor as the wagon approached the town. They thanked the husband, paid him, and walked into a small restaurant in which there was a pay phone.

They were quite stiff from the long, uncomfortable ride. They stretched, rubbed their backs, and made little grunting noises as they stepped up to the phone that hung from a wall. There were six small tables in the room, and three persons were dining.

Don picked up the receiver, threw some coins into the slot, and dialed the operator for the number of the police department in Lima. A police sergeant answered, and Don anonymously described where Diego Gonzales would be found. Although Don tried sounding as urgent as possible, the sergeant didn't seem overly concerned. He said he'd have someone check it out, but he was accustomed to receiving crank calls. Most of these calls were checked out, but few led to anything of consequence. The sergeant relayed the message to a police car that periodically patrolled the general vicinity described by the anonymous caller. The car responded that they would attempt to get up that way as soon as possible.

Don hung up, and he and Steinert decided to grab a bite to eat and then call the taxi company whose phone number was pasted onto the telephone. Afterward, they would return to Steinert's hotel, the Hotel Cuzco, which they believed would be safe since no one knew where Steinert was staying and he was registered under the pseudonym of Karl Grosz.

Earlier that same day, after attempting again, to no avail, to locate Diego, Jose Marin feverishly dialed every auto rental agency listed in the telephone directory. After several calls, he found the dealership that owned the car.

Marin was jubilant at first with the information but was soon told that the agency wasn't allowed to divulge confidential rental records to anyone, especially not over the phone. Marin immediately sensed what the person meant by emphasizing the "not over the phone" phrase. A little palm grease might do the trick.

Marin rushed to the agency and, without too much persuasion in the form of a modest sum of money, managed to obtain the information from the agent.

Unlike the hotel, in which Steinert was able to register as Karl Grosz, auto rental required presentation of a valid driver's license, which of course showed the name of Anton Steinert with his New York address. Steinert had also been required to include on the application the name of the hotel he was staying at, which he did. Steinert had little reason at the time to suspect that his rental car would be used as an instrument in tracing him to his hotel by thugs.

Marin immediately dialed the hotel from a pay phone and asked for Anton Steinert, but he was informed that no one with that name had registered there. Marin figured that either Steinert had never checked into the hotel or he had used a phony name. Marin then spent a good part of the afternoon dialing every respectable hotel in Lima, asking for Anton Steinert.

Finding nothing more, Marin decided that his best bet was still the Hotel Cuzco. Maybe this Steinert guy had in fact used a fictitious name. It was at the Hotel Cuzco that he would snoop around and see what he might stumble upon. If he was really lucky, those two Americans just might be caught entering or leaving the hotel.

Later that same day, as afternoon gave way to early evening, Marin, Alcalde, and Hernando took up places inside and outside the hotel, watching and waiting.

Still later that evening, at nearly the same time that Don and Steinert were finishing their meal at the small restaurant and preparing to take a taxi back to the hotel, two police officers, attempting to locate a person buried up to his neck, decided that their search would have to wait until morning. They had come within two hundred feet of finding Diego. Diego was able to see the beams of light of the car's headlights and the dimmer lights of the flashlights carried by the officers as the lights became broken, moving patterns through the trees, when it began to rain, an unusual event in the arid climate of this part of Peru. The officers felt that it would be fruitless to search in the dark and rain for nothing larger than a human head. The search would have to wait until morning.

As Diego felt the cold rain drops fall onto his face, his momentary excitement at seeing the attempted rescue gave way to despair. It had been a day and a half since he'd eaten or drunk anything, and he began to shiver as the cold water began penetrating the soil.

At eleven p.m., Don and Steinert's taxicab approached the Hotel Cuzco. It was totally dark now and had just begun raining, and the streets were almost deserted. Steinert asked the driver to stop at the corner, one block from the hotel. They could see the blurred lights of the hotel through the streak marks of the windshield wipers.

"Why here, Anton? Do you think there might be trouble?"

"It might pay to be cautious."

They paid the driver and splashed into puddles of rainwater. The lights reflected off the mirror-like wet streets as the rain continued to fall, and they walked close to the buildings, trying to avoid the raindrops. They didn't know that they weren't avoiding detection by Alcalde, who was standing in a darkened doorway across the street, watching them as they walked through the entrance of the hotel. Alcalde knew that Marin and Hernando were waiting inside to greet them.

Inside the well-lit lobby, two persons were sitting on chairs chatting while a hotel receptionist stood behind the counter. A doorman opened the door for Don and Steinert.

Marin and Hernando were sitting in a corner of the lobby, half pretending to be reading magazines, when they noticed two men walking into the lobby from the entrance.

"It's them," Hernando said in a loud whisper. Reacting purely on instinct, the two men stood up and took two steps toward the oncoming Don and Steinert, who saw their path blocked by Marin and Hernando. They stopped and faced each other with only fifteen feet between them.

Steinert looked into the cold, steely eyes of Marin and then at the cut and badly beat-up face of Hernando. Marin saw that no box or cylinder was being carried by either man.

Marin and Hernando had their hands in their jacket pockets, indicating to Steinert that pistols were being pointed at them. Alcalde now stood behind them, blocking their exit from the hotel.

Don and Steinert whirled around with intentions of attempting to escape through the entrance, but Don immediately saw Francisco Alcalde blocking their path, and he shouted the name, "Alcalde."

Steinert was familiar with the name, if not the face, of the man who had tortured Don. Catching everyone off guard, he pulled Hernando's gun from under his jacket and, in a flash, aimed it and pulled the trigger at a distance of only five feet from Alcalde. The shot rang out and caught Alcalde in the neck, just below his Adam's apple. He gasped, made a gurgling sound, and fell backward through the plate glass door, shattering it behind him as he fell through and toward the outside. He came to a halt on his back among the shards of glass.

Hernando and Marin stood motionless, frozen for a few seconds as they watched Alcalde smash though the glass door, immediately followed by the two Americans, who leaped over the body and past the horrified doorman.

Composing themselves, Marin and Hernando ran through the doorway in pursuit of Don and Steinert, who had a one-block lead. Don and Steinert turned the first corner, but Steinert, being much the oldest and hobbling badly, was already feeling his legs weakening and his breath becoming shortened. He yelled to Don that he wouldn't be able to go on at that pace and that he intended to hold them off while Don escaped.

"Keep going. You can make it," Don implored.

"I can't," a breathless Steinert managed to pant.

Marin and Hernando were only a half block behind and closing fast.

Steinert suddenly stopped at the next corner, wheeled around, and fired a shot at the oncoming Hernando and Marin. Hearing the errant gunshot, Marin and Hernando crouched down behind a parked car. The gunshot bought a few precious moments of time for Don and Steinert as they stood against a building around the corner from Marin and Hernando.

"Don," gasped a heavily breathing Steinert, "I cannot go on. Save yourself. Save the cylinder. I can hold them off, maybe kill them and escape myself. You cannot help me. We only have this one gun. You can outrun them."

Don looked at Steinert, who was still trying to catch his breath, and he knew that Steinert couldn't go on. The rain was coming down harder now, and the streets were deserted. No one could help them here in this dark corner of the streets of Lima. Don nodded. "All right. But I'll try to get help."

"Just save the cylinder. The cylinder. Now go!"

Don took one last look into Steinert's eyes and then turned and ran down the block into the wet shroud of darkness.

During this time, Hernando had been creeping up toward the corner on the street side of the parked cars. He was almost to the corner by the time Don began running down the block.

Steinert stood leaning against the building, still desperately trying to catch his breath, when he caught a glimpse of Hernando's large bulk turning the corner. Steinert fired and hit Hernando in the chest at almost point-blank range. Hernando had his gun raised and, in a reflex action, let loose with three rapid-fire shots before falling face down at Steinert's feet. He was dead.

But one of the shots had caught Steinert in his left side, and he dropped to his knees, staring hypnotically at the drops of rain as they hit the sidewalk. He still had managed to hold on to the gun, but then a tremendous blow to his head sent him reeling backward. His spectacles were knocked off his face, and the gun flew out of his hand. Marin had turned the corner and had powerfully kicked the kneeling Steinert in the head with his boot.

Marin reached down and grabbed the collar of Steinert's shirt. With his left arm, he pulled Steinert's head toward the gun in his right hand.

"Where's the cylinder, old man? Where is it?" he snorted contemptuously.

Steinert was stunned from the blow and bleeding from the wound in his side, but he was lucid enough to see the barrel of the gun pointed at his chest. He heard Marin ask for the cylinder, but Steinert believed that either way he was a dead man. He would never tell this repulsive animal where the greatest prize in the history of mankind could be found.

People have claimed that in moments such as this, one's life passes before one's own eyes, but Steinert saw only brief flashes of indelible moments and thought it remarkable how the tables had turned. The irony of his plight was crystal clear to him: his own death might mimic what he himself had done to stay alive in another time, another lifetime ago.

It had come full circle. He had fulfilled the promise he made long ago in the killing fields of Poland, to live long enough to see some of the injustices repaid. Many Nazi leaders had committed suicide; others were executed or served long prison sentences. Others lived their lives hiding in constant fear of detection from the authorities. Unfortunately, some escaped prosecution, and a few had become corporate leaders in some of the largest companies in Germany. Being a noncommissioned officer, Steinert was part of a cast of thousands who, willingly or not, had helped the Nazi regime to carry out their ungodly mission but who never needed to run from the authorities. They would have been a far lesser adversary than was his own conscience. He took solace now in the fact that if this was how he was to die, it would at least be for a lofty cause; the lives he had helped take were wasted on nothing.

Steinert looked the evil Marin in the eye and spat in his face. Marin, reacting impulsively, pulled the trigger, firing a shot that blasted a hole above Anton Steinert's heart.

Marin let go of Steinert's collar as Steinert's limp body slumped to the pavement, crimson blood flowing from the gaping wound in his chest and mixing with rainwater to be washed into the sewer system of Lima.

Marin stood up and disdainfully half kicked Steinert's head while wiping the spittle from his face. He muttered, "Filthy old man," and then spat back at the motionless form. Then, looking down the dark, empty street in the direction that Don had vanished, Marin fumed, "When I find you, you'll wish you were never born."

But Don had escaped. He'd heard the shots and hoped that the worst hadn't occurred. Steinert's gun had only three shots left in it, and Don had counted a total of five gunshots. But he knew he must go on, find the cylinder, and discover its meaning for the world. If Steinert were killed, that achievement would stand as a monument to his mentor, his friend, this brave and complex man who, from a different point of view, could have been branded with the ignominious label of mass murderer.

Don would spend the remainder of that night hiding in a rear hallway to an apartment building. He would catch a few hours of restless sleep, awakening with every noise or slamming door. He was wet, cold, and tired but more determined than ever to go on. His plan was to find a taxi, retrieve the cylinder from the ruins, and somehow escape from Lima, hopefully with Steinert at his side.

He then did something he couldn't remember doing since his childhood. He prayed. He prayed for the life of Anton Steinert.

He would sleep fitfully and dream of the old man.

CHAPTER 21

COUNTING SHEEP DIDN'T WORK. She was living proof of it. During these past few days, she hadn't had one decent night's sleep. The bags under her eyes were a glaring testimonial to that fact, and all the makeup in the world couldn't do for her what one night's restful slumber would.

Over the past two days Diane had called Block repeatedly to ask what was being done to locate her husband and Anton Steinert—and what the meaning of all that cylinder stuff really was. But each time, Block's responses were vague, and Diane was no closer to getting answers or receiving help than she was before.

Finally, partly out of pity for Diane and because he didn't believe all that "national security" garbage he knew the boys in the Pentagon always threw around, Block told Diane that it was out of his hands and that the entire affair had been turned over to someone at the Pentagon. He did not divulge Rawlings's name.

Diane attempted to contact the Pentagon and see what was being done about the return of her husband, but she was unable to reach the proper department, and her questions went unanswered. The grim prospect that something dreadful may have happened to Don brought her closer to the realization that she loved Don for who he was, not who she thought he ought to be. She hadn't understood until now that a loving, understanding, and sharing companion provided more security than all the money in the world. She vowed to do anything within her power to ensure his safe return.

She now believed that the powers that be were stonewalling her, purposely withholding precious information from her. The only positive thing that had lately occurred was that Frank Craine was avoiding her like the plague and gingerly tiptoed around her whenever it became necessary to speak with her. He had thought, *if she wants to wait for that jerk of a husband of hers, so be it. There are plenty of women left in this city.* He rubbed his arm, where the bite marks had almost healed.

One of Diane's coworkers, Cindy Dunham, stopped at her desk. "Ready for lunch?"

Diane glanced at her watch, which read twelve thirty. "I'm starving. Where to?"

Cindy, a plain woman whom Diane felt wore her hair too short for her plump face, answered, "How about Steak and Ale? I'm in the mood for a beer."

Eating had recently become a necessity rather than an enjoyment for Diane. She ate to conquer hunger, not to please her palate, and would have agreed to any culinary suggestion from McDonald's to Sardi's. "That's fine."

Diane fetched her jacket from the closet, and the two women exited at Fifty-First Street and then walked up Madison Avenue. It was brisk out, but the temperature felt good to Diane, reminding her that she was still a vital human being. Being cooped up in the office gave her too much time for worrying. The sunlight burned off some of the cobwebs.

The restaurant was brimming over with luncheon patrons, many of whom sat at the bar and paid no particular attention to the game show that was playing on the huge TV that sat on a shelf in the corner.

Within minutes, the two women were seated at a table near the bar, and they ordered two light beers.

Diane had confided in Cindy, and Cindy knew that Diane desperately needed someone to talk with and be consoled by. Diane had told her of the strange letter from Anton Steinert and the discovery by her husband of what he believed was an alien object. Of course, Cindy met her remarks with skepticism, much as she had when Diane informed her of her premonition.

Diane had always been an upbeat person, and seeing her so depressed bothered Cindy, but she knew she could only serve as a sounding board for Diane, someone for Diane to work out her emotions with. As much as was possible these past few days, Cindy had tried to get Diane's mind away from Peru and premonitions, and their discussions usually centered around work and work-related problems.

"I hear Capwell awarded their account to L. J. Simmons," Cindy remarked.

"Big account?" Diane fingered her glass.

"One of the biggest. John was hoping he could land it for us, but what the hell. You can't land every fish. Problem is, this one was a whale."

"Maybe we should've called in Captain Ahab if we wanted to catch Moby Dick," Diane quipped.

Cindy smiled. "We don't need to catch Moby. We have our dick, in the form of Frank Craine."

Diane laughed. "Dick head is more like it."

"Been leaving you alone?"

"He thinks I'm Dracula's daughter now."

"Maybe he'll pay some attention to me now," Cindy said, tongue in cheek.

"Come on," Diane answered, questioning if Cindy really meant what she'd said.

"Just kidding. The man's an animal, but unfortunately he's one who happens to be our superior."

"Boss," Diane corrected.

"What?"

"Please don't say the word 'superior' where Frank is concerned."

Cindy smiled. "Boss it is."

Diane was suddenly peripherally aware that something was different. The game show that had been shooting out a barrage of staccato questions and answers had abruptly ceased. She casually glanced at the TV screen and could see that a special bulletin had interrupted the local program.

Cindy was startled as Diane impulsively leaped out of her chair, rushed over to the bar, and yelled, "Make that louder!"

The bartender responded, "Sure, Miss," and obliged her by turning up the volume with the remote control.

On the screen a local newscaster was speaking next to an enlarged, superimposed photograph of an elderly man. Below the photo was a name that rippled through Diane's brain like an electric shockwave—Anton Steinert. She gasped as she heard, "Steinert, who taught at New York University for many years and was a world-renowned archeologist, was killed during a gun battle in the capital city of Lima, Peru. Police are theorizing that a terrorist group may have had a hand in what appears to have been an assassination, as Steinert's wallet and money were found intact on his body."

Assassinated! Diane felt faint and muttered, "Oh my God" as Cindy grabbed her from behind. She helped Diane back to her seat as the bartender asked, "Is she okay? Too much to drink?"

Cindy waved him off. "It's fine. I have her." She then helped a limp Diane into her seat and stood next to her, avoiding the eyes of curious onlookers.

"Diane, what is it?" she said in a loud whisper.

Diane looked up at Cindy and answered dispassionately, in shock, "That's him. He's the one."

"Who is him?" Cindy implored. "I don't follow you."

Still dazed by the broadcast, she answered, "Steinert. The man who went to find Don. He's been murdered."

"Dear Jesus," Cindy said. There could be no whitewashing of this event. "I see what you're getting at." She grabbed Diane's hand as she sat down across from her. "But that doesn't mean anything has happened to Don. I mean, did they say anything about him?"

Diane had now recovered from her initial shock and said, "No, but I've got to make a phone call."

"To whom?" Cindy asked as she watched Diane stand up and put her jacket on.

"Some asshole named Block, or someone else who can tell me what the fuck is going on here."

The adrenalin began to flow. Yes, they hadn't mentioned Don, but she was determined to do something, anything, that would help get her the answers she needed to know. If making phone calls were her only hope, then she would continue making them all the way to the White House, if need be. "Tell them I'm going home. That I got sick. I can't sit in that office today."

"Where will you be?"

"I'll make the calls from my apartment. I've got to find out what the hell is going on."

She rushed out without asking Cindy if she would mind picking up the check.

The two police officers, who the night before had given up their search for a man purportedly buried alive up to his neck, returned in the morning in order to follow up and close the book on what they were certain was another crank call. They turned up the dirt road, drove the anonymous caller's designated distance, and stopped the car.

"You see anything?" the big, heavyset driver casually asked.

"No," answered the other officer, also heavyset but on the short side. Both men were characteristically barrel-chested, as were most people of the area, whose ancestors had evolved increased-capacity, barrel chests as compensation for the rarefied atmosphere of the lofty, mountainous region.

The driver wearily said, "All right. We're here. We searched. We saw nothing. Now let's get the hell out of here and eat breakfast. I'm starving."

The shorter man answered, "Listen. We might as well take a look around. What if that call was for real?"

The big man scratched his ear and examined his finger. "No way. Who the hell would bury somebody way up here and then call us to tell us about it? Come on. I'm hungry."

The smaller man was hungry too, but he pleaded his case. "Maybe some kidnapper or terrorist group did this for ransom." He opened his car door. "I'm getting out. You can stay if you want, but if they do find this guy later and he's dead, we can kiss our badges good-bye, especially if the dead person is someone important. Besides, if he is important and we save him, we'll be heroes."

The larger man laughed. "Heroes? Us? Yeah, that would be great." Seeing the smaller man's point, he offered, "But I'm giving you fifteen minutes, and that's it, because in sixteen minutes my stomach will start to erupt from hunger. And if my stomach erupts, I start to belch, and then watch out! Remember, you've got to drive in the same car as me."

The smaller man looked up toward the sky. "There is a God, because I just asked him to make sure that your gas didn't come from your other end, and he granted my wish." He laughed at his own remark.

"Very funny. Very funny," the large man deadpanned.

The two men got out of the car and began to scour the woods for a head. The caller had said to walk about one hundred feet from the dirt road, off to the right.

The big man asked, "Hey, did he mean to the right from inside the car, or facing the car?"

The smaller man answered impatiently, "How should I know? He said right. The right. The right is this way, I think."

The big man called out, "What's that?"

"Where?"

"Over there." He pointed out the direction, about thirty feet away. "It's a head!"

With a sense of urgency, the smaller man responded, "I see it. God, I hope it's still attached to a body."

The two men jogged to Diego and knelt down. Diego's eyes were closed. The big man gingerly pushed at Diego's forehead with his index finger, and Diego's eyes sprung open, looking like two white automobile headlamps against his filthy face. He'd heard them but was almost delirious from two days of exposure, dehydration, and insect bites.

"He's alive!" the big man exclaimed.

"Let's dig him out," the smaller man suggested.

"Let me get this tape off." He removed the tape with a scratching sound, and Diego gulped his first full breath of air in two days.

The two men didn't take long to dig him out of the shallow hole. They untied the damp and dirty Diego, whose muscles were stiff now, and carried him from under his arms to the rear seat of their car.

"Hey, man, can you speak?" the smaller man asked.

Diego, his mouth parched, answered with a scratchy voice, "I ... I think so."

The larger man retrieved a canteen that they always kept in their trunk, and offered it to Diego. "Here, take some of this. But slowly, very slowly."

Diego grabbed the canteen and guzzled the water.

"Too fast, man. Take it easy."

Diego stopped only to take a breath.

"Who did this to you? What happened?" the big man asked.

Diego coughed, and his chest heaved, but he managed to get his words out. "Two men ... Donald Carter ... Anton Steinert. They intend to ...

smuggle ancient—" he coughed again. "Ancient relics out of Peru. Americans. I tried to stop them."

At that moment, Diego felt no remorse in betraying his former friend who had almost let him die in that stinking hole. Now they deserved something in return.

The two officers jumped into the front seat of the car and drove off. This was extremely interesting news, as they had heard on their radio that an Anton Steinert had been found shot to death in the streets of Lima in a gun battle that also killed two other men who were known criminals. The connection seemed obvious, and their next destination was police headquarters. Heroes didn't need to stop for something as trivial as food.

After spending a terrible, restless night hiding on the floor of a rear corridor to an apartment building, Don awoke and immediately began to wonder what had happened to Steinert. Did he manage to escape? He thought, *If the old man had died saving me, how would I ever forgive myself?* But his immediate concern now was escape for himself. If Steinert had escaped, he would know where Don was going, and that was back to the ruins to retrieve the cylinder.

He caught a taxi and was well on his way back to the ruins when a newsflash on the radio interrupted the local music. Don leaned forward in his seat as he heard of the deaths of Alcalde, Hernando, and internationally known archeologist Dr. Anton Steinert and of the bizarre discovery of a man near death, buried up to his neck, named Diego Gonzales. The newscaster said the police believed both incidents to be related to a former employee of the University of Lima named Donald Carter. It was believed that Carter was armed and should be treated as a potentially dangerous person. It continued to say that Carter might also be involved in a smuggling ring, stealing ancient artifacts from the government of Peru.

Don slumped back in his seat. Depression over the confirmed death of Steinert and fear for his own life soon gave way to apathy. Don pondered the possibility that it was finished. Perhaps he should simply turn the box over to the Peruvian government and give himself up. He felt that he could explain the strange events of the past weeks and that the cylinder might be vindication enough.

The ride toward the ruins in which they'd buried the cylinder was long enough for him to regain his composure. He knew there was no one left in Peru for him to trust. Diego was now a mortal enemy, Steinert was dead, Marin was probably still looking for him, and now the police and government of Peru wanted him as though he were a common criminal. But Don remembered the face of the old man as he charged him with the task of saving the cylinder. Tears for Anton Steinert welled up in Don's eyes. He clenched his fist and slammed it down onto the car seat, angered by the thought of those animals taking the life of that kind, tormented old man. *Bastards!* he thought. Steinert was right. They should have let Diego die.

It was then that Don decided he must not succumb. He would try to contact the one person in the world whom he knew he could trust, the same person who Steinert had told him knew the complete story of the cylinder. He would go back to that same little town where he and Steinert had first called the police to notify them about Diego's whereabouts, and he would call Diane. Don desperately needed to talk with her, to hear a familiar voice carrying fond memories of a past that now seemed light-years distant.

The taxi passed the partially hidden, white rental car and then stopped near the site of the ancient ruins. Don told the driver to wait; it would take maybe five minutes for him to retrieve the "tools" that he'd left behind.

A few minutes later, Don returned carrying the lead box in his arms. The driver then drove to the little town, and as he paid the driver he realized that he had almost no money remaining. Don knew that he must hide in this town, where he might be able to get a room and some food. Using a fictitious name, he would try to get an odd job, either working in the fields or within the town itself. He believed he could go unrecognized even if his wanted photograph were to appear, as he had now grown a full beard, not having shaved for more than a week. His hair had also grown longer since his arrival in Peru, and any photo on file with the government or university would show him as clean shaven, with short hair neatly in place. His command of the language was perfect now, and he believed he would have no trouble blending in to this town.

Don decided to keep the box and cylinder with him, hiding it in the small room that he rented above the restaurant. He wanted the cylinder with him in case of any escape route out of Peru that might arise unexpectedly. Holding on to it was also a source of strength to Don, as though he were holding a family member, one whom he might even be willing to give his life for.

In his room, Don moved a small dresser away from the wall and, using a metal rod that he found outside, managed to work a couple of floorboards free. He placed the box into the hole, replaced the floorboards, and moved the dresser back into place.

Don then went downstairs, bought a pack of local Canela cigarettes, lit one with a deep drag, and watched its smoke rise, which made him feel as though he were seeing a long-lost friend. He then walked to a pay phone hanging on the wall and dialed Diane's telephone number, collect. While waiting for the connection, he nervously tapped his foot and uttered to himself, "Please be home". The phone rang once, twice, three times, and then four. Then came an answer, a simple "Hello." It was Diane's voice, sounding sweeter than he had ever remembered, and Don's spirits immediately soared.

The operator said, "I have a collect call from Peru. Will you accept the charges?"

Diane shouted, "Yes, I accept."

"It's me." His face wore a look of someone who was either about to laugh or cry.

Diane practically dropped the phone and screamed, "Don! Oh my God. Where are you? Are you all right?" She began to shake.

Don clutched the phone with both hands and replied, "So far, I'm okay. But I need help, need it badly."

"Of course. Anything. I heard about Dr. Steinert, and I've been worried sick. I thought the worst. If Steinert was killed, you might also be dead. Where are you right now?" She was still shaking uncontrollably.

"Still in Peru in a small town not too far from Lima. Everyone is looking for me—the police, the guys who killed Steinert. Diego Gonzales told the police that we were attempting to smuggle ancient Peruvian artifacts out of Peru. In a way, he's right. Only it's not an ancient artifact. I believe it's an alien cylinder left here for us to discover it and decipher its secrets."

"And you really believe it's an alien thing?" She wondered whether it was worth Don's risking his life for.

"More than ever."

"Do you still have it?"

"Yes, and I've got to figure a way to get it and myself out of this country, but there's no one left here who can help me. That's why I called you. Not only to tell you I'm safe but also because you're the only person I know who knew about the cylinder, and I …" Don hesitated. Although he didn't how Diane would react, he still managed to continue and say, "I trust you … I missed you a lot. Maybe what I really should be saying is that I love you."

Diane felt like crying but controlled herself. "And I've missed you more than I ever thought I would. Let's get you home, and we'll go out to dinner and get drunk or something and discuss our future together."

"I wish that could be tonight."

He was beginning to sound depressed, and Diane decided to change the subject and discuss the main issue. "I spoke with a Charles Block in Washington. He said he'd give the information to the proper authorities and make calls to the American embassy in Peru. I've made several calls, but no one's telling me anything. Maybe now they will. I'll call Block again and see what he's done and what we should do to get you out of there."

"Sounds like a good start. I'll call you tonight and each subsequent night at six. You're usually home at that time, aren't you?"

"I'll make it my business to be here. Six p.m. on the dot."

Don felt he had to say something more. "Great, and I want you to know that I meant what I said before."

"And I still love you. Tonight at six."

"At six."

They hung up their phones, awash in tear-filled emotions.

Miles away from Diane's apartment, two men with earphones and a tape recorder sat inside a smoke-filled room. Sandwich wrappers, old newspapers, and empty beer and soda cans littered the place.

One man turned to the other and said, "That's it. Call Central and let them know."

Diane's phone had been tapped.

That afternoon, Diane called Block in Washington. Block seemed pleased to hear that her husband was safe, but he was evasive in his answers. What Diane didn't know was that Block was under strict orders not to discuss the case with her anymore. But upon insistence by Diane, and because he felt sorry for the sexy little lady and was tiring of her phone calls, he offered one piece of information: that a Colonel Tom Rawlings was now handling the case. He gave her Rawlings's telephone number. Rawlings's secretary answered her call and told Diane that Rawlings was on his way out of town on an assignment and couldn't be reached.

"Where did he go? Will he be gone long?" Diane asked.

"Col. Rawlings will be gone for an indeterminate length of time," was the reply.

"May I ask where he went?"

"I've only been told that he's leaving for a country somewhere in South America."

Diane hung up. So Rawlings was on his way to Peru. She was certain of it.

That night, at precisely six, Don called Diane, who promptly informed him of her conversations with Washington.

"I'm afraid for you. This Rawlings guy isn't on his way to rescue you, you know that."

"Believe me. I know I'm expendable. The only card up my sleeve is that I still have the cylinder. But if someone else gets their hands on it, I can't be sure what will happen with me."

"Then why don't you just get out of there without the cylinder? Then you can make some kind of deal, since you're the only one who would know where it's hidden."

"In the first place, I don't think I could get past immigration. I don't have my passport anymore, and there's no way I could go back to my old apartment to get it. I'm sure the police have confiscated everything by now. Besides, they're sure to be looking for me at all the airports. But most of all, I'm not leaving the cylinder. It might sound silly, but until you've seen it for yourself, you can't fully understand the feelings I have for this thing. I'm not giving up the greatest discovery in history without a fight. And Anton's last words to me were, 'Save the cylinder.'"

Diane understood and didn't try arguing with him.

Don continued. "Besides, I have almost no money left. I'll have to get an odd job just to survive. There's no way for me to get out of this hole without money."

Diane knew what she had to do. "Don, as soon as I can, I'm going to book a flight to Lima. My passport is still valid."

The suggestion took Don completely by surprise. "What? No way. I don't want you here. It's too dangerous."

"But I'm in no danger. You are. I can bring you some clothes, money. I can be your contact, your agent. In any event, there's no one left to help you. No one you can trust. How will you ever get yourself and that cylinder out of there with no help? You have to let me help you."

Don thought for a brief moment. He knew he desperately needed help. No one was looking for Diane. Maybe she was correct. She'd be in no trouble, and he longed to see her, to hold her in his arms. After briefly weighing the situation, Don said, "Okay. Come to Peru."

Diane was ecstatic. "Just tell me what to do."

"I'll have to contact you. There's no phone in my room, and I'm not even sure if I'll still be in this dump by tomorrow. Once I know you've arrived in Lima, I'll call you."

"How?"

"You'll check into the Miramar Hotel. It's a very nice hotel in downtown Lima. I'll call the hotel and ask for your room."

"The Miramar. Let me hang up and start making arrangements. Call me back at ten tonight if you can. By then I should be able to find a flight to Lima."

"I'll call at ten."

Only hours earlier, an entourage of twelve from the United States, headed by Col. Tom Rawlings, had made plans to board an army transport plane bound for Lima, Peru. Rawlings had already been informed by aides of the loss of the cylinder back into the hands of Donald Carter, and they further related the story of Steinert and the rest. Therefore, he wouldn't be able to examine the cylinder at the present time, and, of course, no deals were possible now with Julio Mendez.

Rawlings was further informed that Carter had contacted his wife and that she intended to fly to Lima to help him. Rawlings knew he could block her trip out of the country, but he decided that she could be a useful instrument in leading them to her husband. Once she checked into the hotel, Rawlings would have her phone tapped—illegally, of course, but he thought it was justified under the circumstances. For the right price, the wiretap would be easily accomplished.

Rawlings's intelligence sources revealed that a small Soviet contingency could be expected to arrive in Lima for the same purpose as Rawlings's group: to find and verify the authenticity of the so-called alien cylinder before it fell into enemy hands.

Tom Rawlings, like the average person, didn't believe that the cylinder would prove to be from an alien world. But the mere thought that it might be alien, and the prospects that could arise from it should it prove to be so, were enough to make him want to locate and secure the cylinder for the United States. But it was more than just a job to Rawlings. He was in competition with the Communists, and he knew that even if it were a hoax it would be a matter of principle that the United States discover and prove it as such instead of being outmaneuvered by the Russkies.

He had no set plans now that the cylinder couldn't be examined by his group. They would set up temporary headquarters at the Royal Hilton Hotel, taking up several rooms and a suite. There they would await any word from the local police, the Peruvian government, or their own intelligence services. But most of all, they would look forward to the arrival of their trump card, one that they knew the Russians didn't have: Diane Carter.

At ten that evening, Diane received the collect call from Don. She had contacted the airlines and booked a flight from JFK to Lima via Miami that would depart at nine thirty a.m. the next day and arrive in Lima at five thirty p.m., and she was already packing for the trip. She had also called the Miramar Hotel in Peru and confirmed her reservation there. She would call her agency in the morning and inform them of her sudden need for an indefinite amount of time off. She wasn't sure how her supervisors would react to the news, but the possible loss of her job didn't seem to matter much right now.

Don reiterated the plan for her to wait for his call at the Miramar. He would give her further instructions at that time. Don told her that he would periodically check the airline at the Jorge Chavez International Airport to see if there were any delays.

They wished each other good luck, kissed into the phone, and said their good-byes.

These same messages, now recorded, were immediately relayed to Rawlings. He would be waiting for her, eagerly.

CHAPTER 22

DIANE'S FLIGHT DEPARTED JFK the next morning and arrived in Lima at 5:10 p.m., having made good time due to favorable headwinds. She caught a cab and traveled toward the Miramar Hotel, a modern, high-rise hotel in the heart of downtown Lima. The taxi ride to the hotel was highly interesting for her as she had never before been to a country in South America. The sight of a relatively modern city calmed her nerves a bit, as she had naively pictured Lima as being similar to the Spartan cities in Bolivia that she'd seen in the movie *Butch Cassidy and the Sundance Kid*.

On her way to the hotel, Diane absorbed everything around her as the taxi passed through the bustling streets of downtown Lima. She could smell the fragrance of anticuchos—hearts of beef roasting over eucalyptus embers—in a street-side brazier. She heard the chiming of church bells and the sound of a man dutifully sweeping the street. A vendor of fresh bread passed by on bicycle as other vendors made musical sounds with their voices, yelling "Para hoy, para hoy" to attract attention to their wares. And everywhere were buses, taxis, and people milling about on the sidewalk. Diane found it all fascinating.

Once at the hotel, a bellman helped her with her luggage to the front desk, where she was greeted in Spanish by one of the clerks.

"I'm sorry," Diane responded, "I don't speak Spanish. Do you speak English?"

"Of course, Señora. Many guests speak English, and all the persons at the front desk speak English."

"That's a relief. I'm Diane Carter, and I made a reservation yesterday."

The clerk thumbed through a bunch of papers in a file, had Diane fill out the appropriate forms, and then called over the bellman and handed him the keys.

"Room 615," said the smiling clerk to the bellman.

Diane began to follow the bellman, who had placed three pieces of luggage onto a cart. Then she suddenly turned to ask the clerk if there were any messages for her, hoping there might be one from Don.

"No, I do not believe so." He turned and checked the box to room 615. "There is nothing here for you. But someone ask a little time ago if Diane Carter check in today."

Diane's spirits rose. Don had already called to check if she had arrived. She could hardly contain her jubilation at the thought of seeing him soon.

"Did he leave a phone number where he could be reached?"

"Phone number?" the clerk replied. "No, he ask if you arrive and then walk away with no message."

"Walked away?" Diane was confused. "You mean he was here in person, not on the telephone?"

"Yes. I believe he was expecting you."

After the importance of secrecy that Don and she had discussed only the night before, why would he take the risk of showing up in the middle of downtown Lima in plain sight of any of the many people searching for him?

"Señora, you seem … worried. Is anything wrong?"

"Mr. …?"

"Blancas." He pointed to his name tag pinned to his breast pocket.

"Mr. Blancas. What did this person look like?"

"Vamos a ver. He was well-dressed, about forty-five, maybe fifty years old. Glasses. He wore glasses. I do not remember more."

Diane spun around and scanned the lobby. It wasn't Don. Someone else knew of her pending arrival. Could it be a friend of Don's? Or someone he simply sent over to ask about her arrival? She noticed the bellman waiting patiently at the elevator with her luggage and realized that she had better get to her room and wait for Don's call, but she began to think defensively. She turned to the clerk for one last question.

"This man. Could you tell if he was from Peru, or somewhere else?"

"Definitely an American. I know the American accent. I watch many English-language American movies on the television. They have subtitles in Spanish, but I find watching them improves my English." He had a broad grin on his face and was proud of his English speaking abilities.

But Diane hadn't noticed. She'd already turned and begun walking toward the bellman—who was still waiting at the elevator—steeped in her own thoughts and anxieties.

Within minutes, she arrived in her room and began to unpack her clothes. She would wash up, change into something more comfortable, and try to relax while waiting for Don's call. She had been in Lima for less than an hour but already had been made aware of the possibility of danger. Diane hoped that the unidentified person had been sent by Don. She looked at the door and impulsively walked over to it, double locked the door, and latched the chain.

One hour passed by, but each minute seemed an eternity. She paced the floor, having already unpacked her things.

The phone rang. Diane leaped across the bed, flopped onto it, and grabbed for the phone on the night table on the opposite side of the bed.

She practically shouted the greeting. "Hello!"

"It's me," Don said cheerfully.

Diane was relieved. "Of course it's you, you dummy. Thank God you called and you're okay. I was worried sick about you."

"But didn't you just arrive? I called the airport and knew the plane had landed, and I tried to estimate how long it would take for you to get to the hotel, check in, and have some time to unwind."

"I'm sorry. I was okay, I really was, until I spoke with the clerk at the front desk. He said someone was asking if I arrived. Some American, forty-five or fifty years old, wearing glasses. Did you send someone?"

There was silence at the other end of the telephone. Don began to speak with a serious tone. "Go to the lobby, now! I'll call the hotel and ask them to page you. Pick up one of their house phones. Understand?"

"Yes, but—"

"Just do it. Can you get to the lobby in three minutes?"

"I … I think so. Yes, I can get there."

"Three minutes. Expect my call."

Diane heard the click of the phone, hung up the receiver, quickly unbolted the door locks, and ran to the elevator, inadvertently pressing both the up and down buttons in her haste.

"Come on, come on," she mumbled to herself, urging the elevator on.

It seemed much longer, but within a minute the doors to the elevator opened and she stepped in. A man standing inside smiled at her, but she paid no attention. She pressed the button for the lobby. The doors closed, and the elevator began to move up instead of down.

"Oh, shit!" she exclaimed, totally ignoring the presence of the man. Realizing that she'd entered an elevator on the way up, she frantically pressed several buttons higher than six, watched curiously by the man. The doors opened at the eighth floor, and Diane rushed out. She pressed the down button as the doors closed, slowly obscuring the man, who was shaking his head in wonderment.

"Damn it!" she shouted. She waited a few seconds and then thought, *the hell with it*. She ran down the hall toward the stairwell. She opened the door and rushed down the eight flights to the lobby, arriving perspiring and out of breath.

As soon as she emerged from the stairwell, she heard her name being paged and ran to the front desk, appearing disheveled and panting heavily.

"Mr. Blancas, that's me."

"You been out jogging, Señora Carter?"

In other circumstances, she would have found the statement humorous, but she ignored his question and demanded, "The phone. Which phone?"

"Here. You can use this one," he said, baffled by her appearance, as he placed the telephone on the countertop. "Line three."

Diane pressed the button for line three. "Don?"

"What took so long?"

Slightly embarrassed, she said, "I got on an up elevator by mistake."

"Jesus. And you're here to bail me out?"

Diane, having caught her breath and happy to hear Don's voice, inhaled deeply and tried to relax. "Yeah, some heroine. But what's wrong? Why all the cloak-and-dagger stuff? And who was that man?"

Don became serious. "First of all, I sent no man to meet you. Someone must have known you were coming here, someone from the United States."

"But how? We only discussed this last night. How could someone possibly know about it all the way here?"

"I can't be certain, but it's a good bet your phone was tapped."

"You're kidding." She was only slightly surprised.

"You gave those papers I mailed Steinert to the government. They probably bugged your phone and heard our arrangements. I'll bet the phone in your room is bugged, too. That's why I asked you to grab a house phone."

"If they know I'm here, they're probably watching me right now." She glanced around the lobby, examining the faces of several persons but not actually knowing what to look for.

"That's right," Don said. "That's why you've got to find some way of getting away from them. Our best bet is the phone, but we can't even be certain that they're not listening on some extension right now."

Nervously, Diane asked, "Do you think they'll try to capture me?"

"No, I don't. They could have done that already if they wanted to. First of all, they're Americans. They have no jurisdiction here, and besides, you don't even know where I am, or where the cylinder is. They're probably hoping you'll lead them to me. We have to outsmart them."

"But how? What can I do now? I don't know who they are, where they are, or even how many there are of them." She glanced around the lobby again but, again, could detect nothing unusual.

"Tonight, call for a cab to pick you up at the hotel at ten. Go to Café Enrico on Avenida Arenales. I'll call there and let you know what to do at that point. Expect my call at ten fifteen. Got it?"

Diane repeated, "Ten p.m., go to Café Enrico on Avenida Arenales. You'll call me with further instructions."

"Good. Love you."

"Love you too." She handed the phone back, thanked Mr. Blancas, and hurried to the elevator and up to her room, where she readied herself for her hoped-for rendezvous with Don, purposely dressing in a blouse and skirt that she knew Don admired.

At nine thirty she called for a taxi to be waiting for her in front of the hotel. It arrived just before ten. As she walked through the lobby, she felt as though eyes were following her every move, but she wasn't sure that her feeling wasn't just paranoia.

Her taxi was waiting for her, and she was helped in by an accommodating doorman. The taxi drove through the brightly lit streets of nighttime downtown Lima and within minutes came to a halt in front of Café Enrico, a very pleasant-looking, relatively high-class restaurant and bar. She entered and asked to be seated at the bar, noticing that the time was already 10:12. She glanced around the restaurant as casually as she could to try to determine if she was being watched or followed.

Several people were finishing dinner, and the place was only about one-third full. A man and a woman sat at the other end of the bar. Two men entered the café and also sat at the bar, closer to the couple than to Diane.

Diane tried catching a glimpse of the two men without being conspicuous. It was difficult to get a good look at their faces, as they seemed to be facing each other in active conversation, but she thought they looked like Americans.

A phone rang behind the bar. The bartender asked for Señora Carter, and Diane stammered slightly, "Me ... that's me." The bartender handed her the phone.

"Diane, say nothing. Only listen. Order a drink, if you haven't already, and then ask where the ladies' room is. The restrooms are toward the rear, down a small corridor. There's another doorway that leads to a street behind the restaurant. A taxi will be waiting for you. Get in quickly and check to see if any other car follows you. I doubt there will be. There's no way for them to know of this back exit. Understand?"

Diane nodded and said, "I understand."

"The driver already knows exactly where to take you. If you think, even for a second, that you're being followed, tell the driver you changed your mind and return to your hotel. Is that clear?"

"Very." She was trying to appear as nonchalant as possible but was sure she wasn't succeeding at it.

"See you in a while. Be careful. Very careful." The concern reflected in Don's voice made Diane feel all the more tense.

Diane heard the click of the phone, thanked the bartender, and ordered a glass of white wine. But before the bartender could pour the drink, she asked where the restrooms were. The bartender gestured with his hand and said, "Around the corner and down the hallway."

Diane rose from the stool, walked past the two men and the couple who were still sitting at the bar, and turned down the corridor toward the rear door. She paused for a second to look behind her and, seeing nothing, opened the door, stepped out into the night, and closed the door quietly behind her.

As soon as she turned around, she saw a taxi parked at the curb. She hurried over to it and got in. The cab smelled of liquor.

Apprehensively, she asked, "Do you know where to take me?"

"Si, Señora. I been told. No problema." The driver looked at her through the rearview mirror and smiled, revealing a gold tooth.

The taxi pulled away and Diane scanned the streets for any sign of being followed. She continued doing so for about ten minutes until the taxi entered a dark road. She could clearly see that she wasn't being followed. She sat back, sighing with relief as a sense of exhilaration came over her. She had lost them, she thought, and in only a short while she'd be seeing Don.

The taxi continued toward its appointed rendezvous while the driver made all sorts of small talk in very halting English. Diane politely attempted as best she could to satisfy the driver with brief remarks. She was in no mood for the taxi driver's broken English chatter.

Occasionally, Diane would turn around, still checking behind to see if she was being followed, but each time she detected nothing unusual.

The taxi began to slow down and then pulled over to the side of the road, about one hundred feet from an isolated intersection.

"Where are we?" Diane asked, looking all around at the dark and deserted roadway, surrounded by sinister hills that loomed eerily into the darkness.

"This the place, Señora. He say go this place."

Diane hesitated for a moment. The dim light that had just been turned on inside the taxi obscured the outside, making it appear darker than it was. But Diane knew she must follow instructions. She paid the driver, adding a fair tip, and the driver thanked her. He rushed outside and opened the rear door, and Diane stepped out. The driver got in, turned the taxi around, and sped off back toward Lima, leaving only the odor of exhaust fumes lingering in the cool black of night.

She heard sounds of rustling in the underbrush and became nervous at the noises, but she talked herself into believing that it was only some small animal or birds moving through dead leaves.

There was still no sign of Don. Suddenly, a car's headlights could be seen in the distance. Diane instinctively backed into the underbrush as the car sped by. If it was Don, he'd know where to stop—or at least she prayed that that would be the case, as doubts began to fill her head. She thought, what if she was dropped at the wrong spot by that dumb driver, or what if Don couldn't make it here for some reason? She hadn't the faintest idea of where she was or how far she was from Lima or any sort of town or city. How would she get back to Lima? The thought of hitching a ride less than thrilled her. Thoughts of rapists picking her up made her feel even more uncomfortable. In this place, someone could imprison her in some deserted farmhouse and keep her there and do anything he wanted with her, and no one would ever know what happened to her. No, if she had to she would stay off the road, away from sight, and try to make the most of the situation in the morning, when she would at least be able to see something.

Her thoughts were interrupted by the sound of footsteps approaching. Her heart began to pound in her chest, and she crouched down until her bare knees touched the cold, damp underbrush.

She could hear only the footsteps now; all other sounds were blocked from her mind, even her own breathing, which she attempted to silence. Suddenly, she heard her name being called out in a loud whisper. "Diane. Diane. Where are you? It's me, Diane. It's me."

"Don!" Diane shouted, rising from her knees. "I'm over here." She felt as though the weight of the planet had just lifted from her shoulders. She began to tremble joyously with relief.

Don heard where her voice came from, rushed to the side of the road, and spotted Diane emerging from the underbrush. The two met head on and clutched each other in bear hugs fashion at first. Then they tenderly kissed each other on the face and on the lips. Their emotions began to overwhelm them, and Diane began to cry. Don's eyes, too, had misted, but the urgency of the situation forced Don to quickly compose himself, and he spoke first, his hands on Diane's quivering shoulders. His voice was pressing.

"We've got to get out of here. I have another cab waiting for us around the bend in the road, just up ahead. I had to be certain no one followed you. I waited until I saw your cab pull away and that other car pass by."

Diane was now ready to get down to the business at hand. "I don't think I was followed, but I'm fairly certain some men were watching me in that café."

"I know. Let's get out of here. We can talk later."

They walked quickly up the road. Diane was having trouble keeping up with Don in her dress shoes. They turned onto another road and walked another seventy-five yards to where another taxi sat waiting for them. They got in, and the taxi sped off toward Don's room in the little town. Diane touched Don's newly grown beard and smiled playfully. "My, how manly you look."

"This will be my disguise. You like it?"

"Do I have a choice? But right now I'll take you any way you look." She thought he appeared somewhat older now but wasn't sure if it was only the beard that was making him look that way.

Don lit a cigarette and blew the smoke out the half-open window.

Diane remarked, "I see some things haven't changed."

Don shrugged and then looked at Diane, trying to sound serious as he said, "If I didn't find you I'd have been in big trouble."

"Why is that?" She sounded concerned.

"I don't have enough money left to pay for this cab. I hope you don't mind the Dutch treat." He smiled.

"Maybe I'll let you wash dishes to pay for this cab," she quipped as she poked him in his side with her elbow.

Don winced, faking pain. It felt good for the two of them to joke together again, and they both laughed out loud.

They arrived at the town and got out near the rooming house. Diane paid the driver, and they walked to the second floor, where Don opened the door to the small room that contained a bed and a dresser. There was no closet and no bathroom. A communal bathroom was down the hall.

Once inside, Don and Diane sat at the edge of the bed and began to discuss their next move. Don said, "We need to be more mobile than this. Tomorrow we should travel back to Lima, where we can rent a car."

Diane answered softly, "Okay, but right now, are you okay? What happened to you, and what happened to Dr. Steinert, and why are you being sought by the police?"

"It's a long story, but first I was double-crossed by my best friend, Diego Gonzales, who intended to have acquaintances of his sell the cylinder to the highest bidder. Fortunately, after I dug up the cylinder, I threw a bunch of stamps on the package I sent Anton and dropped it off at a mailbox before they kidnapped me. The rest you know something about. Steinert had some things I sent checked out, and when he didn't hear from me, he contacted you and flew down here. He followed Diego and managed to find out where I was being held and rescued me. Anton had to smash some big jerk over the head with a whiskey bottle."

"My God," she replied, astonished.

"We found Diego and forced him to tell us where the cylinder was by burying him up to his neck and threatening never to return if he lied."

"Jesus! So then what happened?" She could hardly believe what Don was telling her.

"We found the cylinder, but were chased by Diego's friends into the hills. We outran them, but our car blew out two tires. We buried the cylinder and then made our way back to Lima. They somehow learned where Anton was staying and were waiting for us. Anton shot one guy with the gun he took from the big jerk, and we ran, but Anton couldn't keep up. The rest made the news. He saved my life ... twice." Don's voice trailed off as he recalled the old man. He stared straight ahead as if focusing on nothing.

Diane reached out and touched his arm, which brought Don back to reality.

"I'm sorry, but I just can't get Anton out of my mind."

"I understand," she said tenderly.

"Anyway, the next thing I know, they find Diego, and I'm being sought as a criminal for attempting to steal ancient relics from Peru. That's when I called you."

"And that's when I realized our government couldn't protect you, at least not here, in Peru. They want that cylinder and intend to get it. Do you have a plan?" But before Don could respond, Diane put her hand up and said, "Wait. Before you say anything, where is the cylinder? Can I see it?" There was a hint of anticipation in her voice.

"It's right here, with me."

"Here?" She glanced around the tiny room.

Don stood up and went to the dresser, pushed it aside, pulled up the floorboards, and lifted the lead box out. He carried the box to the bed and placed it on the floor next to Diane.

"Someone could find it here," she said.

"I know. I thought about burying it again, but I wasn't sure I'd be able to get back to this area. If I'm able to make my escape, I want this thing with me. Where I go now, it goes." Don smiled as he corrected himself. "Rather, where we go."

He took the cover off the lead box, exposing the shiny, golden metallic cylinder.

Diane looked down at the cylinder while Don stared at her, waiting for a reaction.

She looked up at Don and spoke with disappointment. "That's it? It looks so ... so plain."

"What did you expect?"

"I don't know. I guess something with little antennas and things coming out of it."

"That's the beauty of it. It's complexity in a simplistic package. This thing is far more advanced than anything our own technology has been able to produce. Can you imagine what we might learn from this?"

"You're really convinced that this is no baloney? That it's the real McCoy, an alien thing?"

"I'm sure of it."

"How do you know?"

"Lots of things. But the main reasons are the metal, which is made of a material we cannot identify and seems indestructible. It has the ability to give off enough radiation to melt solid rock into liquid and then go back to almost zero radiation levels while remaining untouched itself. We found it embedded in solid rock. An earthquake revealed it to a young cousin of Diego, who was killed trying to pry it loose from the rocks."

"Can I ... I mean, is it dangerous to touch it?"

"Not at all. As long as you don't bang on it. It seems to have a protective device against someone destroying it. Striking it violently makes it give off immense quantities of radiation."

Diane again looked down at the cylinder, only this time with a newfound sense of awe. "Can I touch it now?"

"Go ahead."

Diane reached down and touched it reverently with her fingertips.

Don said, "Everyone seems to have that same reaction. Sort of a religious experience, isn't it?"

Diane, still staring at the cylinder, responded, "In a way, I guess. But I'm thinking about the people, or whatever they are, that made this. What are they like? Where are they now? Where are they from? Why did they leave this?"

"And these are the kinds of questions I hope to discover answers to. Not, 'How can I use this to gain an advantage over my enemies?' or, 'How can I use this to destroy my enemies with the information I might obtain from this?' That's what our government wants it so badly for."

Diane placed her hand behind Don's neck. "And that's why you're in so much danger. They'll stop at nothing to get their hands on it. You know that. But even if you escape with this, you can't hope to keep it from our government forever." She removed her hand.

"I know that. But my biggest fear is that in their zeal for strategic information they'll destroy its true scientific and historic value. We need to know more about these aliens, whatever they are. It's sort of like uncovering the burial chamber of an ancient pharaoh only to find that some thieves, looking for treasure, have plundered the tomb. The gold or whatever they find is only worth so much and can always be sold, although if melted down, it loses much of its historic and true value. The knowledge that's lost by desecrating the tomb is invaluable, priceless, and irreplaceable. Once they've plundered the cylinder for its 'gold,' so to speak, we might never be able to retrieve the priceless information about these aliens. The scientific community should have the right to examine this thing before the military."

"I agree one hundred percent. But you're a wanted man. How can you get yourself and the cylinder safely out of here?"

"That's where I'm hoping you'll come in. You're my only ally now, and so far, you're a really good one. You'd make the most beautiful CIA agent in the world."

Don moved closer to Diane. They stood next to the bed beside the cylinder. He placed his arms on her shoulders while staring at her face. His hands began to unbutton her blouse, one button at a time, from the top down, revealing a lacy bra that clipped in front. Diane didn't move. She stared at his hands as they performed a familiar task that nonetheless felt to her like a new experience. Watching him unclip her bra, freeing her breasts, aroused her as she hadn't been for months. As Don began to probe her breasts and nipples with his fingers, she could stand it no longer. She looked up at Don and asked him to kiss her. He willingly obliged.

Embracing, they guided each other slowly onto the bed. Diane looked at Don and asked, half kidding, "You don't suppose that cylinder thing can see us, do you?"

Don smiled and said, "I don't know, and right now, I don't really care."

The two of them then made love with more passionate abandon than ever before.

CHAPTER 23

TOM RAWLINGS WAS FURIOUS. His two CIA agents, posing as "aides" to Rawlings, had been assigned to keep watch of Diane Carter but had lost her almost immediately. She was to be his main hope of contact with Donald Carter, but now he was back to square one, for apparently Diane Carter knew she was being followed. But his anger soon mellowed to disappointment. After all, his entourage consisted mostly of scientists, negotiators, and aides, with only two of those aides being trained CIA agents.

After discussion with Major Craig Styles, his chief non-CIA aide, it was decided that Diane Carter would eventually return to her hotel room for her baggage. They would either attempt to convince her to help them with this situation or, in the event they were unable to speak with her, slip an envelope under her door containing a letter detailing the benefits of having them help her and her husband out of their predicament.

Major Styles cautioned Rawlings that since they were in a foreign country on unofficial business—they weren't even allowed to wear their uniforms—the type of aid that could be offered to the Carters was limited. The Peruvian government wouldn't allow Donald Carter, now a fugitive from the law, out of the country, at least not legally. And more importantly, the Peruvian government wouldn't allow the cylinder out of the country.

Rawlings knew that his group would have to locate the Carters in order to obtain the cylinder. Once that had been accomplished, the entourage's scientists would then have to determine whether this cylinder thing was even worth the effort, which Rawlings was certain it was not. But if by some miracle it was deemed worthwhile, with help from Washington they would smuggle first the cylinder out of Lima and then the Carters, if at all possible. The cylinder at that point would have top priority; the Carters would not. The group was also aware that the Soviet Union now had a group in Lima, which would represent another potential obstacle to their plans. The Commies wouldn't give up on the cylinder easily, hoax or not.

Still another obstacle, though this one was judged less dangerous, was the group that originally had the cylinder and lost it to Carter. Precisely what their role would be at this juncture was uncertain. It was possible that they would be out of the picture, considering recent events.

In brainstorming possible future actions, the Rawlings group negated the idea of following Diane Carter again, should they have the opportunity, because she would probably be able to lose them as easily as she had the first time. They also tossed around the idea of kidnapping her and either forcing her to tell them where her husband was or using her as a bargaining chip for the cylinder. But this plan, too, was negated for several reasons. First, kidnapping an American citizen and keeping her hostage in a foreign country did not sit well with most of the group, though Rawlings and a couple of others felt they could justify it. Second, if she didn't talk or if Donald Carter didn't take the bait, what would they do then? They doubted either Diane or Donald Carter would believe that they would torture or kill her, which is precisely what they would not have done, at least not in this particular situation. And should the whole affair prove to be a hoax, they wouldn't want to be embarrassed or, worse still, cited or prosecuted for acting too rashly. And lastly, the group needed an ally in this affair. They didn't want to lose any confidence the Carters might have in the group as potential allies in their cause.

Therefore, it was decided to write a letter that detailed the intent of the United States government to bring the Carters and the cylinder safely back to the United States and pointed out that their resources were far better than the Carters'. The letter was slipped under Diane's hotel door that afternoon.

Meanwhile, Diego was being released from the hospital, where he had spent the night recovering from his ordeal in his would-be grave. He was met outside by an angry Jose Marin, who was waiting in his car. Diego opened the door and got in, nervously unsure of Marin's reaction at first. He saw the half-crazed look on Marin's face and immediately knew what the reaction would be.

"Fool! Why'd you tell them where the cylinder was?" Marin's body shook with rage, and he felt like strangling Diego but managed to control himself.

Diego responded sheepishly. "They would have let me rot in that hole. I had no choice. That old man really knew how to get to me. I—"

Marin abruptly interrupted, waving his hand for Diego to be silent. "Your excuses mean nothing now. Alcalde is dead, Hernando is dead, and the old man is dead. But we're alive, and Carter still has the cylinder. We need to find him and kill him this time, slowly if possible." Marin clenched his teeth and tightened his hand into a fist as he shouted, "And get that cylinder back."

Diego spoke softly, acting prudently subservient. "But Jose, how do we start? We won't see Don simply strolling down the street carrying the cylinder under his arm."

Marin enjoyed being in control of situations, and he spoke calmly. "Here's my plan. I've been in touch with Julio Mendez, who informed me that both the Americans and Russians sent people here to negotiate for the cylinder, but, of course, they were informed of the loss instead."

"And now they're back home, I guess."

"You guess wrong. The amazing thing is that they're both still in Lima."

"Why?"

"Apparently they were impressed enough with the information Mendez and Solars gave them to be willing to stay. I think both groups will try to devise a plan to capture the cylinder for themselves."

"What about our own government? What are they doing?"

"Mendez told me they're working with the Lima police, hoping that Carter can be located and taken into custody. Our government won't allow the cylinder out of Peru if they can get their hands on it. Now that Carter has it, they think they'll eventually catch up with him. In any event, they're keeping a watchful eye on the Americans and Russians. They're not going to let them smuggle the thing out of Peru."

"So with three governments and the police all looking for Carter, what chance do we have?"

Marin smiled menacingly. "Ah, you think Jose Marin doesn't have a plan? Well, he does."

"I'm listening." Diego leaned in closer.

"First, we know what Carter looks like, both with and without his beard and long hair."

"Big deal. He's still not going to show up at our doorstep."

"I know that. But I think we can make him show up at our doorstep with the cylinder."

Diego asked skeptically, "How can you do that?"

"It might be a long shot, but you just might be the key."

"Me?"

"Yes, you. You told me that Carter was married and showed you several photos of his wife."

"So?"

"So you've got to find this wife of his."

"What are you talking about? She lives in New York."

"She does, but right now she's here, in Lima."

Diego was surprised at the information. "How do you know that?"

"Mendez has had a man who works at the airport keeping tabs on every American or Russian entering or leaving the country during the past few days. One name stuck out like a cockroach floating in a glass of milk: Diane Carter."

Diego's eyes opened wide. "So she's here to help Don. Do we know where she is right now?"

"No, but if we can get to her, we'll get that cylinder back, I guarantee it. Carter will fear no one more than he fears us. He knows what we'll do to his wife if he doesn't play our game. We can always amuse ourselves with her before torturing and killing her. He knows that." Marin had an ugly sneer on his face.

Diego was alarmed by Marin's callous remarks. Torture? Death? These were terrible acts of violence that Diego wanted no part of, yet he knew they were ones he could easily be drawn into by his acquaintance with Marin, whose wanton disregard for others Diego was now coming to understand. Out of fear of drawing the wrath of Marin, he hesitated, but then he decided to attempt softening the brutish heart of Jose Marin.

"Jose, it won't be necessary to do anything terrible to Don or his wife, I assure you. I understand you may have to threaten her, scare her a little, to get the cylinder, but I'm sure you won't have to hurt either one of them. Besides, Don was my friend." He'd said what needed to be said and hoped he didn't need to pile drive it home to Marin. But curiously, he detected a puzzled expression on Marin's face, one whose meaning Diego couldn't determine. Nervously facing Marin, he hoped Marin was considering his plea and would break the tense silence with an affirmative answer.

Instead, Marin scowled. "They're scum," he said, speaking with such vehemence that spittle flew from his mouth and landed on Diego's shirt.

Diego ignored its presence as Marin continued.

"You care about scum?" he screamed. His face was flushed with rage.

Startled by the reaction, Diego meekly tried defending his remarks. "But they're not really—"

Marin shouted, "Don't tell me they're not dirt, Diego, because I don't want to hear it. Your so-called friend stole that cylinder from you not once but twice, and he's your friend? He's like all the rest of them, spitting on peasants like us and then telling the world how sorry they feel for us. Your *friend* will never tell us where it is unless he knows we mean business."

"But Jose," Diego pleaded, "we can threaten them first. Then maybe they'll be frightened enough to tell us what we want."

Marin shook his head in disbelief. "You don't understand, do you? I don't care if they do tell us. Either way, they deserve to die. Besides—" His eyes bulged. "I'm going to enjoy fucking the shit out of that gringo woman. I've never had an American woman before, and I'm going to enjoy it just like the others." His face bore a sick smile.

Diego shuddered. "What others?"

"Other women, of course. I've raped lots of women. Sometimes I made them do things they'd never done even with their own husbands. And you know what? They loved it! They said they didn't, but I know they did," he said with demented pride.

Diego blinked several times in uncontrollable succession. He knew Marin to be a thief who was possibly involved in small-time drug deals, but this talk of wanton rape and murder was a deplorable revelation to him. Minutes before, he had thought he was dealing with a man to be feared; now he knew that he was dealing with an out-of-control monster.

Marin continued with his frenzied tirade. "We owe them nothing. No mercy. They wouldn't care if we starved to death, so why should we care how they die? You see my point, don't you?"

Diego nodded weakly in agreement, knowing that there would be no sense in arguing with Marin in his crazed state. Diego could only pray that if and when the time came for Marin to make the choice between life and death, he would be more rational. Diego hoped that somehow they would find the cylinder without hurting Don and his wife. In the meantime, he figured she was safe. Marin didn't know where she was.

Diego then asked, almost wishing that Marin would have no answer, "But how do we find her?"

His anger vented, a now calmer and more calculatingly rational Marin answered, "My guess is that she's staying in a hotel in Lima. Probably a nice one in the downtown area. I suggest you keep an eye out for her. If you get really lucky, you just might spot her on the street or in a restaurant. Who knows?"

"I've only seen photos of her, but if I get close enough, I think I could identify her. But I don't like our chances."

"I agree. It's a long shot. But what we can also do is call every hotel and ask for Diane Carter. Maybe she was foolish enough to register under her own name. In fact, maybe she would, thinking that no one was looking for her or even knew she was in Lima."

Diego drew a deep breath and said with resignation, "Sure, we can try that."

Marin put the car in gear and drove to a local restaurant, where he broke some bills for change for the phone booths. He opened the phone book and ripped out the page that listed the larger hotels in Lima. Then he ripped it in half, giving one half to Diego and keeping the other half for himself. They both began to make their calls to the various hotels in an attempt to locate the one in which Diane Carter was registered.

It didn't take long. After several calls, Marin called the Miramar, and yes, the hotel operator would put the call through to her room. Marin hung up. Diane Carter was staying there.

Marin was elated. His plan now was for the two of them to go to the Miramar immediately, attempt to rent a room as close to Diane Carter's as possible, and wait and watch for her. They knew that she might never return or take days to return, but it was worth it, they felt. What did they have to lose? They would take turns watching for her with no real risk. After all, she didn't know what either of them looked like.

The two men registered for a room, requesting a room on the same floor as Diane. The rooms on either side of hers were occupied, but they arranged to get one across the hall, two doors down from hers. This would serve as their headquarters for the time being. They felt that, provided she was alone, kidnapping her somewhere outside the hotel would be no problem. Inside the hotel would be no place to attempt to capture her; there would be too much security and too many people around. For now, they would wait and see.

But for Diego, the wait would be filled with mixed emotions.

CHAPTER 24

DIANE AND DON AWOKE to a gloriously clear morning. The night before had been the most wonderful since their honeymoon, maybe better. They lay in bed for an hour, reminiscing about good times and enjoying each other's company. But eventually, the idle talk turned to serious discussion. They decided that they would wait for late afternoon and take a taxi back to Lima, where they could rent a car. Diane would continue on in the taxi to her hotel room, where she would pack all of her belongings and check out, grab another taxi, and meet Don at a certain location, making sure she wasn't being followed.

They tossed around the idea of Diane wearing a disguise of some sort but negated the thought as they figured that if the Americans were watching her hotel room, any disguise would be fruitless.

After checking out of the hotel and reuniting, they would drive back to their little room and make further plans. The thought that Marin and Diego might be the ones to be watching her room never occurred to them.

Before leaving, they wrapped the lead box in brown paper to make it appear like a package. Late that afternoon, they set out for Lima in a taxi. Don was dropped off at an auto rental agency with the box, and Diane proceeded on to the hotel to carry out the plan of packing and meeting Don near the Café Peligrosa.

Diane entered the hotel and, looking to see if she was being followed, took the elevator to her room. She placed the key in the door and opened it, unaware that she was being watched through a crack in an almost-closed door by Diego, who called out in a loud whisper to Marin, "It's her. She's here already." It had only been five hours since they had taken the room.

Marin jumped out of the chair he'd been sitting on, threw a newspaper onto the floor, and ran to the door. "Where is she?"

"She's in the room."

"Alone?"

"No one with her."

"Good. Now we wait for her to leave. It might take all night or even tomorrow, but we'll have to wait and see—and we'll watch for anyone else who might enter her room. Maybe even Carter himself?"

"He's not that stupid."

"You never know. Keep an eye on the door. I'll relieve you in an hour."

"Okay." Diego then sat back in the chair that he'd placed next to the slightly ajar door and peered through the crack while Marin went back to reading his newspaper and smoking his cigar. They both settled in for what they knew could be a long and dull wait.

But they wouldn't have long to wait. As soon as Diane entered the room, she began making plans to vacate. She would pack quickly, call for the bellman, call for a taxi, check out of the hotel, and rendezvous with Don.

She had just begun to pack, throwing everything back into the suitcases, when she glanced over toward the door and noticed an envelope lying on the floor beside it. In her haste, she hadn't noticed it when she entered the room.

Diane picked up the sealed envelope, tore it open, and extracted a hand-written letter. It was addressed to her. The letter read:

Dear Mrs. Carter:

The US government has sent our group to Lima in an attempt to determine whether or not a certain cylinder is genuine or a hoax and, if genuine, to secure the same and return it to the United States.

We know you are here to help your husband. We do not think you can be much help in getting him safely out of Peru. We have the resources to get you, your husband, and the cylinder out of Peru.

Please allow us to extend our help to you. We know you are trusting no one at this point, but please think this over carefully and discuss it with your husband. If you decide to avail yourself of our help, please call this telephone number: 386021. Someone will answer that number on a twenty-four-hour basis.

Remember, we only want to help you. God bless you, and God bless America.

Sincerely,
Col. Tom Rawlings

Diane didn't know whether to greet the message with relief that possible help could be found or to be nervous knowing that she was probably being watched at this very moment. She wondered whether they would in fact help Don or only use him to get their hands on the cylinder. This remained to be seen.

She folded the letter, placed it in her purse, and continued to pack.

A few minutes later, she called for a bellman and a taxi. The bellman arrived shortly and knocked on her door, under the watchful eye of Diego.

"She's checking out. There's a bellman at her door."

Marin thought for a moment and answered, "Let's beat her downstairs and wait for her there. I'll get the car and park it in front. You wait in the lobby for her. Follow her out and watch where she goes. I'll be waiting for you in the car."

With that, the two men rushed out of the room and took up their positions.

Two minutes later, Diane rode the elevator to the lobby with the bellman. Within five minutes, she was checked out of the hotel and helped into a waiting taxi, with her luggage placed into the trunk. She was watched carefully by Marin, who was parked two cars behind her taxi.

Diego quickly spotted Marin's car and jumped into the front seat as the taxi pulled away from the curb, followed by Marin and Diego.

Marin spoke devilishly. "You didn't tell me she was so good looking. I can't wait to fuck the hell out of her. Maybe even in front of her husband, just before I slit both their throats. You'll join me in the fun, eh, Diego?"

Diego now realized how deeply he'd involved himself in this affair. He held no animosity anymore toward his ex-friend and certainly none against

Diane. Hadn't Don carried out his end of the bargain and notified the police to find him? Diego was no killer, and he knew Don was in this mess because of him, but he feared the half-crazed man sitting next to him. So, as convincingly as he could manage, he nodded and replied, "Sure, Jose. Sure."

Sitting in the lead car, Diane was wary of her situation, but not of Diego and Marin. She expected the possibility of being followed by one of Rawlings's group, and peered behind to see if any car appeared to be following her. It didn't take long for her to notice that a car was mimicking each and every turn that the taxi made. It was turning to dusk, but she could plainly see that the men appeared to be local, not American, and wondered if it wasn't simply a coincidence.

But uncertainty wasn't what she needed at the moment. Diane desperately needed to be with Don, and she decided to gamble and outrun these two if need be, with Don at her side, rather than attempt to make the taxi driver outrun them or have the driver drop her off by herself. *Besides,* she thought, *how do I know the driver would be willing to risk his own life in a high-speed chase?*

Thus, Diane chose to continue on to meet with Don. Perhaps, she thought, they weren't following her at all.

The taxi pulled over to the corner near the Café Peligrosa, the designated meeting spot.

Diego and Marin pulled over to the curb about one block away and saw Diane and the driver get out of the cab, open the trunk, and place the luggage by the curb. Diane was aware that the car that was following her had pulled over to the curb, one block away. She told the driver to wait a moment.

She scanned the area for Don, thinking that if she didn't see him immediately, she would have to tell the driver to place the luggage back into the trunk and take her somewhere else, perhaps back to the hotel, where there would be enough people around to ensure some protection for her.

As Diane was paying the driver, another car pulled up to the adjacent corner of the cross street, about twenty feet away. It was Don in his rented car. He gave a brief whistle as Diane turned and spotted him waving at her.

Diane yelled, "Quick, get over here!"

Don jumped out of the car and ran to the luggage as Diane asked the driver to help her throw her luggage into Don's car.

"What's wrong?" Don shouted.

"There's a car down the block. They might be following me."

They threw the luggage into the trunk, and Don slammed it shut. As Don and Diane jumped into the car, Marin's car began pulling away from the curb.

"That's the car, but I don't think they're Americans."

Don looked back at the car as he turned the corner. "Christ, it's Marin's car."

Don floored the accelerator, wheels spinning and rubberized smoke flying. Looking in the rearview mirror, he could see Marin's car behind him.

"Who's in the car?" Diane shouted as the two cars sped through the streets.

"I can't see their faces, but one of 'em's got to be Marin; it's his car."

Diane was terrified. The cars were streaking through the streets, passing other vehicles at breakneck speeds. "Don, we can't keep going like this. They're still right behind us. If they get to us, will they just take the cylinder and go?"

Don didn't answer, concentrating on his driving and not really knowing what to say to her.

Meanwhile, in the chase car, Marin was gleeful. "I can't believe she led us right to him. If we can get them, we'll get that cylinder easily."

"Yeah," Diego answered nervously, "if you don't kill us first with your car." He was biting his fingernails and having mixed emotions, but he hoped to be able to get the cylinder and somehow leave Don and his wife unharmed. He'd have to try to convince Marin not to do anything drastic.

In the lead car, Don yelled to Diane to jump into the backseat.

"What?" asked a confused Diane.

"Just do it," Don snapped.

Diane turned around and slithered on her stomach over the back of her seat. Then she turned and asked, "Now what?" She was sitting on the front edge of the rear seat, next to the wrapped lead box that was securely seat belted in.

Don yelled, "Take the paper off the box, open it, and take out the cylinder. Place it, very carefully, on the front seat next to me."

Diane asked no questions. She did precisely what Don asked of her and, considering the speed of the vehicle, placed the cylinder as gently as she could on the front seat, next to Don.

"What do I do now?" she yelled from behind his ear.

"Stay where you are, and keep low. If I'm right about this thing, we possess a more powerful weapon than any gun they might have. I've got to use it properly and figure out a place to use it."

The cars were now into the outskirts of Lima, almost into farm country, and the roads were incredibly dark.

Marin was getting edgy and beginning to lose patience. He opened his jacket and pulled out a gun from his belt.

Seeing this move, Diego apprehensively asked, "What are you doing?"

"Throwing a scare into them. If I'm lucky, I'll hit one of their tires."

Marin reached out of the open window with his left hand holding the gun and took aim at the lead car, about fifty yards ahead. Accelerating, he moved his car closer and then fired a shot at the rear of Don's car. The bullet missed.

"Damn it," exclaimed Marin. "Not easy to shoot like this."

But the shot was clear warning for Don and Diane. At the sound of the shot, Diane gasped and then screamed, "They're shooting at us."

"Stay down," Don barked. He knew he had to attempt whatever he could right now. The next bullet could hit Diane or him. Holding his right hand on the cylinder, he turned onto one of the smaller dirt roads and shouted, "When I stop the car, you open the passenger-side door, jump out, and run as fast and as far as you can into the brush on the side of the road. Got it?"

But before she could respond, Don pressed down hard on the brake. As the car screeched to a halt, he quickly turned the car around to face Marin's oncoming car, stopping in an almost diagonal manner and effectively blocking the narrow dirt road, his high beams shining brightly at Marin's car.

Don saw the headlights of Marin's car pull up to the front end of his car and come to a skidding halt. Dust and dirt filled the air as the headlights of the two cars shone eerily through it.

By the time Marin's car stopped, Don and Diane were already out of the passenger-side doors, the side angled away from Marin's car. Diane leaped off the side of the road and into the dark underbrush, tearing some of her clothing as she attempted to follow Don's order of going as far as she could.

Marin and Diego saw the ghostly image of Diane disappear into the darkness off the side of the road, but with the bright lights of Don's headlights shining in their eyes, they couldn't see which direction Don went.

"Should I go after her?" Diego asked.

"Stay here. We don't know if Carter has a gun. Do you see him?"

Suddenly, the sound of shattering glass filled the car. The two men instantly wheeled around in their seats. In the dim, red rear lights of the car, looking through the gaping opening of what was once their rear window, they saw Don run down the road and then jump into the underbrush. Marin attempted to peel off a shot at Don through the shattered window.

Diego saw him take aim and yelled, "No!" as he struck Marin's gun with his hand. The shot caromed harmlessly off the dirt road.

Marin smacked Diego across his face with the butt of the gun and screamed, "You fucking moron! Why'd you do that? I ought to—"

The odor of smoke and a feeling of enormous heat began to fill the car. Diego and Marin looked down behind the front seat. There, on the floor of the rear seat, in a magnificent glow, lay the cylinder that Don had thrown through the rear window.

"It's the cylinder!" screamed Diego, knowing full well how potentially lethal the cylinder could be.

As she ran deeper into the brush, Diane heard the gunshot and then the screams. Fearing for Don, she instinctively turned around and saw an eerie, luminescent glow fill the other men's car. Against that backdrop she could see one man exit the car and vanish into the darkness while another man slumped over the back of the front seat. Thinking that it couldn't be Don in that car, she turned and ran deeper into the brush, feeling her way toward sanctuary.

Don hid in the brush behind a rock, breathing heavily. He felt his heart pounding within his heaving chest. He knew the cylinder was potentially lethal, but had no way of knowing if the men had gotten out of the car or not. He listened for sounds of movement or of talking, but he heard nothing. His hiding place was downwind from the cars, and the gentle breeze floated the putrid smell of burning flesh past his nostrils. In another time it would have nauseated him, but now it brought a cognizant smile across his face. *They're dead,* he thought. *No one could withstand a dose of radiation such as that.* But still he thought he should wait a while longer, just in case. He desperately wanted to call to Diane but knew he shouldn't give away his or her location. *Stay where you are, Diane,* he silently implored. *Stay till I call you.*

Diane had run for several hundred feet in the dark, groping through dense brush and around small hills and boulders, tearing her clothing and scratching herself. She'd heard the sound of shattering glass followed by a gunshot, some shouting and screaming, the ghostly images, and then absolute silence, except for her own panting, which she tried unsuccessfully to control, fearing they might hear her. She knew there was nothing for her to do but wait. She trembled at the thought that Don had been shot and was lying by the roadside bleeding or already dead.

Her premonition had come true at its worst! Don was dead, and she was being sought by two maniacs. *Stop!* she ordered herself. If Don were dead, the two men would pick up the cylinder, get back into their car, and drive off. And why was it so deathly quiet? What was Don's plan? Using the cylinder as a weapon? Had it worked? She wanted to call Don's name but thought better of it. She'd have to wait, even if it meant waiting for daylight, when she could see what had happened. Darkness would shield her for now.

But Diane needed to know something, anything. She slowly, quietly, stood up high enough to see over the shrubs. In the distance she saw only one set of headlights, not two, but thought she saw the dark image of the other car. Why were the lights off? She had no answer. She crouched down again to wait.

Don decided he'd waited long enough. He was certain they were dead and called Diane's name.

Hearing Don's voice, and believing that he'd discovered the two men dead, she shouted, tenuously, "Over here. Are you okay?"

"I'm fine. What about you? Did you shield yourself from the radiation?" he shouted.

Diane yelled back, "There must a zillion bushes between me and that thing. Besides, I'm real far away. But what about those men? Are they both dead?"

"I'm sure they're dead. I could smell burning flesh."

Dear God, she thought. She tensed. He smelled but didn't actually see them? She became frantic. "Don! I saw one of them run from the car. He could still be around."

"You're sure?" His senses were now on alert.

"Yes."

"Find another spot right now, and don't give away your location until you hear from me."

"I understand."

They both silently moved to new positions and wondered if one of their enemies could still be alive. If so, they would have to be extremely careful, as he might be armed.

They sat still for the next interminable minutes among the silence of the night sounds. Only the headlights of Don's car still shone as the radiation from the cylinder had cooked and shorted many of the wires and fuses of Marin's car.

Don decided to get up and slowly walk toward the cars in a crouched position, hidden by darkness. His only weapon was a rock that he'd picked up. He could see smoke coming from the inside of Marin's car as he approached and looked into the open front door. He saw the badly burned body of one man slumped over the front seat, head and arms hanging down toward the floor of the rear seat.

Don froze. Where was the second man? There were definitely two of them. He began to back away into the darkness once more. Then he heard a sound by the side of the road. Fearing that he'd been spotted, he raised the rock over his head in readiness to throw it. He cautiously crept backward. Every muscle and fiber in his body tingled from the adrenalin that now pumped through his rapidly pulsating arteries. He had no fear of dying now as the animal instincts passed on to him from his caveman ancestors gave him the courage that arose from the blind reaction of defending his mate. Without actually thinking it, he was ready to defend Diane to the death.

Don squinted but saw nothing. Where was he? He heard a sound. Then another came. Was it Marin? Did he still have his gun? But then he heard what sounded like a moan. There was another moaning sound. He moved toward the sound and then spotted the second man lying face down in the underbrush. Don could plainly see that the man posed no threat, and he pushed the man's body with his foot, turning the man over, face up.

Don gasped. "Diego!"

Diego, near death, managed to open his eyes and look at Don. He appeared to be attempting to speak, and Don knelt down on the ground next to him

Diego managed to raise his hand, loosely grabbed Don's shirt, and muttered softly, "Forgive … forgive me."

As soon as he'd spotted the cylinder, Diego had fumbled with the door handle for a few precious moments before finally managing to open the door and fall out of the car while Marin stared spellbound at the sight of the cylinder's glow. The heat from the radiation quickly filled the car as Marin, although near unconsciousness, still attempted to reach down and pick up the cylinder. Instead, he slumped dead over the front seat, his head, arms, and torso hanging over the floor of the rear seat, burned almost beyond recognition, as the cylinder melted its way through the bottom of the car and onto the dirt road below.

Diego, though not nearly as badly burned, had received too massive a dose of radiation for any human to withstand and had stumbled to the side of the road, already vomiting.

Don stared at his former friend, badly burned on the outside and scarred still further on the inside from the penetrating radiation. Don felt absolutely no animosity toward Diego, in spite of all that had occurred. Don gently replied, "All is forgiven, Diego. All is forgiven."

Diego's arm dropped to the ground, and he was now gasping for air.

Don heard his name being called by Diane, and he looked up and shouted, "Over here, by the cars. It's all right."

Diane's shoulders slumped. *Thank God it's over,* she said to herself. She got up and rushed out of her hiding place as swiftly as she could. She couldn't wait to see Don and throw her arms around him.

Diane followed the headlights as she walked out of the underbrush and over to where Don knelt next to the dying Diego.

She had expected Don to rush into her arms, but when she saw his melancholy expression, she asked, "Who is that?"

"It's Diego Gonzales. He's dying." Don couldn't help feeling sorry for his one-time best friend.

"Look at him," Diane said, grimacing. "He's all burned up. The cylinder did that to him?"

"It did, just as I knew it could. But I didn't expect to be killing Diego. I never meant to hurt him." He shook his head.

"But he's not dead. Maybe we can get him to a hospital."

"No chance. The amount of radiation he took was immense. He's laboring for oxygen already. I think he's unconscious."

Diego wheezed slow breaths in and out for another minute as Diane and Don watched in silence. Then the wheezing stopped, and Diego's body stiffened up and then relaxed. Diego lay still.

Don looked up at Diane and said sadly, "He's dead." Don looked down again at Diego with sagging shoulders.

Diane immediately understood the depression that was coming over Don, and she attempted to snap him out of it. Placing her hand on his shoulder, she spoke sympathetically but with authority. "I know how you feel right now, but this is no time to give up."

"I know, but I'm sick of this garbage. I don't think the cylinder is worth it anymore. I feel like walking into the police and saying, 'I'm Don Carter, and here's the lousy cylinder. Do what you want with it.'"

Diane walked over to the car and reached inside.

Don watched her and asked, "What are you doing?"

"I'm getting my purse."

Don smiled to himself. *Just like a woman. People dying in one of the most incredible ways possible, and she's probably looking for her lipstick.*

Diane walked back to Don and said, "I think it's time we trusted someone enough to let him help us."

Don was surprised at the remark. "What are you talking about?"

"In my purse is a letter that was slipped under my door." Diane reached inside her purse and handed him Rawlings's letter. "Read it and tell me what you think."

Don stood up, walked closer to the headlights, and began to read the letter. Upon finishing, he thought for a moment and looked toward Diane. "I think you're right. I don't know how in hell we're gonna get ourselves or the cylinder out of this country, and I'm sick of being chased and shot at. Let's find this Rawlings guy and see what he can offer us."

"I agree. It's the only choice we have."

"But one thing," he said with determination. "I'm not simply handing the cylinder over on a silver platter. I want assurances first about our safety, and I want to know of his intentions for the cylinder."

Diane placed her arms around Don's waist and rested her head on his shoulder. "We have to trust someone. We can't go on like this."

Don kissed Diane on her forehead and then walked over to Marin's car, crawling underneath in order to retrieve the now cooled and quiescent cylinder. After placing it back into the lead box, the two got into their car and rode past Marin's car and Diego's body, saying nothing to each other.

Don wondered whether or not Diego had gotten what he deserved, his mind now beginning to fill with self-recrimination. For that matter, his thoughts continued, did anyone ever get what they deserved? At that moment, death seemed the only reward, no matter how one lived his life. He'd lost a father figure in Anton Steinert, and now the only real friend he had in Peru was gone; both were dead because of him. He banged the steering wheel with his hand.

Empathizing with him, Diane said, "Talk to me. God knows you need to talk it out, with all you've been through."

"The priest in Ochoa was right. Strive for excellence at something worthwhile. If money comes along, great. The quest for wealth at all costs will lead to no good."

Diane nodded. "It might surprise you, but I actually agree with you."

Don looked at Diane. She appeared beautiful to him, even now, disheveled and tattered. "And Anton and Diego—if I'd never come to Peru, they would both be alive right now."

Diane answered gently, "You can't blame yourself. You know that."

"Maybe yes, maybe no. If I had turned the cylinder over to the authorities immediately, none of this would've happened."

Diane touched his arm. "How could you have known in your wildest dreams that this thing would be from another world and that you'd be involved with animals such as those men?"

"Not Diego." He shook his head. "Not Diego. The others, yes. But not Diego. I believe he got into something that was way over his head. He was an acquaintance of Marin, not a true friend."

Diane said nothing. Allowing Don to air his emotions would serve as his catharsis.

Don continued. "And Anton. What about him? He spends decades studying early man and then spends two days with me here and gets killed for it. I must be some great good-luck charm." He was hardly noticing the road ahead.

"You're my good-luck charm, and don't you forget it." She briefly thought of discussing her premonition with him, and possibly the one concerning her father, but quickly changed her mind. The ordeal wasn't yet over. Maybe by telling Don about it she would jinx it. Yes, Don was in trouble, and yes, she did go to Peru exactly as she had predicted, but she never foresaw the outcome of her premonition. If they were to come out of this okay, they would need all the luck they could find. Besides, she knew Don would dismiss her premonitions as coincidence or exaggerations, and maybe that would place a whammy on it, too. No, it was better to leave it unsaid, at least for now.

Having Diane at his side, someone close in whom he could confide, refueled Don's rehashing of the past. "Anton would be alive if it weren't for me."

"Come on, he made the choice to come here himself. You didn't force or ask him to do it. And what in the world was a man of his age doing playing cops and robbers and shooting guns, anyway? I still can't believe he was involved in a shootout. Did he even know how to use the gun he had?"

Don didn't answer. If he had, he would have lied and told Diane that Steinert really didn't know how but learned on the fly. Don was the only person Steinert had ever confided in. That same man had saved his life not once, but twice, and had paid the supreme price for it. Telling anyone, even Diane, of the horrors that Steinert had participated in, would take the only thing that remained of Steinert on the face of this earth: his legacy. Yes, Don thought, Steinert had committed terrible and deplorable acts of horror. But that wasn't indicative or representative of the real Anton Steinert. The true Steinert had died saving Don's life on the streets of Lima. He was Don's hero, and Don would see to it that he was remembered as one.

Diane didn't press him for an answer. It didn't matter. What mattered to her was that they were on their way to being saved and could now begin their lives together again. She smiled to herself, thinking, *Love will be lovelier, the second time around.*

Having somewhat spoken it out, Don relegated the past events to history and concentrated on finding a telephone to call this Colonel Rawlings. Self-preservation was now foremost for the two of them.

Tom Rawlings sat on a couch in his hotel room with his bare feet resting on a coffee table. He was wearing trousers and an undershirt and was comfortably watching the TV, which was playing an old rerun of *The Maltese Falcon*. Rawlings laughed at seeing Humphrey Bogart and Peter Lorre speaking fluent Spanish with highly unsynchronized lip movements. It was late, and the television was doing its job: His eyes were beginning to droop. Soon he would roll over onto the bed and dream of killing Viet Cong.

The ringing phone startled him. *What does Styles want now?* he thought. He picked up the phone. "Yeah, what?"

"Is a Colonel Tom Rawlings there?" a man's voice asked.

"This is Rawlings. Who's this?"

"Don Carter."

Rawlings didn't allow his voice to betray his emotions and asked, with his best military tone, "Carter. Where are you?"

"It doesn't matter. I'm with my wife, now. She gave me your letter."

"You'll allow us to help you?"

"Maybe. No promises. Meet me at two p.m. in Simon Bolivar Park tomorrow afternoon. Alone. If you're not alone, you'll never see me or that cylinder again. Is that clear?"

"Yes, loud and clear, and I agree to your terms."

"Seat yourself on the green bench between the concession stand and the soccer field. I want you to wear something that will make it easy for me to identify you."

"I understand. A ... uh ... a yellow plaid shirt with tan slacks."

"Good. Two p.m. Alone."

Rawlings heard the line go dead, and he hung up his receiver. He hadn't revealed the excitement he felt at that moment.

CHAPTER 25

THE NEXT MORNING, NEWS of finding two badly burned bodies on the roadside, identified by their driver's licenses as Diego Gonzales and Jose Marin, hit the local radio and TV stations. The surprising thing, the broadcasts continued, was that the car they were driving had a hole burned through the floor, and yet no evidence of a fire, or at least one large enough to burn two men so badly, could be found. Police were investigating further.

This news was heeded by the Peruvian government, the Russian contingency, and the Rawlings group. The Russians had been sent to meet with Julio Mendez to verify and negotiate for the cylinder, much as the American group had done, except that the Russians had no substantial leads to follow until now. They knew from Mendez that Diego Gonzales was Don's closest friend in Peru, and hearing of his and Jose Marin's deaths and, more importantly, the manner in which those deaths occurred only increased their desire to locate and secure the cylinder for the Soviet Union.

The leader of the Russian group was Boris Vasilyenkov, a member of the Soviet secret police, the KGB. The Russians felt it wise to send a man knowledgeable in covert actions in dealings such as this. Two of Vasilyenkov's aides were also from the KGB and were highly trained in clandestine work. The remainder of the group consisted of persons with similar backgrounds to the Rawlings group: scientists, aides, and negotiators.

Vasilyenkov was a highly trained man accustomed to dealing in result-oriented tasks. It was always easy for him to justify the means by using the catchall phrase, "For Mother Russia." The Communist Party and country always came first, even if it meant that some individuals had to give up their rights, including their right to live. His duty in Peru was to obtain an object deemed important enough by his government to send secret police all the way there. He knew there would be little, if any, questioning of the methods used in accomplishing his task, as long as there was no embarrassment to the Kremlin. No matter what events occurred, Vasilyenkov knew that he was prepared to do anything in his power to ensure that the outcome didn't embarrass his government and, therefore, him.

Vasilyenkov further knew from both personal experience and history that "might makes right." He'd read Machiavelli's, *The Prince* which drove home the message that a leader must gain support by the force of arms or the power of money. The leader must gain support of the strong by cajolery or, if that is ineffective, by deceit or force. Since appearances very often mean more to people than substance, the leader must appear devout and loyal, even if he is not. But in the final analysis, Vasilyenkov read, it is better for the leader to be feared than loved.

Vasilyenkov thought that he was The Prince reincarnate, and he felt no remorse in arresting "enemies of the state" whether he knew they were innocent or guilty of true crimes. If they were shot, fine. Sent off to a gulag in Siberia, fine. Being released unharmed was also fine, as long as it was the decision willed by the government and not the individual exerting his "rights" on the government. As far as Vasilyenkov was concerned, the Party had all the rights. The individual had almost none. This was, after all, what had made the Soviet Union emerge from the medieval form of government of Czarist Russia to become the nuclear superpower that it was today.

Vasilyenkov gave his two KGB agents the job of collecting information as to the possible whereabouts of the cylinder. They believed the best place to begin was with the Americans. It was concluded that the Carter fellow, being an American, would eventually make contact with the Rawlings group. When and if he did, Vasilyenkov wanted to make sure he knew about it. They would then decide what further course of action to take. In the meantime, they would keep an eye on Tom Rawlings and his group.

One of the scientists sent to authenticate the cylinder was a man named Vitale Mischkin. He knew of Boris Vasilyenkov's reputation as being a no-nonsense, party-line man who couldn't be trusted by the scientific community, which, throughout Communist Russian history, was always a necessary body of more free-thinking individuals that the Soviet government was consistently forced to keep wraps on. Scientific advances were of number-one importance to the propaganda machine in Moscow, yet many of the tenets of pure science too often seemed to run counter to the dogmatic ways of Communism. Normally, Mischkin would never have accepted any mission that included a man like Vasilyenkov, but the lure of possibly obtaining or, at the least, being able to view an object purportedly from alien intelligence was more than enough inducement in spite of his apprehensions.

Mischkin had on occasion overheard conversations between Vasilyenkov and his two other KGB agents. It was clear to Mischkin that Vasilyenkov had no scientific interest in the cylinder. Only the accomplishment of his mission mattered. It soon became apparent to Mischkin that if the Russians couldn't obtain the cylinder, they must make sure no one else was to have it, especially the Americans. Mischkin didn't express his feelings on the matter openly with anyone. For the time being, he would wait and keep a watchful eye on the situation.

Later that day, Tom Rawlings sat on the bench designated by Donald Carter, in the middle of Simon Bolivar Park. He had only a sketchy idea of what Carter looked like, but with Don's newly grown beard and long hair, Rawlings wouldn't have been able to recognize him.

There were several benches with a variety of different people sitting on them as Rawlings surveyed the tranquil scene about him. Some people were purchasing food at the concession stand, some thirty feet behind him. Several teenagers were kicking a soccer ball on a large field, about thirty yards in front of him.

A young man with a beard approached Rawlings's bench, sat down at the opposite end of the bench, and opened a newspaper to read. Rawlings glanced at him, but the man made no acknowledgement and continued reading the paper.

Rawlings had two of his men follow him. Promises meant nothing in relation to his service to his country, and he wasn't one to let his guard down.

If any unforeseen action was necessary, he wanted to have help nearby. His eyes squinted past the soccer field. Just beyond were a row of hedges, and somewhere behind them were his two men. On a signal from him they could be summoned in seconds. He left the capture of Carter as his final option, and this meeting would determine if the option needed to be exercised.

Five minutes passed with no sign of Carter, but Rawlings was a patient man and was willing to wait a great deal longer; he'd waited for two years in Vietnam. Then he heard his name called.

"Rawlings, don't look my way. You're alone, as I'd asked?"

The bearded man had spoken. It was Carter, and Rawlings knew how cautious Carter felt he must be at this point.

Rawlings opened a book and pretended to read. Speaking without moving and in a soft voice, he answered, "I'm alone. Our only intentions are to help you. You need our help. We're willing to give it."

"For a price, of course."

"The price of a certain cylindrical object, yes."

"How do I know you won't double-cross me?"

"I'm not sure what you mean. What do you want?"

"I want safety out of this country for me and my wife. I want the cylinder out, too, but I want to be involved in its study once we get back to the States."

Rawlings, somewhat familiar with the fine art of negotiation, needed to instill some sense of trust in Carter. He didn't want to start off on the wrong foot and lose Carter altogether. Therefore, he candidly responded, "I won't lie to you. You know I can't guarantee what our government will do with the cylinder, but I can promise you all the help the government can provide in getting you, your wife, and the cylinder safely out of Peru. You are, after all, American citizens. But first, we don't even know if this cylinder is worth all this effort. We need to examine it before we can proceed. I've brought some experts down with me."

Don thought for a moment and then said, "Will you at least guarantee that I'll be in on any and all research when you examine the cylinder here?"

"Of course. We need all the help we can get to determine its value."

"Okay. I'll meet you with the cylinder and my wife tonight in front of the Hotel Miramar at nine."

"Twenty-one hundred hours in front of the Hotel Miramar. Alone?"

"You might as well bring help. You never know when you'll be needing it around here."

"By the way. That incident outside Lima with the two burned-up guys and the car with the hole in it—that wouldn't have involved you, by any chance?"

Don rose from the bench without answering. "Nine tonight" was all that he said as he walked off.

Rawlings remained for a few seconds and then left for his car. He was pleased that he would soon know whether this cylinder thing was a hoax or the real McCoy and, if genuine, how valuable from a security standpoint it actually was. He'd told Carter that he would see to their safety, but Rawlings knew that the more valuable the cylinder, the less critical it was to worry about the return of the Carters to the United States. The security of the United States came first.

Don had left the rented car parked on a side street near the park. He cut across the main parking field in a crouched position, hidden between cars, knowing that if Rawlings or some of his men attempted to follow him, he could lose them. They would never be able to see where he exited from the park, and he knew that he could lose himself in the crowded streets. He wasn't sure why he thought he had to do this, since he was meeting them that evening, but these past weeks had taught him to trust no one, and he doubted Rawlings had actually been there alone.

Safely back in his car, Don drove off to meet Diane, who was waiting for him with the cylinder, which was hidden once again under the dresser in his room in the little town.

Once back in the room, he told her of the meeting with Rawlings.

"What did you think of him?" she asked. "I realize we don't have much choice, but can we trust him?"

Don sat on the floor with his back against the wall, and Diane sat down Indian style, facing him. "He's military through and through. These guys have been trained to follow orders, not to think. If his orders are to get the cylinder and return us to the United States, he'll do it. But if it's only to get the cylinder…"

"Would there be any reason for them not to help us?"

"I don't think so. At least, I hope not. But what will they do with the cylinder once they get it? That's the biggest question of all."

"It won't be long now. In a few hours we'll know." She sounded relieved.

The Russians were now watching the Rawlings headquarters, but they didn't have a large enough staff or equipment to determine what the Americans were doing. They hoped to be able to monitor large-scale movement within the Rawlings group, perhaps signaling some type of significant discovery. At that point, the Russian group would have to play it by ear, determining their next move with each successive event.

Waiting to leave made the hours pass excruciatingly slowly for Don and Diane. They left for Lima with the cylinder at six thirty p.m., stopping along the way to pick up some sandwiches.

Later that evening, precisely at nine, with the cylinder snuggled safely between them on the front seat of the car, they spotted Rawlings and another man standing in front of the Hotel Miramar. Don slowed to a halt and looked at Rawlings standing fifteen feet away on the sidewalk.

Rawlings said nothing as he approached the car and got into the rear seat. Major Styles followed with Rawlings's car.

Diane glanced back at Rawlings, who acknowledged her with a nod of his head. Diane nodded back and looked forward again, saying nothing.

Rawlings directed Don to drive to a secret location chosen by the group where the examination of the cylinder would take place. The hotel in which the group was staying would be too risky for the event.

Styles, following close behind, had been instructed to fake a stall on a predetermined street as precaution against Don's car being followed. His job was to lead interference for the Carter car by blocking the cars behind him while the Carter car sped off. Styles would then return to the hotel. With this accomplished, the Carter car made its way alone toward the clandestine, makeshift laboratory.

They soon arrived at an abandoned factory building in the northeast section of Lima. Rawlings led them by flashlight into the basement through a dark and damp staircase. Don held the lead box containing the cylinder in his arms, being careful not to trip or drop it.

Farther ahead, down a long corridor, they could hear what sounded like a gasoline engine and could see a beam of light emanating from under a closed door.

"You have a generator?" Don asked Rawlings.

"We bought it today. It runs the lights and a few electrical devices."

Rawlings knocked on the door, giving three taps followed by one tap and then two more. The door was opened by one of Rawlings's men, and the three entered a room of dimensions approximating twenty by twenty-five feet with a high, pipe-filled ceiling and no windows. The generator made a muffled noise, as it was in an adjoining room, the exhaust fumes piped to a room above. Electrical extension cords ran under the door into their room and led to three lightbulbs, which hung from nails at three different parts of the room. The room had one large table in the middle and a few folding chairs scattered about.

Diane looked around the room, which was damp and filled with dust. There were cobwebs in all the corners and crevasses of the cement-block walls. She felt uncomfortable in the decrepit surroundings.

Don counted six other persons in the room besides themselves and Rawlings. All wore normal street clothes. There was one woman in the group.

As they entered the room, no one spoke; all eyes appeared to be focused on the dark box that Don cradled in his arms.

Rawlings spoke first in an almost cheerful and perhaps triumphant tone. "Gentlemen, and lady," he said, purposely turning toward the woman, "I give you Mr. and Mrs. Carter and the elusive cylinder."

Several of the group now began to smile and speak as they moved closer to Don. One of them, a fifty-six-year-old research scientist named Oscar Weinberg, spoke directly to Don.

"Mr. Carter, please, set the box down on the table and relax. We're your friends here. We hope, as I'm sure you do, to discover just what this cylinder is all about."

"Call me Don. And this is my wife, Diane," he said, gesturing with his hand toward her. "And this is the cylinder, which I guarantee won't disappoint you."

Don walked to the table and set the box down.

Rawlings took charge again. Speaking to the group, he said, "Okay, let's get down to business. Let me introduce the team to you. You of course know me, and the gentleman who just spoke to you is Dr. Oscar Weinberg, a researcher who works for the Pentagon. Over there," he said, pointing out the rest of the group one by one, "is Dr. Alicia Sadowski. There is Dr. Frank Corsica, and over there is Jim Fielding, one of my aides. That's David Crossman, another aide. And last but not least is Dr. Hank Gruen. These people were sent with me for the expressed purpose of determining the validity of the rumored alien cylinder. Another aide and a negotiating team—people with, shall we say, a bit of diplomacy in their repertoire—are back at the hotel along with Major Styles. The negotiators were sent with us to attempt a purchase of the cylinder once we determined its worth. Of course, at this point, we don't require the services of that team. What we do need is to begin discovering exactly what we have in that box and decide whether or not the two of you have been beating your brains out over something worthwhile or just a pile of junk. We also have a man standing guard outside who will call us on our walkie-talkie if there's any trouble."

Don responded with confidence. "That suits us just fine. How do you suggest we begin?"

"I suggest you begin by filling us in on all the details of how you came to discover the cylinder and anything you believe you've found out about it. Evidence is what we need. Then we can proceed further, together."

Don replied, "Right. Sounds like the best thing to do. This way you'll also be aware of the dangers in working with it."

Don sat down on one of the folding chairs and motioned for Diane to sit next to him. The two faced the group that had now spread itself around the table. Some sat, while others chose to remain standing. Don then reiterated the story from the beginning, discussing Paco Rivera and Diego Gonzales, the cylinder, the melted rock, the dots, the radio signals, the strange metal, the ability to emit immense levels of radiation, and of course, Anton Steinert. Don became solemn as he recalled incidents involving Steinert and how he had saved Don's life at the cost of his own.

The story took several minutes to complete, taking it to the present. Don paused and said, "That's all she wrote. You now know as much as I do." His voice had a sad quality to it, and Diane placed her hand in his. He glanced at her and gave her a small smile.

Rawlings once again took charge. "Okay. I think we need to have a look at our would-be alien. You can have the honor," he said to Don while gesturing toward the box.

"Sure." Don rose from the chair and glanced at the faces of the group. His story had evidently whetted their appetites, and he could see the excitement of anticipation in their eyes. This made him remember how important a discovery the cylinder truly was, and it renewed him in his quest to discover its secrets.

Don slowly lifted the lid, placed it on the table, and then lifted the cylinder out, placing it gently onto the table, next to the box.

The group stared in silence, with each one of them crowding in a bit closer to get a better view of the shiny, golden metallic object. A Geiger counter that had been turned on prior to their entering the room was brought closer to the cylinder by Dr. Gruen, with no noticeable difference in measurement.

"It doesn't appear to be emitting any detectable radiation levels," Gruen said with skepticism.

"It won't," Don replied, "unless … provoked."

"Provoked?" Dr. Alicia Sadowski said with a wry smile. "You make it sound like it has a mind of its own."

"Maybe it does," Don answered.

The group set up receivers attached to a tape recorder and TV monitor. They then recorded the signals that Don had described to them. The signals, when played on a cassette, revealed the same strange language that Don had told them that Steinert had discovered resembled Quechua, whose translation roughly meant, "Those who can enter, receive God".

Don addressed the group about this. "I've had a lot of time to think about the meaning of that translation. I now believe that the true meaning might make sense only in a more modern, or rather, more technological setting."

"Meaning what?" asked Weinberg.

"The aliens who landed here had only the language of ancient Peru to use to relay their message to us. That language had no words for technologies that didn't exist then, such as 'computers' or maybe even 'the universe' as we know it today. Maybe their word for universe was synonymous with God or the heavens. I believe that the message that was meant for us, using the closest words that were available in the ancient Quechua language, would be, in a more modern sense, 'If you can gain access, you'll find answers about the universe.' In other words, if we have the capabilities to work with this unit, it will yield information. But it's rigged so that it can't be entered in the normal sense. There are no written messages inside, so to speak, no pieces of paper for us to get at. We can't just open it up; it prevents that with immense radiation. We have to use signals to do that, signals that will trigger some response by the cylinder. Again, we must, to use the modern vernacular, gain access by using the correct coded signal, as though entering the memory of a computer."

"Interesting hypothesis," Dr. Gruen said. "But we're still quite far from proving that this thing is actually alien."

"What would convince you?" Don asked.

"Well, I'd like to examine the metal, but you said it responds violently. I'd also like to witness some of this power you told us about. That would certainly help, but with the dangers involved, how do you suggest we do this? You've had several firsthand experiences with this."

"I'm sure some of you could devise a small experiment," Don responded. "It seems to give off radiation commensurate with the amount of force exerted on it. You might try just light tapping at first and then heavy banging. Of course, we couldn't be in the room while this is going on."

Dr. Frank Corsica responded first. "I think we could rig up a quick experiment. We could leave the tube of the Geiger counter in the room, by the door, and leave the rest of it outside, enabling us to monitor the radioactivity. These cement-block walls ought to shield us." Pointing to another Geiger counter, he continued. "If not, we'll know it soon enough by the readings on this second Geiger counter, which we'll keep with us in the hallway."

After a few side discussions, the team devised a pulley system using a fifty-foot extension cord draped over a pipe which ran across the ceiling, with one end leading out of the doorway and the other end tied to a hammer. The hammer was attached to the table in such a manner that when the end of the cord was pulled from the outside hallway, the hammer would strike the cylinder. The weight of the hammer itself would make the hammer drop back to its original position once the tension on the cord was relaxed.

After accomplishing this, everyone in the group left the room with their flashlights, entered the hallway, and closed the door almost fully, leaving only enough space to allow the cord through. The first Geiger counter's tube was left just inside the doorway, resting on the floor, while the control box, which contained its meter, was placed in the hallway with the group. The second

Geiger counter was placed entirely in the hallway to monitor the radiation levels there. It was decided that Don should pull the cord while the others examined the readings on the Geiger counters.

Rawlings saw that everyone was in place and asked Don if he was ready. Don responded affirmatively. Rawlings then gave the word to begin, and Don gave an easy pull on the cord. The cord yanked the hammer, which lightly tapped the cylinder. No measurable difference in meter readings was observed.

Gruen said, "Try it again, harder this time."

Don again pulled on the cord. The hammer hit with more force, and a reading was picked up by the Geiger counter. Its tell-tale clicking could be heard by everyone as Dr. Gruen recorded the meter reading on a pad.

Don yanked much harder on the cord next time, and a loud clanging noise was heard as the hammer crashed into the cylinder. The Geiger counter reading jumped to a dangerous level inside the room, but the thick cement wall was enough to prevent the radiation from entering the hallway. The hallway Geiger counter showed safe, although slightly elevated, levels of radiation.

Don looked at Rawlings. "Ready for the big one?"

"Sure," Rawlings replied. "Let's see what that baby can really do."

Don grasped the cord with both hands and yanked the cord as hard as he could five times in rapid succession.

The Geiger counter in the room jumped to the highest level possible for that machine, clicking wildly amid mumblings of the group, including some nonscientific expletives such as, "Holy shit!"

Suddenly, the hallway Geiger counter began to click wildly. Frank Corsica warned, "Let's get out of here!"

The group turned and ran down the corridor with Corsica carrying the hallway Geiger counter. The few flashlights lit the hallway in haphazard fashion as the group hustled its way through it. Corsica, watching the meter, yelled out, "It's okay here. We're okay."

The group, with some panting—either from running or pure excitement—stopped and turned. Several brief discussions arose among the group members. Corsica asked for one of the flashlights, which was handed to him, and he carefully made his way through the corridor back toward the cylinder, monitoring radiation levels as he approached the doorway. The group followed close behind.

As he walked, Don spoke to the group, saying, "It's probably all clear by now, even in the room. The cylinder doesn't take long to return to normal."

"We'll see," Corsica replied, still watching the meter.

Smoke was emanating from inside the room as Corsica walked to the door and placed the Geiger counter tube by the opening. He noted a normal reading. Standing by the side of the door, Corsica kicked the door open with his foot, glanced inside the room, and yelled, "The level's okay, but the table's on fire!"

The group ran into the room en masse to see the table burning around a hole in the middle of it. Below the hole lay the cylinder in a pool of melted cement. The plastic coating of the electrical cord that was tied to the hammer was completely melted away within fifteen feet of the cylinder. Fumes filled the room as some of the men turned the table upside down and began stepping on the burning parts, putting out the fire.

Don suggested that they carefully roll the cylinder out of the melted cement before the cement cooled and hardened into a rock-like mass. This was accomplished by gently pushing the cylinder with one of the legs broken off the burning table.

The room was now buzzing with the chatter of amazed persons. Rawlings walked over to Don and Diane and said, "Unbelievable. The damn thing gave off enough heat to melt the cement, yet the cylinder itself seems untouched."

"Just as I told you it would be," responded a cocky Don.

Rawlings asked, "Can we examine the metal? You think we can try to determine what it is without it going hog wild on us?"

"It's been done before. Just don't bang on it."

After allowing the cylinder to cool off, the group prepared to use test kits with which they would attempt to classify and identify the metal. They used a variety of acids and other chemicals and attempted to scratch the metal, but no mark was left, and the conclusion was made that it was harder than any known mineral or metal on earth. Their attempts to identify the metal were fruitless, just as Solars's had, to the amazement of each and every person except Don and Diane, who expected as much.

Weinberg suggested that it was getting late and that perhaps they should call it a night and continue the next day. This led to a fairly heated discussion. Alicia Sadowski turned to Don and said loudly enough for all to hear, "It's your opinion that these aliens came here several thousand years ago, as dated by that star chart, correct?"

"That's what I believe."

Sadowski continued. "And that they've left us with some sort of device that will ... educate us, I guess is a good way of putting it, about things of the universe that we don't understand?"

"Yes, that's about it."

Sadowski looked at Rawlings. "Tom, I believe we may have actually discovered an object sent to us by some alien being. It behooves us to continue working on this as diligently as we can, even if it means working through the night. I, for one, don't think I could even begin to sleep knowing the exciting work that we could be accomplishing right now."

A discussion followed with varying opinions. Finally, Rawlings raised his arms and loudly said, "Hold it. Hold it, everyone. Look. We don't know how much longer this could take. It's now oh two hundred. I think we need to get some good rest, and I believe that we need some more equipment than we have here."

"Like what?" asked his aide, Fielding.

Weinberg answered, "Like a computer that we can program to make a transmitter give off continuous signals in a sequential fashion at a far greater speed than we can figure out. It seems that we must somehow unlock the code needed to, as Don aptly put it, gain access to its brain."

Crossman asked, "Do you think it's smart to continue to research the cylinder here? Now that we have it, maybe we ought to get it to the United States as soon as possible."

Rawlings thought for a moment and then answered. "But we also know we might not be able to get it out of Peru at all. If we can't, I want to know now what the cylinder can tell us. We might not get out with the cylinder, but maybe we can get out with notes, or better yet, recordings of information."

There was general agreement to this suggestion, and the group decided to stash the cylinder above some pipes in the factory. Don didn't want to leave it and expressed his concern. He'd been double-crossed before, but the group's members reassured him that they could be trusted. Two aides would take turns standing guard during the night. The prospect of losing the cylinder due to foul play on the outside was far greater, they said, than losing it from someone's actions on the inside. Besides, it was generally thought that the cylinder was far too dangerous to be carried around so much.

Don begrudgingly agreed to leave the cylinder, not that he had much choice in the matter, and they packed up their things and left for the hotel. Rawlings had made arrangements for another room for the Carters under assumed names. It was no problem for them to enter the hotel unnoticed at half past three in the morning.

Both Don and Diane had trouble falling asleep. These past few days had been terribly taxing, and the remembrances of it kept them tossing and turning. Even when they eventually did manage to sleep, theirs was a fitful sleep filled with dreams of past horrors and future fantasies.

CHAPTER 26

THE NEXT MORNING, THE group had breakfast downstairs while Rawlings ordered breakfast in bed for Don and Diane, not for sentimental reasons but rather because he wanted them to be as invisible as possible. The way Don and Diane felt, it was a most welcome suggestion. After eating, they were extremely relaxed.

The plan was for the Carters to wait for word to walk down the stairs and over to the rear of the hotel, where a car would pick them up and take them back to the factory. This would be done after the appropriate items needed for the research were bought and delivered to the factory by the group.

Don sat on the bed and watched admiringly as Diane brushed her long, black hair in the mirror above the dresser at the foot of the bed. Diane sensed him staring at her and asked, "Penny for your thoughts?"

"In addition to wanting to ravish your body, I was thinking that it looks as though we'll really be able to get out of here. Can't wait to get home."

"Me too." She continued brushing her hair while looking at Don in the mirror.

Don said, "I wouldn't care if I never laid eyes on this place again. A perfectly wonderful experience turned out to be sheer hell."

"I know." She put down her brush and turned toward him. "I lived through part of it, remember?"

"I should never have let you come here." Holding his index finger to his thumb, Don continued, "You got this close to being killed and God knows what else."

"But we made it. And you've discovered something that'll make a great name for you. So maybe it'll all work out for the best after all."

"That doesn't exactly sound like the New York ad exec I once knew."

"Maybe, maybe not. What we went through made me realize that there are more important things in life than money." She paused and then said with a wink. "Hmm. Seems I've heard that somewhere before."

"But it's also a necessary commodity that people are willing to die for. Just ask the Spanish conquistadors."

"Or Marin and Diego."

"But what about all the governments? They're not looking for money; they're looking for power."

"Money is more important than power," she casually said.

Surprised, Don asked, "Why do you say that?"

"Money buys power."

"Meaning?"

"I see it every day in my business. Little jerks with even smaller brains who inherited daddy's business throw their weight around everywhere and on everyone, and they get away with it because of the weight of their bank accounts."

"Ah, but they can fire you, so it's power after all, not money." He expected Diane to agree with him.

Instead, she answered, "Not only my boss. I'm talking about all the idiots that I come across day in and day out who work for other firms."

"No kidding? You see that kind of guy often?"

"Often enough."

With a slight twinge of jealousy, Don asked, "Anyone like that ever try to hit on you?"

"Quite a few times, believe me. They think they're big ladies' men just because they drive around in their flashy Benz." Then she affectionately added, "Don't worry. They couldn't hold a candle to you."

Appreciating the remark, Don said, "Boy, am I going to get a swelled head."

"I'm in trouble if that's all I can make swell."

They both laughed. Then Don continued, "But still, it's power that they're exerting, isn't it? And doesn't power get you money?"

Diane thought for a moment. "Maybe they're really one and the same. But it seems to me that money is easier to get than power. Look at how many know-nothings have money—"

"And some of these know-nothings become politicians," Don replied.

"There are a hell of a lot more people with tons of money than politicians with real power."

Don said, "Maybe you're right. I guess the United States is really as powerful as it is because it has so much money to spend. Who was it that said, 'The business of America is business?'"

"I don't know, but it sure sounds right."

"But now you've got me confused. Do you want to be rich or don't you?"

"I'm only saying," she replied, "it seems that the result of having so much money isn't really worth giving up your life for, both literally and figuratively. If money comes along, great. I know now that living, loving, and sharing are far more important than the greedy lust for money. It sure can't bring back the dead who strove all their lives for it, can it?"

No answer was given, nor did one have to be spoken. Each had learned something about the other during their ordeal, and it had brought them closer to each other. The rest of the morning and early afternoon was spent talking, discussing, communicating, and enjoying each other's company more than they had ever realized was possible.

At two p.m., the phone rang. Don picked it up, watched by Diane. Don hung up and said, "They're ready."

Craig Styles drove them while another car led the usual interference behind their car. Within thirty minutes, they arrived at the factory, and Styles, a pleasant enough man of few words, pulled away.

A disturbing thought crossed Don's mind, but he didn't relate it to Diane. This could be some kind of trick, he thought. It was possible that no one would be there. But his fears soon abated as he walked down the corridor and heard the sound of the generator.

He knocked three times, once, and then two times. The door opened, and they were greeted by a cheerful Rawlings.

"Come on in. We just got set up and are ready to try to program the computer so the cylinder will open up to us." Rawlings felt like a kid again. He couldn't remember the last time he had felt so good, so full of purpose, but he knew it had to be some time before Vietnam.

Rawlings guided them over to the newly purchased personal computer, which was being worked on by Oscar Weinberg, who considered himself something of a whiz kid with these things.

"You see," Weinberg said, "I'm programming the computer to rapidly change the frequency of the transmission for this transmitter set. It will go up and down the frequency scale and then change the order in which signals are given out. Now, depending upon just how tough our alien friends wanted to make our entry into the cylinder, we might have to wait a long time for the right frequency and sequence of signals to make the cylinder respond. My guess is that they were only concerned with us having the right technologies to make proper use of their information. I don't think they wanted to make it difficult for us at all. Otherwise, why leave the cylinder behind in the first place?"

Don agreed with Weinberg. He didn't think it would take very long either. "Unless," he said, "we've misinterpreted the meaning of their message altogether."

"Possibly," Weinberg replied, "but I don't think so. This was left for someone to find, on purpose."

Weinberg gave the command for the transmission to begin. He sat back and said, "We can do nothing more for now but wait and watch. We've got the recorder ready with the TV monitor if by some chance an image should appear on the screen."

For the next few hours, the group took turns watching the monitor while some talked, some toyed with sequencing ideas, some played cards, and others drank coffee from thermoses. The two women naturally gravitated to each other and made small talk about things in the United States.

As night began to fall, some of the group became hungry and began to discuss plans for dinner. Someone would have to go to a restaurant and get some food to take back for the rest.

Just as the food orders were being taken by Crossman, Gruen, who'd been taking his turn watching the monitor, shouted. "We got it! We got a transmission!"

Chairs were knocked aside and cards dropped onto the floor as the frenzied group scurried over behind Gruen to view the monitor and listen for any other voice transmissions.

"What do you have?" shouted Don.

"Look," Gruen said, "this is amazing. It's a panoramic view of an ancient city of Peru, probably one near that town of … you know, the one where you found the cylinder."

"Ochoa," Don replied.

"Yeah, Ochoa."

The group stood transfixed as they viewed a video of a village and people of ancient Peru that had existed about four thousand years before the camera was invented here on earth, two thousand years before the birth of Christ. What they viewed wasn't so amazing in itself; the main thing was that they were privy to viewing it at all. This was a kind of "home movie" taken by a being from deep space showing human beings as they actually appeared, four thousand years earlier. These were no actors.

They continued to watch as people walked about, seemingly performing their daily chores, walking among the thatch-covered stone houses that dotted the hillside. The women were bare-chested, and one young woman sat in front of a small house, breast-feeding her young infant.

One man, appearing about fifty years of age, although it was difficult to tell and he could have been much younger, walked directly up to the camera and began speaking in the tongue of the ancient Quechua language as if on cue. He had the bearing of someone of importance, possibly the chief of the village.

He stood there and spoke for about five minutes, occasionally gesturing with his hands, changing expression from smiling to frowning, from happy to sad, as if he were retelling a personal oral history of himself and his people.

"My God," Alicia Sadowski excitedly said. "Can you imagine what he must be telling us? I can't wait to get this tape interpreted."

There was general provocative agreement among the group.

Suddenly, the transmission went blank.

"What happened?" the group demanded. Gruen, still at the controls, assured them that he touched nothing and that maybe that's all there was to the transmission. But no sooner had he said that when a second transmission began.

What appeared on the screen was enough to make everyone in the room gasp dumbfounded, with each and every eye nearly popping out of its socket. Exclamations and expletives filled the room as all eyes were glued to the image on the screen. What they were viewing went beyond anyone's imagination. No one had even dared suggest that this might be possible. There, on the screen, was a full-body view of an alien being, a thing, a creature, a monstrous life-form of unimaginable beauty from another world.

"Jesus, look at it!" Gruen exclaimed.

Rawlings spoke gleefully, practically shouting, "All those years working with UFOs and now this!"

All eyes remained glued to the screen as each person was lost in the wonderment that was before them. They spoke as one.

"Unbelievable."

"Fantastic."

"Who would have believed …"

"Pinch me, I'm sure this must be a dream."

"This is no dream," Rawlings said. "Wait till Sloan and the others view this. I can't wait to see the expressions on their faces back in Washington."

Weinberg was busy jumping up and down like someone who had just opened his Christmas presents and had gotten everything that he'd asked Santa for. The sight of the alien had affected the group like nothing else could have, even winning the lottery, for they had hit an even bigger jackpot: the jackpot of the cosmos, the dream of the ages.

Don looked at Diane and said with enormous excitement but a touch of regret, "If only Anton were here to see this. This is incredible."

The alien on the screen that had unknowingly caused grown people to act like children, resembled a cross between an insect and an octopus, almost like something out of a science fiction movie. It apparently wore no clothing or other protective covering. It had several arms with many finger-like projections protruding at the end of each arm. The arms radiated from a central body that appeared to be more rigid and solid than the arms, which had a rubbery, flexible sort of appearance, and they moved in coordinated rhythm with each other. Crossman had been counting and estimated that there were about twenty arms.

The alien had what some in the group thought were eye-like openings, or at least light-sensitive organs, spread throughout its body. But nothing resembling ears or a mouth could be seen.

The camera moved back and exposed the inside of an alien ship equipped with many flashing lights, including what appeared to be ultraviolet and infrared lights. Apparently the alien could detect infrared and UV light, invisible to the naked human eye.

The alien moved easily on several of its arm-like projections. It then entered a small, pod-like vehicle and sealed itself inside. A door to the craft opened, and the pod-like vehicle moved out of the craft, followed by the camera. The pod moved with a smooth effortlessness as though floating on air. The pod was now outside the spacecraft and apparently protected the alien from what must have been, to it, a harsh environment.

When the vehicle emerged, the group members realized with surprise the great size of the alien. A person stood perhaps half the size of the alien. Then the monitor went blank again.

The group stood and watched, hoping for another transmission, while speculations concerning what they had seen filled the room: Perhaps some sort of ionized particles powered the pod; maybe the alien had a brain that filled the body, giving it the capacity of a computer; perhaps it could read minds and didn't need a mouth or other earth-like speaking or hearing organs; maybe its great size meant that it came from a larger planet than earth, or one which simply had more gravity; were there more of these creatures on board, or was it being filmed by remote-controlled camera? Why did it wear no clothing? Did the aliens not need to be covered at all on their own planet and therefore have an environment that was either never harsh to them or permanently controlled by them? Did the alien hope to study us? Did it take some humans back to its planet, and if so, are their descendants still alive four thousand years later? Did these aliens land in other places on earth? Did they land at other times? Would they ever return again at some future time, perhaps with the descendants of the Indians that they might have taken with them?

These and other titillating questions were being bounced around the room when a new image appeared on the screen amid shouts urging everyone in the room to be quiet. This time the alien was back inside the spacecraft.

One of the arms picked up a card that had a symbol on it, sort of a design or diagram. No one in the group was quite sure. One of the other arms touched something and held it toward the camera. It was a bolt-like object. The alien put both down and then picked up a new card and a new object. This card had a new, though similar, symbol pictured on it, and the object was a larger version of the same bolt-like object. A third card was picked up, and a still larger bolt-like object was shown.

"What's it doing?" Diane asked, but no one answered, for each had the same perplexing question in mind.

Now the alien picked up a different card and an object that looked like a piece of wire. Then it picked up another slightly different card and a slightly larger wire. And then it showed a third, though similar, card and an even larger wire.

Weinberg exclaimed, "Jesus. You know what it's doing? It's teaching us its written language. It's teaching us to read, in its own tongue."

"Why?" asked Crossman.

"For communicating with us, of course. I think it intends to teach us its language and then use it to communicate information to us. Remember, the original message is, 'If you can enter, find God,' or as we now believe, 'the universe.' I think the next step will be for our friendly alien to tell us much of what it knows about the nature of its own world and of the universe."

General agreement and enthusiastic responses met this hypothesis.

Rawlings interrupted while the alien continued its language lesson. "Do you think it's possible it'll give us information concerning energy, atomic fusion, or even something more powerful?" The soldier in him was emerging. *Weapons,* thought Rawlings. What powerful weapons might they be able to produce with the information gleaned from this four-thousand-year-old alien?

As the alien continued as would-be tutor, discussion arose as to the amount of tape they would require to capture all of the transmission on their video. They also suspected that this process could take a long time and so decided to man the monitor round the clock if need be, taking turns at the monitor. But regardless of how long it would take, plans would have to be made to spirit the cylinder out of Peru and safely onto American soil. They couldn't remain in the factory undetected forever. At any given moment, they would have to be prepared to pack up, vacate, and make their way back to the United States.

Rawlings said that he and Major Craig Styles would handle the arrangements via coded messages to Major Sloan in Washington. He was depending on Washington to give him further instructions on the best procedure to accomplish the mission.

Rawlings left the factory, taking his aide, David Crossman, with him, and headed back to the hotel in one of their cars. At the hotel he contacted Major Sloan in Washington, informing him in sketchy, coded detail of the events that had occurred. Sloan replied that he'd get working immediately on a plan and would get back to Rawlings ASAP via coded phone messages.

Major Sloan knew he had his work cut out for him. He had to find a way to get the cylinder, the twelve people of the entire Rawlings contingency, and the Carters, in that order of importance, safely out of Peru, and if possible, he had to do it without creating an international incident. Sloan rushed the information over to CIA headquarters at Langley. This was a job that had to be carried out as discreetly as possible.

The authorities, understanding the importance of the mission, afforded it top priority and devised a plan within the next four hours, which was then communicated back to Rawlings, who'd been pacing the floor of his hotel room waiting for the orders to arrive.

The phone rang, and Rawlings grabbed it. He was given a coded message, which he immediately began to decode. After thirty minutes of concentrated effort, the message was clear. Rawlings would take his group to a remote beach approximately fifty miles outside of Lima. Inflatable rafts would be waiting to take them off shore to a submerged submarine that would surface briefly to take on human cargo and materiel and then vanish once again into the dark depths of the ocean. The rendezvous would take place in a day and a half at 0200 hours in total darkness. They were to watch for a signal by flashlight. There would be a margin of error of only one hour. If no contact was made by 0300 hours, the plan would be scrubbed. The Carters were not a priority but would be extracted at a later time.

Following military procedure, Rawlings took out a book of matches from his pocket and lit the paper that the message was written on. He dropped the burning paper into the wastepaper basket. The message had been committed to memory and shared with Major Styles, who also memorized it.

Rawlings was eager to tell the others of the plan, but he didn't know how he would break it to Don and Diane. He thought it best to wait for the last possible moment to spring the unfortunate news on them. They would have but one more day at most to work with the cylinder before packing up their gear and preparing to depart.

Rawlings told Styles he would be back as soon as possible. But first, Styles would have to go downstairs with Rawlings to run the usual interference with a second car. Rawlings told Styles to tell Crossman to order some food for him. It was already eight thirty p.m., and he was starving. He realized that with the excitement of the day, he hadn't eaten since before noon.

Styles told Crossman to go downstairs and get some sandwiches for them while he and Rawlings were gone. As Rawlings and Styles rode the elevator down, Rawlings wondered what new, out-of-this-world things they were videotaping back at the factory. He smiled to himself as he realized the unintended pun he had just made.

Rawlings walked out of the hotel and up the block toward his car while Styles walked off in the opposite direction to his car, parked around the corner. They would meet at the corner for Styles to play the usual stall game to ensure Rawlings wasn't followed to the factory.

Rawlings approached his car and placed the key in the door. Cars were passing him in the street, but one stopped directly behind his back as he was about to unlock the door. Thinking that it was someone looking for his parking space, Rawlings began to turn around and signal that he was getting out. They could have his spot.

But he never managed to convey the message. A sharp pain shot though the back of his head, and Rawlings saw his car appear to fall away from him. *What an odd thing,* he thought before blacking out.

Major Styles waited for several minutes, around the corner, for Rawlings to pull up with his car. As each minute passed, he became increasingly anxious. Finally, he decided to walk around the corner past the hotel entrance and down the block to where Rawlings's car was parked. Styles approached the car, but he didn't see Rawlings. Scratching his head, he wondered if Rawlings had run upstairs for something he might have forgotten, or maybe the car wouldn't start. Styles waited a few more minutes and then decided to call upstairs with a house phone in the hotel lobby. Crossman, who hadn't yet left for the sandwiches, answered.

"You see Rawlings?" Styles asked.

"He left with you, didn't he?"

"I don't know. I'm waiting down here and don't see him."

"Is his car still there?"

"Yes."

"I don't know what to tell you. If he comes back or calls, I'll be sure to tell you right away. You sound worried."

"It's not like him not to follow procedure. Let me go. I'll check outside again and wait. I'll call back as soon as I find him."

"Okay."

Styles walked out of the hotel. *Where the hell is he?* he wondered. Styles leaned against Rawlings's car and waited for another five minutes. Feeling impatient, he decided to walk into the middle of the street and look up and down the street to try to see whatever he could. Could Rawlings have forgotten where his car was and be walking up and down the wrong block? The thought seemed ridiculous, but Styles was willing to try anything at that point. Seeing nothing from the middle of the street, he began to walk back to the sidewalk when he noticed something dangling from the door of Rawlings's car. It was Rawlings's keys still sticking out of the keyhole.

"He's been kidnapped!" Styles said aloud, concluding the only thing that seemed possible. He grabbed the keys and ran as fast as he could to the elevator and up to the room. Barging in on Crossman, out of breath, he gasped, "They've got Rawlings."

"What?"

"He's been taken. Kidnapped."

"By who? How do you know for sure?"

"I don't know, but I found his keys still sticking out of the lock in his door." Styles held out Rawlings's keys.

Crossman pounded his fist into the palm of his other hand. "Shit! We'd better notify the guys at the factory to pack up and get out of there."

The two men strode out of the room toward the elevator.

Crossman tentatively asked, as Styles pressed the down button, "You don't think he'd tell them where the group is, do you?"

Styles was annoyed at the question. "How do I know? I doubt he would say anything. He was a POW in Nam, you know." The elevator door opened, and they stepped into the empty elevator.

"Yeah, and I heard he wasn't a model for the school of name, rank, and serial number."

Styles angrily retorted at the insinuation. "That's bullshit. By the time they got anything out of him, it was of no use to the gooks anyway."

The door opened to the lobby and they began to walk toward Styles's car. Apologetically, Crossman said, "Sorry. I didn't realize I'd hit a sore spot."

"Well, you sure did. He deserves better." Styles was still angry.

As they reached the sidewalk, Crossman replied, "We don't have time to stand here and argue. We don't know who has him or what they'll do to him, but we certainly can't afford to take any chances."

Composing himself, Styles replied, "You're right. It's just that he's lived with a bum rap for a long time. No one knows what it's like to be tortured by animals except the POWs themselves."

"Okay, listen. You stay and gather up the guys here while I take off for the factory."

"I'll make sure you aren't followed. I'll meet you at the corner with my car. Here are Rawlings's keys." He handed Crossman the keys and pointed toward the corner up the block.

Crossman opened his jacket to reveal a .38 caliber pistol. Patting it, he said, "I'm taking no chances. Don't worry. I'll be looking at every shadow from now on."

After the usual stall tactic, Crossman arrived at the factory, where his ominous news quickly brought everyone to their feet and then scurrying around to pack things up and get out of there.

Don regretted having to leave, as he believed they were well on their way to learning the alien's language. He'd hoped to begin learning what knowledge the alien had to offer, but he knew that after the news of Rawlings's disappearance, that would have to wait.

Once safely back at the hotel, the group decided that the evacuation plan would have to be cancelled. There was still no sign or word from Rawlings, and it would be far too risky now to carry out the original plan of a rendezvous with the submarine in the event that Rawlings did talk.

They hid the cylinder in one of the closets, guarded by several members, and decided to contact Washington. They would have to sit it out and wait for word as to their next step or as to the whereabouts and well-being of Tom Rawlings.

CHAPTER 27

A CHILL SHOT THROUGH his body as he gasped for air. He was tied to a wooden chair as two men watched him slowly return to consciousness after throwing cold water onto his face and chest.

Tom Rawlings was dripping wet, and his head throbbed from the blow he had taken earlier that evening. He looked up at the two men who smiled, not at Rawlings but because they could now begin to interrogate the American.

Rawlings sat silently, staring straight ahead. He'd been in this sort of predicament before and had a fair idea of what to expect. He also knew what they were after. What he didn't know was who they were or represented. Both men appeared to be Peruvian, and one of them began to speak in Spanish, to which Rawlings responded disdainfully in English, "Sorry, my Spanish is terrible."

The shorter of the two men moved in closer and said, "So I talk in *Ingles*. Where is it?"

"Where is what?"

"Where is it?" the man angrily repeated.

"I don't know what you're talking about."

The man stepped closer and, with an open hand, smacked Rawlings across the face. The side of Rawlings's face stung from the blow, but Rawlings continued to stare straight ahead.

"You talk, eh?" the man said.

But Rawlings didn't react. His mind wandered back to Nam, and he knew he could take whatever these shits could throw at him, and—

A blow from the man's fist caught Rawlings on the side of his mouth, loosening some old bridgework he'd had done several years back. He could taste the blood that was beginning to flow on the inside of his mouth.

"You talk now? Where is it?" The man's face was close enough for Rawlings to feel the man's hot, foul breath.

Rawlings looked up at him and angrily asked, "Who are you? Who do you work for?"

But the man only snarled and repeated, "Where is it?"

Rawlings could tell that these were absolute amateurs at interrogation. He'd been through it all in his two-year imprisonment in South Vietnam. Upon his return to the United States, he had read as much as he could on the fine art of interrogation, which more often than not was synonymous with torture. He knew that during the Korean War the Chinese were more adept at securing information from POWs than were his Viet Cong captors. The percentage of those who spilled their guts to their captors, and also those who died in captivity, had been much greater among POWs in Korea than in Vietnam. In Vietnam they primarily used physical torture: beatings, cigarette burns, and the like. He'd read that psychologists found that when face to face with his torturer, a POW is less apt to succumb to his demands. The angry POW wants to take revenge on his torturer and, paradoxically, this motivation gives the POW a purpose for survival. Ironically, physical torture often hardens the victim against his captors rather than softening him up into informing, or makes him concede to anything he believes his captors want to hear. Almost no useful information is gleaned in this manner.

On the other hand, Rawlings had learned, the human mind can become a person's own worst enemy. The Chinese isolated many prisoners during the Korean War, keeping them in solitary confinement and darkness so that they could not differentiate between day and night. They spoke to no one, not even their captors, for long periods of time, being fed through a slot and seeing no human face. They lived with their own excrement in the total blackness with no enemy to confront and no individual to turn their hatred against. They lived with body sores and among the flies, insects, and other creatures that crawl, serving as a constant reminder of the level of deprivation they had sunk to.

All they had were their own thoughts—thoughts of never returning and of suicide. And every so often their captors would feed "information" to their depressed prisoner, such as "We hear the Americans are losing the war, and you might have to remain here for the rest of your life." And the final blow would be when the prisoner was told, fictitiously, that his wife and son had been killed in a car accident. News such as this in such a state of mind would make most any man crack.

Rawlings knew it wasn't the beatings or physical torture that had made him talk in Nam but the attack on his psyche when he was threatened with being dropped head first into a bucket filled with human excrement. *Everyone has a breaking point.*

But Rawlings vowed that these men facing him now would never get a word out of him. These were Neanderthal assholes. He clenched his teeth, waiting for another blow, which viciously struck him across his nose and left eye. Rawlings smiled to himself. *Go ahead, hit me again, harder this time. See what Rawlings is made of. But don't let me loose, because I'll rip your faces apart with my bare hands. I'll cut your balls off and feed pieces of your body to the dogs.* The adrenalin surged through his body as he waited silently for the next powerful blow, and then the next, until his face became a bruised and bloody mess. One of his molars was knocked out, and he spat it onto the floor.

Through hazy eyes, Rawlings could see the man rubbing his sore fists and staring at a crack in the almost-closed door that led to another room. He was gesturing with his shoulders as if asking someone what his next move was.

So that was it. Someone else was calling the shots, someone who didn't want to be seen. He knew these were total amateurs.

The man left the room through that same door and closed it behind him. A few moments later, he returned with a gun in his hand, showed it to Rawlings, and placed one bullet in its six-chambered barrel.

"You talk," the man demanded again.

You talk. How stupid, Rawlings thought. *The moron probably got the expression from some second-rate spy movie.*

The man spun the barrel and placed the gun against Rawlings's head. Rawlings could feel the cold metal against his temple.

The man asked again, "Where is it?"

Rawlings didn't reply, and the man pulled the trigger.

Click was all Rawlings heard. He knew the game very well: Russian roulette. There was one bullet in a six-chambered gun. Which chamber had the bullet? There was no way of knowing—except that after one pull of the trigger, your odds of having your brains blown out were one in five instead of one in six.

"You talk. Now!" the man shouted at Rawlings.

Again, Rawlings merely sat. His mind was already made up. He was ready to die and began to mumble a prayer. It didn't matter anymore whether it was this bullet or the next. He was prepared to die, here and now. He would never talk.

The man squeezed the trigger, slowly. *Click.* One in four now.

"You talk or muerte," he said, mixing up his English and Spanish. Again he squeezed the trigger, and again came that tell-tale click. One in three.

Rawlings now knew that the man was asking him something, but he didn't hear him anymore. His eyes were closed as the man's finger squeezed off another round. Again there was a click.

Rawlings, not listening to the man's order to talk, waited for death. Except for a run of some bad luck resulting from his years as a POW, life had been generally good to him. His work in the military was important, and his family was the best there was.

The trigger was pulled again, and again there was another click. There was one chamber left.

Rawlings felt the man grab him by his hair and yank his head back, so that he was forced to look up at the man. The gun barrel was now aimed right between Rawlings's eyes, and the man screamed at him to talk.

Rawlings closed his eyes just as the man began to squeeze the trigger for the sixth and final time. Rawlings remembered his family, his wife and his two beautiful daughters, and was momentarily saddened at the thought of never seeing them again. But he felt an inner peace and thought to himself, *I am ready to meet my maker.*

The man squeezed the trigger, and the barrel turned as the last chamber was struck by the hammer. But to Rawlings's great surprise, only another dull click was heard. Unnoticed by Rawlings, his captors had taken out the bullet.

Rawlings opened his eyes, realizing that they weren't going to kill him. Perhaps he would win this time. He breathed in deeply and looked at his interrogator. The man was again staring at the doorway as if asking for further instructions. He walked to the door and then came back. He said something to the other man in Spanish, and then the two of them turned the chair so that Rawlings was facing away from the door.

The two men stepped back, away from Rawlings. Rawlings heard the door open and then the footsteps of someone entering the room and stopping somewhere behind him, out of his vision.

"Very good, Colonel Rawlings," a man's accented voice said. "They train you good."

Rawlings instantly recognized the accent as being Eastern European, probably Russian. *Of course. The Russians are here too.*

"Who are you?" Rawlings asked.

Answering in acceptable English, Vasilyenkov said, "It no matter. We want item we believe you already have."

"We have nothing."

"No? Why have people been very invisible in past days? Our sources say you find object with help from Mr. Carter."

"I don't know what you're talking about."

Vasilyenkov's tone turned serious. "We no play games, colonel. I no have time to waste. We never wanted harm you. Certainly, we all civilized men here."

Rawlings sarcastically responded, "Right."

Almost apologetically, Vasilyenkov said, "And if you in my position, you would have done same."

Rawlings ignored the last statement and said, "We're finishing up some loose ends here. The cylinder thing is a hoax. We're getting ready to leave the country soon. I suggest you do the same and go home to something more useful."

"Hoax? The automobile with hole burned through floor, and two burned men, one who was friend of Carter, that is hoax?"

"So two jerks fooled around with some explosives or acids or something and got themselves killed. Does that mean Martians came to earth and cooked them? Come on, sir, be reasonable. Do you really believe that some alien did that?"

Calmly, knowing perfectly well what Rawlings was attempting to do, Vasilyenkov answered, "Then why you also here? For holiday?"

"Like your people, we got word that some crazy person was trying to blackmail our country with some idiotic story about an alien object. My job, just as yours probably is, is to check out the story. They always come up phony. It's all a hoax, just a goddamn hoax."

"We will see. For now, I leave you with thought. If our intelligence reports are correct, and if cylinder is genuine, Peruvian government will no allow out of country. You will no get past metal detectors at airport. And my government will do all in power to see your country no receive it."

"You don't have to worry. There's nothing going home with us except what we came with."

"We will see, Col. Rawlings, we will see."

Rawlings heard the sound of footsteps leaving the room and felt as though someone was doing something with the ropes. Then he heard more footsteps, followed by silence in the room.

Rawlings began to struggle with the ropes and realized they'd been cut. He was now alone in the room and able to free himself. His head throbbed in synchronized unison with the pulsing of his blood, and his jaw hurt more than several root canals performed without Novocain. Yet upon realizing that he'd won this battle, that they hadn't been able to make him talk, that he wasn't broken, and that he had been complimented by the Russian on his performance, he felt more exhilarated, more alive, than he'd felt in far too many years.

He stood there, alone in that room, and his sweat- and blood-soaked face broke into a smile. He began to laugh, lightly at first, and then more and more loudly until he was laughing uncontrollably, almost maniacally. He pumped his fist high into the air and roared with a booming voice, not caring who might hear him, "That's the stuff Tom Rawlings is made of, you bastards. That's the real Tom Rawlings!"

Years of disgrace lifted from his shoulders. He turned and walked triumphantly, head held high, down the stairs. He could hear the trumpets and see the throngs of people throwing petals of flowers at him, shouting joyously, "Raw-lings, Raw-lings, Raw-lings ..."

Within a minute, he was down in the street. He caught a taxi and made his way back to the hotel room. As the door opened, Gruen gaped at Rawlings's face and said, "Holy cow! What happened?"

"Aren't you gonna ask me if I got the number of that truck?" Rawlings quipped.

He entered the room, greeted by all the others who had gathered to await his hoped-for return. Rawlings quickly related the story and, after finishing, asked, "What about the sub? Are we ready for it?"

The room became dead silent until Styles finally said, "Cancelled."

"Cancelled? Why?" He cocked his head to the side.

Styles sheepishly said, "When we knew you were kidnapped, we were forced to go to an alternate plan."

At first, Rawlings felt chagrined. *They thought I would talk!* But after a moment he realized that they were following correct procedure. The whole mission couldn't be jeopardized simply because one man's feelings might become hurt.

"You did right to cancel, Craig. What alternative, if any, did they come up with?"

"We're still waiting to hear from Washington. We expect an answer shortly."

"All right. I'd better wash up and change. Is everyone and every*thing* here?"

"All set. Just get yourself ready," Styles answered.

A short time later, the phone rang. Rawlings ran for the phone with a towel still in hand, watched eagerly by the entire group. He snapped his fingers, and someone handed him a pen and pad. Rawlings wrote the new coded message on the pad and hung up.

"We've got work to do, Craig."

Rawlings and Styles then sat down together a table and pored over a small code book in order to interpret the coded message. Within fifteen minutes, the decoding was completed.

"We have our new orders," Rawlings said to the anxiously waiting group. He stood up and held the paper. "It reads, 'Air Force C130—'" Rawlings looked up at Don and Diane and said for their benefit, "that's a military transporter— 'will make emergency landing at Lima for repairs tomorrow, p.m. Meet at next oh three hundred hours on airstrip undetected.'" Rawlings paused, glanced at the Carters, and continued to read the message. "It goes on to say, 'Carters no clearance. Not priority. Extraction later.'"

Diane shouted, "What the hell does that mean? Carters not priority."

Rawlings looked at Diane and Don, visibly embarrassed. "I'm sorry. It means that they feel that you can only jeopardize the mission at this point. You're wanted by the police here, and neither of you is military or important to this mission, at least as far as Washington is concerned. They're ordering me to get my staff and the cylinder safely back to the States. They obviously don't realize how much help you've been to us. But even if they knew, I doubt they'd risk, even slightly, the mission for two civilians."

"So you lied to me," Don said, his voice raised. "You said you'd get the cylinder and us out of Lima. Christ, I'm the one who found the damn thing and went through hell to hold on to it." His face was flushed with rage.

Rawlings knew he had to defuse the situation. "And we will. It says you can't go with us. It doesn't say you can't go at all. We'll figure a way to get you two out of here. The major obstacle as I see it is your passports. Without them you won't clear immigration, and you're a wanted man, Don. If we can't figure a way to get you home, 'extraction later' means the government will get you out, I guarantee it."

Alicia Sadowski spoke up. "I have an idea, Tom. We won't be needing our passports if we're sneaking out of the country. We can get a Polaroid shot of each of them tomorrow and replace the new photos on two of our passports. I guess Diane will have to use mine since I'm the only female. We do sort of resemble each other, at least enough to get by immigration."

"Great idea, Alicia," Styles said. "And with Don's command of the Spanish language, they should have no problem getting through."

Sadowski replied, "And he'll never be recognized with that beard and long hair."

There was general agreement with this plan, including begrudging agreement by both Don and Diane, who knew they had little choice in the matter. It was also decided that airline tickets would be purchased for the first available US-bound commercial plane to take the Carters out of Lima.

The next day, they carried out their plan of exchanging Don and Diane's photos on David Crossman's and Alicia Sadowski's passports. They also arranged for a flight to New York via Miami for nine o'clock the following morning.

The group readied everything for the departure, including packing the cylinder inside a wooden crate, cushioned with foam rubber. The remainder of the day was spent making small talk, much of which concerned the cylinder and the alien teacher.

Rawlings had missed much of the last taping and asked Don what he thought of it thus far. Don thought for a moment and then responded, "The major impression I get is that our alien friend is giving us a kind of Rosetta Stone enabling us to understand his language. It's my guess that the next step will be for it to allow us to read important material that it's prepared for us, books perhaps, that will, in fact, give us a deeper understanding of matters of the universe."

Rawlings wore a broad grin and leaned back in his chair. "I can't wait to get this back to the States and rub the Russians' noses in it. What a coup this is. This could give the United States a huge edge over the Russians if it really does contain information about energy."

Don stared at Rawlings and thought that Rawlings truly didn't know what an amazing find the cylinder was. The most incredible discovery on earth, contact with intelligent alien beings, was happening before his very eyes, and all Rawlings could think about was the advantage it might give the Americans over the Russians.

Don's earlier fears arose again, those concerning the ultimate use of the cylinder, but he knew there was nothing more to be done here. First he must escape; then he could appeal to the scientific and military communities concerning the ultimate destiny of the cylinder.

CHAPTER 28

VITALE MISCHKIN WAS DISCUSSING nothing of any importance with one of the other Russian scientists in his group, Dr. Tsialonen, when Vasilyenkov walked into the room with the two other KGB agents. They had paid two locals to interrogate Rawlings, achieving no positive results, and now they sat down to discuss their next steps.

Mischkin continued conversing with Tsialonen while intently straining to listen in on the three agents. What he heard struck him like a bolt of lightning. He heard them say that the leader of the American group, Rawlings, had been interrogated but had disclosed nothing. But Vasilyenkov and his men were certain that something major was about to occur, as they had received word that a US C130 had been forced to land at the airport in Lima due to "mechanical problems." He listened carefully as he heard them toss around several ideas, one of which nearly turned his stomach. They were planning the potential destruction of the plane in order to ensure that the cylinder, if it was indeed on that plane, would never arrive on American soil.

Against his better judgment, Mischkin couldn't contain himself. He walked to where Vasilyenkov was sitting and stood there momentarily as the three men halted their discussion and looked at Mischkin.

Vasilyenkov stared at him, and then asked, "What is it?"

Mischkin was outraged and spoke in a manner in which Vasilyenkov was never addressed by anyone. "You barbaric fool! I overheard your discussion.

How could you even dream of destroying what might be the only piece of evidence of intelligent, alien life that exists in the entire world?"

Vasilyenkov stared frigidly into Mischkin's eyes. He was always a man in control and didn't intend to be intimidated by a naïve scientist, a man, Vasilyenkov felt, who knew about books and formulas but surely not about people or politics. Mischkin was a dreamer, like so many other scientists, not a realist. What did Mischkin know about things that truly affected the world?

Everyone in the room was hushed in fragile silence as they watched for Vasilyenkov's response.

He didn't keep them waiting long as he spoke with almost no emotion. "So, this cylinder, which we don't even know for certain is actually from some foreign world, is more important to you than the security of Mother Russia?" Vasilyenkov always knew just the right phrase to use in any given situation.

"I didn't say that," Mischkin snapped, pointing a finger at Vasilyenkov.

Still calm, Vasilyenkov replied, "But you implied it, which is the same thing among intelligent men."

Mischkin spoke slowly and deliberately. "This could be the most important object ever found in the history of mankind. Don't you see that?"

Vasilyenkov knew that Mischkin would be putty in his hands, and he spoke with an almost fatherly, advisory tone. "Vitale, don't you think I know that? But what good is this object to us if the Americans get it and use its information to gain a military advantage over us? When the Soviet Union is blown off the face of the Earth and your family is dead or groveling in the streets for scraps of rotten food, what will you say then? Will you say it was worth it?"

Mischkin knew that it was useless to argue with a man such as Vasilyenkov, and he also knew his career could be badly damaged if accusations of treason were lodged against him back home. Therefore, out of fear, he responded, "I apologize for my outburst, Boris. It's simply that the excitement of obtaining the cylinder, and the thought of then losing it, was too much for me. You're correct, of course. The security of our country comes first. But I implore you, if there's any way to save the cylinder, please try to do so. This is incredibly important to us."

"And exactly who is 'us'? Isn't 'us' the Soviet Union? We're in this together, Vitale. I assure you, I will try to do all I can."

"I hope so. I sincerely hope so." With that, Mischkin turned and sat down, still visibly shaken by the confrontation. He knew that Vasilyenkov would do as he pleased, and Mischkin made plans to keep an even closer watch on Vasilyenkov's next moves.

Later that night, at approximately one a.m., the group bade farewell to Don and Diane and left with all their belongings.

"See you in about a day," Rawlings said as he shook hands with Don. He kissed Diane on the cheek and then looked at Don and said, "That's some girl you got there."

"I know," Don said proudly. "Believe me, I know."

"Oh yeah. One more thing," Rawlings added as he began to exit the room. "If you ever get the itch to join the military, Uncle Sam could sure use a couple of good eggs like you."

"Fat chance," Don replied, smiling.

"No way," Diane said. "Unless they allow me to choose my uniforms from Bonwit's." She chuckled.

Rawlings genuinely laughed and then, changing to a more serious expression, and in an almost touching manner, saluted the two Carters, holding his hand at his forehead for several seconds before snapping the arm down to his side in true military fashion. He turned and exited the room.

Diane turned to Don and said, "You know, I could almost learn to like that man."

"I know what you mean," he said, feeling a bit empty now that the group and the cylinder were gone. But he still had Diane to worry about, and he and Diane would now try to catch a few hours of sleep. They would be up at six thirty a.m. to prepare for their flight home.

Meanwhile, Rawlings's group of twelve piled everything into two minivans that they had rented for the evening's trip to the airstrip. Styles and Crossman, earlier that evening, had scouted the area surrounding the airport and had seen the C130 sitting on the tarmac near one of the cargo terminals. The airport was completely fenced in, but Styles and Crossman were able to cut a hole in the chain-link fence not far from the parked plane.

The plan was to drive the vans up to the fence, unload, cross the darkened airstrip at 0300 hours, and load everything, including themselves, onto the plane. They expected help to be waiting inside.

At 0230, they were in position outside the fence. It was decided that each person would carry enough items to ensure that only one trip would have to be made and that they would cross the tarmac to the plane one at a time to avoid too much commotion. They couldn't afford to be detected by anyone.

At precisely 0300, Styles ducked through the ripped fence and scampered as quickly and quietly as possible toward the plane, some two hundred yards away. At this hour of night, the airport was closed, and only a few night watchmen patrolled the airport, mostly inside the terminal building.

Rawlings decided that he'd be the last to go. He watched as each member reached the waiting plane and was helped up an emergency ladder and onto the darkened plane.

Finally, it was Rawlings's turn. He stepped through the fence and then replaced the fencing in a manner that would make the opening hard to detect, especially before dawn.

Rawlings crossed the tarmac, climbed the ladder, and was helped into the plane by Major Mark Watson, who welcomed him aboard. Watson told Rawlings that they had clearance to leave after dawn, at 0700 hours. Watson suggested that the group sit down, relax, and try to catch some sleep, if possible.

The crate containing the cylinder was placed onto one of the seats, seat belted in, and further tied to the seat with rope for added security. The group then settled in and waited for runway clearance.

It was now four a.m., and all was quiet and still in the predawn darkness that surrounded the airport, except for a shadowy, stealthy thirteenth figure that quietly ran across the tarmac and up to the wheels of the C130. Standing on top of one of the wheels, the man reached up into the landing gear housing, completed his job, and then silently returned to his companion, who was waiting in a car at the other side of the airport fence. The car slowly pulled away, out of sight of the airplane.

At seven a.m., final clearance was given for the C130 to taxi onto the runway. The plane's engines revved up to their proper RPMs, and the plane took off with no complications.

Rawlings sat back and sighed with relief. In a few hours he would be safely back in the good old US of A.

Don and Diane had awakened at six thirty to prepare for what they prayed would be an uneventful trip home. They were beginning to pack the last of their belongings when the phone rang. It was 7:10. The ringing bell startled them as Diane exclaimed, "Oh no. I bet it's Rawlings. Something's gone wrong."

Don nervously reached for the phone as he replied, "Here goes nothing" and then spoke anxiously into the phone. "Hello?"

An unfamiliar voice on the other end answered in soft, measured phrases in fairly decent, Eastern European–accented English, "I must speak with person in command."

Confused and apprehensive, Don cautiously probed the caller for more information. "In charge of what?"

"I have only little time. Please. In command of Americans to find very important thing."

Don paused, and then said, "I'm in charge here. Who are you and what do you want?"

The voice continued. "I tell you only this. Airplane at airport ... in large danger ... must no leave airport."

Don was becoming frantic. "Why? What danger? What will happen?"

"Bomb," Mischkin answered as he hung up the phone. *Mother Russia and talk of national security be damned,* he thought. The cylinder had to be saved.

Diane nervously asked, "What is it?" She could plainly see how upset Don was.

"Maybe nothing, maybe plenty. Some guy with an accent that could be Russian was warning us that the plane, the C130, will be blown up!"

"Fucking bastards," she screamed. "Blow up the plane? What do we do? It's probably already taken off."

Don tried to calm her. "Maybe not. We can call the airport. Maybe it's still on the ground."

"Who was that guy? Do you think it was the one who captured Rawlings?"

"I don't know." He picked up the telephone. "Why would he warn us?"

"Maybe it's the Peruvians who want to blow up the plane, or ... I don't know. None of this makes any sense."

Don thought for a moment. "Maybe it's a trick. Maybe the Russians, knowing we have the cylinder, figure that if they tell us there's a bomb on board, the plane would either never take off or turn back and lands in Lima again."

"But if anyone were to find the cylinder at the airport, it would be the Peruvians, not the Russians."

Don thumbed through the plane tickets and itinerary for the phone number of the airport. "But at least they'd figure they still might have a chance to get it."

"Did you find the number?"

"Got it." Don dialed and was transferred to flight information. After a wait of two seemingly interminable minutes, Don was informed that the plane had already departed.

In Spanish, Don said, "Hold on a second, please." He cupped his hand over the mouthpiece and told Diane in English, "It took off already. What do we do?"

"Tell them there's a bomb on the plane. They'll definitely relay the message to them."

"Okay." At this point, he would have listened to any suggestion.

Don put the phone back to his ear and said in Spanish, "Hello, are you still there?"

"Yes, sir, still here."

"Listen carefully. We have reason to believe that there is a bomb aboard the American C130 that just took off."

"One moment and I'll connect you to security."

"Please hurry."

Don heard some clicking noises and then heard, "Please connect this call to security."

"One moment," the operator replied.

"Security," a man answered.

Don wasted no time. "There's a bomb on board the American C130 that took off within the last hour."

"Who is this, and how do you know about this bomb?" The man at the other end was very calm.

"I received an anonymous phone call regarding that plane."

"What is your name, sir?"

"My name is …" He knew he couldn't reveal his true identity, but he also knew that Rawlings would have to know who the message came from. "Don … Diane."

"Mr. Diane. I myself do not have the power to recall an airplane. Understand that almost all of these calls have no basis of truth to them. What I must do now is contact my superior, who will then contact the tower to discuss the recall of the plane. Airports receive so many crank calls that they usually inform the plane that a call has been taken, and the personnel on the plane then check the plane for mysterious-looking objects."

"Please hurry. I have great cause for concern that this call may, in fact, be the real thing."

"Is there a number that I can reach you?"

"No, I … I'm calling from a phone booth. I'll call you back."

"All right, Mr. Diane. I'll get going on this."

Don hung up.

"What did he say?"

"He'll work on it right away. Let's hope they notify the plane and it'll turn back or that the whole thing is a ploy or hoax. Or maybe they'll actually find some kind of bomb and defuse it."

"There's nothing more we can do except get to the airport. No matter what, we've got to catch our plane."

"God, I hate leaving like this. So much uncertainty."

"We have to. Besides, if the plane comes back, we can do nothing anyway. And if … if the plane is blown up, we're better off back home."

Don mulled over Diane's remarks. "You're right. Let's get the hell out of here."

They finished packing and left for the airport.

The C130 sped toward Andrews Air Force Base in Maryland. It was a reliable flying machine and had logged thousands of hours. But tucked into the landing gear housing was a new addition. The ticking was very quiet.

Rawlings spoke with Styles while some of the others played cards or made small talk and a few tried to catch some well-deserved sleep. The mood inside the plane was high, and each person was excited to get home and tell the world of the group's discovery. What other amazing things would the cylinder reveal? Even their imaginations wouldn't do justice to the revelations the cylinder might have in store for them.

Alicia Sadowski wondered if the Carters would make it safely aboard their plane. She had grown to like the Carters and planned to see them as soon as she could back in the States.

Weinberg, Corsica, and Gruen discussed the possible effect of the cylinder's existence upon the world of religion, debating whether the revelation that life indeed existed on some other planet in the outer reaches of space would be able to coexist with current religious dogma or would have an adverse effect upon religious beliefs. Although hailing from quite diverse religious backgrounds—Oscar Weinberg being Jewish, Frank Corsica Catholic, and Hank Gruen Lutheran—the three highly educated and experienced PhDs were able to discuss the oftentimes volatile and explosive subject of religion openly and with little outward emotional involvement, though the inner ghosts of their religious upbringings may have haunted any one of them.

Corsica remarked, "Look at the way the church treated Galileo in the seventeenth century when he published his *Dialogue Concerning the Two Chief World Systems*."

"You mean," Weinberg replied, "when he disputed the then-accepted theory that the earth was in the center of the universe?"

Gruen interjected, "Actually, with his telescope he provided evidence supporting the Copernican theory that placed the earth as just one of several planets orbiting in space about the sun."

"Yeah," Corsica responded, "but it took the church two hundred years to accept that fact. I can't imagine what effect the revelation of thinking beings from a foreign world might have."

"Oh, I don't know, Frank," Gruen commented. "The Church has changed dramatically since the days when they took Galileo to view the torture chamber in the Vatican basement in order to induce him into writing a retraction of his book. His book was heresy, they said."

"And they placed a great man under house arrest for the rest of his life," Weinberg stated.

"Science and faith have always made strange bedfellows," Corsica said.

"I agree with you," Weinberg said. "But I also agree with Hank that the church has become more receptive to less dogmatic ways of thinking."

"Listen," Corsica said. "I suppose if we were to walk into a room with some alien-octopus—"

"That talks," Gruen joked, and the three men smiled.

Weinberg added, "That can make advanced transistor TV sets—"

"And put the Japanese out of business," Gruen interrupted. They laughed heartily.

Corsica finished his statement. "That's smarter than us, it would be pretty difficult for someone to dispute its existence, wouldn't it?"

"No, of course it would," Corsica responded. "But in the case of Galileo, no one was disputing the existence of God. But the centuries-old religious dogma behind it was threatened, and, therefore, the clergy who expounded these dogmas felt threatened. They feared that the masses' belief in them would be shaken. Perhaps modern religions will also feel threatened."

"I believe the human race is ready for this event," Weinberg said. "I don't think our discovery will affect religion much, one way or the other—that is, unless this alien creature has all the answers for us ... answers concerning God, creation, death, and so forth."

"I guess only time will tell us," Corsica said. "Our friendly alien would have to provide us with a lot of proof, wouldn't it?"

"He sure would," Gruen said.

Excitedly, Corsica said, "I can't wait to see the faces of people when they see our video."

The three men smiled with satisfaction and sat back in their seats. They hoped the answers would be revealed soon enough.

The pilot flying the plane, Major Mark Watson, was sitting next to the copilot, Major Alan Norris, when a message was received over their radio from the tower at the Lima airport. The message, heard by both pilot and copilot, was taken with little outward expression of concern by either man. Watson spoke first.

"I'd better go back and relay this to Rawlings."

"Okay," was all Norris replied.

CHAPTER 29

AT EIGHT THIRTY A.M., Don and Diane Carter, now traveling as Alicia Sadowski and David Crossman, after standing in a long line, handed the immigration official their passports. He glanced at the photos and then their faces, stamped the passports, and waved them through to the gate. They sat down, saying little to each other out of nervousness, and waited for the call to board their plane. Two pair of eyes darted in watchful harmony for any approaching harbinger of detection.

One of the officials, who had been alerted to check for the names of anyone from Rawlings's group departing Peru, routinely reviewed each plane's manifest, which now revealed the names of David Crossman and Alicia Sadowski.

Don and Diane were waiting apprehensively when the public address system blared twice in succession, "Will passengers Sadowski and Crossman please step up to the customs desk."

Don grabbed Diane's hand. "We either walk out of here and get lost in the crowd outside the terminal, or we step forward and gamble."

Diane bit her lip, knowing the decision would have to be made within seconds to avoid suspicion. "I'm for taking our chances with the plane. We have no other way of getting out of here, and it's the only passport you've got."

"All right," he answered. "Let's play it cool. Remember, Crossman doesn't speak Spanish."

They walked over to the customs official.

"I'm David Crossman."

"I'm Alicia Sadowski."

"Is there a problem?" Don asked, in English.

"Come to my office, please," he answered in English. The official's name tag identified him as Sergio Rolon.

"Sit, please." He motioned, and they sat down on two chairs facing a desk. Rolon stood leaning against the desk, and they waited for him to come to the point.

"I understand you come to Peru with a Col. Rawlings, is this so?"

"Yes, it is," Diane answered.

"And you now leave without him?"

"Yes, we are. We were recalled to Washington," she said, as calmly as possible.

"On what business?"

"Private. Government business. That sort of thing." She wasn't as calm, now that he began to probe more deeply.

"Then why is your destination New York City if you were recalled to Washington?"

Don quickly interjected. "We live in New York. We don't have to report to Washington for another two days. Gives us time to relax and take care of personal things."

Rolon stared at the two of them as if sizing them up. He had dealt with so many people attempting to smuggle undeclared items, from trinkets to drugs, that he believed he could always tell if someone was lying, and these two looked like liars to him. "Do you have luggage with you?"

"We do," Don answered. "It passed through customs already."

"We know that customs does not always do a full job with each and every piece of luggage. In your case, I would like to reinspect them. It seems my government is very concerned with the smuggling of, como se dice, important items out of Peru. May I have your claim stubs, please?"

Don reached into his coat pocket. "They're stapled to the ticket jacket. I have them here." He handed Rolon the jacket and stubs.

"Let us find these bags together, yes?"

They followed Rolon out of the office and into a baggage holding area down the hallway from the gate area.

"Do you see them?" Rolon asked.

Don and Diane scanned the area. They were relatively at ease realizing that Rolon would find nothing, certainly no cylinder or ancient Inca artifacts. Diane spotted her pieces. "Over there. The gray ones over there."

Rolon ordered a sky cap to place the luggage on a counter top, which was done immediately.

Diane momentarily froze. She grabbed Don's arm and whispered urgently, "The name tags. If he looks at them, we're finished."

Don inhaled deeply and walked over to the counter. "Need some help?"

"Si." He waved his arms across the three bags. "Which is you and she? They are a matching set."

Don and Diane's thoughts were one. Crossman and Sadowski. Two separate travelers. Why would they have the same luggage, and how could they tell them apart unless they checked the name tags, all of which read, Mr. and Mrs. Donald Carter!

Diane replied, "They're all both of ours."

Don glanced at her, not fully understanding.

"Both?"

"Yes," she answered sheepishly. "We live together. Never took the time to get married."

"I see," Rolon remarked, looking at Don, who managed a weak smile.

Reacting instinctively, Diane said sternly, "Can we get on with this? My plane is about to board, we're both exhausted, and now you want to mess up our suitcases."

Rolon merely nodded. He would know soon enough if the young lady was grandstanding or not. He unzipped each suitcase and rummaged through them, finding only clothing and assorted paraphernalia. The name tags dangled like red flags to Don and Diane, but with the claim tags matching the numbers on the suitcases, Rolon had no reason to examine them, and they went unnoticed.

"I am sorry for the inconvenience, but we have to be careful these days. You understand, of course." It was a statement that had been repeated many times before, always with the same lack of sincerity.

"No problem," Don answered as he zipped up the suitcases and handed them back to the sky cap, who threw them onto a conveyor belt that whisked them away, to the relief of Don and Diane.

They sat down once again to await the call to board their plane, proud of their successful performance.

They hoped that by 9:45 they would be boarded and would later be safely in the air, on their way to Miami and then New York. Even the smell of New York seemed enticing to them.

It had been one hell of a trip, Don thought. One hell of a trip. But this was perhaps only the beginning of greater things in store for him, for Diane, and maybe even the entire world. He prayed that there was no bomb on that plane.

Rawlings was sitting and talking with Styles when Watson approached. "Excuse me, gentlemen. Can I speak with you a moment?"

"Sure, what's up?" Styles cheerfully replied.

Watson moved in closer toward the two men and spoke loudly enough for only them to hear him. "We've just received a call from the tower at Lima. They said they got a call from someone who said he got word that there was a bomb on the plane."

The two men's backs stiffened up, and Styles demanded, "Who told them? Did they give you a name?"

"Yes. A Don Diane." Watson saw Styles and Rawlings give each other a look of recognition and asked, "You know that name?"

"Yeah, we know it," Rawlings said, appearing more concerned now. "It's Don and Diane Carter. What do we do now?"

Watson said, "The tower suggests we turn back."

"Turn back?" Styles retorted. "How do we know this isn't some phony deal?"

"But what if it's true?" Rawlings asked.

Watson calmly answered, "Look, I've been through this before. Airports get calls like this all the time."

"But not from the Carters," Rawlings stressed. "And only a few people have any real knowledge that this plane was at the airport. I doubt it was coincidence that the caller specifically named this plane. I'll bet the Russians are behind this. In fact, I'd bet my life on it." It was perhaps a poor choice of words, but no one paid it any mind. They had a potentially life-threatening situation on their hands and were determined to defuse it.

Styles asked, "How do we know it was, in fact, the Carters calling? Could it be the Russians using their name? They know about the two of them."

Rawlings interjected, "Or the Peruvians, who may have only just realized that we're gone."

Watson then spoke. "Well, wherever the call came from, they did use that name and specified this plane. The prudent thing is to turn back."

Rawlings spoke directly at Styles. "The cylinder, Craig—what if it's a trick, meant to get us back to Lima?"

Now it was Styles's turn to play devil's advocate. "And what if it isn't? We're responsible not only for the cylinder but for the lives of everyone on this plane."

Watson decided to make the decision for them. "Listen, I realize that this is obviously an important mission—"

Rawlings interrupted. "You don't know how important."

Watson continued. "Maybe not. But I'm still the captain of this craft and suggest we do the following. We turn this plane around and head back for Lima while searching every square inch of this plane. But even if we find no bomb, we should still make for Lima."

"Why?" Styles and Rawlings asked simultaneously.

"We might not be able to find it. It could be on the outside of the plane, under the wing, tucked into the landing gear, or who knows where?"

"And if we do find it?" Rawlings asked.

"We can open an emergency door in the rear of the plane and jettison it. We then bring the craft around for another one-eighty and head for the stars and stripes."

Styles and Rawlings glanced at each other knowing that Watson's plan made the most sense. Maybe the threat was a trick. Maybe it wasn't.

Then Rawlings got an idea. "Hey, wait a second. Why land back in Lima? We're closer to the airport in Quito, Ecuador, than to Lima. Let's land, check out the plane, and take off."

Watson shrugged his shoulders. "Great idea."

"I agree," Styles chimed in.

Enthusiastically, Rawlings said, "Let's do it. We'll inform the others of what's going on and have everyone turn this plane upside down."

Rawlings called all the others to attention and informed them of what had occurred. Some were visibly nervous at the news, but all were able to keep their composure. Fourteen enervated persons now began to search the entire plane with a fine-toothed comb as Norris, the copilot, headed the plane back for the coast of South America.

For the next ten minutes, they scurried around looking under all the seats, in all compartments, in the toilet, and even in their own luggage in the unlikely event that someone had slipped a bomb into one of their pieces back at the hotel. They came up empty.

Watson returned to the cockpit and informed Norris that they'd found nothing thus far.

Norris, sounding very casual, remarked. "I didn't think they would. Did you?"

"Not really. But just to keep 'em honest, I think we oughta check the landing gear," Watson replied.

"You think it's necessary? I'm sure this is nothing more than another imbecile calling in a bomb scare."

Watson thought for a second and said, "After speaking with Rawlings and Styles, I'm not convinced that's the case here. They're into some top-secret shit that may include the Soviet Union. It couldn't hurt to check out the underbelly and landing gear."

"If you feel so strongly about it, fine. We'll have to drop down to under ten thousand, even five thousand. I want to be able to breathe in there."

"You? I thought I'd go," Watson said.

"I'm tired of sitting, and my ass hurts already."

"Fine. I'll take the stick."

Watson took over control of the plane while Norris grabbed a small toolbox and a flashlight and then waited at the back of the plane for Watson to descend to an altitude that would provide enough oxygen and warmth in the plane's belly. Norris would have to open up a trap door that led from the rear of the cabin down into the fuselage below. Rawlings and Styles looked on as he dropped down into the belly of the plane and began treading his way along the superstructure in the rear of the plane toward the landing gear, which was tucked into the plane between the wings.

"Colder than a witch's tit in here," he mumbled to himself.

The noise of the engines was deafening inside the fuselage as Norris stepped from one strut to the other while holding on to the cross-members of the superstructure with one hand and the flashlight with the other. The toolbox was tucked under his arm.

He examined the area with his flashlight as he made his way toward the landing gear. It took over a minute for him to arrive between the left and right wing landing gear housings. Using his flashlight inside the terribly loud, vibrating plane, he scanned the area all around the huge, tucked-in left wheels. When satisfied, he muttered, "Nothing here" and switched over to the right landing gear and began to scan it with the flashlight.

He started whistling the tune, "Just Whistle While You Work," but he stopped in midtune at the sight of a strange-looking object fastened with two bolts onto a metal strut just above the landing gear.

Norris stared at it for a few seconds, not wanting to believe what was before him, but he couldn't avoid the inevitable conclusion. "Holy Jesus, Joseph, and Mary! They really did it," he exclaimed in disbelief.

Perspiration began to bead up on his forehead, and he could feel his palms becoming sweaty, even though it was extremely cold in the plane's belly. As far as Norris was concerned, he might as well have been inside the belly of the Beast.

The object Norris stood mesmerized before was black and appeared to be a shoebox with tape wrapped around it. Attached to the device was an old-fashioned alarm clock, which he shined his light on. The time on the clock read 9:12. He strained to see the setting of the alarm dial. He stared intently at the tiny arm, which appeared to be pointing to approximately 9:15. There was no way for Norris to be certain of the exact minute of the alarm setting, nor was he certain that the alarm dial had anything at all to do with triggering the device. He thought about opening the box and attempting to defuse the bomb but thought better of it, as he'd never been trained in demolitions and knew that pulling any wires or opening the box could set the bomb off. He thought about getting help but knew there might be precious little time. Besides, he thought, the area he was positioned in was only large enough for one man to adequately work.

Norris placed the flashlight next to him on a ledge where it would shine its light on the device. He began to unbolt the device from the strut. Using a pliers and a screwdriver, he unscrewed the first nut. He then began to unbolt the second one, but this one was tighter, and his sweaty palm strained to turn the pliers, which twice slipped off the nut of the second bolt. It was in a more difficult spot than the first bolt, and he stretched to get a better grip on it.

He could see the clock. 9:13. His breathing increased while straining to loosen the nut. It began to turn, and in few seconds he had it. He gingerly lowered the device, crouched down, and placed it on the floor of the fuselage.

9:14!

He knew he had to get it out of the plane now. Norris believed that the quickest way was to open the housing for the landing gear and drop the bomb out of the opening. For a split second, he was caught in a terrible quandary between attempting to make his way back toward the trap door and shout for them to tell Watson to drop the landing gear or opening it himself with the emergency crank. He spotted the crank directly above him, and he chose to begin turning the crank by hand in order to open the doors to the landing gear. As soon as he could get it open about one foot, he could drop the device safely out of the plane.

He turned the crank as hard as he could, and the housing began to open, resulting in a tremendous blast of cold air rushing in. The frantic Norris paid no mind to the wind or the temperature as he concentrated only on turning the crank.

"Turn, you bitch, turn!" he shouted at the stiffly moving crank as the housing continued to slowly open wider amid an ever-increasing whoosh of frigid air.

It was now 9:15.

Watson was sitting at the controls when a red warning light and buzzer went off, indicating that the landing gear housing was being opened. Watson knew that it had to be Norris opening the doors. He knew he could open it all the way automatically by simply pressing a switch, but he quickly thought better of the idea, not knowing the consequences it might have on Norris if the housing were to suddenly open.

Confused, Watson placed the plane on automatic pilot and walked back toward the rear of the plane.

The plane was only ten minutes from the coast in its flight path back to South America and was still over the open waters of the Atlantic Ocean as Watson approached the trap door leading to the fuselage.

Rawlings was speaking to Styles about how anxious he was to see his wife and two girls. "You know, Craig, if it wasn't for my family, I probably wouldn't have had the guts to stick it out in Nam. I needed to see them so badly that survival became a must for me. You have kids, don't you?"

"Two teenage boys and a ten-year-old girl."

"Funny isn't it?" Rawlings remarked. "I've known you for what, two, three years, and I never thought to ask you about your family until now."

"I guess it's all in the nature of our work, Tom. We—"

The ticking stopped.

An explosion ripped through the belly of the C130 and ignited the plane's fuel, causing a further explosion and shattering a good part of the aircraft. What remained of the plane and its passengers plummeted into the ocean depths, ending the lives of Rawlings, Styles, Weinberg, Sadowski, Crossman, Gruen, Corsica, and the rest.

The now glowing hot cylinder sank through a cataclysm of boiling water to the bottom of the ocean, where it came to rest in the cool sands of darkness, thousands of feet below the surface.

Undisturbed, it sat quietly on the calm ocean floor, waiting patiently, just as it had for thousands of years embedded in the solid rock of the Peruvian Andes.

CHAPTER 30

NEWS OF THE WRECKAGE of the plane with the loss of all those aboard, and the disappearance of the elusive cylinder, reached Charles Block at his apartment in Washington as he was lying in bed during the early morning hours, just after dawn, the next day. The call had come from Code Green of the Central Intelligence Agency, a division of the department that Block knew was involved in covert operations. He was ordered to break the news to the Carters immediately.

Block stood in his pajamas next to the bed, waiting for the phone connection to be made as his wife rolled over, trying not to become fully awakened by her husband's phone calls. Minutes before, she had heard him receive a call from someone at the Pentagon, and now he was dialing to call someone else.

Block heard the phone ringing at the other end. A groggy Diane answered, and Block identified himself.

"Mr. Block, what's wrong?" A call at this early in the morning made her fear for the worst, and she tensed up.

Uneasy in this situation, he broke the news swiftly and to the point. "I'm sorry to inform you that the plane carrying the entourage from Peru has been lost at sea, possibly as the result of sabotage. All those on board are presumed to be dead. I'm terribly sorry."

Diane didn't even blink. Don saw her blank expression, sat up in bed, and asked, "What's the matter?"

Holding the phone and automatically cupping her hand over the mouthpiece, with Block waiting for a response, she said limply, "They're all dead. The bomb. It blew them up."

"Hello, Mrs. Carter," Block called out.

"Yes."

"Is your husband all right?"

"He's right here, with me."

"At least that's good news. You went to Peru to find him, and you did."

Almost numb, she answered, "That's right. Thank you."

She hung up and stared at Don, who could only stare back, lost in his own short-circuited emotions.

The terrible news threw the two of them into a disbelieving, almost catatonic state for a short while. They didn't know how to react and didn't want to allow the full impact of what they had just heard to sink in too suddenly. The pressures of the past few weeks, coupled with the devastating news of the sabotaged plane, was more than either of them was willing to bear at that moment, and all they could do was cry and find comfort in each other's arms, saying little.

Mrs. Block was now totally annoyed with her husband. First was the ringing phone. Then there was a call out, and now came another call out. In her half sleep she thought it was something concerning a plane but was too tired to ask. "Charlie," she mumbled. "Come on. Go back to sleep,"

"In a minute, hon. Just one more quick call."

"Code Green," a man answered.

"They're home. Both of them. And even though she put her hand over the receiver, I managed to hear something about her knowing that a bomb blew up the plane."

"Anything else?"

"That's it."

"Thank you, Mr. Block. You've been a great help to us."

The line went dead. Block hung up and climbed back into bed, grumbling. Those guys in the Pentagon were always playing these damn mysterious games. *Must make them feel real important,* he concluded as he pulled the blanket over his head to shield him from the early morning light.

Code Green picked up the phone and dialed out. "It's go," he told two men at the other end, over their car phone.

"Understood," the driver answered. Then he hung up.

Code Green's suspicions had been confirmed by Block. The Carters were the only ones not on that plane, and they knew of the bomb aboard but did nothing except strike a deal to save their own skins. How else could they have gotten out of Peru with the Peruvian government searching for them at every point of departure? They had sold out, probably to the Russians. There was no telling what else they knew of the covert operations and how much more help they could be to the Commies. In any case, Code Green knew he had to send a message that the enemy would not soon forget. He couldn't allow the transgressions to go unanswered.

Although believing their circumstantial evidence would never hold up in a court of law, the CIA needed far less justification to eliminate persons they feared were jeopardizing the security of the United States.

As soon as the message had been received that a bomb might be planted on the American C130, airport security had notified the American embassy of the threat to one of its planes. The embassy then called the State Department in Washington, repeating the information. Hours later, when the plane was confirmed to have vanished from all radar systems and was declared missing and then a fishing boat reported plane wreckage floating in bits and pieces on ocean waters, a Col. James Highsmith, proud to be the first African American appointed to a post at the US embassy in Lima, was dispatched to the airport in an attempt to unravel the strange events that led to the fatal crash.

Security at the airport logged written records of all incoming calls, and it didn't take long for Highsmith to discover that the call warning of a bomb had come from a man identifying himself as Don Diane.

Highsmith relayed the information back to Washington, where it was swiftly channeled to Code Green.

"Are you certain of this information?" Code Green asked. "A Don Diane tried to warn that plane?"

"Positive."

Code Green dialed the number of the car phone in order to rescind the two men's orders. With this new information, it was now doubtful that the Carters were aiding the other side.

But the two men were already taking up their positions outside the Carters' apartment building. Their car was parked out of sight, around the corner. Their silencers were tucked inside their jackets, as was a small amount of cocaine, which would be planted and construed as evidence by the police that the Carters were involved in the smuggling of drugs out of Peru and had been killed in a busted drug deal. Not wanting to be seen by anyone, they would avoid the elevator and walk the seven flights of stairs to the Carters' floor.

Code Green then contacted one of their operatives in downtown Manhattan. "This is Code Green. I'm giving you the address of a Donald and Diane Carter. Two of our agents must be told that their objective has been cancelled. This has top-shelf priority. Our estimate is that if you don't get there within the next ten minutes, the two subjects will be inadvertently processed. Is that clear?"

"Very." The operative wrote down the address, 121 W. Twenty-Eighth Street, apartment 7D, threw on a pair of pants and a shirt, set the timer on his watch at 0:00, rushed out of the apartment, and hailed a cab. It took more than a minute before a taxi pulled over to the curb, and he jumped in, noticing that four minutes and fifteen seconds had already passed. He was only about twenty blocks away, but with early morning traffic beginning to build and the possibility of being caught by several stop lights, he knew it would be close.

"Step on it, Mack. There's an extra ten spot if we get there in less than five minutes."

"You got it, buddy. This cab don't fly, but I'll do what I can."

After a few precious moments of shared grief, Don began to reminisce about the past few weeks, and Diane, knowing how much Don needed to talk problems out to get them off his chest, lay next to him, watching him and being the good listener.

"Anton, Diego, Rawlings, and the rest. Their lives were lost for nothing. In the end, we don't even have the cylinder for the world to know what they gave their lives for, and to study and marvel at. To know that out there, somewhere, is alien intelligence. My God, who knows what grand revelations they could have shared with us about the nature of our universe, about life, maybe even death, or … or even God? Damn those sons of bitches that did this! Goddamn them." He pounded the mattress with his fist as the anger raged within him.

Diane, understanding and empathizing with Don, asked, "Who do you think killed them?"

"Does it really matter? Probably the Russians, who couldn't bear to let us get our hands on it if they couldn't have it. But it wasn't really the Russians. I hate to sound like I'm philosophizing, but mankind killed those people and lost the cylinder. All of us. If the situation were reversed, would the United States have allowed the Russians to walk off with the cylinder?" Don walked over to the window and stared blankly at the checkerboard-patterned windows of the building across the narrow street.

"Probably not. You're right. Governments are all alike. We'd probably have blown a dozen Russians out of the sky as easily as they did." Diane walked over to Don, stood behind him, and placed her arms around his waist.

"Damn right they would. National security and all that crap." He was still angered, but the emotion had softened. Disbelief and anger were giving way to acceptance.

"What about the possibility of finding that cylinder?" Diane asked. "I'm sure it's still in one piece."

"Yeah, but where?" Don turned around and faced her. "They have trouble finding whole ships at the bottom of the ocean, like the Titanic. How are they gonna find something a little larger than a football in several thousand feet of water? They can't even pinpoint the exact location of the crash. All they found were pieces floating with the ocean currents."

"But the cylinder sends out signals."

They walked away from the window and sat on the bed with their backs against the headboard as Don answered, "But only very weak ones. And it can shut down." Then, with a trace of disgust in his voice, he added, "And if this thing has been programmed to comprehend the recent events, it'll probably be another four thousand years before anyone finds it."

"Do you think there may be other cylinders around?"

"I guess it's possible, but only time will tell us that. But who knows? Maybe the world is better off without the cylinder and the power it might've given us. But my biggest problem is to convince people that the damn thing ever existed. Damn it!" His frustration was palpable.

Diane offered, "But we have the original tape, the one you recorded with Diego. It's still at the Pentagon or somewhere like that."

"Yeah, great. But without the cylinder, you think anyone's going to believe it?"

"Do you think they might try to contact … visit us again, these aliens?"

"If they do, it won't exactly be those aliens. The alien we saw has probably been dead for thousands of years."

"That's if their lifespan is like ours," she said.

Don looked at Diane, feeling enlightened by the remark. "I never thought of that. Maybe they can live for thousands of earth years."

"Or never die at all. Can you imagine if they could've shared the secret of longevity or immortality with us?"

"You mean permanently, like the fountain of youth?"

"Maybe," Diane replied. "Although I'm not sure I'd want to live so long."

Don kidded, "Or do you mean like Dracula or some other unworldly zombie?"

"I really don't think I'd go around sucking people's blood." Then more seriously, she continued, "I prefer to think of it as bearing witness to remarkable and wonderful revelations of the universe that have yet to come."

"You sound almost poetic. I didn't know you had it in you."

"I'm deep, Don, really deep," she answered with a mock-serious expression on her face. Diane then asked, "You know that book you once talked about writing?"

"So?"

"So I think this story just might be worth writing a few thousand words about." She was serious.

"You think so?" he said, agreeing with her statement but needing the incentive of her approval and support. Her encouragement would mean everything to him.

"I certainly do."

Don thought for a moment. "Yeah, I could write a book, couldn't I? In fact, we could write it together." He began to sound excited, and Diane smiled as he continued. "At least the story would go on record. If they don't believe us, who cares? That's their loss. But you and me, we know. We touched it. We saw it. We know what the alien looks like, and they can never take that away from us."

"Carter and Carter. Sounds like a pretty good team to me," Diane said as she placed her hand lovingly on the back of Don's neck.

The two agents exited the stairwell at the seventh floor and peered in both directions. Seeing nothing, they ducked back into the stairwell and began to screw their silencers onto the barrels of their .45s.

The operative's taxi turned up Twenty-Eighth Street. His watch read ten minutes, thirty seconds. He knew it may already be over, but then again, maybe not. *I'm only an avenue away ...* His thoughts were jarred by the sudden halt of the cab. "What's the matter?" he shouted.

"Sorry, buddy. Garbage truck. No way around it. Unless you want to get out and—"

The operative had already thrown a twenty-dollar bill over the front seat. He leaped out of the cab and ran up the street in the direction of the Carters' apartment building.

The agents noiselessly approached the Carter door. The routine had been thoroughly practiced until it was now a matter of precision teamwork. They would knock at the door, someone inside would ask who it was, they would respond, "Telegram," and the door would open a crack, enough for the two burly men to hit the door with their shoulders. The door would either be unchained and offer little resistance or, if chained, would snap under the combined weight of the coordinated ramming. Guns drawn, the man on the right would fire three shots in rapid succession, immediately neutralizing the person answering the door. The other man would rush past, seek the second target, and, catching it by surprise, instantly open fire, eliminating it.

The operative didn't wait for the elevator. He bolted up the steps, three at a time, and was rounding the stairs on the sixth floor, one floor below, when Don and Diane heard a knock at their door.

"Who could that be at this hour?" Diane asked.

"It's gotta be related to the crash. I'll get it."

He walked to the door and asked, "Who is it?"

"Telegram."

Don began to unbolt the locks on the door.

The agents heard him unbolt the locks. They drew a deep breath and crouched in readiness to strike, expecting little resistance.

The operative leaped out of the stairwell, panting heavily, and, spotting the two agents at the Carter door, shouted, "Code Green cancelled!"

The door swung open.

The two agents had heard the shout a split second before the door opened. The words "Code Green" made them wheel around. Seeing a man with his arms raised above his head, clearly unarmed, again shouting "Code Green is cancelled," they immediately thrust their guns inside their jackets.

"What's going on here?" Don asked, looking at the two men's backs and seeing a third man rushing toward them shouting something about the color green.

One man turned and calmly said, "Is this 221 West Twenty-Eighth Street, apartment 7D?"

"It's 7D, but this isn't 221. That's up the block."

"Sorry," the man said.

Don closed the door.

"Who was that?" Diane asked.

"Some idiots in the wrong building."

Talking about the events and planning for the future helped Don and Diane, and their anger and frustration were somewhat vented, at least for the time being.

He knew the old adage that time heals all wounds, but Don had lost something that would remain in his thoughts for the rest of his life. He thought about the cylinder, and then he looked over at Diane, his beautiful wife, who had gone to Peru at the risk of her own life to rescue him. Now he spoke to her as though a remarkable revelation had just occurred to him.

"You know, we just lost the greatest find in the entire world, but there is one large consolation."

"What's that?"

She was beautiful to him in more ways than one; she was his companion for life. "Maybe my greatest find was finding you again."

She knew he truly meant it and looked at him tenderly, clearly touched by his remark. "What a lovely thing to say. But you really don't mean it, do you?" She wore a charming, little-girl expression on her face.

"Could I sleep with a stupid old cylinder?" Somehow, through it all, he was happier than he'd been in longer than he chose to remember.

Diane laughed. "No, no, I guess you couldn't."

Diane, too, had found an inner peace and contentment that she hadn't known since her father's death.

Don smiled broadly and said, "I guess we really do have a cosmic relationship."

Diane cocked her head to the side. "Cosmic?"

Don lovingly embraced Diane. Thoughts of losing the cylinder could wait for another time.

EPILOGUE

STEVEN CARTER FINISHED THE manuscript. Now he had an enlightened understanding of his father's life-long quest, of his need to finally be listened to and believed.

He decided to write an epilogue to his father's tale and sat down at his computer. He wrote the following:

If modern man had the power of a god and could peer into the vastness of space many light-years from his solar system, he would see a civilization far more advanced than his own, waiting and wondering when it might be hearing from the human race.

One of these aliens' ancient voyages had left messages and information for the strange human beings that they encountered long ago in ancient Peru. These humans had apparently evolved enough to obtain the powers of thinking and reasoning, and the aliens hoped that they would one day develop enough technological know-how to make contact with them and exchange ideas, cultures, and perhaps thoughts on the universe, creation, and the nature of life.

Apparently, modern man had developed enough technology to understand the alien messages, but this same technologically adept human had not yet learned to get out of his own way. In spite of all of Man's relatively recent inventions and technological advances, which, in some cases, lengthened his lifespan and improved his physical quality of life, the effect of these improvements on his mental being—his soul, as it were—was still uncertain. Progress in terms of the physical world seemed to have had little effect upon Man's primal fears and instincts.

The great eternal answers, and perhaps some of the questions, were still unknown to him. After all, modern, technological Man was still in his infancy.

The future of mankind is not nearly as certain as its past, which has its roots enmeshed and intertwined with those of the animal kingdom. Primitive survival instincts still pervaded Man's very soul, enough so that they blinded him from the greater gifts the universe had to offer.

Steven turned off his computer. He walked into his parents' bedroom, watched solemnly by a forlorn Diane, who was sitting in a chair by the bed. Don's breathing was becoming more and more labored. His years of smoking were exacting their final toll.

Steven bent down and gently shook his father. Don was barely able to open his eyes, but his face clearly showed that he recognized his son.

Steven said, with great conviction, "Dad, I believe your story. I know it's the truth. Now I understand."

A small smile crossed Don's face. He could now die in peace.